SOUTHERN STORMS

"We're organizing a campaign," Cara announced.

Lee looked quickly up. "Against Lone Star Partners?"

"*For* the mustangs."

Lee released a light laugh. "You've got nerve, lady. I'll grant you that."

"Don't you *dare* treat this issue lightly," Cara went on. "Walking Dune has existed for centuries—unspoiled, unbridled. The people who make their homes here endure blistering summers, savage winter storms, hurricanes, power outages. I doubt your fancy resort folk will last through one northeaster. Where will that leave your multimillion-dollar development? And as for the horses, this is the only place in the world where Spanish mustangs live wild and free. They've been here on the island four hundred years. Lone Star has been here four weeks. Just who the hell do you think has more claim?"

Lee studied her, his thoughts darting between what she'd said and the inescapable idea that, with her color high and eyes flashing, she was the most magnificent thing he'd ever seen . . .

ALSO BY MARCIA MARTIN:

SOUTHERN NIGHTS . . .

The dazzling story of a woman's mysterious inheritance—and the one man who knew the secret of her birthright.
"Truly a great book!"—*Rendezvous*

SOUTHERN SECRETS . . .

After years of intrigue, the belle of the town is reunited with the man who has always loved her.
"Compelling . . . emotionally charged . . ."—*Rave Reviews*

SOUTHERN STORMS

MARCIA MARTIN

JOVE BOOKS, NEW YORK

SOUTHERN STORMS

A Jove Book / published by arrangement with
the author

PRINTING HISTORY
Jove edition / May 1992

ISBN: 0-515-10870-7

Jove Books are published by The Berkley Publishing Group,
200 Madison Avenue, New York, New York 10016.
The name "JOVE" and the "J" logo
are trademarks belonging to Jove Publications, Inc.

PRINTED IN THE UNITED STATES OF AMERICA

10 9 8 7 6 5 4 3 2 1

Dedicated to
the endangered Spanish mustangs
of North Carolina,
and those fighting to save them.

Acknowledgment and thanks to
Stephen P. Griffin, A.I.A., Architect
and
The Corolla Wild Horse Fund

PART ONE

Sleep hath its own world,
And a wide realm of wild reality,
And dreams in their development hath breath,
And tears, and tortures . . .

—"The Dream"
Byron

Chapter One

The alley behind Mott's Grocery smelled of onions and ill-mannered cats.

Light trickled down the dead-end wall, casting the boys in dark relief. There were five of them—four bullies circling the smallest of the group. Nick.

Cara moved forward. The heels of her patent leather shoes clicked along the concrete, and she was suddenly aware of what she was wearing—frilly white dress, lacy gloves. Both were too small, long ago outgrown.

The boys looked up. One of them was Mitch Lincoln.

Fear shot through Cara, pounding in her ears so that she failed to hear Nick's cry—though she saw his mouth form her name.

She tried to stretch taller as she came to a stop before Mitch. She was big for twelve; he was bigger. Heart thundering, she stared him straight in the eye.

"We Malloys stick together," she said. "Would anybody care to take me on?"

Mitch threw back his head and laughed. The sound howled along the alleyway. Cara's skin erupted in chills.

"Yeah, baby," he grinned. "I'll take you on." Reaching out, he tweaked her left nipple.

Cara lunged back, eyes flying open, shoulders banging against the brass headboard.

"It's okay, honey."

3

Her head swiveled.

"Just a dream," Tom added.

The words floated from the dark mound beside her. Cara's wide eyes adjusted, and then she saw him, moonlight turning his fair hair to silver, outlining the bare shoulders above the sheet.

She drew a long, shaky breath. Just a dream, she repeated, her heart slowing to the magical phrase. Just a dream. And it hadn't even been one of the bad ones. But it had been so long since she had one that she'd begun to hope maybe they were gone for good.

Shifting down on the pillow, she ran a palm over her swollen stomach. The doctor had said it could happen. Pregnant women were known to have rowdy dreams. Maybe that's all it was. Hormones.

"Don't worry," mumbled Tom, his voice barely audible.

Cara extended a hand, her fingers making contact with the charmed flesh. He'd never had a nightmare in his life. Settling on her side, she watched his chest rise and fall, rise and fall. Her eyelids grew heavy and finally impossible to hold open.

The image of Mitch Lincoln waited in the blackness, beckoning her to sleep.

*   *   *

"Aren't they beautiful?" he asked.

Cara smiled. It was like Tom to see beyond the filthy condition of the mustangs. They'd taken a mudbath somewhere on the island then migrated to the beach, their favorite haunt when the wind blew hot from the southwest, bringing mosquitos and biting flies and other summer pests to the Outer Banks. The sun was going down, shimmering on the ocean, painting the shore in a flattering light. Still, she wouldn't call the dozen or so wild horses "beautiful."

"Yes," Cara lied. "They are."

Just then, the black stallion raised his head and looked in their direction, a breeze catching his mane, fanning it like a dark flag. Suddenly she glimpsed the beauty her husband tended to see in most everything.

"They really *are*," she added with a note of surprise.

The stallion mosied toward them. It was not his height but the powerful neck and shoulders that gave him the look of what he was—the unchallenged leader of the herd.

Tom looped an arm around her shoulders. "Wonder how close he'll come this time."

They stood very still; the stud came to a halt mere yards away. Beneath streaks of mud, he was solid black but for a white splash on his forehead—Star, Tom had named him many summers ago, when he was a teenager, and the stallion, a yearling colt. Three years they'd lived in Walking Dune, and Cara had seen the mustang approach Tom many times—never anyone else.

"Hello, Star," Tom offered quietly.

The mustang's ears pricked, and then he turned and ambled back to his herd, where he paused to nuzzle a big-bellied mare.

"June's a little late to be foaling," Tom said. Shifting behind Cara, he stretched gentle arms around her altered breadth. "Guess Star's offspring will be arriving about the same time as my own."

Cara settled against him, enjoying the feel of his hands. She was due in two weeks and was huge. It would have been easy to feel clumsy and dowdy and altogether unappealing. But Tom had never allowed her to feel that way. Since the first time they met, he'd made her feel beautiful.

Her thoughts turned back to that spring day in her final semester at Virginia University. It was raining. Head bent, she darted down the steps of Chastain Hall and collided with someone coming along the path. He lost his footing and ended up on his backside. Looking down with an apology on her lips, she extended a hand, halting as she recognized Thomas Ward Chastain III.

A series of unflattering contrasts blasted through her mind. She was a nobody from nowhere; he was a Chastain from snooty Warrenton. She was at the university by grace of a loan; he was of the family for whom a portion of the campus was named. She was standing there with her long black hair shedding streams down a cheap parka; he was sitting in a mud puddle that was making a mockery of what looked to be a designer topcoat. She couldn't afford to have that coat cleaned.

And then he smiled. "Hello, gorgeous," he said.

Shortly after graduation, they married.

An ocean breeze stirred her hair; Cara sighed in sublime peace. That was when she'd come to the Outer Banks for the first time—to a stretch of North Carolina coast as wild as it was beautiful, a quaint village as old as the legends of colonists and Indians. That was when she'd come home to the towering, Victorian house that had presided over Walking Dune for a century.

The name Chastain went back four generations in the island village. There were families who claimed a longer history, and the Chastains were, after all, "summer folk" who spent most of the year in neighboring, refined Virginia. Still, over the decades, the family had attained a position of leadership. It had been the Chastains who founded the town council, set up the post office, and organized the fire department coveted by other small towns along the Banks. It had been the Chastains who opened their house to victims of hurricanes and north-easters and other disasters.

Even now, the villagers wouldn't think of gathering any-where else in an emergency. Built by a master craftsman at the turn of the century, the Chastain house was positioned a safe distance from the shore and was braced and underpinned in a way Tom said couldn't be duplicated these days. From the widow's walk, one could see the Currituck Sound to the west, and to the east, the blue Atlantic, stretching all the way to the horizon.

Cara loved the feeling of security she had within its walls—the lofty grace of the high-ceilinged rooms, the smell of cedar that crept from closets to waft throughout the house, the comforting presence of antiques and heirlooms that had been handed down through generations.

The pleasant curve of her mouth drooped as her thoughts took a turn. Tom's mother had given him the summer house, had made him a graduation present of it. Mere days later, she must have felt like chopping off the hand that signed the deed.

Abigail Chastain. Revered widow of Judge Thomas Ward Chastain . . . dignified first lady of dignified Warrenton. Cara could just picture her face when Tom called her long distance, announcing first that he had no intention of attending law school, but was planning to write a novel . . . then, that he'd gotten married and was moving to Walking Dune. His description of his mother's sputtering response had been hilarious.

But there was nothing funny about the night he took Cara to Warrenton. She'd known Mrs. Chastain was a widow, Tom her only child, the house "kinda big." But nothing had prepared Cara for the stateliness of the mansion or the sting of blue-blooded contempt. Tom had none of that in him. His mother had enough for the whole state of Virginia.

She was slight of stature, but one tended to forget that in the face of everything else—the regal carriage and refined accent, the impeccable grooming that spoke of generations of breeding. That night she wore basic black and classic pearls.

They retired to supper at a banquet-sized table set with china and crystal. Chandelier light sparkled on Mrs. Chastain's clipped silver hair and diamond-decked fingers, illuminating the warm smiles she turned on Tom and the frozen ones that made their way to Cara. Summer afternoons; icy mornings.

Minutes after they sat down, the conversation took a turn and stayed there. Cara's grasp of the situation was immediate. In the short time since receiving news of her son's marriage, Abigail Chastain had checked up on his unsuitable bride.

Carolina Malloy—named for her father's home state—had been raised in a small town in western Virginia, the daughter of a coal miner and a schoolteacher, both deceased.

"I'm so sorry, my dear . . ."

There was a brother, Nick, three years her junior.

"And where is *he* at present?"

Cara had no idea—Nick came and went like the wind.

The woman even knew about the Indian blood that ran in Cara's veins, and made a great deal of it when Tom voiced surprise. Cara had few answers to their questions. Someone in the Malloy line—her father's great-grandmother, she thought—had been Cherokee. Cara had inherited her father's black hair and olive complexion. Maybe *that* was the Indian influence. Hell, *she* didn't know!

"A native American. How very unusual, Carolina . . ."

Temper flaring, Cara briskly informed "Madame" that no one had called her Carolina since her toddler brother shortened the name. The infuriating woman merely arched a brow and continued using the full appellation as though Cara had never spoken.

Throughout the miserable evening, Abigail Chastain's manner remained superficially unimpeachable, but Cara had heard—loud and clear—the sneering message beneath the veneer. No one was good enough for her son, and Carolina Malloy *definitely* was not.

After that, there had been a dearth of communication from Warrenton. Cara liked to think of it as a cold war, waged as much from her side as her mother-in-law's. Unfortunately the chilly silence had melted in the past months. Since learning of the pregnancy, Abigail had deluged them with phone calls. And the nursery positively bulged with expensive gifts.

Hope she doesn't think that means she can drop in any time she damn well pleases, Cara thought.

"Hey, what's the sour face about?"

She looked over her shoulder to see Tom's eyes on her. They were the color of azure water—much lighter than her own, which Tom delighted in calling "violet."

"Oh, nothing," she answered. "A pregnant lady has the right to get a bit moody now and then, doesn't she?"

Tom seemed appeased. He ran a palm across her full stomach, smiling as he felt the baby stir. Cara hoped the child would inherit that smile, as well as Tom's fair hair and pale eyes . . . everything about him. At six feet, he was a few scant inches taller than herself, but perfectly formed from the tip of his aristocratic nose to the sole of his foot. If she'd dreamed up a Prince Charming, she couldn't have outdone her husband.

"I love you," she murmured.

His hand moved to her breast, kneaded it so that she caught her breath. "Do you have any idea how much I love *you*?" he whispered.

Cara grinned as a wishful thumb brushed across her nipple. "I'm beginning to get an idea."

He turned her around and looked into her face. "*Are* you?"

Tom's fingers rested on her shoulders, his thumbs stretching to continue their erotic play.

Cara closed her eyes. She knew how much he wanted her. She wanted him, too. It had always been so. When they kissed, there were fireworks. When they made love, the earth moved. In all the time they'd known each other, there never had been a time when his touch failed to rouse her.

"Where are you?" lilted Tom's voice.

Cara chuckled and opened her eyes. "If I told you, I'm afraid our child would receive an intrusion he doesn't deserve."

He smiled—one of those white, flashing things that made her heart skip.

"I guess I'd better hit the road," he then said.

He was driving down to Manteo to pick up some research books. Cara locked her wrists behind his neck.

"Must you go?" she asked.

"I need those books, and Manteo's Booksellers is the only place around here I can get them."

She frowned, but then caught herself. She ought to be supportive, oughtn't she? Tom had yet to finish a single one of the four manuscripts he'd begun since they moved to the Banks, and he refused to let her see what he'd accomplished so far. She'd been an English major in college and was well read in the masters. "Let me get something good down first," Tom always said.

"You know, honey," Cara said with sudden alertness. "With all the research you do—all the books you need—wouldn't it be great if we started a shop? Nothing big, mind you, but an outlet that would allow you to order what you please, when you please?"

His face lit up. "You're a genius!" he pronounced. "Not only a book shop, a library! Walking Dune Library and—"

"No," Cara broke in. "Something simple. Something named for the man who made it happen. Tom's Books. I like the sound of that."

The light in his eyes was brilliant, pure, so full of love that it warmed her from head to toe. "Tom's Books," he repeated softly, and gathered her close for a kiss that left her tingling.

By the time they started across the sand, arms linked about each other, the sun had dipped below the dunes. Up the way, the stallion neighed. Tom and Cara turned to look as the herd fell in step to follow his lead up the beach.

It was almost as if Star were calling goodbye.

Cara pulled her husband's arm closer and smiled to herself. Tom's fanciful imagination was rubbing off on her.

* * *

Night had fallen, but after the crispness of the Rockies, the Houston air was oppressively hot and smoggy. Lee Powers hailed a cab at the front of the bustling airport and slipped out of his jacket before climbing in the back.

As the driver took him closer to the fashionable Galleria area, he peered out the window, watching landmarks flash by, remembering the times Marilyn used to pick him up when he returned to the city. The first couple of trips had been happy events. They'd stopped off at Carrabba's on Kirby to get a bite, then gone back to the apartment and made love. The third trip, after they quarreled long distance, she met him with a strained look. No food. No sex.

After that, it was understood. She didn't offer to pick him up; he didn't expect it.

As the cab skirted past the brightly lit skyline, Lee absently focused on the tall tower of the Lone Star Partners building. It was sleek and impressive, just like the real estate developments in which the conglomerate specialized.

At twenty-nine, he'd been the youngest architect ever offered the opportunity to act as Lone Star field representative. It meant he was the top on-site authority, boss of the development. Frank Winston himself, CEO, had given him the shot.

"Just get your feet wet," Frank had said. When the project went flawlessly, he made the appointment permanent.

"After all," sneered Lee's rivals, "he's Frankie's boy."

Marilyn had been proud of the promotion, thrilled with the salary jump that enabled them to move to a luxury apartment. Two developments later, she'd changed her tune. Out of eighteen months, her husband had been absent a total of ten. Lee realized she had reason to be angry. On the next job, he flew her out to California for a week. They had fun, but the trip proved no more effective than a bandaid on a festering wound.

The fights got louder. Last winter, they'd reached a crescendo.

"What the hell do you want me to do?" he'd shouted.

"Leave Lone Star."

Lee looked into her pretty face, peachy gold with a sprinkle of freckles. She was dead serious, and although perhaps he shouldn't have been surprised, he was.

"Are you prepared to give it all up?" he demanded, spreading his palms. "This place? The new BMW? The country club?"

It was more for himself he hammered the questions. Marilyn had been raised by well-to-do parents who'd given her everything; he'd grown up on the hard side of Pasadena and made it through Rice University by working his ass off. The lifestyle they'd achieved was nothing new to her. It was everything to him.

"One of these days you'll realize some things are more important than money," she returned with bright eyes.

It was a sensitive button. She knew it. She pushed it anyway.

"I'd wager the people who say that about money have never had to do without it!" he fired.

"Something's got to give," Marilyn retorted. "Leave Lone Star."

"No."

She whirled out of the room. He stomped after her and patched things up by pulling her into his arms. The love they made was hot, passionate . . . desperate.

That was six months ago. He'd been gone the past four, overseeing the latest Lone Star expansion in Colorado. It was a resounding success; yet as the cab turned into the ritzy apartment complex, Lee was melancholy. He was thirty-three years old, and his career was skyrocketing. His marriage was another matter.

Producing a smile and wave for the doorman, he strode through the posh lobby and stepped into the equally posh elevator. As he rode to the seventh floor, he wondered if Marilyn was home and if so what kind of reception she would give him.

Intuition had been nagging him; still, he was unprepared for the sight of her luggage in the foyer. All lined up in a row like that, the stylish pieces had a solemn air of finality about them. Lee's heart began to thud.

She came out of the bedroom, her purse slung over her shoulder, her fair hair bouncing as she walked up to him. He was reminded of the first time he saw her. His throat went dry.

"Hello," she offered. "I was waiting for you."

Lee set down his bags. They looked rumpled and meager next to the column of designer luggage.

"Waiting?" he voiced.

Marilyn looked up and caught her breath. In her opinion, he was still the most handsome man on earth. She'd always loved his hair—a brown so dark it was almost black, thick and waving back from prominent cheekbones, a high forehead, a face that wore the constant burnish of sun. His nose was straight and strong. Above it, dark brows furled over equally dark eyes; below it, a thick moustache covered his upper lip, curving to points below the corners of his mouth, evoking an almost dangerous look.

Caballero . . . The word chimed in her mind, accompanied by the memory of the black leather jacket in Lee's old trunk. She'd found it one day in the front closet of the modest rooms he rented before they married.

"What's this?" she'd asked casually, unprepared for the haunted look that came over him when she held up the jacket with "Caballeros" emblazoned on the back.

"There are things you don't know about me," he returned bluntly. "I grew up wild. The Caballeros were a street gang, and I ran with them until I was sixteen, until . . ."

Years passed before Lee would divulge what came after that "until." It was a girl, some rich little princess with whom he'd had the audacity to fall in love. "They said I wasn't good enough," he concluded in a fierce tone, and would go no further.

Whoever "they" were, they'd turned his life around at the tender age of sixteen. Eight years later, Lee Powers was the most success-driven man Marilyn had ever met. He was working the rodeo circuit back then, financing his final year at Rice. She and her girlfriends ogled him from the moment he stepped into the arena, proceeding to impress the crowd with a spectacular display of rifle marksmanship. Her friends dared her to go down and introduce herself. Marilyn took the dare.

Later, she hadn't been able to tell what stole her breath more, his dark good looks, smooth-talking charm, or the sort of raw, streetwise masculinity that emanated from him like a sexy scent. Once she'd met Lee, no other man had been able to do so much as turn her head.

And it was still the same, Marilyn thought. She'd planned this for weeks, but now the sight of him shook her resolve.

"I'm leaving," she said hurriedly.

"Where?" It was all Lee could manage.

"Back to Austin. I'll stay with Mom and Dad until I get my feet on the ground."

He looked sharply away, blinded by sudden images from the past—Marilyn laughing as they ran through a flash rain, Marilyn smiling as he put the wedding band on her finger, Marilyn moaning as he moved on top of her.

"We both knew this was coming," she added quietly.

He nodded, but couldn't bring himself to meet her eyes.

A knock sounded on the door. Lee stepped aside as a taxi driver came in with a dolly and loaded Marilyn's bags. Within minutes the man was gone, and although Marilyn continued to stand before him, Lee found the place suddenly, chillingly empty. He looked at her, opened his mouth, but ended up merely shaking his head.

Marilyn stepped swiftly forward, reaching up to cup his face in her palms. "I know," she said. "In spite of the angry words, in spite of everything, I still love you."

"Well, then—"

"But it isn't right. It hasn't been right for a couple of years. You know that. I'm going to be thirty in a few months, Lee. I don't want to spend any more of my life playing wife to a husband who isn't here."

He raised his hands to cover hers. "Maybe I . . . could . . ." He stumbled to a halt, unable to force the words past his throat.

Marilyn could almost smile. "No, you couldn't. Maybe some day, when you've put to rest all those little-boy demons inside you, maybe then you can leave Lone Star. But not now. Now, you won't be happy—you won't be *you*—unless you're setting that place on its ear, dazzling everybody, raking in a fortune." Her eyes filled with sympathy, regret, and a dose of anger. "Maybe you can leave when you've proven to yourself what I already know. You're as good as anybody, Lee. Better than most."

He bent to kiss her. Marilyn backed away.

"Sorry," she said. "I don't think I'm up to that."

"I can't believe this is happening," Lee rumbled. "After all these years, you'd think we could work it out."

"Like I said—lousy timing. Right now, the things we need are just too different."

Marilyn was right, he knew. Yet something inside him rebelled against accepting that it was over. Lee stared at her, the moment stretched out . . . She stepped around him to the door.

"Goodbye, Lee."

He didn't turn, didn't move a muscle. He didn't want to see the door close behind her . . . but he heard it.

When she was gone, he slumped against the wall and covered his face with his hands.

A nearly full moon was high. Its soft light filled the sky, overflowing to spill on the rippling Currituck Sound.

John and Amos Wilkes made it a point to go crabbing a couple of nights a week each summer. Virginia Seafood bought all the crab they could catch, and paid a tidy sum for it. Besides, crabbing gave the brothers an excuse to take off from the wives and kids, and spend the night drinking beer and swapping tales.

It was after ten o'clock when they heard it—a long, screeching noise . . . followed by a crash.

Amos set aside his beer. "Now what do you suppose that was?"

John tugged the brim of his baseball cap. "Reckon somebody had an accident?"

In the ensuing silence, a blood-curdling cry resounded along the shore. The brothers stared at each other, the hair bristling along their limbs. Just as the goosebumps died down, the cry came again, splitting the quiet moonlit night.

"That ain't human," Amos remarked.

The two men pushed to their feet, staring through the darkness in the direction from which the sound had come, taking a few hesitant steps. The ringing cry came once more, and they broke into a run.

The roadside scene they came upon was one of which stories would be told for years. Tom Chastain's fancy convertible was lodged halfway up a cedar by the road. The headlights glared into the ancient branches—raining a glow on the motionless man that lay below . . . and the mustang herd that was gathered about him.

John and Amos turned to each other with wondering eyes, looking back in time to see the shape of a horse materialize on the nearby road. Struggling to its feet, it skittered into the circle of light. The black stallion came forward and nudged the newcomer, a mare, into the fold. Then he looked at John and Amos.

They took a fearful step back as the powerfully built stud came forward, stopping at the feet of Tom Chastain. Suddenly the stallion threw back his head and released the same chilling cry that had brought the men running. The dark eye he then turned on them was ringed with white. They froze where they stood, but the black mustang only backed away, rejoining the others who waited . . . quietly . . . expectantly.

John and Amos looked at each other and in silent agreement sidled a step toward the stricken man. Their movement had the effect of a pistol shot; the herd whirled en masse and thundered into the night.

The Wilkes brothers hurried the rest of the way and dropped to their knees. Tom Chastain's head was turned at a crazy angle, and he was dead still.

The funeral of Thomas Ward Chastain III would have been held in Warrenton, Virginia, but for the fact that his young widow insisted that he be buried in the ancient Walking Dune Baptist Church graveyard. She brooked no argument— not even from Abigail Chastain, who may have pushed the matter if she hadn't been forced to admit that Cara simply couldn't travel, not three days after bearing Tom's child.

The news had come to Abigail in one shocking phone call. Her son was dead; her grandson was born. There was an indecency in the way fate had thrown the two together— death and life, despair and joy. Abigail teetered between the two until she thought she would be sick. Then she *was* sick.

It took two full days for her to gather herself sufficiently to make the trip. Now she stood with a sizable crowd in the black-iron-fenced cemetery—listening to old Reverend Stowe, breathing air laden with ocean salt and crape myrtle, being consumed by a feeling of hate. Abigail bit her lip to keep from screaming.

She hated the damn air! She hated the damn Outer Banks! She hated the damn mustangs Tom had swerved to miss!

"Ashes to ashes," the minister pronounced. "Dust to dust . . ."

As soon as the news reached him in Virginia Beach, Nick Malloy had raced to Walking Dune. Now he stood beside his sister and studied her from beneath lowered lids. All in black, she was as straight and still as a statue, except for the occasional times she rocked the infant cradled in her arms.

Nick looked at his nephew, Thomas Ward Chastain IV, a big, healthy boy despite his harrowing entrance into the world. The shock of her husband's death had triggered Cara into early labor. The doctor said that if the sheriff hadn't had the presence of mind to call him and request his attendance when he told Cara the news, there could have been a double tragedy that night.

Nick broke out in a sweat that had nothing to do with the summer heat. He mourned the loss of Tom Chastain, who had been a good friend as well as a brother-in-law. Three years back, Tom had staked him in a charter fishing business. Nick worked hard and turned it into a success, the first thing of any substance he'd accomplished in his life. Tom had given him that chance.

But at the moment Nick's concern was with Cara. She'd always been invincible, the tough older sister who never backed down. He remembered the time when he was nine, and the bullies of that hell-hole town they grew up in chased him down an alley. Cara had walked right up to them. "We Malloys stick together," she'd said. "Would anybody care to take *me* on?"

One of the gang had been Mitch Lincoln. Nick's hands convulsed into fists. He couldn't think the name without feeling the urge to kill. He'd been too young, too damn young to do anything. Dad was sick, Mom distraught to the point of madness. By the time he grew up enough to realize what had occurred, Mitch Lincoln was gone.

Cara had handled the horror alone.

Later, when Dad died and her hopes for attending college went up in smoke, she got herself a scholarship. Two years after that when Mom died, she swiftly took her minor brother into her own small apartment. "We'll make do," Cara had said. And they had.

She had steel in her veins, he'd often thought. But this was different. He'd never seen Cara like this, not even after that hellish summer that scarred her life as well as her voice.

Nick reached out and closed a hand about her arm, willing strength and comfort to flow from his fingertips. His sister never looked his way.

Reverend Stowe went on and on about Tom.

Dahlia's eyes were stinging with memories—she, Tom, and Louis . . . racing through the shallows of the sound, laughing in the summer sun. She glanced aside at Louis. A breeze lifted his light brown hair, and his jaw rippled as if he'd clenched his teeth. She longed to touch him, but knew she wouldn't. Her heart ached.

Dahlia Dunn. Louis Talbot. She couldn't remember a time when she hadn't known him, hadn't loved him. She still remembered the days when their future together was something she'd taken for granted—girlhood days she should have outgrown and never had.

Their forefathers had been friends, had come to Walking Dune together a century ago, built lodges and indulged in the gentlemanly pastime of duck hunting. The Banks once had been a haven for the sport. Times had changed, but a few well-to-do families from those days had settled. The Dunns, Talbots, Quincys. They were island gentry, if there was such a thing.

Dahlia and Louis grew up together, and in the summertime Tom Chastain had filled out their trio. The three of them had been inseparable, and although Tom was more classically handsome than Louis, there never had been a question of who held Dahlia's heart. Why? she'd often wondered. Tom was charming. Louis had a temper and a sharp tongue, and the most maddening way of treating her like a kid sister, and . . . his faults made no difference.

At eighteen they went their separate ways to college. She and Louis returned to Walking Dune single and unencumbered, much as they'd been when they went away. She took over running the inn and stables that evolved from the Dunn hunting lodge; he took over his daddy's real estate business. Tom came back with Cara.

Dahlia had liked her from the first. It was impossible not to like Cara with her low-pitched voice and easy laugh— even though she *was* a damn voluptuous beauty who drew men's eyes like flies . . . even though one of those foolish men turned out to be Louis.

Tom had never been aware of it, Dahlia thought. Cara was too adept at carrying off Louis's lovesick, moony eyes as friendship.

But now Tom was gone.

The minister finally concluded his eulogy. The widow turned and began to walk away. Dahlia watched Louis scurry like a damn rat after a prize piece of cheese. Her blood slugged through her veins, weighted by a leaden feeling of jealousy.

Still, infuriatingly enough, she couldn't not like Cara.

Hundreds turned out for Tom Chastain's funeral—nearly all of Walking Dune, as well as many attendants from Virginia. Most stopped by the house afterward to pay their respects, murmuring among themselves, exchanging understanding looks when the widow and mother of the deceased excused themselves and went upstairs.

The village womenfolk bustled about, uncovering platters of sliced ham and deviled eggs, casseroles and finger sandwiches, cakes and pies. There was a quiet hum among them as they buzzed to and fro—kitchen, dining room . . . kitchen, dining room.

Like a bunch of bees, Nick thought, watching as they laid out a spread on the dining room table that would feed an army. He'd never understood the custom. Why did everybody bring food to a funeral? Who the hell felt like eating? Apparently a lot of people did. No sooner had the women completed their task than a file of people began to form at the table, plates in hand.

Walking out of the adjoining parlor, Nick stopped in the foyer and cast a worried look up the staircase. Cara had been so stiff when she disappeared up the stairs. So far he hadn't seen her shed a tear. That was like Cara. She'd be far more likely to cry out of anger than sorrow. But this time her restraint worried him. She'd loved her husband to the point of obsession. She was bound to crack. He put an anxious foot on the bottom step.

"Let her be, Nick."

He turned to find that Dahlia Dunn had come up behind him.

"She might need someone," he said.

Dahlia cocked her head to one side and studied the man before her. Like his sister, he had raven hair and deep blue eyes. Nick Malloy was a looker. If her heart weren't already consumed, hook, line, and sinker . . .

"Interested in a woman's point of view?" she asked.

"All right," he surrendered slowly.

"She needs some time alone, Nick. Ever since this thing happened, people have been milling around her."

"But I'm not just people. I'm her brother."

Dahlia gave him a small smile. "Even that doesn't give you the power to take away the hurt. You can't battle her grief for her, Nick. She's going to have to do that herself. And it's going to take a long time."

Nick took his foot from the step and turned to face Dahlia. What she said made sense, and the way she'd said it touched him. His gaze roamed over the pert face, green eyes, red hair. Not for the first time, he thought Dahlia a fine-looking woman, even though she did have a big streak of tomboy in her, and insisted on acting like a man to the point a guy tended to forget she was a woman. But right now, she looked soft, feminine. . . .

"Why don't you come with me?" she said.

The suggestion went through Nick with a pleasurable tingle. A lazy smile came to his mouth.

"Where to?"

"The study. A few of us are gathering around the poker table. We need a fifth."

The smile faded. "Poker?"

"That's right," she answered with a jerk of her head toward the dining room. "It's no less disrespectful than filling our bellies with those vultures over there. Besides, Tom liked poker. I have a feeling he'd like it if we dealt a few in his memory."

Nick hesitated only an instant. "Why not?"

The Chastain house study was a holdover from another era. Like an old-fashioned gentleman's smoking room, it was dark with wood paneling, quiet with plush carpet, studded with sportsman prints of fox hunts and steeplechases. At the far end by the fireplace was Tom's desk, topped with typewriter, stacks of paper, and an eight-by-ten picture of Cara in a silver frame. She'd given strict orders that nothing on Tom's desk was to be touched.

Across from the doorway was the circular game table with its inset of green leather, probably an antique like everything else in the house. Jack Quincy was seated there; a heavy-jowled man in his fifties, he'd been mayor as long as Nick had known about Walking Dune. At Quincy's right was Ned Crockett, a friendly guy about thirty-ish who was with the sheriff's department. Louis Talbot sat next to Crockett. Dahlia was the only woman.

Nick seated her in gallant fashion, then turned the empty chair and straddled it. "Well? Are we here to play some cards?"

Talbot dealt. Quincy squinted at his cards. Dahlia leaned back in her chair. Nick arranged his hand. Full house, kings and fives.

Taking on his best poker face, Nick willed himself to think of other things as the others drew cards. The thought of Cara put a crease between his brows.

"That's two to you, Malloy. What do you say?"

Nick looked up into Louis Talbot's hazel eyes. They were steady, demanding. He'd played cards with Talbot once before, in a private club on the Virginia coast, hundreds of miles north of the Outer Banks. Nick's boat had been in dry-dock for repairs. He had no idea what Talbot had been doing there.

"I'll see you," Nick said, "and raise you five."

He didn't miss the obvious surrender of the other players. Jack Quincy folded his hand. Ned Crockett looked at the ceiling. Dahlia dropped her cards to the table in a show of disgust.

Only Talbot remained. A single hand cradled his cards—carelessly, confidently. The man was from old money. It didn't matter what he lost.

"I'll call you," Talbot uttered with a gleam in his eye, and tossed the necessary five chips into the pot.

Nick spread his hand. Talbot looked, closed his cards, and smiled with the utmost courtesy.

"Whose deal?" he queried.

Cara settled the sleeping baby in the basinette and stepped out of her pumps. Leaving them where they fell, she walked to the dressing table with the oval mirror of beveled glass. Black didn't suit her, she thought mindlessly. The dress and hair were one color . . . like a witch.

Stripping off the hated garment, she was confronted with her reflection in a slip. Tom had liked her this way, had said she reminded him of Sophia Loren. Cara examined herself scathingly. All she saw were full breasts and hips, skin the hue of milk, eyes like hard sapphires—suggesting no feeling, no emotion, because she had none. She would never have feelings again.

She spun back to the basinette and peered down on the babe. *This* is feeling, she insisted desperately. *This* is love. The moment was broken by a rap at the door. She knew who it was.

"Come in," she bade curtly.

Her mother-in-law strolled in with the regality of a queen. "How is my grandson?" she asked.

Her grandson! As if Tommy had no other function in life!

"Sleeping," Cara snapped quietly.

"Good. I want to talk to you, Carolina."

Looking away from her scantily attired daughter-in-law, Abigail meandered to the bay window. "This . . . *tragedy,*" she supplied after a moment, "is nothing to be taken lightly."

Anger hardened the limbs sapped by emotional fatigue. Cara straightened. "Of course it isn't."

"Tom's son should be reared where he can be given everything—"

"Everything Tom would have given him," Cara broke in.

Abigail whirled. "I suggest that the two of you come back to Warrenton with me, where Tommy can be—"

"We're not leaving."

The older woman's nose plumbed the air. "You're being stubborn. This is no place for a child. I don't know what I was thinking when I gave this house to Tom in the first place. The weather is savage, the conveniences deplorable. Why, if a northeaster hits Norfolk, you'll have no power for days. Be sensible, Carolina. Bring your child to Virginia, to the upbringing he deserves."

Rage knotted Cara's stomach and reverberated in her voice. "We're *not leaving,*" she repeated.

Abigail scrutinized her for a moment, then strode across the room. "Bitch," she muttered as she whipped open the door.

"What did you say?" Cara demanded.

The elder Chastain widow turned in the doorway. "I said I hope you'll come to your senses."

The door closed, and Cara took a helpless step toward it, ruing the departure of the woman she despised. Now she was alone, but for the sleeping infant and the attentive specter of grief.

Cara walked woodenly to the bed, fell across it, and caught the scent of Tom's cologne on the silken spread. A fierce fist plowed into the covers. Suddenly Tommy erupted in ragged, heart-rending wails. Cara scrambled off the bed and gathered him up.

Tears streamed down her face as she put her son to her breast.

"There we were down at the Currituck, along about ten o'clock. It was real quiet and peaceful-like when all of a sudden the most godawful sound you ever heard come ringin' through the trees. The hair on the back of my neck stood straight up, and then it come again. 'That ain't human,' Amos said. Isn't that right, Amos?"

"Yep."

The afternoon was drawing to a close. Most folks had already left the tall house with the white wreath on the door. Those who remained had split up, the men retiring to the front porch while the women tidied up the kitchen and rounded up children.

"What do you reckon he was doin' out on Highway 12 at that hour?" Jeb Smith asked.

"His missus said he was on the way back from Manteo," John replied. "We figure Mr. Chastain was comin' along the road, the herd crossed in front of him, and he tried to miss 'em. One of the mares musta got grazed but not hurt bad. Right after we got there, she scrambled up from the road and pranced over to the others, pretty as you please. Didn't she, Amos?"

"Yep."

"I'll never forget it," John went on. "There was poor Mr. Chastain lyin' on the ground, and the whole danged mustang herd standin' around him. About that time the stallion steps up, throws back his head, and lets go with one of them cries. I tell ya, I never heard the like, and never want to again."

The other men shook their heads in respectful acknowledgement of how horrifying such a sound must have been.

"There he was, that big black stud—standin' ten feet away and just lookin' at us. That was when I knew. He wanted us to *help* Mr. Chastain. Dangedest thing we ever saw, wasn't it, Amos?"

"Yep."

Walking Dune was rich with history, and the wild horses were part of it. The mustangs' ancestors had arrived in the 1580s with English colonists who brought them from Spanish settlements. Once there had been thousands. Seventy-five or so survived into the twentieth century, the majority having taken refuge in timberland near the Virginia line. A dozen remained in Walking Dune, roaming the shores and village as they pleased, part of the only known Spanish mustang herd living in the wild.

Old-timers passed down stories of how fishermen once had used the mustangs to drag loaded nets ashore . . . of the coast guard riding "Banker ponies" to patrol the shore during wartime. There was even a story of one indomitable horse who saved eight shipwrecked men by carrying them on his back.

The island lore of Walking Dune was spiced with tales of the wild horses. And after that tragic June, there was one more.

Tom Chastain had given his life for the mustangs, and their leader had called for help.

Chapter Two

"Come on in, son," Frank said.

Lee liked the way he called him "son." It could be just a colloquialism, but Lee preferred to think the endearment carried more weight. Frank's only son had been killed years ago in a plane crash. Frank Winston, widower, millionaire cofounder of Lone Star Partners, had been left entirely alone. He'd gravitated to Lee, virtually adopted him—which suited Lee fine, considering that both his ill-fated parents were dead, and his older sisters had long since moved away from Texas.

"Have a seat," Frank invited.

Lee sank down in a plush, leather chair and looked up. Frank continued to stand before the panel of windows overlooking the city. Below him, San Jacinto Drive bustled. Behind him, the sun was blinding, firing his white hair to brilliance, casting his creased face in shadow, though Lee had the distinct impression that the smile he'd seen on entering the office lingered.

"How's Margo?" Frank asked.

"Margo?" Lee repeated with a blank look.

"For God's sake, Lee! It was just three weeks ago!"

Lee resurrected the memory of the New Year's Eve party at·Frank's sprawling ranch. "Oh, *that* Margo," he crooned. "She's fine, I suppose."

Frank scowled. "You suppose?"

25

Lee stifled a grin. "I haven't seen her, Frank. Sorry."

"Sorry? You're sorry?" Frank shook his head condemningly. "I've set you up with the loveliest ladies in Houston, and believe me, they're among the prettiest in the world! What's the problem?"

Lee allowed the grin to break. "No problem," he replied. "I enjoy myself. She, whoever *she* is, enjoys herself. No problem."

"No longevity!" Frank accused. "Ever since Marilyn left—"

"Marilyn," Lee interrupted, no longer grinning, "has nothing to do with this."

Frank recognized that stony look. For the most part, Lee Powers was smooth-talking and easygoing, his business success owing much to a laid-back brand of Southern charm. But there were times when that forbidding look came over him, reminding Frank that there was a dark side to the typically sunny man. And lately Frank sensed something else, a restlessness that had him worried. He'd thought a woman might make a difference.

"You're right, son," he admitted and, moving out of the glare, came to sit on the corner of his desk. "Forgive an old man, eh?"

Lee studied the craggy features he'd come to love. "Always."

"Good." Frank smiled and clapped his palms together. "Because I've got something new for you."

"What's that?"

"Walking Dune."

"What the hell is Walking Dune?"

"Just wait 'til you see. Thickets of cedar and oak and pine. Mountainous dunes. On an island between the sound and the sea."

"An island where?"

"North Carolina. Let me tell you, son, it's a real coup to gain entrance to an area that's been existing outside the mainstream for hundreds of years. I've already signed a contract for the first parcel of land—it was owned by an out-of-state family that came on hard times. I figure it's enough to accommodate Phase One, but I envision full-scale development. That'll mean dealing with the locals, and the state . . ."

Frank went on as Lee's thoughts took off on a flight of

their own. *North Carolina?* Yet he shouldn't doubt. He had the greatest respect for Frank Winston's instincts. Years ago, when Houston was in an upward spiral that showed no sign of ending, a few business leaders had begun branching out. One of them was Frank Winston.

When oil deregulation hit, and the Houston boom ended with a bankrupting bang, Lone Star Partners rested comfortably on a broad, diversified base extending across a half dozen states. Frank was a mystic. North Carolina, huh?

"I've got agents down there optioning land as we speak," Frank was saying.

"Already?"

Frank nodded.

"So when do we leave?" Lee asked.

"We don't."

"But the geotechnical survey—"

"Has already been done."

Frank retrieved a file and handed it over. It was brimming with charts, maps, blueprints. Lee frowned.

"Now, wait a minute. I—"

"You were in Louisiana."

Frank reached out and placed a hand on his shoulder. "Look, son. I know you've always been in from the beginning, overseen the coring, charted the topography yourself. This time I couldn't wait. This time I'd like you to make an exception and do the preliminaries according to the stats in that file." Frank straightened and stuffed his hands in his pockets. "I sent Jay Lambert. He did a good job."

Lee thumbed through the intricate papers and nodded. Lambert was a fine civil engineer. Everything seemed to be in order. His pique dying in the face of a new challenge, Lee glanced up.

"What kind of development are you looking for?"

"The best . . . only the best. This place deserves nothing less. Wait till you see it. It's like another world."

"How the hell did you get a fix on something in North Carolina?" Lee asked curiously.

Frank settled on the edge of his massive desk. "A friend. She's going to be a silent partner in this one, in fact."

Lee's brows rose. "She?"

"Come on now," Frank blustered. "I'm not so old that I don't know a *few* ladies!"

Lee set aside the file and folded his hands across his stomach, eyeing the older man with a teasing disrespect he knew he could get away with.

"I never would have thought otherwise," he said.

February 3

Morning sunlight streamed through the chintz curtains on the eastern window, glancing off the spotless counters of the cozy Chastain house kitchen. Cara approached the breakfast table and set a plate in front of Louis.

"Homemade scones," she announced. "If these don't make your mouth water, nothing can."

Looking up, Louis thought how wrong she was. Her hair was pulled back, accentuating the perfect shape of her face, and the blue turtleneck she wore made her eyes look almost purple. *She* made his mouth water. But he knew better than to say so, and hid his feelings by taking a long sniff of the pastry before him.

"Elsa must have made them," he said with a grin.

Cara pursed her lips, then slipped into a good-natured smile as she sat down across from him.

"I admit it," she said. "I'm no cook. Elsa is a godsend."

"How long has she been with you now?"

"Four years. I don't know how I ever got along without her." Cara took a bite of the delicious fare, rolled her eyes, and grinned. "Tyrant though she may be."

"Tyrant? That sweet old woman?"

"Don't let those twinkling eyes and silver hair fool you," Cara responded with a wagging finger. "Elsa runs this house, she runs Tommy, and she does her best to run *me*—what I eat, when I sleep . . . what I do, what I don't do. 'You're a young woman. You need to get out more!' "

She knew she'd made a mistake when Louis's expression turned suddenly serious.

"It sounds like good advice," he said.

"Not you, too!" Cara said to fend him off.

Louis sat back in his chair. Since Tom Chastain's death, the men who had gathered the courage to approach his widow had been turned deftly away. Their numbers included himself. At the New Year's Eve party a few weeks back, he'd kissed Cara at the stroke of midnight; but when he warmed to her lips, she'd broken away and fairly run out of the room. Neither had spoken of it since.

"You know, Cara," he said carefully. "It's been almost five years—"

"I don't think anyone is more aware of that than I."

"It isn't normal," Louis insisted, his temper stirring.

"No one but me can decide what's normal for me."

"But five years—"

"It wouldn't matter if it were a hundred."

Cara's voice, though characteristically low, seemed to ring in the sunny room. Louis looked between her shining eyes. When she got that look, there was no pushing her.

"Where's Tommy this morning?" he asked after a moment.

"On the beach with Elsa."

They finished the scones in relative silence. Cara replenished his coffee, resumed her seat and watched him take a sip.

"All right, let's have it," Louis said, replacing the cup in its saucer. "Why did you invite me over this morning?"

"I'm worried, Louis."

"About what?"

"Lone Star Partners."

His mouth formed a silent *O*.

"They're going to rip this place to shreds."

"Rip it to—" Louis chuckled. "That's a bit melodramatic, don't you think?"

"Is it?"

Louis shrugged beneath her steady look. "Maybe Walking Dune could use a little new blood, a little new money."

"What do we need with new money?" Cara challenged. "We get along fine, don't we? We have our own council, our own fire department, church, school, post office, library . . ." She leaned across the table, her eyes searching his. "I love Walking Dune the way it is. The old buildings of the village. The quiet streets. The thickets of cedar and crape myrtle, wild stretches of beach—"

"Okay, okay. I get the picture."

"It will never be the same, Louis. They've already secured a significant amount of oceanfront, and that's only to be Phase One. Lone Star is optioning other property and planning to cut a deal with the state for that wilderness acreage north of town."

"Maybe it won't be as bad as you think. I hear the houses they're planning to build are mansions."

"Is that supposed to make a difference?" Cara asked, arching a brow. "What are you saying? That we should be grateful that the hordes of strangers who will descend on this place have got plenty of money?"

Louis flushed uncomfortably. "I didn't mean it that way. At least Lone Star won't be putting up row upon row of cheap condominiums and motels. At least if Walking Dune has to change, it can change in an upscale way."

Cara wasn't at all placated, but she could see that Louis simply didn't sense the danger that had been making her skin crawl ever since she heard of Lone Star Partners.

When he left, she slipped on her jacket and stepped out back. The February morning was clear and cold, the ocean air biting. Down below, flumes of pampas grass waved in the wind, interrupted every so often by a clump of crape myrtle that would bloom fuchsia in the spring. She moved onto the elevated walkway, which stretched a football field's length from the house to the gazebo. Straddling the dunes, the peak-roofed structure was topped with a weather vane that was spinning round and round in the breeze. Beyond that, sunlight sparkled on the deep blue water.

When she reached the gazebo, she shielded her eyes and scanned the blinding sand. Elsa was near the foot of the gazebo stairs, her long green coat flapping as she bent to pick up a shell. A short distance up the beach, Tommy was drawing in the sand with a piece of driftwood. Cara smiled ruefully. She'd told him to keep his jacket hood up on such a chilly day. But it was down, his unhampered blond curls glistening in the sunlight.

Tom, she thought, accepting the pain that came with every memory she allowed herself. *He's so like you . . . so very much like you.*

Her reverie was interrupted by a misplaced rumble of thunder. Cara turned sad eyes toward the noise. The mustangs were racing across the distant turf toward the beach. They tended to be frisky in the wintertime. Cara's vision went suddenly sharp, darting from the speeding herd to the stretch of beach where a break in the dunes marked the mustangs' path. Her breath froze in her lungs, and for an impossible instant she was unable to move. Once she could, she was down the steps like a streak of lightning.

"Tommy!" she cried, unaware of Elsa's bewildered expression as she raced past, her bootheels digging into the sand, slowing her progress as if in a bad dream. "Tommy!" she shrieked.

He looked up, then turned his head in the direction from which the herd made its thrashing entrance onto the beach.

Time went into slow motion. Cara's frantic eyes relayed her son's small frame, so tiny against the advancing horses. She saw the spray of sand kicked up around them, the frosty clouds puffing from their nostrils. She could no longer feel her churning legs. Her lungs burned. Her ears roared.

Tommy took a fearful, backward step, and they were upon him.

"No!" Cara didn't know whether the word made it past her lips or simply tore through her mind.

At the last second, a black horse separated and galloped round the fringe of the herd. In fluid obedience, the mustangs turned, bypassing the boy in a speeding blur.

Cara lurched the last few yards and grabbed Tommy up into her arms. He threw his arms around her neck and began to cry.

"Shhh, baby," she murmured on a racking breath. "It's all right now." A sob shook her. She grasped him more tightly. "Hush now, Tommy. It's okay."

A moment of knee-buckling relief passed before Cara had the presence of mind to notice they were not alone. Several yards away stood the black stallion.

She looked over Tommy's shoulder with blurred vision, her tearing eyes locked with those of the horse, and . . . an odd sensation swept over her, stilling any movement, tingling along her limbs. For a split instant something passed between them—some recognition . . . some understanding . . . *something*.

The spell was broken as Elsa hurried up, and the stallion turned to trot in the direction of the herd.

"Lord have mercy," Elsa groaned. "Lord have mercy—"

"He did that on purpose," Cara gasped.

"Who?" Elsa queried, her eyes wide with fright.

"Star."

"What?" Elsa shrilled. "*What* star?"

Cara made a sound that fell somewhere between a laugh and a sob. Burying a hand in Tommy's fair curls, she pressed her wet cheek against his.

June 29

Lee pushed aviator glasses up his nose and depressed the accelerator. There was no one on the highway, the speed limit of fifty-five miles per hour seeming ill-applied. The needle climbed to sixty-two, past sixty-five. The sleek car raced through the countryside.

He'd insisted on flying into Asheville and driving the breadth of the state to the coast. He liked soaking up the feel of a place, and he'd never traveled in North Carolina before. But what he'd discovered in a week-long exploration was that he couldn't pin a tag on the changeable region.

A Texan tended to think there was no place as big as Texas; and, of course, in terms of square mileage, North Carolina didn't come close. But the way he'd zigzagged across the state left him with the impression he'd been clear across a country.

The Great Smoky Mountains of the west were hazy shapes against the sky, not as new or jutting as the Rockies—where he'd overseen a development a few years back—but majestic in a way that only the most ancient mountains of America could be.

He'd driven a ways north on the Blue Ridge Parkway and found it breathtaking—lined with trails leading through the fragrant trees that gave North Carolina its nickname of "Pine Tree State" . . . dotted with picturesque villages of chalets bearing names like Blowing Rock . . . conjuring the scent of woodsmoke though, of course, not a chimney was smoking in the advent of summer.

From there he'd darted south into the Piedmont and skirted through the stately city of Charlotte, its modern skyline rivaled by neighborhoods of curving drives and monumental oaks.

The *trees!* God, the *trees!*

Tuesday he'd headed northeast to Chapel Hill and Durham, university cities . . . Wednesday, to Raleigh, the state capital and home of yet another university . . . on to smaller Rocky Mount, which was graced with architecture from the turn of the century. When he left Rocky Mount this morning and continued east, it was like leaving civilization as he knew it.

Let's face it, Lee thought. *I'm a city boy.*

For he had no comprehension of what made up the lives of the people who tended the tobacco fields that were beginning to top on each side of him. Like leafy sentinels, they lined the highway, and there was no one in sight who seemed responsible for the green fields that stretched acre after acre, broken every so often by tall stands of corn . . . a dilapidated silo . . . a seemingly deserted, black-windowed farmhouse. Where the hell *was* everybody?

Afternoon sun broiled from the west. The top was down, and hot wind raged across the car, sweeping the hair from Lee's forehead, tugging at the glasses perched on his nose. A trickle of sweat slipped down his back. The engine hummed; the wind roared; his thoughts wandered.

Houston and Lone Star seemed light years away from these quiet, sunlit fields. Yet he thought of Frank, his penthouse office overlooking the city, his tantalizing farewell the previous week.

"Got something special waiting for you at the Asheville airport," he'd said.

"What?"

"Never you mind." Frank smiled. "You'll see."

The "something special" turned out to be a brand-new Jaguar XKE convertible. Forest green with tan leather interior, the thing was shaped like a missile and moved like one.

Lee smiled. In the years they'd known each other, he and Frank had talked about a lot of things: sports, politics, cars. Frank knew the XKE was Lee's dream car. The smile disappeared. Lee was damn fond of Frank and didn't like the idea that he was beginning to make noise about retiring from Lone Star Partners. On top of that, he was hinting that Lee should take over when he left.

CEO of Lone Star. Damn! Just thinking it took his breath. To reach such a pinnacle had been his dream, his obsession, for as long as he could remember. But somehow, now that it was within reach, things were different.

The truth was, the career that had seemed so glamorous eight years ago was losing its luster. Traveling around the country and overseeing multimillion-dollar developments had given him a breadth of experience few architects could claim. It also had cost him a wife . . . a normal kind of life.

Until recently, Lee hadn't questioned the direction his life had taken. But when he returned to his posh Houston apartment this past winter after polishing off the development in Louisiana, he'd had the odd sensation he didn't belong there. The rooms had been empty, alien. Gradually the feeling had stolen over him that it simply didn't feel like home—worse yet, there was no place that did. He'd found himself itching to get back out of town where he had legitimate cause to feel like a stranger.

So, he'd jumped at the North Carolina project, spearheading the design process, producing elegant plans that rivaled any he'd ever seen. Phase One called for a dozen three-story resort homes with thousands of square feet, patio decks, whirlpools, wet bars . . . plus a full-scale beach club. Phase Two featured chip-putt golf, swimming pools, shops, and restaurants; Phase Three, more mansions.

He glanced again across the green fields lining the highway. Picturing the ritzy development against such a backdrop, he was disconcerted to find it seemed a little gaudy.

The farmlands stretched on toward the coast, interrupted now and then by a small town, eventually giving way to lush swamp. On each side of the road, the trees were tall and green, the water still and shining. Passing through Plymouth, he drove on toward Pleasant Grove. To the north was the Albermarle Sound; ahead, a treacherous coastline notorious for shipwrecks stretching back in time from World War II to the beginnings of American colonization. And on the fringe of that coast was the barrier of islands known as the Outer Banks . . . home of Walking Dune.

Led by Joe Conover, one of the best project managers at Lone Star, the construction crew had moved in weeks ago to clear the land, grade, and start pouring foundations for the luxury homes that would go for close to a half-million dollars a pop. As usual, Lee would arrive in time to oversee the actual building.

Normally at this time he felt like a general arriving to direct his troops. He hadn't anticipated the undermining nuances that had beset him since he'd started cross-country through North Carolina. Somehow, in a matter of days, the land had impressed him with the notion that it should be left alone.

The feeling intensified as he approached the Alligator River and passed a jeep labeled North Carolina Conservancy. They were a legendary group. Working within industry, they'd managed to save several hundred thousand acres as habitats, just within the past year. Their current effort in the area had to do with the endangered Red Fox. As he sped by in the flashy car, the two officers gave him sullen looks. Lee slowed the Jaguar and approached the sprawling bridge across the Alligator at a respectful speed.

To call it a river seemed an insult. After having been in Louisiana, where the river water was a dull brown, he thought the Alligator looked more like an ocean—blue, choppy, topped with cresting waves. The smell of ocean brine was strong.

Leaving the bridge, he passed a sign announcing Dare County—named, he supposed, for Virginia Dare, the first English child born in America. Green forest bordered vast stretches of marsh grass rippling gold in the sun. It looked untouched, virginal, and he found himself wondering if it had changed at all in the four centuries since those first settlers arrived—the Dare family, and the others who had met such a mysterious end in the Lost Colony of Roanoke Island.

He'd read about it only last night, in a promotional book tucked away in the bedside table of the Rocky Mount Motel. Four centuries ago, the English had left a group of a hundred colonists on Roanoke Island. They'd dug in, built Fort Raleigh, waited for the return of the English ships that would bring them the necessities for continuing life in the New World. But war broke out with Spain. By the time the English returned three years later, the colonists had vanished. All that remained was a cryptic clue, part of a word—*CRO*—carved on a tree.

Historians maintained it was the beginning of the word *Croatan,* the name of an Indian tribe who had been friendly to the English from the beginning. But no one could be sure. The Lost Colony remained a mystery.

Roanoke Island. It lay ahead, just across the Croatan Sound.

Lee threw a long-ranging look across the tidewater lands that struck him as both savage and pristine. "Another world," he murmured against the wind and, with a smile, picked up speed.

The dusky light gave way, casting shadows through the rustic, shelf-lined room comprising *Tom's Books.* Cara flipped on the overhead light and returned to the meeting table. Somehow her heart felt both heavy as lead and weightless as fire.

"Two mares in three weeks. We must do something."

Cara's voice was typically low and rasping, but as she looked from one face to the next, her eyes communicated turmoil. Last night another mare had been killed on N.C. 12. Like the last one, she too had been with foal; like the last one, she'd fallen victim to the caravan of heavy equipment that had been streaming into Walking Dune since May.

Cara started making calls as soon as she heard the news. Deputy sheriff Ned Crockett had driven down from Corolla. Doc Simpson—the ageless vet whose first name Cara didn't know—had come from Nags Head. Jack Quincy, Dahlia, Louis . . .

"I don't see that there's anything we can do," Jack responded. "They have the proper permits. As far as I can tell, they're going about their business in a completely businesslike fashion."

Louis gave the older man a scathing look. "Your supportive attitude wouldn't have anything to do with the fact that you're making a fortune off them, would it, Jack?"

"What the hell's that supposed to mean?"

Louis shifted and slung an arm around the back of his

chair. "Come on, Jack. Everybody knows that since Lone Star Partners showed up, your hardware business has gone through the ceiling."

"What about you?" Jack retaliated. "I hear they optioned that worthless tract of yours down by the sound! I'd say you'll be making a killing—"

"Hold on," Cara intervened. There was a grudge between the two men—Louis claiming Jack swindled some Talbot land out of his ailing father shortly before his death, Jack maintaining he'd done the Talbots a favor by taking it off their hands.

"Let's not squabble among ourselves," she continued. "The issue is not how their presence is affecting us, but how it's affecting the mustangs. This is just the first wave. If these resort homes go up the way they've planned, it's going to change Walking Dune forever. More people. More traffic. If we don't stop this thing now, the mustangs of Walking Dune will be picked off like targets at a turkey shoot. How about it, Ned? Is there any sort of citation or limitation or *something* you can serve on these guys?"

The deputy sheriff tipped the hat back on his head. "Not that I know of. It doesn't appear they were speeding. Neither driver had been drinking."

"Unfortunately, there's no law against stupidity," Dahlia said.

Cara considered the caustic comment. "This is no solution," she began slowly, "but at least we could make a concerted effort to educate the people coming in here."

"How do you propose to do that?" Jack demanded.

"Print flyers. Put up posters. Maybe schedule a few meetings."

"What you're talking about takes a lot of time," Jack said.

"Maybe we could take up a collection and reimburse you," Louis sneered.

Jack came to his feet. "I've had enough of you for one day, Talbot. And as for your concern, Cara, I find it admirable, though misguided. You said earlier that Walking Dune is going to change forever. You're right. It's no place for wild mustangs anymore."

"They were here long before any of us," she reminded.

"Look!" Jack retorted. "We all know how you feel about the horses . . . how Tom felt about the horses. But fact is fact. If you really want to do something to protect the mustangs, move them the hell out of here. Transplant them to the northern hills where there isn't a highway for miles."

"That could be just as risky as what's happening here," Dahlia observed. "Right, Doc?"

The vet nodded. "At the very least, changing habitats would be a big adjustment for them. I'm no fortune-teller. Maybe they'd acclimate. Maybe not."

"Well, maybe we should just let things take their course," Jack returned. "That's my two cents' worth."

"I'd call that an accurate estimate," Louis taunted.

Jack flashed him an angry look. "You people can waste your time on this if you like. I have more important things to do."

His footsteps thudded across the slatted floor, and the shop door slammed behind him. Cara slumped in her chair.

"I didn't anticipate his point of view," she said. "Do the rest of you feel that way?"

"Hell, no!" Dahlia snorted. "I say we hire a couple of thugs to beat the hell out of those two drivers, and promise more of the same to anybody who comes close to a mustang!"

"An interesting notion," Ned commented with a grin. "But not exactly legal. By the way, I reckon you all know of the picnic Lone Star is throwing tomorrow."

"I heard," Cara muttered.

Flyers had been posted around town for more than a week. Starting at noon tomorrow, the event was to be held at Slater's Beach—a stretch of undeveloped coast at the south end of town, wild and free until it was caught up in the nets of Lone Star's initial purchase.

"A bit obvious, wouldn't you say?" Dahlia offered. "Actually fatting the 'fatted calves'?"

Cara chuckled. Ned guffawed. Louis took a playful swat at the redhead's shoulder.

"I say we do what Cara suggested," Doc remarked thoughtfully.

The other four, caught in the midst of sarcastic mirth, turned in unison.

"Let's make an effort to educate these people," the vet went on. "I could draft a list of safety and first aid tips. Dahlia here, with all she knows about horses, could write something on their general behavior and habits. Ned? You could put together a statement of the laws that exist to protect the mustangs."

As she considered his suggestion, Cara's gaze darted over the salt-and-pepper hair, the eternally mild-mannered smile, the middle-aged serenity that fairly glowed about Doc Simpson.

"That's great!" she exclaimed. "You've just organized the beginning of an entire campaign!"

"Not really," Doc returned. "Much as I'd like to, I can't be here to run any campaign. Money will have to be collected, a kind of wild horse fund. Printing must be overseen, distribution taken care of . . . If we're serious about this, we're going to need a chairperson, someone on call twenty-four hours a day. Someone to manage the whole thing."

There was an instant of silence.

"I'll do it," Cara volunteered.

Doc smiled. "Thought you might."

"And I can help with the legwork," Louis put in.

Doc's smile grew. "Thought you could."

"I still say a good, healthy beating could work wonders—"

"Dahlia," Doc broke in gently. "Let's give this a try first, hmmm?"

When the meeting broke up, it was after eight o'clock. Ned and Doc Simpson walked off together. Dahlia and Louis waited on the boardwalk as Cara locked up.

The last glow of sunset stole across the empty street and lit on her bare arms and legs. She was wearing khaki shorts and a matching sleeveless shirt tucked in at the waist—a completely casual ensemble that in its very simplicity, Louis thought, showcased her body to magnificence. She ran almost every day, and it showed—in her muscles, which were elongated and defined . . . in her skin, which was an even, glowing brown. She began tying a red bandanna around her head; it streaked above black brows, confined black hair to the back of her shoulders. Louis thought of Indians—maybe Aztecs . . . some noble tribe.

"Well!" Cara said, dropping her hands from the knot in the

bandanna. "I'd call that a productive meeting, wouldn't you?"

"Productive?" Dahlia questioned. "It's a start."

"But a good start," Cara insisted and started to move away.

"Want a ride?" Louis asked.

"No, thanks. I'm going to run." She put a hand on her abdomen. "Work off the huge supper Elsa laid out tonight. See ya!" she tossed and trotted down the steps.

"As if you need to work off anything," Louis muttered.

Dahlia looked up and saw the ardor in the eyes following Cara Chastain's bouncing progress along the roadside.

"Don't you ever give up?" she asked.

Louis glanced over, clearly piqued. "Screw you, Dahlia."

He spun away and took swift strides up the boardwalk.

"I wish." Dahlia sighed and turned in the opposite direction.

Lee had stopped at a seafood place called RJ's—where his attractive waitress, Sandy, had given him her phone number— before crossing the Roanoke Sound and broaching the Outer Banks. Now he drove north along N.C. Highway 12, the only road spanning the string of islands that stretched a hundred and seventy-five miles from the Virginia state line south to Cape Lookout.

Behind him lay Nags Head and the typical commercialism of East Coast beaches. When he hit Southern Shores a half hour back, he'd noted a change—the advent of extravagant mansions folded into land swells along beach and sound.

Money . . . it was almost as if it paid homage to a longitudinal line. For a while the luxury structures had graced the desolate coast. But for the past ten miles, there had been nothing but rolling dune.

It couldn't be much farther, Lee thought, his memory drifting to Joe Conover. He and Joe had worked together a half dozen times, always smoothly. Lee almost purred, thinking of the accommodations Joe had arranged. He'd talked to the man just last night.

"Right on the beach, boss," Joe had said. "Part of the tract Lone Star nailed down and just two doors down from the biggest house in town."

To Joe, big meant grand. Of course, the rented house would be home to a collection of construction workers brought in from Texas with their superintendent. Lee didn't care about big or grand or the workers, as long as his bed had clean sheets. The day had been long, and he was stiff from driving. He could use a good night's rest before sinking his teeth into Walking Dune.

He'd just completed the thought when he rounded a curve. The sun was a fading orange glow in the west, casting dubious light across the highway. One second Lee looked across the dunes to his right, the next he looked back to the road. But it was no longer empty. He didn't know when she'd appeared, but a woman stood smack in the middle of the road—feet planted, arm raised in the universal signal of STOP.

Lee slammed on the brakes, screeching to a halt some twenty feet before her. The stop was so quick that the Jaguar's engine died.

He looked up to register the sight of a spectacular female, scantily covered in a strip of shirt and shorts that barely reached the beginning of her thighs. Tall, bronze, long-limbed, she stood like a defiant sentry, her black hair whipping in the wind.

A damn *Amazon!* Lee thought. And then the sound reached him . . . like the echo of cannon shot, only continuous, building. A breath later, a herd of horses galloped across the road, led by a big black no darker than the mysterious woman's flowing hair.

In an instant, it was over. The woman looked his way, and though Lee couldn't read her expression in the dying light, he got the distinct feeling it was filled with loathing. Seconds later, she launched into a running motion and followed the horses out of view toward the sea.

Lee blinked. The road was once again quiet and still. He had nothing to show for his fast-beating heart but the memory of a wild woman who seemed part of a herd of horses.

"What the hell?" he sputtered to no one.

Reaching for the ignition, he started up the engine and, with a last wondering look across the dusky dunes, shifted into gear.

"She's causin' trouble," Joe concluded.

Lee set aside the last of his bags and looked at the older man with tired eyes. The oceanfront house—announced as

Fast Break in a lazy scrawl across a good breadth of the front exterior wall—was huge and rustic. But it was clean. Lee wanted nothing more than to strip down and climb into the master room's double bed, which looked too short to accommodate his six-foot-two frame. Still, he supposed he shouldn't ignore talk of trouble.

"What kind of trouble?" he asked.

"Talkin' up the local folk. Urgin' 'em not to sell. She wants Lone Star the hell outta here."

"And who the hell is *she?*"

"Cara Chastain. Widow to the biggest money in these parts."

Lee sank to the bed, a weary smile on his face. "Widow?"

Joe grinned around tobacco-stained teeth. "Far be it from me to downplay your influence, boss, but she's one hard nut to crack."

"And the—uh—*nut* lives just two houses up the beach?"

"That's right. She got particularly riled up about them horses."

Lee's ears pricked up. "Horses?"

"Yessir. Believe it or not, they got mustangs living around here, running wild. A couple of the boys were bringing in equipment late at night, and the danged things ran across the road right in front of them. They couldn't do anything to miss them."

Lee recalled the unnerving experience of just two hours before. "I can see how that might happen," he said.

"Two mares have been killed."

A look of regret furrowed Lee's brow. "Damn," he muttered. "And damn again, considering public relations."

"Exactly. I hear tell Mrs. Chastain called a meeting for tonight. She ain't going to let this thing about the horses pass."

"Okay. I get the message. Is everything lined up for the picnic tomorrow?" It was a traditional thing. Lee always threw a get-acquainted party when Lone Star came into a community. It helped to get things off on the right foot.

"Yessir," Joe answered. "The caterers are driving up from Kitty Hawk first thing in the morning."

"Kitty Hawk," Lee repeated. "Nags Head . . . Walking

Dune. They've got the damnedest names for things around here."

Joe nodded, grinning. "I even hired a local bluegrass band to play some music. They're happy to do it for a few hundred bucks."

"Good," Lee mumbled around a yawn. Succumbing to the draw of the mattress, he stretched out and crossed his arms behind his head. "I'll just have to make a public apology about the mustangs and see if that will soften up the little widow."

Joe's brows went up at the thought of Cara Chastain as a "little widow." He started to tell Lee Powers he was off the mark, but then saw that the man's eyelids had dropped.

Across Lee's memory thundered a herd of horses—bays, chestnuts, sorrels, a single black no darker than the raven hair of the champion standing in the road. Damn, she was something. . . .

"Boss?" came Joe's quiet voice. A peaceful snore answered.

"Nite, boss," Joe added, and retreated from the private chamber.

Chapter Three

Cara picked up the coffeepot and began to pour, her back rigid as petrified wood.

"You know how I feel about those people," she said, calmly replacing the pot and lifting her mug. "I'm not going to their blasted picnic, and that's the end of it."

"Then I'll take the boy."

The mug halted at Cara's lips. "You will *not*."

"I will, *too*."

Cara turned, rested her hips against the kitchen counter and—not for the first time—imagined Elsa Logan's tortuous demise. Why the devil did she love the cantankerous old woman so much?

"Elsa," she sang. "You're overstepping your bounds again."

"My 'bounds' include taking care of Tommy, and it's wrong to keep him from going to this party. They're planning games for the children—"

"Please, Mom," Tommy piped in.

Cara's gaze swung to the breakfast table. He was sitting there in his jammies, his hair still tousled from sleep, his cereal spoon lifted halfway to his mouth and forgotten.

"I'll be good," he added with a look of shining hope.

Cara melted like a pat of butter thrust in the path of sunshine. She turned frustrated eyes on Elsa, who should have known better than to bring up the subject in front of the boy.

"You do understand," she said in a near whisper, "that Lone Star is out to castrate our town, *rape* the land we live on."

"Castrate and rape," Elsa smirked quietly. "Now, there's a pair of words. What have you got on your mind this morning?"

Cara eyed the shorter woman meaningfully. "You don't want to know."

Elsa dismissed her mistress's unspoken threat with an uncaring snort. Cara looked across the room at Tommy; her eyes probed his, and she was lost.

"Well, go ahead and put on your shorts!" she huffed. "If you're set on going to this . . . this bacchanalian feast for the enemy!"

Tommy had no idea what his mother meant, but he was up the stairs like a shot.

Lee contemplated the long tables covered with red-and-white-checked cloths. They were laden with Southern picnic fare—fried chicken, cole slaw, hush puppies, watermelon . . . enough to feed half the coast. Pitchers of iced tea laced the tables; tubs of ice sat at each end, brimming with beer; Joe and a group of the friendlier men hovered about, ready to carve watermelons, replenish chicken, or do whatever else was required. Adjacent to the tables, a half dozen musicians tuned up on the bandstand Joe had rented from some place in Nags Head.

Lee's assessing eye swept the expanse of Slater's Beach. Stands of cedar provided shady strips from the road to the dunes. Within their dark green boundaries, the sand had been raked a smooth white, forming a dance floor before the bandstand, and a playing field near the dunes. Beyond the play area, a slatted walkway offered access to the beach.

The setting looked perfect, but Lee sensed he'd made a mistake. It was almost noon, people would be arriving any minute, and the sun was broiling—pouring from a pale sky, reflecting off the sand in shimmering waves.

He was wearing a cool white shirt, jeans that were worn thin, and lightweight boots. Even so, Lee was sweltering. Inside the boots his feet burned. Sweat gathered under his arms and beaded on his forehead. He passed a disgruntled hand across his brow. He'd have done better to plan the damn thing for the evening.

A chugging sound pierced his reverie. Lee glanced over his shoulder to see a truck pull off the road and stop behind the Jaguar. Too late now, he thought and, hiding his misgivings behind a smile, went to greet the first of his guests.

As things got underway, however, he saw that his worries were misplaced. It appeared the entire population of Walking Dune—a whopping two hundred fifty-three—had turned out, and they were taking the heat completely in stride. Dressed in cool clothes and sunhats, they milled around the picnic tables and before the bandstand, where they tapped their feet to lively bluegrass tunes. The majority of children had gravitated to the sandy field where a mix of Lone Star and village people had organized relay races.

After an hour or so, Lee took a break from diplomatic mingling and stepped into the meager shade of a cedar. He was hot and sweaty and tired of smiling, but he'd succeeded in meeting a good many of the residents from whom Lone Star had optioned property. The Quincys, Bradfords, Hales, and Freemonts, and a giggling spinster by the name of Nettie Wolf. All of them had been friendly.

Louis Talbot, whose optioned property would be a corner lot in Phase Three, was a bit reserved. But so far the only hostile note had come from Talbot's feisty companion, Dahlia Dunn.

"Put a muzzle on your bulldozers," she'd said. "We like our mustangs up and running."

Lee's mouth twitched good-naturedly at the memory. It was still early in the game, but as he reviewed the general consensus, he was pleased. On the whole, he liked the people of Walking Dune. They not only had a down-to-earth way about them, but also an air of refinement enhanced by the distinctive Outer Banks accent—a drawl edged with a clipped British ring.

Propping a shoulder against the tree, Lee surveyed the milling crowd. Yes, he decided. He liked them. Better yet, he got the impression they liked him too. If a sour remark from a redhead was the only negative of the day, he'd consider it a success.

A short while later the band announced a break. Speech time. Straightening away from the cedar, Lee waded through the crowd, vaulted onto the bandstand, and stepped up to the microphone.

"Afternoon, folks," his voice resounded. "For those of you I haven't had a chance to meet yet, my name is Lee Powers. All of us from Lone Star welcome you here today."

He smiled across the blur of faces turned up to him. "Everybody got plenty of chicken?"

There was a murmuring response.

"Plenty of watermelon?"

The murmur swelled.

"Plenty of beer?"

The crowd erupted in laughter. Lee joined them.

At the back of the audience Cara tipped her head in Dahlia's direction. "Boy, *he's* a smooth one, isn't he?"

"Oh, yeah," Dahlia murmured. " 'Put a muzzle on your bulldozers,' I told him. 'I'll be sure to consider that, Miss Dunn,' he says."

The speaker wiped a hand across his brow. "Whew, it's a right hot day! You people have got a pretty island here, I grant you. But one thing I gotta know—is it always this hot?"

"Just wait 'til you see your first nor'easter, boy!" an old-timer called.

Lee fanned himself. "I'm ready right now," he said with a grin.

The crowd laughed again. Cara grimaced. "He's certainly charming the pants off everybody."

Dahlia nodded. "Half the ladies here would drop theirs, that's for sure. I thought Nettie Wolf was going to bat her lashes right off her eyelids. I must admit, he *is* a damn good-looking man."

"Really?" Cara replied disinterestedly. She shielded her eyes to get a better view—not of the "damn good-looking man," but the top representative of Lone Star Partners.

"Seriously, folks," he was saying, "I just got in last night, so I haven't had time to get to know you or the town. But from what I've seen so far, Walking Dune is a unique place. I want you to know that we at Lone Star intend to preserve that uniqueness."

"The only way they can do that," Cara muttered, "is to get the hell out—"

"I heard some bad news last night. Our project manager, Joe Conover, informed me there have been two accidents. Fortunately no people were hurt. Sadly, two of the wild horses were. All of us at Lone Star are deeply troubled by these incidents—"

"I think I'll leave before this stuff gets too deep to walk in."

Dahlia responded with a roll of her eyes and a smile.

"I've got some work to do at the shop," Cara added. "See ya."

Dahlia raised a hand in farewell and, as Cara moved away, began scanning the crowd for Louis.

"On a brighter note," Lee went on, "I think you can take heart from the fact that what we do at Lone Star we do well. The company has a nationwide reputation for quality design and construction. You can rest assured that our plans for Walking Dune will yield one of the finest developments in the Carolinas."

He paused to let the drama of his statement sink in. The crowd hummed, Lee's gaze tripped across the nodding heads, and . . . he saw her.

The black hair was pulled up in a ponytail instead of hanging free about her shoulders. And she was wearing white, not that tan color which, from a distance, made her appear nude. But the long arms and legs were the same . . . and the body. Damn, if it wasn't the *Amazon*! Taking off at a clip toward the dunes! Suddenly aware that he was staring off into the distance, Lee brought his view back to the crowd and found them regarding him curiously.

"Well, I guess that's all that needs saying," he finished with a quick smile. "Please . . . eat up, drink up. Have a good time. I'm looking forward to getting to know all of you."

There was a polite round of applause as he jumped down from the bandstand and moved to the edge of the crowd, his eyes searching, zeroing on the distant figure. She was kneeling, talking to a small boy as fair as she was dark. Lee strode in her direction. She straightened and turned to a round, grandmotherly type with silver hair knotted on the back of her head. He was making good progress when Jack Quincy flagged him down.

"Nice speech, my boy—"

"Thanks, Mayor."

Lee cut off the surprised man with a passing nod and moved on, looking up to see that the mystery woman was no longer at the children's playing field, but was making a beeline away from the beach. He halted in midstride and watched her merge with the swell of the crowd—invisible but for an occasional bob of her head. Picnic tables and a sea of people separated them.

Reversing his pace, Lee swore as he tripped over a tree root. He glanced up and saw Jack Quincy's questioning eyes leveled on him, as well as those of the mayor's wife and several others. Tendering a vague smile to the lot of them, Lee walked on a bit more sedately, and made up time by skirting behind the bandstand. Hurrying into the open, he paused to scan the entrance area, his gaze lighting on her just as she disappeared around the screen of cedar lining the road.

"Damn," Lee muttered under his breath.

He must have spotted her—what?—five minutes ago? It felt like he'd been tracking her for days. Striding into motion, he cut across the sandy field, closing the gap so that when he rounded the stand of trees, she was only meager yards ahead. He didn't notice Joe Conover until the man stepped directly in front of him.

"I was just coming to ask you something, boss. The crew was wondering—"

"Can it wait, Joe?" Lee interrupted, peering over the shorter man's head. "There's somebody I'd like to meet."

Following his line of vision, Joe glanced up the road.

"You *do* know who that is, don't you, boss?"

"Who?"

"Cara Chastain."

Lee's gaze swerved. "The *'little widow'*?"

Joe flicked the ever-present cowboy hat off his forehead. "Been meaning to fill you in on that . . ."

Lee stepped around and took off with long strides. Joe followed for a few steps, watching curiously. He'd seen a number of ladies chase after Lee Powers, but never the other way around. With a rumbling chuckle, Joe craned for a better look.

She was just ahead, coming up on the Jaguar parked by the road.

"Hello!" Lee called. She didn't slow, didn't show any sign of having heard him. He trotted a few steps and caught her trailing arm with a light, detaining hand.

"Excuse me," he said a bit breathlessly. She turned, and whatever breath he'd been drawing stopped halfway down his throat.

The brows were black slashes above deep blue eyes . . . the cheeks high and glowing with sun . . . the lips, full and red and shaped so perfectly they looked as though they'd been drawn there with a ruddy pencil.

"Excuse *me,* Mr. Powers," she returned.

Unusually low and husky, her voice set Lee's spine tingling. She glanced pointedly at the hand on her arm. He saw the gesture but failed to register its meaning.

"*Excuse* me?" she repeated.

This time, her sharp tone broke through. "Oh, sorry," Lee muttered, releasing her arm . . . scrambling to gather his wits.

He offered a smile. She didn't return it, only continued looking up at him with unnerving steadiness. Half a head shorter than he, she was tall for a woman, which might account for his initial impression when she surprised him on the road. Today she was wearing an equally casual shirt, shorts, and sneakers, but . . . today he was close enough to pick up a pungent air of dignity. If she *had* been an Amazon, she'd have been their queen.

"Nice to see you again," he said.

"Again? I wasn't aware that we'd met."

They were standing next to the Jaguar. Lee shifted back against the hood and draped an arm over the windshield.

"In a way we have," he said. "Last night on the highway."

Cara glanced at the car, remembered it, and looked back at the man's face. There was the hint of a grin there, shining in the dark eyes, lifting the corners of the dark moustache. It occurred to her that he was pleased with himself, as if his allusion to a near tragedy were somehow exceedingly clever.

"So that was you," she remarked. "I should have known."

Lee's friendly grin settled to half-mast. "Should have known what?"

"That it was one of *you* people. No one from around here comes barreling up Highway 12 at that speed."

The grin disappeared altogether. "I was going the limit," he replied. "No faster."

"A convenient excuse."

Excuse! Lee's brows shot up for an instant, then drew together in a dark line.

"I'm not making excuses," he said evenly. "It's a public road."

"No doubt . . . and due to become a veritable freeway if you have anything to do with it."

Her highfalutin way of speaking fanned his irritation. "You are, of course, entitled to your opinion," Lee drawled with misleading courtesy, "however misinformed it might be." Surprise flickered over her set features. Probably unaccustomed to anybody taking her down a peg . . .

"If anyone's misinformed," Cara flared, "I should think it's you. Anyone who *is* informed knows better than to go the full speed limit on that road, *particularly* near a crossing, *particularly* at that hour. If I hadn't been there, we could have chalked up another mustang or two."

She hadn't raised that sexy voice of hers, yet it rang in Lee's ears. Her cheeks had turned crimson, her eyes to blue fire. She was as high-spirited as one of her damn mustangs. Irritation dissolved in the luscious taste of challenge. Before he realized what he was doing, he slipped into a smile. She seemed to take it as a slap in the face.

"Good *day*, Mr. Powers," she snapped.

Whirling around, she moved away, her long legs carrying her swiftly up the roadside. Lee straightened away from the car.

"Hey!" he called, his insolent smile broadening. "Can I give you a ride home?"

She glanced over her shoulder—"I have my own transportation, thank you!"—and kept going.

Lee backed along the line of parked cars, watching with lingering interest as she stopped some six cars up the road and drove away in a red Wagoneer. When he pivoted near the entrance to the picnic area, he all but collided with Joe again. The older man grinned up at him.

"Seems the 'little widow' don't take to you much, boss," he teased.

Lee raised a rebuking finger.

"Nor to convertibles," chimed a male voice.

Lee turned to see Louis Talbot swaggering toward them, proferring a cold-eyed smile that smacked of a declaration of war. Lee's pleasant expression faded.

"She doesn't like convertibles?" he repeated.

Talbot shook his head, still wearing the crocodile smile. "Her husband was killed in one. It'll be a cold day in hell when Cara Chastain rides in that topless machine of yours."

"We'll just have to see about that, won't we?" Lee sparred.

Hiding a merry look, Joe stepped aside and bowed out of the confrontation. Talbot lost even the semblance of friendliness.

"If you've got anything on your mind besides passing curiosity," he said, "you're barking up the wrong tree."

"Are you telling me you've staked some kind of claim on the woman?" Lee returned, his eyes narrow and drilling. Talbot returned the look with good measure.

"As much as any man *can*," he snarled and stomped away.

The picnic broke up around four. Lee bid farewell to the guests, shaking hands, introducing himself when he noticed someone he hadn't met. Through it all, his secret thoughts kept returning to Cara Chastain.

She was not like any woman he'd ever seen. Tall, muscular, eyes blue as the Atlantic, hair black as night. She emanated a sort of untamed power. Yet her manner was reserved to the point of iciness, her high-brow speech like a sword . . . wielded, he mused, to cut down anyone who dared cross her.

The last of the picnickers departed. Joe went off to get a clean-up detail underway. Lee decided to take a look around town. Passing up the Jaguar, he left Slater's Beach and walked north along the road.

It was hot and quiet, sandy wilds stretching hundreds of yards in every direction. The first house he encountered was Fast Break, with towels hanging from balconies on both levels, and the yard littered with vehicles bearing the Lone Star logo. Thicket covered the next lot, then a beach house similar to Fast Break, and then . . . a stately Victorian that loomed like a castle over its fellows.

The Chastain house, Lee thought, his architect's eye scanning the full three stories, the shape of the roof with the widow's walk. He'd guess it was built around the turn of the century.

The elegance of the estate—and it seemed right to label it such—started long before he reached the house. A white picket fence defined the grounds, enclosing a manicured lawn, fluffy stands of pampas grass, clusters of palms. Crape myrtle lined the roadside, reaching over the white fence every ten feet with branches of purplish pink blossoms.

Lee paused at the front gate. A long, bricklaid path paved the way to the house, continuing as steps to a veranda detailed with a gingerbread pattern from the 1890s. He was drawn to take a closer look but couldn't quite swallow the idea of showing up unannounced on Cara Chastain's doorstep. With a final longing look he moved on.

There were a couple more cottages, small and modest next to the Chastain house. Then he hit "town," if you could call it that. It was really nothing more than two rows of buildings lining N.C. Highway 12, which was renamed Main Street for the duration of the town limits.

Flags flew before the post office and firehouse, the most modern-looking structures of the group. The rest looked as though they were from another era, when shaded porches served as gathering spots for folks who made the trip "to town."

Granted, some of the town buildings had been given facelifts of natural wood and glass angles. Granted, pine and cedar bestowed a clean freshness on the seaside air, a carpet of fragrant needles on the sandy ground. Still, Walking Dune was nothing more than a pretty ghost town, trimmed with boardwalks and a quiet desolation announcing: Closed on Saturday.

Wolf's Fabric and Notions . . . Quincy's Real Estate and Hardware . . . Freemont's General Store and Pharmacy. Every building seemed to house at least two functions, and every one was shut tight. During the entire fifteen minutes it took to walk along one side of "town," Lee didn't see a single person; nor did a single car pass. What the hell did people *do* around here? Back at the Fast Break the boys would be breaking out the leftover beer from the picnic.

The image of Houston broke into his mind's eye, a dream or—depending on your point of view—an obscenity. Skyscrapers and steel had no place here. This was, he reminded himself, "another world."

Pausing at the end of the boardwalk, Lee cast a look up the highway. A comfortable distance away was an old, whitewashed church topped with a steeple, surrounded by a fenced-in cemetery, shaded by gigantic live oaks. Across from the church stood a three-story brick schoolhouse that looked as though it had been built in the forties. Beyond the facing structures, stretching north as far as the eye could see, was a wilderness of sand dunes interspersed with pine and cedar.

Crossing the road, Lee skipped two steps up to the boardwalk—which was just as empty as the one across the street—and headed back the way he'd come. His bootheels clicked an unrequited message; his thoughts drifted.

Walking Dune . . . That afternoon, in making conversation with Jacob Abernathy, who doubled as postmaster and choir director, Lee had learned the logic of the strange name. "In these parts," northeasters and hurricanes caused old inlets to die and new ones to be born. Fierce winds caused dunes to march across the island.

"Sounds like the place is alive," Lee had commented.

"And so it is, my boy," Abernathy had returned. "So it is."

Walking Dune—home of island storms, Spanish mustangs, and . . . Cara Chastain. Just then, Lee came across a shop with an open door, the sign announcing: Tom's Books. Open till six.

He stepped inside, the back of his mind lingering on the image of deep blue eyes and a body that ought to be outlawed.

Cara was perched on the stool behind the counter, trying to make heads or tails of the inventory list.

"Ten volumes of Shakespeare's complete works?" she muttered, and slashed her pen through yet another entry that had nothing whatever to do with the shipment she'd received the day before. A noise came from the shop door. She glanced up distractedly.

"Well, *hello.*"

The lilting greeting suggested both surprise and pleasure. He strolled—no, swaggered—toward her. Cara was immediately annoyed.

"Hello, Mr. Powers." She looked back at the papers in her hand. "I'm afraid you've caught me at a bad time."

"That's all right. I can wait."

She flashed him a look of aggravation. Lee crossed his arms across his chest, rocked on his bootheels, and smiled. She made him feel downright wicked. With exaggerated deliberation, she set aside her papers, rose from the chair, and moved from behind the counter, bringing the incredible body into view. Damn, she was *something.*

"What exactly may I do for you?" she asked.

The image that popped into his mind was shameless. It must have shown. Her expression took on the fierceness of a glare, a single coal black brow lurching into a severe arch.

"Well?" she prodded.

"Well, I was just looking around. What *is* this place, anyway?"

Cara gestured to the walls lined with bookshelf upon bookshelf. "We have books here," she said with mock pleasantness. "We sell them, we loan them out. Tom's *Books* . . . Get it?"

Suddenly it hit him—*Tom.*

"Named for your husband?" Lee asked gently.

She seemed to flinch, though what gave him that impression, Lee couldn't really say; a mere second after the thought occurred to him, she was regarding him levelly, the blue eyes calm and cold as a frozen lake.

"That's right," she answered. "Would you like to buy a book? Borrow one, perhaps?"

"Not really." Lee took a slow step closer, the feeling of wickedness having dissolved in an urge to connect with her. "As I said, I just happened by. But now that I'm here, I'd like to take the opportunity to mend the breach that seems to be springing up between us—"

"There's nothing at all springing up between us," Cara interrupted. "Mr. Powers, you have—"

"Lee," he corrected. She arched that damnable brow again.

"As I started to say, *Mr. Powers,* you have a nice, friendly way about you—"

"Thank you." Her nostrils flared.

"And you make pretty speeches—"

"Thanks again." Lee smiled.

"But a picnic doesn't obscure the harm Lone Star Partners is doing here in Walking Dune."

She made the statement in that soft-spoken way of hers, but the look on her face was vehement. Lee smoothed his moustache, the smile disappearing beneath his fingers.

"It wasn't meant to obscure anything," he said. "Just help things go a little more smoothly."

"For whom?"

He shrugged. "For everyone. The townspeople, the crew—"

"The mustangs?"

"So we're back to that. Look, I can't tell you how sorry I am about the two horses that were hurt—"

"Killed."

"All right, killed. I wish it hadn't happened, but from what I heard, my men weren't driving recklessly. The horses darted out in front of them on a dark road—"

"Ten yards beyond a 'horse crossing' sign—"

"There was no avoiding the accidents—"

"Folks around here pay attention to those signs. A little caution would have prevented those *'accidents'*."

Lee slumped to one leg and eyed her. She was immovable as a mountain.

"Look, lady. There are costs when a major development gets underway—on all sides. Walking Dune is moving into the twentieth century, and Lone Star is picking up the tab. Did you think it would be painless?"

Cara folded her arms. "The price of progress, huh?"

"You could say that."

"What if we're not willing to pay that price?"

Lee propped his hands on his hips. "Judging from the reaction at the picnic this afternoon, I'd say most people are willing."

"Most people don't grasp the full scope of what's happening here."

"And you do," he concluded.

"You're damn right I do."

The hushed words rang with adamance, defiance . . . the threat of an iron-willed adversary. Lee stifled the impulse to whistle, low and long. She was *something*, all right.

"I hear you called a town meeting last night," he said after a moment.

"Not a town meeting, but yes, a few of us got together."

"A few?"

"Ned Crockett, Doc Simpson . . . Louis, Dahlia—"

"Dahlia? The redhead?"

"She's very knowledgeable about horses."

"Great," Lee muttered, glancing at the floor.

"We're organizing a campaign," Cara announced.

He looked quickly up. "Against Lone Star?"

"*For* the mustangs."

His gaze hovered between her eyes. "It amounts to the same thing, doesn't it?"

"Yes. I guess it does."

Lee studied her, and the hot stirring began anew, reminding him of the first time he looked into her face.

"I reckon that puts us on opposite sides of the fence," he said.

"I reckon so." An idea burst into Cara's mind. "Unless . . ."

"Unless what?"

Her gaze swept over the Texan, top local authority for Lone Star Partners. "Unless you'd be willing to come around to our side."

"Come around . . ." Lee released a light laugh. "You've got nerve, lady. I'll grant you that."

"Don't you *dare* treat this issue lightly."

Though issued in her usual low-pitched murmur, the command wiped the grin off Lee's face.

"You have no concept of what you're jeopardizing," Cara went on. "Walking Dune has existed for centuries—unspoiled, unbridled. The people who make their homes here endure blistering summers, savage winter storms, hurricanes, power outages. I doubt your fancy resort folk will last through one northeaster. Where will that leave your multimillion-dollar development? And as for the horses, this is the only place in the world where Spanish mustangs live wild and free.

They've been here on the island four hundred years. Lone Star has been here four weeks. Just who the hell do you think has more claim?"

Lee studied her, his thoughts darting between what she'd said and the inescapable idea that, with her color high and eyes flashing, she was the most magnificent thing he'd ever seen.

"They've been here four hundred years?" he managed.

Cara sighed with obvious exasperation. "The mustangs have a very long and illustrious history, Mr. Powers. Perhaps you should learn something about them before you so blithely decide they're an acceptable casualty in the name of your beneficent progress."

"Perhaps *you* could enlighten me. Over dinner, maybe?"

Surprise infused her face, followed by something he had no time to read before she turned swiftly away. Selecting a booklet from the counter, she thrust it into his hands.

"This volume is well documented," she said. "It will enlighten you far better than I can."

"Though not so . . . inspiringly."

Lee supplied the word in a low, intimate tone. She peered for a moment as though she'd been insulted, then stepped aside to a table covered with books.

"If you'll excuse me, Mr. Powers, I'm very busy. I was intending to close up just before you came in."

"The sign says open till six." The blue eyes snapped at him like a couple of angry watchdogs.

"It's *my* shop, *my* library. I can close it whenever I like."

Lee raised his palms. "What are you so mad about?"

"I'm not mad."

"It sure seems like it."

Cara began stacking returned books in a meaningless pile. "I hardly think you know me well enough to judge my moods."

"All I did was ask you to dinner."

She stacked faster. "Your ulterior motives seem clear."

"My what?"

Cara slapped a hand on the top book and met his eyes. "As you said, we're from opposing camps. You don't care to change your position, and I assure you I'm not going to change mine. I intend to do everything in my power to deter

Lone Star's development of this island. No picnic, no pretty speech, and no dinner invitation will change that."

"I see," Lee said slowly. "Well, you're right. I *do* have ulterior motives." She smirked with satisfaction. "But they have nothing to do with Lone Star."

He was watching her with an expression that appeared half-teasing, half-serious. Cara saw his lips part in a smile, creating a white strip beneath the dark moustache. Something rippled through her, something . . . startling. She turned her back and moved away.

"If you're trying to flirt with me," she tossed over her shoulder, "you're wasting your time."

"Really?" came the deep voice behind her.

"Yes. Really." Cara stepped behind the counter, feeling infinitely more comfortable by putting a barrier between them.

"And why is that?"

"I don't go out with men. For dinner, or anything else."

Lee's gaze dipped from her eyes to her mouth and back again. "That's a shame."

The same discomfiting sensation swept over her. "I don't happen to think so," she countered. "I'm quite content with the arrangement, and have been for quite some time."

"How much time?"

"That's not your business," Cara returned briskly. "I asked you to leave, Mr. Powers—*twice,* I believe."

"And I told you, I'm Lee." Shifting the book she'd given him from hand to hand, he took a step forward. "Cara . . ."

He spoke her name. That was all. Yet the sound of it shivered over Cara, like a masculine touch running down her spine.

Her face caught fire in a way she thought she'd forgotten, the comfortable old blinders fell, and she was confronted with . . . a man—big, lanky, handsome to the point of absurdity. His dark hair was thick and wavy, his eyes almost black and lined with the most amazing fringe of lashes. Awestruck, Cara was unaware of the way her gaze went racing over him— broad shoulders, narrow hips, long legs. . . .

"Do you think you might reconsider about dinner, Cara?"

Cara lifted stunned eyes and found his sparkling with amusement. Of *course* he was amused! Hadn't he just caught her in the midst of the most disgraceful study of a man she'd ever undertaken?

"The name is Mrs. Chastain," she announced.

Though her cheeks were bright with flustered color, her tone was cool and imperious, her proud stance nothing short of majestic.

"All right," he said after a moment. "If that's the way you want it."

Cara raised her chin.

"Thanks for the book," he added.

"My pleasure."

She said it while looking somewhere beyond his shoulder. Lee didn't want to leave, but damn if he knew how to stay any longer. He waited for her to meet his eyes. She didn't.

"Well then, until the next time—"

"There will *be* no next time, Mr. Powers."

He turned and walked away, but not before Cara saw the flash of a grin beneath his moustache. Pausing at the open doorway, he looked back.

"You're wrong about that, Mrs. Chastain," he said and, with a passing salute, sauntered out.

She waited—giving him time to get far away, shutting out the sight of him each time it flashed before her memory's eye. When a full five minutes had passed, she grabbed her purse and darted around the counter. But as she reached the door, the unwelcome image returned—*him* filling the doorway, blocking the golden sunlight until it haloed his tall frame.

Cara fumbled with the lock, cursed under her breath, and fled the shop. But she couldn't escape the cloud of self-reproaching shock that followed her along the sunny boardwalk.

Lee Powers had forced her to look at him as a man. And for the first time in five years, the woman in her had come alive.

Lee shared a beer with the boys, but declined their invitation for a night on the town down Nags Head way. He didn't begrudge them the chance to let off steam; it was Saturday night, and come Monday, they'd be working their asses off.

So would he, but right now he wasn't in the mood for a tour of loud, smoky bars.

With a last round of catcalls and warnings of what he was going to miss, Joe and the rest of them drove away in a bevy of trucks and left the Fast Break quietly empty. Withdrawing another beer from the ice chest, Lee went out back.

It was nearly seven o'clock. The heat was letting up, the light turning soft. He walked across the deck supported by ancient pilings, and rested a hand on the cedar rail, long since bleached silvery white by sun and salt air. A strip of walkway repeating the color stretched ahead of him, and beyond that, steps that led down to the beach.

Lee took a swig and looked to the right. As far as he could see, there was nothing but rolling ocean, deserted beach, sea oats waving atop the dunes—wild coastline stretching all the way to Slater's Beach. Soon, that would change—replaced by mansions with carpets of grass tucked around them, and half-million-dollar views from every balcony. At the moment the prospect chimed with a solemn note.

A puff of sea breeze stirred his hair as Lee mosied along the walkway. When he reached the steps, he went most of the way down, took a seat, and looked out across the beach. At this hour the ocean was dark and calm, its rhythmic lapping like a restful, end-of-the-day song. With a sense of surprise, he felt tension leave his neck and shoulders, not having realized it was there until it melted away.

Noticing a piece of driftwood resting in the nearby sand, he set aside the beer and fished the old pocketknife from his back pocket. Turning the wood in knowing fingers, he found a likely spot and switched the knife open with the practiced flick of a wrist. A whistle filtered from his lips as he applied the blade. Minutes later he heard something and looked up to see a towheaded kid approaching at a gallop across the sand.

"Hello," he greeted, coming to a stop at the base of the steps.

It was the boy he'd seen with Cara Chastain. "Hello," Lee replied. The boy's pale curls and eyes were completely unlike the woman, but something about his face . . .

"You're one of those Lone Star people, aren't you?"

"That's right. My name's Lee. What's yours?"

"Tommy Chastain. We live just over there."

He pointed to where the tall roof of the Chastain house pierced the sky.

"Who's 'we'?" Lee asked.

"Me and Mom. Elsa lives with us, too. She's our house-keeper."

So, he *was* her son.

"I heard Mom tell Elsa something this morning. She says you're going to castrate us."

"What?" Lee sputtered, his brows flying up.

"She says Lone Star is going to castrate the town."

Lee couldn't hold back a peal of laughter.

"What's so funny?" Tommy asked a little fiercely.

"Oh, nothing," Lee said, his chuckles dying down. "It's just a funny expression. That's all."

"What does it mean, anyway?"

There was a hint of Cara in the steady way the boy looked him in the eye. "I think your mom meant she likes Walking Dune the way it is," Lee said.

"Oh." Tommy cocked his head to one side, his gaze falling to Lee's hands. "Whatcha doin'?"

"Whittlin'." Lee took a few demonstrative strokes at the wood.

"Do you like whittlin'?"

"Um-hmmm. I bet I've liked whittlin' for—well, let me see—more than twenty-five years now."

"Wow!" Tommy breathed.

Lee nodded in amused agreement, realizing twenty-five years sounded like a century to a kid Tommy's age.

"Is that your knife?"

"Um-hmmm." Lee held up the switchblade with the pearl handle. "It belonged to my dad, and his dad before him. Pretty, isn't it?"

"Could I hold it?"

Lee recalled asking the same thing in the same mesmerized way about a lifetime ago. "How old are you, boy?"

Tommy stretched as tall as he could. "Five."

Lee appeared to consider his answer with great seriousness. "Well, partner," he then said, "I'll tell you like my daddy told me. A knife is not a toy. I had to wait until I was ten before he let me hold this one."

"Oh." The word was filled with disappointment.

Lee hid a grin. "I tell you what I'll do, though."

"What?" the boy voiced hopefully.

"I'll whittle you something. Would you like that?"

"Sure!"

"Okay. What'll it be?"

Tommy squinted his eyes as he thought about it. "How about a horse?" he suggested.

"A horse," Lee repeated slowly, his thoughts darting to the boy's mother. "That figures . . . Okay, a horse it'll be."

Tommy's eyes fixed on his hands, as if he expected the carving to spring forth at any moment.

"I'll have to get a nice piece of wood," Lee grinned. "It's going to take a while. Okay?"

"Okay." Tommy's face broke into a beaming smile. "Hey, Lee! Would you like to see the Portuguese man-'o-war that washed up on the beach?"

Lee closed the knife and tucked it in his back pocket. "Sure," he replied, rising to his feet and taking a downward step.

"Well?" Tommy questioned, not moving from the base of the stairs.

"Well, what?"

"Aren't you going to take off your boots?"

Lee's gaze fell to the boy's bare feet. "Oh, is *that* the way it's done?"

Tommy looked up with an expression of grave concern. "I can see you need somebody to show you the ropes."

Lee threw back his head and laughed heartily. "I guess you're right," he admitted and, stripping off his boots and socks, followed the boy onto the cooling sand.

Cara walked onto the gazebo and searched the stand. Tommy knew better than to leave the house without telling anyone, but these days he seemed prone to forget. In fact, she suspected he got a kick out of putting one over on Elsa.

She spotted him some fifty feet up the way, where he and . . . *somebody* were kneeling over something they'd found on the beach. As the two of them straightened, Cara recognized Lee Powers.

It had taken her no longer than the drive home from the shop to discredit her silly reaction to the man. But now, as she saw him unexpectedly, her heart skipped in the most stupid way.

She sidled up to the rail, watching them. Tommy was talking animatedly, then opened his arms wide as if demonstrating the size of something monstrously big. The man laughed and, applying his hands to Tommy's, corrected them to a more diminutive measure.

An odd yearning flared within Cara, something wrapped up in the idea of men and boys . . . fathers and sons. She took an impatient step toward the stairs, intent on breaking whatever spell had come over her. But as she looked once more in Lee Powers's direction, her pulse fluttered warningly.

"Ridiculous!" she muttered, and yet decided she wasn't setting one foot on the steps to the beach. She'd simply have to call Tommy and hope he heard her. She put her hands to her mouth in the shape of a megaphone.

"Tommy!" she yelled. Both of them looked over. "Tommy! Come on! You're late for supper!"

Her son said a few words, turned, and started sprinting toward the gazebo. Cara's gaze shifted to Lee Powers. He was looking in her direction, then disconcerted her by raising a hand in a long-distance greeting.

Hesitantly, Cara lifted an answering hand, then jerked it out of the air, feeling foolish and not certain why. She turned her attention to Tommy as he hurried up the stairs.

"Hi, Mom!"

"Hi." Cara put an arm about his shoulders and propelled him onto the walkway.

"That's Lee, my new friend," Tommy bubbled. "He's going to whittle me a horse!"

"Oh, really?" Cara cast a look over her shoulder. The man continued to stand there, watching as they walked toward the house. She looked quickly ahead once more.

"Maybe we could have Lee over for supper some time."

"I don't know about that, Tommy."

He frowned up at her. "Why not?"

"Well, I'm sure Mr. Powers is a very busy man."

Tommy considered her words. "He has to eat supper, doesn't he?"

"I suppose so," Cara allowed.

"Then he could eat it with *us,*" her son concluded brightly.

"Really, Tommy!" Cara ushered him quickly across the deck to the kitchen door. "Can we talk about this later? Elsa is positively in a swivet about her soufflé getting soggy!"

"Soufflé?" Tommy repeated, passing dutifully inside. "What's soufflé?"

Closing the screen door behind Tommy, Cara backtracked a few steps across the deck, a willful impulse making her scan the beach. He was there, but far in the distance. Having turned his back to the house, he'd moved to the water's edge, where he appeared to be staring out to sea. There was something lonely about the solitary figure, something touching . . . Cara caught herself, her brows knitting in a quick furrow.

"Ridiculous!" she muttered once more, and couldn't decide with whom she was more annoyed—Lee Powers or herself. Turning away, she went inside to be greeted by Elsa's impertinent scolding.

During the next few days Lee spent most of his time getting things in gear at the site. Each day unforeseen needs arose, and he found himself running into town for one thing or another. Most times Cara Chastain's Wagoneer was parked outside Tom's Books; one morning a half dozen cars were parked along with it.

Having picked up a few things at the hardware store, Lee deposited them in the Jaguar and ambled across the street. The grandmotherly woman he'd noticed with Tommy at the picnic was standing by the open shop door.

"You must be Elsa," he said, joining her on the boardwalk.

"And you must be Lee Powers."

She'd seen him from a distance at the picnic, of course. Close up, the tall Texan was dashingly attractive, in spite of the coarse work clothes he was wearing. The shirt, once blue, was faded to near white; the pants, an indiscriminate dark color, were threadbare at the knees and tucked into construction boots. On second thought, Elsa decided, the clothes actually enhanced his appeal. There was something about a working man.

"What's going on?" he asked with a curious look toward the book shop entrance.

"Children's hour. It's about over now, but Cara has storytime for them every Wednesday morning during the summer."

"Is that right?" Lee murmured, propping himself against the rough cedar wall and peering unabashedly over Elsa's shoulder.

There was a woven rug in the center of the floor. Cara was seated cross-legged at the head of a circle of eight or nine children sitting the same way. Like a bunch of little Indians at a powwow, Lee thought.

The notion intensified as Lee's gaze narrowed on Cara. Her black hair was in braids, and the sleeveless shirt she was wearing looked like buckskin trimmed with fringe. Holding a book open in one hand, she gestured gracefully with the other, as if drawing a picture in the air. The children were hanging on her every word.

Her side was turned to the entrance. Lee leaned brazenly into the doorway, picked up the husky stream of her voice, and realized the reason behind the Indian getup . . . *Hiawatha!*

"And the forest dark and lonely," she was saying,

> *Moved through all their depths of darkness,*
> *Sighed, 'Farewell, O Hiawatha'!*
> *And the waves upon the margin*
> *Then rising, rippling on the pebbles,*
> *Sobbed, 'Farewell, O Hiawatha'!*
> *And the heron, the Shuh-Shuh-Gah,*
> *From her haunts among the fen-lands,*
> *Screamed, 'Farewell, O Hiawatha'!*

Cara's hand fluttered to her side. She closed the book and set it aside, her gaze traveling round the circle of children.

"Thus departed Hiawatha," she began once more in a voice that gave Lee chills.

> *Hiawatha the beloved,*
> *In the glory of the sunset,*
> *In the purple mists of evening,*
> *To the regions of the home-wind . . .*

By the time she finished, her final words ringing against absolute silence, Lee was as enthralled as the children. There was a moment of suspended time before the magic she'd spun loosened its hold, and the children began to stir.

"She tells a good story, doesn't she?" Lee murmured to Elsa.

"You should have heard *The Legend of Sleepy Hollow,*" the woman returned proudly. "Every week it's the same. Cara dresses up to fit a new story. The children love it."

Lee shook his head, faintly smiling at this unexpected side of "the little widow." Even now, as mothers joined their children in a chattering group around her, a kind of radiance lingered about her smiling face.

"Guess I'd better collect Tommy," Elsa said.

Lee stepped out of the way, his gaze lingering on Cara.

"She puts up a tough front," he commented, "but I get the impression that behind it she's as soft as they come."

Elsa's parting glance turned into a shrewd look of assessment. The man was very handsome, the finest-looking specimen she'd come across in quite a while . . . maybe ever.

"You a single man, Mr. Powers?"

"I'm single," Lee answered with an amicable smile. "Why?"

"Just curious," Elsa murmured. "You've got a good eye for a single man. Cara Chastain *is* soft, as you put it. She's also smart as a whip and stubborn as a jackass. Make no mistake about it."

Lee's brows rose as Elsa walked past. Watching a moment as the perky silver-haired woman passed inside and joined the throng, he dropped down from the boardwalk and returned to the Jaguar. Executing a U-turn in the middle of Main Street, he cast a bemused look at the front of the book shop. Cara

Chastain was one of a kind. That was for sure.

The timbre of her voice—rasping, but somehow silky at the same time—stayed with him as he returned to the noisy construction site south of town.

Chapter Four

"No, Abigail . . . Yes, I know I turned you down for the Fourth of July, but it couldn't be helped . . ."

Glancing across the kitchen, Cara saw Nick at the back door and motioned energetically for him to come in.

"Tommy is fine," she said into the receiver, her gaze on Nick as he stepped inside and walked toward her. "Growing like a weed . . ." She hadn't seen her brother in several months; he looked suntanned and vital and was grinning from ear to ear. Cara matched the expression, though she rolled her eyes in a show of frustration.

"Abigail, I simply can't get away right now . . . I told you a bunch of developers from Texas have descended on Walking Dune. This is a critical time . . . What I have to do with it is that I've been put in charge of a committee to protect the mustangs . . . Well, why *not* me? . . . I'll bring Tommy up to Warrenton some time before school starts, I promise you . . . That's right. He's in kindergarten this year. Look, Abigail, I really must run. Nick has just arrived."

Swiftly hanging up the phone, Cara reached for her brother and enfolded him in a hug. "I'm so glad to see you, Nick."

"Likewise."

"How's Virginia Beach?"

"Fine, but I've been hankering to get down this way." Nick planted a quick kiss on his sister's cheek and stepped back. "Let me have a look at you."

Cara struck a cheesecake pose. She was wearing sneakers, cut-off jeans rolled up into shorts, and a sleeveless denim shirt. But her face was alive with excitement, her eyes shining.

"You look different," Nick observed. "Different in a good way. The old sparkle is back. What's going on? Does it have anything to do with what you were saying to Abigail?"

"Maybe, in a roundabout way. I must admit this cause has got me fired up, but the reason for it is nothing short of tragic. Everything's changing, Nick. Lone Star is changing everything. There's no peace in Walking Dune anymore. All you hear all day is the clatter of equipment. The south end of town looks like some foreign place, and two of the mustangs have been killed."

"Two? Your letter said one."

"The second mare was hit just a couple of weeks after the first. They were both with foal."

Nick shook his head. "That's a damn shame. Sorry I couldn't come down any sooner. I had some regular clients who booked the boat months ago."

Cara shrugged. "That's okay. I guess there's really nothing you can do anyway. It's just good to have you here for moral support. How long can you stay?"

"A while." Nick patted his back pocket and grinned. "It's been a particularly lucrative season."

Tommy bounded into the room. "Uncle Nick!" he chortled, throwing himself into Nick's arms.

Nick chuckled and swung the boy around. "Good heavens! This can't be my nephew! Why, *he's* just a kid!"

Cara savored the moment as the two of them embraced. Love welled up within her, encompassing her son, her brother, the feeling of a complete family.

"Hello there, Nick," Elsa said from the doorway.

Depositing Tommy on the floor, Nick reached out and twirled the gray-haired lady in a swift turn about the kitchen.

"Ah, Elsa! A sight for sore eyes. Dare I hope you'll oblige me with some of your famous pot roast while I'm here?"

"Let go of me, you young rogue," Elsa scolded, though her smile revealed extreme pleasure. "You behave yourself, or it'll be nothing but bread and water for you!"

Nick and Cara laughed as Elsa bustled to the sink where she turned her attention to the lunch dishes.

"Want to go out on the beach, Uncle Nick?" Tommy asked. "There was a storm out at sea a couple of nights back. Some really good shells have washed up!"

"Some really good ones?" Nick cast a questioning eye in Cara's direction. "I guess so, as long as it's okay with your mother."

Cara lifted her palms. "Actually, that would be great. Our first promotional materials on behalf of the mustangs arrived this morning, and I need to distribute them in the village. If you like, I'll meet you guys back here for supper."

"Great!" Tommy exclaimed, grabbing his uncle's hand and heading for the door.

"Great!" Nick repeated, allowing himself to be drawn outside.

The door banged noisily behind them. Cara's smile lingered.

"It's nice to hear a male voice in the house, isn't it, Elsa?"

"Your brother's voice is welcome, to be sure. But it isn't the answer to the silence within *these* walls."

The smile disappeared as Cara fired a disgruntled look at the woman's back.

"For heaven's sake, Elsa," she sighed, picking up the shoulder bag filled with newly printed bumper stickers. "Not that again."

"Yes, that again. Louis Talbot positively drools every time he comes around. And if he doesn't suit your taste, I'm sure there are any number—"

"It doesn't matter about the number, Elsa. Honestly, I'd have thought we covered this subject from stem to stern."

Elsa tossed her a sly look. "Things can change."

Cara settled the canvas bag on her shoulder. "Not *some* things," she replied, and walked out of the kitchen.

Lee was so accustomed to the roar of equipment that he barely heard the chugging and clanking. From atop a portable platform he watched the graders move across the land like a team of mechanical mules—heads down, backs humped, pushing brush, trees, and sand ahead of them, leaving behind level, hard-packed turf that showed dark against the snowy dunes. On the fringe, dozers attacked the resulting mountains of debris, their metal scoops swinging up and around, glinting in the sun as they dumped load after load into the beds of waiting pickups.

Lifting his binoculars, he peered into the distance. Commanded by Joe Conover, two armies swarmed about sites where foundations were being poured. There were perhaps thirty men out there, the crews having been rounded out by locals who'd traveled as far as a hundred miles in answer to newspaper ads. The freelancers were not as well-trained as the Lone Star men who had come out from Houston, but Joe was whipping them into shape with typical flair.

Lee was pleased. In five days they'd accomplished a great deal. Next week the foundation for the clubhouse could be staked out.

Now, at four o'clock on Friday afternoon, it was time to quit. They'd been at it since eight, and the sun was grueling. Whipping off the yellow hard hat, Lee signaled "Cut!" to the foreman and climbed off the platform.

The men would come to a stopping point, get cleaned up and probably head out for a rip-roaring night somewhere. That was fine. They deserved it. As for himself, all he wanted was an ice cold drink to wash the dust down his throat. Stripping off a sweat-soaked T-shirt on the way to the Jaguar, Lee tossed it and the hard hat in the back, retrieved a clean shirt, and drove into the village.

It was nearly five when he came out of Freemont's General Store, glanced up the boardwalk, and saw her standing outside the post office with Jacob Abernathy. She carried a sack over her shoulder, and was wearing shorts again. Lee came to a stop, gaze leveling, pulse quickening.

But for the stolen glimpse of her in the book shop, it had been nearly a week since he'd seen Cara Chastain, although her boy, Tommy, had surprised him only the previous evening, showing up at the Fast Break with a conch shell he'd found on the beach.

"It's a trade," he'd announced with the mature air of someone ten years his senior. "How's my carving coming along?"

Lee hadn't been around children much, but it seemed to him that Tommy Chastain was damn impressive for a five-year-old kid.

As for the boy's mother . . . Taking advantage of his sheltered position on the storefront porch, Lee studied her with roaming abandon. The raven hair was pulled up and shining in the sun, the bare limbs gleaming like bronze. Though he was too far away to make out her features, he imagined the high, sun-kissed cheekbones, the startling blue of her eyes. Finishing off his second cold drink, Lee dropped it in a nearby trash barrel and propped against a post, watching discreetly as she shook hands with Abernathy and moved to the street.

Cara placed the sticker on the mail truck bumper, cutting her eyes up the street as she climbed back onto the boardwalk. She'd seen the dark green convertible the moment it rolled into town, from the window of Wolf's Fabric and Notions.

"Oh, my!" Nettie had exclaimed. "Isn't that Powers man just the most scrumptious thing you've ever seen?"

A crease had formed between Cara's brows, quickly dissolving as she took in the sight of Nettie's round face all lit up like a candle. The last of the Wolf family, Nettie had watched alone as her parents passed away, her brother and sister having long since married and moved north. If the lonely woman got a thrill out of ogling Lee Powers, far be it from Cara to spoil it.

"Scrumptious, Nettie?" she teased. "I do believe you've set your cap for the man."

"Why, Cara Chastain!" the older woman tittered. "Don't you think I know he's too young for the likes of me? But there's nothing wrong with dreaming, is there?"

Cara's expression dimmed. "No. Nothing wrong with dreaming."

"I'm definitely on the side of your cause," Nettie had then announced with a bob of her head. "Please *do* affix whatever it is you were talking about to the tailgate of my car."

Cara smiled at the memory, but the expression faded as she focused anew on the Jaguar. She'd hoped Lee Powers would be gone by the time she made her way up Main Street, but there was the flashy car, still parked in front of Hal Freemont's store. She mosied along the boardwalk, her eyes lingering on the sleek vehicle that looked about as much in place in Walking Dune as a damn Lear jet that might have dropped from the sky.

"Hello, Mrs. Chastain."

Cara looked up with a start. He was standing not ten feet before her, in the shadow of the porch outside the store. If she hadn't been so preoccupied, she'd have noticed him the moment she stepped out of the post office. How long had he been watching her?

"Hello, Mr. Powers."

He straightened away from the post, took a step toward her, and moved into direct light. He was wearing a light blue shirt, dirt-streaked work pants, construction boots. His arms and face were the color of mahogany, his cheeks streaked with red. He must have been out in the sun every day.

"I'm glad I ran into you," he said in that distinctive drawl of his. "I wanted to tell you—your son is one hell of a boy."

Of all the things Cara might have expected, a compliment to Tommy wasn't among them. Something warm flickered inside her.

"Thank you," she replied slowly. "Tommy thinks a lot of you, too. He says you're whittling something for him."

Lee drew a block of rosewood from his back pocket. "Just found this in Hal's store. It ought to be perfect."

"A horse, right?" Cara asked with a breaking smile.

The red lips parted, white teeth gleamed, and blue eyes sparkled. A tremor raced over Lee. A simple smile turned her beauty into something dazzling.

"You ought to do that more often," he rumbled. "I see that even a work of art is improved with a smile."

It wasn't until the instinctive guard sprang up around her that Cara realized it had slipped.

"Pretty words, Mr. Powers," she mustered. "I always did say you have a way with words."

The riposte undermined the intimacy of his remark, but he only grinned, the points of his moustache lifting, curling. Cara found the sight fascinating and was appalled.

"A lady should accept a compliment when it's given," Lee chided.

"And especially when given in such a practiced fashion. I dare say, you must have blazed quite a trail from Texas."

He laughed. Cara squashed the impulse to join in.

"Actually," Lee said, "you'd be surprised how little blazing I've done lately."

"Oh, I don't know. You seem to have set a few fires here in Walking Dune." He folded muscular arms across a broad chest.

"Any I'd be interested in stoking?" he asked.

God, he was flirting again. Her cheeks burned.

"I'm sure that's up to you," Cara rallied.

Lee could almost feel the blood racing through his veins. She might be doing her best to cover it, but he wasn't wrong about the crimson blush on Cara Chastain's face.

"Is it?" he asked, searching her eyes.

Cara looked sharply away and made a move for the boardwalk steps. "Excuse me," she said hurriedly. "I've got work to do."

"Wait a minute!"

She looked over her shoulder.

"What the hell are you doing, anyway?" Lee added, his gaze darting to her shoulder bag.

"What I'm 'doing' is spreading the word."

"What word?"

"That of the Walking Dune Wild Horse Fund. We're in full swing now. Flyers are being written, schedules arranged." Cara patted the sack. "Our first effort is underway. A friend up the coast spent all day yesterday printing some bumper stickers for us."

"The Walking Dune Wild Horse Fund," Lee repeated with a smile. "That has a certain ring to it."

"I'm glad you approve." The next thoughtless remark rocketed from some uncharted hole in her mind. "Perhaps you'd like to attend our meeting tomorrow night."

"Perhaps I would. Where is it, and what time?"

Shocked by both her suggestion and his reply, Cara stared for a moment. "I didn't really think—"

"What could be better? Lone Star is your target, isn't it? And I *do* have a certain standing with Lone Star, after all."

He added the last with the challenging lift of a brow. Cara's chin went up.

"The meeting is being held at my house."

"Your house," he voiced with obvious interest. "Well now, that clinches it as far as I'm concerned. I've been hoping for a chance to visit your place ever since I first saw it. Built around the turn of the century, wasn't it?"

"Yes," Cara surrendered.

"Is it listed on the national registry, by any chance?"

"Registry?"

"Of historic places."

In spite of herself, she was impressed. "The house isn't listed on anything as far as I know."

"It probably should be."

"Are you qualified to make such a judgment?" she asked testily.

He shrugged. "I'm an architect."

"But are you a *good* architect?"

Cara felt like biting her tongue. Obviously the man was good, or he wouldn't have the prestigious position he held at Lone Star. She was being a shrew. She knew it but couldn't seem to stop.

"I can hold my own," he answered finally.

Cara glanced away. She'd just insulted the man, and yet he was wearing that same infernal look of amusement she remembered from the book shop.

"Well?" he prompted. "What time is the meeting?"

All she longed to do was get the hell out of his presence; and yet she'd opened the door to having him in her very own home the next night!

"Eight o'clock."

"Good."

"Good!" Cara blasted. "I'll be frank, Mr. Powers—"

"I'd expect nothing less." Her nostrils flared in a way Lee was beginning to find familiar.

"The invitation I extended was less than sincere," she stated bluntly. "I don't know why I did it. Don't you think I see what's happening? You're trying to ingratiate yourself here, become part of something soon to be lost because of Lone Star Partners. The Wild Horse Fund is a dedicated group. We won't take kindly to an antagonistic point of view. Perhaps you should reconsider—"

"If you're trying to finagle your way out of the invitation, however insincere it might have been, it won't work. I'd like to see the house. I'd like to see Tommy . . ."

He trailed off, his eyes probing hers. I'd like to see *you,* the unspoken words whispered. Cara's face scorched with new fire.

"And whether you believe it or not," Lee concluded, "I truly am interested in the welfare of the mustangs."

"Well then," she huffed. "Since you're so supportive . . ." Reaching into her bag, she withdrew a sticker and waved it at the Jaguar below. "May I?" she added.

"If it makes you feel good," Lee drawled.

Leaping down from the boardwalk, Cara peeled the protective layer and slapped the thing on the car's bumper.

"Thank you, Mr. Powers," she tossed, and high-stepped away.

Extending a long leg, Lee left the boardwalk, stepped to the car, and glanced down at the sticker. "I Brake For Wild Horses," it said. He looked up and spotted Cara in the distance, her hips swinging enticingly with her rapid pace.

And wild *women,* he thought with a grin.

The wild horses are descendants of the Spanish mustang and have been a part of the Currituck environment since first settlement of the barrier reef.

In 1523 the Spanish expeditions brought them to the New World. When colonization was unsuccessful, the horses were left behind.

During the period from 1584 to 1589, the English procured a number from Spanish settlements and brought them here with other livestock for Sir Walter Raleigh's colony on Roanoke. The Cherokee, Chickasaw, and Choctaw Indians took many of the horses on their forced migration west, called "Trail of Tears." Some say the Indians' arrival and continued survival was due to these horses.

Later, islanders used them for transportation, to round up livestock and to pull fishing nets. The U.S. Lifesaving Service rode them during beach patrols. . . .

* * *

Lee closed the pamphlet, set it on the table, and slumped back in the wicker couch. Forcing the week-old image from his memory, he saw them once more—a dozen horses plowing across the road, led by a black whose powerful role was obvious at a glance.

It had been a long time since he'd been involved with horses, not since rodeo days. The Texas broncos had been unpredictable and untamed, but they bore little resemblance to the Walking Dune herd that had never known a life other than freedom.

"Mustangs," Lee muttered. Who would have thought when he took on this project that he'd be coming up against a damn conservation issue? Frank sure as hell hadn't said a word about it. Lee tried to picture his boss's familiar features, and found them swimming just outside his reach. The same was true of his Houston apartment. Was it only a week since he'd arrived in Walking Dune?

It was past eleven; the Fast Break was quiet. Everyone else had taken off for Nags Head. His gaze fell to the coffee table where he'd placed the conch shell Tommy brought. Lee fetched the block of rosewood and went out back.

From behind, the lights of the house spilled across the porch. Overhead, the stars twinkled like diamonds on black velvet. From the east came the sound of breakers and the smell of the sea. Lee withdrew the pocketknife and sat down in a weathered rocker.

For a moment he closed his eyes and concentrated. Slowly the image reassembled—the black mustang's height and breadth, the way the wind lifted his mane and tail. The summer night closed about them. . . .

Lee opened his eyes, looked at the wood, and saw a stallion. A low whistle spilled from his lips as he took the first cut.

Surrounded by live oak draped with Spanish moss, the Talbot house faced the sound, its graceful porches and columns offering an antebellum charm unduplicated on the island. Dahlia had always thought it pretty—not so vast as the inn, which had evolved from a Tudor-style hunting lodge—but pretty, particularly now when the setting sun shed a rosy light that made the place look like something out of a storybook.

The notion evoked the little-girl story she once had told herself: one day she'd marry Louis and live in that pretty house. Pursing her lips, Dahlia quelled the memory and, as she drove along the sandy road to the house, turned her thoughts to Louis's call of an hour ago.

"Would you mind picking me up on your way to Cara's?" he'd asked.

"Sure. No problem. Something wrong with the Mercedes?"

"The damn thing's a lemon. No telling how long it will be in the shop this time. Of course, I could take the pick-up, but I'd rather ride in with a pretty lady."

They were casual words, she knew, but even now the memory of his voice saying them made Dahlia quiver. She tried to fight down an accompanying gush of hope, but was no more successful than she'd been thirty minutes ago when she dressed for the meeting.

In a rare departure from jeans and T-shirt, she wore tan walking shorts that clinched her waist and a lime green blouse Louis had complimented her on last summer. "It matches your eyes," he'd said.

Dahlia flashed a look in the rearview mirror. She'd even pulled up her short, flaming curls with combs on each side and affixed gold loops in her earlobes. Looking back at the road, she wondered how long it had been since she dressed up in any way, shape or form. What need was there when all she saw most days were the employees who tended the inn and stables?

Again, irresistibly, she glanced in the mirror. Bright eyes looked back from between lashes artificially darkened with mascara. The tomboy within her rose to the surface and jeered. Flooded with misgivings, Dahlia thought of turning around and going home for a quick change. But it was too late. As she neared the house, she saw that Louis was waiting on the front porch.

She pulled to a stop, and he came down the steps with the swinging gait she knew so well. He was wearing khaki slacks, a white shirt with sleeves rolled to the elbow, and loafers with no socks. Although she couldn't see his face as he approached the car, she imagined its clean-shaven lines, the squared-off jaw, the finely drawn nose and brow.

He climbed in and tossed her a smile of greeting. She returned it, her heart knocking with love and nauseating hope.

"Hi, kid," he said.

"Hi."

Looking ahead, he settled back in the seat. "Ready to go?"

Dahlia's pulse slowed to a disappointed pace.

"Sure," she replied and, as she drove away, cursed herself with practiced expertise for a damn fool.

"Good luck, boss," Joe called as Lee headed for the door. "Trying to get a rope on this mustang thing should be quite a challenge, to say nothing of the 'little widow'."

A few of the men were playing cards around the kitchen table. They looked up and laughed.

"Go to hell, Joe," Lee replied lightly.

The older man had been teasing him mercilessly ever since he found out Lee was going to the meeting at the Chastain house. At first Lee had countered with an explanation of how important it was for Lone Star to be represented, but Joe had only chuckled and continued making sly remarks about the obvious attributes of the woman who chaired the mustang cause.

As the Saturday afternoon wore on and some of the men joined in the banter, Lee had decided to suffer through it without denials. Cara had become somewhat of a legend in the Fast Break. He'd heard comments about her aloofness, her beauty, and her body. He couldn't blame the men for noticing, but some sort of territorial urge had driven him to let it be known then and there that the boss had his eye on Cara Chastain.

It was after seven-thirty, but the July evening continued to shimmer with the heat of the day. As Lee climbed into the Jaguar and drove the short way to the Chastain house, he knew he was unfashionably early. The fact was he'd showered, slicked himself up, and hung around the Fast Break as long as he could stand it. Now he couldn't wait to get inside that house, say hello to Tommy, and most of all, see the woman who had been the cause of such ribald harassment all afternoon.

Parking the Jaguar by the white picket fence, he passed through the gate and walked along the brick walkway, casting appreciative looks across the grounds and up the face of the imposing house. He climbed the steps and rang the bell, noting the frosted pattern on the side panes. Tommy answered the door.

"Hi, Lee! Come on in!"

Lee stepped inside. "Hi, Tommy. How ya doin'?"

"Fine." From behind the boy, a man approached. "This is my Uncle Nick," Tommy chimed.

Even if the boy had said nothing, Lee would have known Cara's brother. Black hair, blue eyes, chiseled features.

"Nick Malloy," he said, extending a hand.

Lee joined him in a firm shake. "Lee Powers," he returned. "Nice to meet you."

"Had time to do any whittlin' lately?" Tommy asked.

Lee looked down at the boy, who had folded his arms across his chest and was regarding him skeptically. Lee dropped to one knee and smiled.

"I've had a lot of work to do, Tommy, but I haven't forgotten our deal." Reaching into his back pocket, he withdrew the block of rosewood and offered it to the boy. "Now, I'm just getting started. It will look a lot better when it's finished, but what do you think so far?"

Tommy's eyes widened as he accepted the piece in reverent hands. The lines of the horse were evident, though rough.

"Wow!" he breathed. "It's going to look just like Star!"

"Star?" Lee repeated.

"The stallion! Wow! Can I go show this to Mom?"

"Sure." Lee straightened, a smile lingering about his mouth as he watched the boy sprint up the nearby staircase.

"You've got a fan there," Nick commented. "I've already heard about this carving thing. Good thing you brought it with you, or you might have been in hot water."

Lee chuckled.

"I was just about to have a drink," Nick added. "Join me?"

"Sounds good." As he followed the man down the hall, Lee turned interested eyes into the rooms they passed. Parlor, dining room, sunroom—all were heralded by arched doorways, furnished with period pieces. They entered a softly lit study that carried on the Victorian theme, though the antiques here were heavy and masculine, as was the atmosphere created by dark pine paneling. Nick moved to a bar in the corner. Lee looked around, thinking the Chastain house surpassed his highest expectations.

"This is some house," he said.

"Isn't it though?" Nick tossed. "Scotch all right?"

"Fine." Lee meandered toward a giant desk and found an elaborately framed picture of Cara. It must have been taken some years back. Her hair was longer, and she was smiling with a kind of dazzling joy that made her look like a schoolgirl. His heart pounded a peculiar beat.

"Water?" Nick asked.

"No. Neat."

"My kind of guy." Nick grinned, joining the other man and offering the drink.

"Thanks," Lee said and gestured to the picture. "Nice shot. When was it taken?"

"Just after they were married, I think. Tom went through a period of photography about then. He's the one who took it."

Lee nodded, raised his glass, took a drink. "He was a photographer?"

"Among other things. Actually, he wanted to be a writer." Nick extended a hand toward the desktop, calling attention to the typewriter and papers that remained exactly as Tom Chastain had left them. "This was his desk. Cara hasn't disturbed a thing here since he died."

"And when was that?"

"Five years ago."

"I heard it was a car accident."

"That's right," Nick replied. "It was late one night. Apparently the mustangs crossed in front of him. He swerved and hit a tree."

Lee regarded the other man with sharp interest. "Well, I guess that sheds some light."

"On what?"

"On why your sister feels the way she does about the mustangs."

"That's part of it," Nick agreed.

Lee took a gulp of Scotch and made his voice as casual as possible. "I suppose a lot of men have come calling since her husband died."

Apparently there was no way to make a comment like that casual. The blue eyes so like Cara's flickered and went narrow.

"So that's the reason you're here tonight."

"Not the only reason," Lee responded. "My company is investing a great deal of money in Walking Dune. This thing about the mustangs is a time bomb. If I can help defuse it, everyone will benefit."

Nick took a drink, though his assessing gaze swept the man from head to toe. He had a strong, solid look about him.

"What's your story, Powers?"

"My story?"

"You married?"

"Oh, my *story*," Lee repeated with a smile. "I was married. I've been divorced several years now. What else do you want to know?"

"Any kids?"

Lee shook his head.

"Where you from?"

"Born and bred in Texas. Came up the hard way, I guess. Pasadena's my hometown. Pasa-damn-dena, they call it. Everybody there works the refineries. I decided real quick that wasn't for me. Worked my way through college, got my degree, got a job with Lone Star. Been with the company about fourteen years now. I live in Houston, when I'm there."

"When you're there?"

"I travel a lot, just like now. I go on location, oversee developments. What about you? What line are you in?"

"Charter fishing," Nick replied. "It was Tom, in fact, who gave me my start. He bankrolled me for the *Virgin*."

Lee's brows went up. "The virgin?"

"My boat. The love of my life, the first thing I ever made good on."

"I see. You live around here?"

"I get down here pretty often, but I'm based in Virginia Beach. What do you want with my sister?"

Lee had been in the midst of draining his glass and almost choked. "I don't know yet," he said.

"You don't know?"

Lee hesitated. Hell, might as well be up front.

"I'd like to take her out, but I've been told that she doesn't go out with men . . . at all."

"That's right."

"Why?"

"Tom. She was devoted to him."

"But he's been gone—"

"Five years. I know." Nick glanced at the man's empty glass. "Want another drink?"

"Better not. Do you mean to say a woman like Cara hasn't been out with even one man in five years?"

"That's what I mean to say."

"Damn," Lee muttered.

Nick cracked a grin. He liked Lee Powers.

"You've got your work cut out for you, buddy," he said.

It was nearly eight. The bell had rung twice more since that initial ring and Tommy's breathless visit to show his mother the carving his "friend, Lee" had brought.

Cara stared in the mirror and frowned. The skirt and blouse with the floral pattern were ridiculous. Stripping them off, she went back to the first thing she'd taken out of the closet— a blue oxford cloth shirt with white pinstripes. Pulling on white slacks and stepping into sandals, she fumed at the jumpy way she was behaving. It had started the minute she caught the sound of Lee Powers's voice drifting up from the foyer.

Well, there was no more putting it off. Flashing a last look at her reflection, Cara left the bedroom with a firm step. She was halfway down the stairs when the door opened.

"Hi, guys," she said as Dahlia and Louis stepped inside, barely getting the words out of her mouth before Louis lit into her.

"Does that car out front belong to who I think it does?" he demanded.

"What car?"

"That damn British green racing machine!"

Dahlia sighed. "You know damn well who it belongs to, Louis."

"What the hell is he doing here?" Louis continued without so much as a glance at Dahlia.

Cara kept her voice low but could do nothing about the heat creeping up her neck. "I wasn't aware we were so well-staffed we could turn away the help of a volunteer."

"Volunteer?" Louis repeated in a sneering tone. "Volunteer for what? Warming your bed?"

The slow-climbing heat erupted on Cara's face. "I'm going to forget you said that, Louis. Why don't you take a seat in the dining room and cool off."

He stared for a moment then whirled away, jerking a hand through his hair as he went.

"What's his problem?" Cara asked.

Dahlia gave her a knowing look. "You don't really have to ask that, do you, Cara?"

Cara's taut nerves tweaked a little tighter.

"But on top of that," Dahlia added, "Louis doesn't like Lee Powers. To quote: 'The man's an arrogant son of a bitch.' "

The sound of men's voices drew Cara's eye down the hall. They were standing outside the study—Ned and Doc, Nick and . . . Her gaze lit on the tallest of the group just as he tipped his head to laugh at something Nick said. He was wearing close-fitting jeans that made his legs look about six feet long, and a short-sleeved black shirt that called attention to his muscular arms and broad shoulders. Her gaze had just risen to his face when he looked her way. Across the distance, their eyes met.

"What the hell *is* he doing here?" Dahlia asked curiously.

Cara pivoted, quickly turning her back on the man. "I invited him, okay?" she snapped. "Is there anything wrong with that? After all, Lone Star is our target, and he *does* have a certain standing with Lone Star."

Dahlia's brows lifted. "What the devil is the matter with you, Cara? Normally you're like some calm lake that even an earthquake couldn't ripple. Tonight your face is red as a beet, and—"

Dahlia broke off, her gaze darting to Lee Powers. He was staring up the corridor, and suddenly she sensed his eyes were lit up with the same brilliance she saw in Cara's.

"Oh, my gosh," Dahlia breathed. "I don't believe it."

"Don't believe what?"

"You and . . . Oh, my gosh."

Cara watched her friend's line of vision return pointedly to Lee Powers. "Don't be absurd, Dahlia." She walked off in the direction of the kitchen.

Dahlia watched her go, unconvinced by the unruffled mask Cara had dredged up at the last second. Casting a look into the dining room, she saw Louis sitting alone at the table . . . stewing. To hell with *this!* Dahlia thought and proceeded toward the study to help herself to a drink.

"Evenin', boys," she tossed as she passed the men.

A round of greetings trailed her into the room, and then the clear ring of a wolf whistle. Dahlia glanced back and saw that Nick Malloy had moved to the doorway. The whistle was a surprise; so was the way he was looking at her.

"Hi ya, Nick," she said casually, though she felt suddenly flustered. "When did you hit town?"

"Yesterday."

Nick walked toward her, noting once again the trim figure shown off by the shorts, the pretty face framed with coppery curls. He thought he saw a blush before she turned to the bar.

"What have you done to yourself?" he asked. "You look dynamite."

She glanced up for an instant. He was right; she was blushing.

"Come off it, Nick," she muttered and went back to fixing her drink. In a noticeable hurry, Nick thought.

"I mean it," he said.

"You gonna sit in on the meeting?" Dahlia asked distractingly.

"Yeah." He folded his arms across his chest, studying her profile. "How long have we known each other now? Seven or eight years?"

"About that, I guess." Dahlia turned and gave him a fleeting look that lasted only as long as it took to remind her just how attractive Cara's brother was. "Well, I'll see you in the dining room. Louis is in there alone, and he's in a foul mood. I'll try and lighten him up before the meeting starts."

With that she walked briskly out of the study. Nick followed to the doorway, pausing to admire her undulating hips as she made swift progress up the hall.

"Looks like *you've* got some work cut out, too, buddy."

Looking around the doorjamb, Nick caught the teasing look on Lee Powers's face and grinned.

The seven of them were gathered around a mahogany dining table that dated back, Lee theorized, to at least the 1880s. He sat at one end, Cara at the other. Nick was on his immediate right, then Doc Simpson and Ned Crockett. On the left was an empty chair, then Dahlia, then Talbot, who'd been firing dark glares his way ever since the meeting began more than an hour ago. Every now and then, Lee returned one. There was no doubt the budding antagonism between them had blossomed into enmity.

A short while back, Tommy had come in to say good night. Cara hugged and kissed him, and Lee had felt a tug on his heartstrings that encompassed the both of them. Now she was bent over a notebook, busily writing down the newest idea that was up for consideration. From beneath lowered lids, Lee watched her, noting for the first time how long and slender her fingers were, and also that she continued to wear a wedding band on her left hand.

"If you ask me," Dahlia said, "corraling them is the worst suggestion so far. Even if we did enclose an area so large that they'd have plenty of room, they still wouldn't be free. Besides, do you have any idea how much something like that would cost? That's the problem with everything we've discussed—money. It's going to take quite a while for the Wild Horse Fund to raise the money to foot any of the projects that have come up so far."

As the newcomer—or more truthfully, the outsider—Lee had kept his mouth shut through the entire meeting. He decided to risk speaking up.

"Can't you get the state involved?" he asked. "Isn't there some sort of conservation agency that could help with funding?"

Louis snorted. "If you knew anything at all, you'd know better than to ask that."

Cara saw the way Lee Powers's jaw clamped in a hard line, but he said nothing. The impulse to take up for him came out of nowhere.

"The state claims no responsibility for the mustangs, Mr. Powers," she explained. "Years ago a law was passed prohibiting people from allowing horses or other livestock to run at large on the Outer Banks. The North Carolina Wildlife Resources Commission has taken the position that the mustangs are descended from domestic stock, and therefore undeserving of state protection as 'wildlife.' Anything we do we'll have to fund by ourselves."

"Sorry," Lee mumbled. "I didn't know."

"There was no reason you should have," Cara remarked with a sharp look for Louis.

"Why don't we get back to the issue of immediate safety?" Doc suggested. "Ned here has done well to draft a list of ordinances, but unfortunately, prohibiting people from touching or approaching the mustangs isn't going to keep them safe. The biggest danger is the highway."

The vet's comment triggered Lee's memory of the two accidents in which his men had been involved. An idea stormed his brain.

"How about paint?" he asked. Six pairs of eyes turned toward him. "Reflective paint. Non-toxic, of course. I talked to the men involved in the accidents. 'It was dark,' they said, 'and all of a sudden the horses were there.' Seems to me the danger would be alleviated if the mustangs could be seen a little more readily at night. Headlights would flash off reflective paint, give drivers a little warning."

"Now there's an idea!" Doc boomed.

"How do you plan to get it on the horses?" Louis put in with a snide look. "Ask them to pose while you go at them with a brush?"

"Paint guns might be easier," Lee returned.

"You ever shoot one of those things?" Ned asked.

Lee glanced at the deputy sheriff. "Not at horses, but yeah."

"And I can get the paint in Nags Head," Doc resumed. "This will be quick, cheap, and possibly damn effective. Good for you, Mr. Powers. It's the best idea I've heard all night."

"I agree," Cara said quietly.

Lee looked quickly her way but was too late to read her expression as she bent once more over the notebook.

The meeting broke up shortly after that. Louis made a hasty exit, and Dahlia followed along. The others remained seated, exchanging a few more remarks about the upcoming project. Cara rose to her feet and began clearing the table, skirting around behind the men, reaching over shoulders to retrieve glasses and cups. She didn't look at Lee Powers but had the feeling he was watching her. When her hands were full, she escaped into the kitchen and found Elsa filling up the sink.

"I believe he's the most handsome man I've ever seen," she said, and squirted a stream of dishwashing liquid under the faucet.

Cara began unloading her burden on the counter. "Who?"

"You know very well who. He sounds smart, too."

"Is Tommy asleep?" Cara parried.

Elsa was not to be sidetracked. "Yes. Tommy likes him, too. He asked if Lee has any little boys of his own. Does he?"

"I haven't the faintest idea what Mr. Powers has," Cara replied, her hands flying back and forth, back and forth, transferring glass after glass, cup after cup, into the sudsy water.

"I can do that," Elsa said.

"I don't mind helping."

"You mean you don't want to go back out there and face him."

Cara spun around, flecks of suds flying from her fingertips.

"I saw the way he looks at you," Elsa added. "And I saw the way you *try* to keep from looking at *him*."

"What have you been doing all this time?" Cara demanded in a fierce whisper. "Spying on us?"

"Do you deny you find him attractive?"

"Honestly, Elsa!"

"That's not a denial."

Piercing eyes targeted Cara from behind Elsa's bifocals. She withstood their scrutiny for a matter of seconds, then yanked the dish towel off the counter and dried her hands.

"Honestly!" she repeated and stalked out of the kitchen.

Yet as Cara entered the dining room, her pace degenerated into cowardly sloth. Ned and Doc were gone, her brother and Lee Powers now leaning against opposite sides of the arched doorway and chatting like old friends. Cara felt suddenly as if she didn't know what to do with herself. She was unnerved and completely maddened with herself for feeling so flustered, but as both men turned to look at her, she knew the only acceptable course of action was to join them. Mustering a cheery expression, she kept her eyes on Nick as she moved across the room.

"So," she said on arriving. "What did you think of the meeting?"

"This guy is quite a find," her brother replied. "Did you know he used to give shooting exhibitions on the rodeo circuit?"

"Oh, really?" Cara's gaze flickered to Lee Powers, but for once he failed to meet her eyes and looked away—a bit uncomfortably, she thought—to the shadows of the foyer.

"That's right," Nick added. "A real sharpshooter. Between him and Ned, your mustangs ought to get quite a coat of paint."

A feeling of admiration bloomed within Cara. She stemmed it with a starched rebuttal.

"They're not *my* mustangs, Nick. They don't belong to anyone. That's the point." Lee Powers's dark eyes turned to her at that. "Isn't anyone else going to pitch in?" she added in her first address to him. "Just you and Ned?"

"I don't think the job calls for a posse, do you?"

There was the hint of a smile in his black eyes. Cara saw it just before they began roaming over her. Feeling the urge to shield herself, she folded her arms across her breasts.

"Surely the rest of us could help," she said. "It doesn't seem fair for you to shoulder the project, particularly when you're not even part of the Wild Horse Fund."

"I don't mind," came the deep voice. "Two men moving quietly at night will draw less attention from the mustangs than a whole crowd trooping around. Besides, maybe this will give me a chance to make up, in some way, for the accidents with the mares."

His eyes were not black as she had first presumed, but had rays of auburn brown shifting in their depths. . . . Suddenly aware of the way she was staring up at him, Cara faltered, her gaze flying away and lighting on Nick, who said, "If you'll excuse me, I've got some shipping logs to look over."

With an aggravating sense of alarm, Cara watched the two men shake hands.

"See you around, Lee," her brother said.

"Take it easy, Nick."

It seemed as though everyone in her household was conspiring to throw her together with Lee Powers. Nick disappeared up the stairs, and Cara was left alone with the tall Texan, who was looking at her in an intense way that made her squirm.

"It's been an illuminating evening," she said.

"Yes. It has."

She took a leading step toward the foyer. "Well, then—"

"It's early yet," he broke in. "Is there any place around here to get a drink?"

Cara's gaze lifted—touching, then racing beyond the dark, curling hairs at the open neck of his shirt. "There's a tavern at Dahlia's inn, if you're willing to settle for beer."

"And are you?"

"Am I what?"

Lee smiled. "Willing."

"Willing," Cara repeated. "To have a beer with you, you mean?"

He propped a forearm on the arch above his head and leaned slightly toward her. "It's not exactly an outrageous idea. People do it all the time."

"I don't," she replied. "I told you before, Mr. Powers—"

"I thought you might have changed your mind. After all, you did say my idea about the paint was the best you'd heard. That sort of makes us comrades, doesn't it?"

Cara hesitated. She didn't know why. She certainly was not about to step one foot out the door with him.

"I must admit you made quite an impression at the meeting tonight," he said in an effort to shift the subject.

"On whom?"

"On everyone, I expect."

"Including you?"

"Of course," Cara returned curtly. "As you know, my concern for the mustangs—"

"I didn't mean just that."

"I know you didn't."

They regarded each other silently. Behind Cara's silence, she nearly gasped as impressions began smashing willfully into her mind—the way the bicep of his extended arm bulged beyond his sleeve, the way his hair curled around the sides of his collar, the way the moustache framed his mouth, calling attention to a sensuous bottom lip.

"We don't know each other very well," she said, her voice sounding shaky in her own ears, "but I'd like to ask you a favor."

"Ask away."

"I'd like you to stop this . . . baiting. It makes me very uncomfortable."

Lee searched the beautiful face; it was flushed like before.

"Uncomfortable in a bad way," he asked, "or a good one?" Her complexion went a shade brighter.

"I didn't know there was a good way to be uncomfortable."

Lee gave her a doubting look and decided to hit point-blank.

"I find you extremely attractive, Cara Chastain," he said in a low voice. "And I want you to have a drink with me. Will you?"

Her heart began to pound. "No. I won't."

"Why not?" he asked after a moment. "You're a free woman. Right?"

The image of Tom flashed before Cara's eyes, steadying her as she looked up into the handsome face of the Texan. "You're being blunt with me, Mr. Powers, so I'll be blunt with you. In the eyes of the world, I may be a free woman. But in my heart, I am not. I'm completely in love with my husband. Memories are all I need or want."

Lee studied her solemnly. "I suppose that's admirable, but all I can think is: What a waste."

"That's a callous thing to say," Cara flashed.

"Maybe. But five years is a long time, too long for a beautiful woman to shut herself away with nothing but memories for company."

"Mr. Powers," Cara began, precisely enunciating each syllable, "I don't tolerate questions on this matter from even my closest friends, and I'm not about to tolerate them from you."

"Okay," he responded slowly. "I guess you've got the right to put me in my place."

"I'm glad we agree on something."

Her expression was pure defiance. Another man might have been put off, but as Lee met her flashing eyes, he was drawn to her so urgently that he nearly reached for her. He stuffed his hands in his pockets instead.

"I'm not usually such a pushy guy," he said. "I just have the feeling we'd hit it off."

"I'm sure there are any number of ladies around here who'd be happy to hit it off with you."

"But you're the one I want."

His words reverberated through Cara, stirring the shakes all over again. "I asked you to stop saying things like that."

Lee leaned back against the doorway. "What are you so afraid of?"

"I'm not afraid," Cara blazed. "I simply do not welcome or appreciate your overtures."

"You might if you gave yourself a chance."

A brow shot up. "Your conceit is truly astounding, Mr. Powers."

"Not conceit," he drawled. "Confidence, maybe. You see, I think I've figured out something about you."

"And what is that?"

"That you're saying one thing and feeling another."

Her first impulse was to launch into a sputtering denial. But as she took in the expression on his face, Cara sensed that was just what he expected. Hanging onto her composure by a thread, she looked him dead in the eye.

"This is exactly the kind of thing I want to come to an end," she said. "I appreciate your help with the mustangs. But if we're to be crossing paths, I insist that you respect my wishes."

Lee considered her thoughtfully. Damn, she was hard! Just when he thought he was getting somewhere, she put up a brick wall.

"I tell you what," he said after a moment. "I'll make you a deal. You say you appreciate my help. All right, then. Agree to celebrate with me after we've finished painting the mustangs. Then, if you don't want to see me again, okay."

Cara shook her head derisively. "Always the diplomat."

"At your service, ma'am."

He finished with a smile. A cocky smile, Cara thought.

"A celebration?" she murmured, her mind clicking away.

"Have a drink with me. The job should be done by next weekend."

His expression was questioning, but he looked damned pleased with himself, too. All right, *Mr. Slick-As-A-Whistle Powers.*

"I'll agree to a celebration," she said ultimately. "Next weekend if the project is finished. We can do it right here."

"We can do it anywhere you like."

The remark carried a sexual undertone. So did his arched look. Cara stepped around him, marched to the door, and opened it. There was nothing Lee could do but follow.

"Good night, Mr. Powers," she said as soon as he stepped up.

"Good night, Mrs. Chastain." He sighed and, stepping outside, found the door quickly closed behind him.

Cara walked swiftly to the study, poured herself a healthy dose of brandy, and swept up the stairs. Once in the sanctity of her chamber, she perched on the bed and took a burning gulp. Her eyes filled with water, and through the haze emerged the image of Lee Powers smiling down at her, the white of his teeth gleaming below the dark moustache. She took another hasty drink.

It was bound to happen sometime, she thought, her mind taking an analytical turn. The man was attractive, and she could see that as well as the next woman. It didn't mean anything. Nothing was going to happen. But as she changed into a nightgown, she found herself pausing, drifting into a daydream as she remembered the way he looked leaning against the doorway, his hands in his pockets.

"What are you so afraid of?" echoed the drawling voice.

Cara jerked the nightgown over her head and made another trip to the study, this time filling her glass to the rim.

Chapter Five

On Tuesday evening, Lee got a call from Ned Crockett. Doc Simpson had delivered the paint pellets, and he had the guns. Would Lee like to get started tonight?

Crockett picked him up around eight o'clock and headed north. Sitting in the passenger seat of the police car, Lee loaded the pistol, which was about the size of a .44 automatic. Seven-inch barrel, five-inch grip . . . He turned it over in his hands, surprised that it felt so familiar. It had been at least five years since he'd fired a gun.

"You seem pretty homey with that thing," Ned commented.

"I hope so. I'll warn you, though. It's been a long time."

"Hell, you know the old saying. It's like riding a bike—once you learn, you never forget."

"Where are we going, anyway?" Lee asked. "Do these horses keep some kind of schedule?"

Ned grinned. "Afraid not. It's gonna be catch as catch can. I thought we'd try the north beach. It's a hot night. What wind there is, is coming from the southwest. Unfortunately that means mosquitos. Fortunately, when the mosquitos come, the mustangs head pretty predictably for the beach."

They banked in on the ocean side of the dunes. Crockett was right—it *was* a hot night. Even when the sun went down, the heat lingered, along with a faint light that radiated from the clear summer sky. He was right about the mosquitos, too. Despite the mild sea breeze, the devils had Lee slapping at his bare arms and neck. He bit his tongue and said nothing until they'd been there a full hour and a half.

"Dammit, Crockett!" he exploded with an angry smack at his forearm. "Do we have to sit here like easy pickin's? Can't we go looking for the damn mustangs?"

"All right," Ned conceded. "We'll give it another ten minutes and then work our way south."

He'd barely gotten the words out when they felt the vibration, then saw the herd canter onto the beach some twenty yards north. Keeping to the dunes, they crept toward the dozen horses who milled along the fringe of the incoming tide. When they'd ventured as close as they dared, the two men nodded to each other in silent agreement and took aim.

Repeating shots split the air, joined by the startled neighs of the horses as Lee and Ned emptied their chambers. Splashes of yellow fluorescence appeared on the sides of four animals, including one of two small foals in the group. The herd scattered and took off up the beach, falling together once more just as they disappeared from view.

"Not bad," Ned offered. "A third of them in one round."

They searched until midnight but never spotted them again. Wednesday night's search lasted until the same late hour but failed to yield even a sighting.

"That stud is pretty smart," Ned hypothesized. "Ten to one, he's got them in hiding somewhere."

On Thursday it rained. There was no work at the site, and Lee spent the day working on Tommy's carving. The sky cleared around dusk, and Ned showed up soon after.

Although the weather had given Lee a respite from double shifts—days at the development, nights on the prowl with Ned—it made the mosquito problem worse. The air was so heavy it was tough to breathe. Sweat dripped from both men, and the damnable mosquitos were a buzzing blanket that seemed to follow them wherever they went—first to the beach, then through the village, and finally to the sound where they caught sight of the mustangs some distance south of town.

Ned was just getting ready to turn around and head north when Lee spotted the animals. It was the yellow paint on a few of them that caught his eye, giving him a small measure of satisfaction in the face of pressing discomfort. Cautiously, he and Ned positioned themselves downwind and crept up on the horses through the cover of cypress. This time they managed to get all but two—the stallion and a sorrel mare—before the frightened horses bolted out of range.

Friday evening was charmed as far as Lee was concerned. He was sitting on the beachfront steps, passing the time before Ned arrived by putting the last few touches on the whittled likeness of Star, when he looked up and saw Tommy hell-bent across the beach in his direction. With the idea of a surprise in mind, Lee tucked the carving under his leg and put away the pocketknife.

"Does it hurt?" the boy demanded on arrival.

"Does what hurt?"

"Does it hurt the mustangs when you shoot 'em with paint?"

Lee smiled. "It probably stings a little. That's all."

"Will it solve the problem?" Tommy asked with a steady look.

Both the look and the mature wording reminded Lee of Cara. "We don't know yet," he admitted. "At least it makes them easier to see at night, or any time for that matter."

"Mom said you're a genius."

A spasm of pleasure gripped him. "Did she, now?"

Something drew his attention beyond Tommy's shoulder, and he saw her, running by the tide at an experienced jogger's pace, and dressed in nothing more than a black one-piece swimsuit. Lee's blood went hot. The boy said something, but he had no idea what it was. His eyes were glued to the spectacle of the woman.

Tommy said something else—apparently in parting, as he moved away at a rapid pace in the direction of his mother. She stopped and raised a hand to her brow, shielding her eyes against the descending sun, looking in their direction. Her son ran toward her. She waited.

Lee came to his feet, watching as she caught the boy up in her arms and swung him around. A mix of longing and lust throbbed to his throat, just as he heard the measured footsteps approaching from behind. He glanced over his shoulder and saw Ned, then looked back to the beach. She wasn't looking his way as she started a slow, trotting pace that allowed Tommy to keep up with her.

He could have caught up to them, but Lee steeled himself against the impulse. One night soon he'd have her all to himself with no chasing. With a resigned grin against the tedious night ahead, he turned and went to join Ned.

But the night didn't turn out to be tedious. Maybe luck was with them; maybe they were simply getting better at their odd task. Lee had developed an instinctive affinity with the stallion; the black stud was downright cunning. Last night they'd found the herd at the sound. Tonight Lee suggested they try the north beach where they located the mustangs the first night.

The sun was still aflame in the west when Ned pulled the police car to a slow stop on the edge of the highway. They crested the dunes not twenty yards south of where the horses were gathered. In unison, the two men dropped to their knees. They were downwind, but close enough that if the breeze took even a slight change, the mustangs could pick up their scent.

"I'll take the stallion," Lee murmured.

"You got it," Ned replied just as quietly.

They moved north behind the dunes and peeked through the sea oats. The horses were still, but for the lazy swish of their tails against the mosquitos and flies that hovered above them like a cloud. All but two sported patches of fluorescence on their coats. The black was out front; likewise, the unblemished sorrel mare stood apart and without cover on the right. The final targets couldn't have been in better position if they'd been directed.

This was almost too damn easy, Lee thought, raising the pistol and feeling as though something were bound to go wrong at the last instant. He was about right, for just as he targeted the stallion, the animal turned and looked straight at him, almost as if he'd known the men were there all along. It was disconcerting. Lee fought the urge to lower the barrel; instead, he fired. A split second later the sound of Ned's rounds joined his own.

The paint-spattered herd galloped away. By nine o'clock, Lee was sighing with relief under the reviving streams of a cold shower.

* * *

Cara had just replaced the receiver when the phone rang.

"Hello?" she said.

"I hope it's not too late to call."

Her heart skipped. She hadn't given him her number, but she'd expected his call. Lee Powers wasn't the type to forget the little rendezvous he'd manipulated.

"Hello, Mr. Powers," she said.

Her husky voice was memorably sexy; even her insistent formality failed to irritate Lee. He propped back on the pillows and gazed unseeingly across the bedroom as he imagined her face.

"I've been trying to get through for over an hour," he said. "Somebody at your house must like to talk."

"I've had a lot of calls to make."

"Horse business?"

Cara glanced at the kitchen ceiling. "Of a sort."

"We shot the last of the mustangs tonight."

"So I heard."

"News travels fast."

"It's a small town," she commented.

There was a sense of intimacy in talking to her over the phone. Lee rubbed an absent hand over his bare chest and was instantly aroused at the thought of her long fingers touching him the same way.

"How about that celebration you promised me?"

"A promise *is* a promise, I suppose."

Lee chuckled. "Please don't overwhelm me with your enthusiasm." He paused, but she didn't reply. "So when can we get together?"

Cara felt a pang of guilt. "How about tomorrow night?"

"At your house?"

"That *is* what we agreed."

Her tone was the resigned one of someone about to face a firing squad. Damn! She wasn't making this easy.

"There's no point in looking at this as some distasteful obligation," Lee said. "You might actually have an okay time if you just relax."

"Can you be here at eight?" Cara snapped, feeling more abominable by the second.

"I'll be there."

"Well, then, good night," she said, hardly waiting for the answering "good night" before hanging up the phone. Staring at the instrument, Cara chewed her lip. After a moment she took a decisive breath and turned.

"What's done is done," she muttered.

"And what exactly is it that you *have* done?" Elsa asked from the kitchen doorway.

Startled, Cara looked up, started to explain, then noted the suspicion on the older woman's face.

"Nothing you need to be concerned with," she replied.

"It has to do with this last-minute shindig you've thrown together, doesn't it?"

"Really, Elsa, I don't know what you mean."

Reaching for the light switch, Cara plunged the room into darkness before those prying eyes looked clear into her guilty conscience.

Lee came down the stairs with a light step, adjusting his cuffs and paying little attention to his surroundings.

"Well, ain't you pretty as a dadburned picture?"

Lee stopped short. He thought everybody had cleared out. Apparently Joe had stayed behind. The old geyser's whistle ended up in a rumbling chuckle.

Lee cast a wry glance down himself and surrendered a grin. He *was* gussied up, having put on the best he'd brought with him—white dress shirt, black sport jacket, matching slacks. A thin black necktie and tooled boots gave the outfit a western flavor, but the stark black and white was decidedly formal.

"Do you think you'll ever get tired of giving me a hard time?" Lee asked.

Joe mosied over. "Ain't likely," he answered and, producing a bouquet of flowers from behind his back, laughed at Lee's surprise. "Me and the boys chipped in. We figure you're out there for the lot of us. After all," he finished with a wink, "she *is* the 'little widow.' "

The July evening was expectedly warm, but somewhat tempered by a breeze. Lee climbed into the Jaguar and placed the flowers on the neighboring seat. Wrapped in green paper, the bouquet was a mix of tearoses and daisies and some blue flower he couldn't put a name to—although it struck him that the deep blue center of the blossom was about the shade of Cara's eyes.

He scratched away from the Fast Break and wore a smile of anticipation as he made the short drive up the highway. But as he drew near the Chastain house, he knew something was wrong. A dozen vehicles were parked by the fence. He recognized Ned's police car, Doc's banged-up van . . . Lee pulled over and nosed the Jaguar neatly in front of the van. Killing the engine, he directed a suspicious look along the column of parked cars.

"What the hell?" he muttered and snatched up the flowers. Pushing swiftly through the gate, he strode along the brick walkway and, as he neared the house, caught the sound of music drifting from the back. Bewilderment mushroomed into anger. He did his best to hide it when Tommy answered the door.

"Come on in, Lee!" he chortled.

"Hi ya, Tommy. I've got something for you." Stepping inside, Lee withdrew the carving from his breast pocket and dropped to one knee. "Here you go," he said. "A promise is a promise."

As soon as he voiced the words, he remembered what Cara had said over the phone: "A promise *is* a promise." Lee fought to keep his face from twisting into a scowl.

"Wow!" Tommy exclaimed. "It's great!"

When the boy looked up at him with shining eyes, Lee found it easier to control his impulse for murder. And when Tommy threw his small arms around him in an enthusiastic hug, he broke into a genuine smile.

"Thank you," Tommy breathed in his ear.

"You're welcome," Lee returned gruffly.

The boy backed off, still beaming. "Come on," he said. "Everyone else is outside."

Lee straightened slowly, the dark anger returning. "Everyone?"

"Yeah. Mom said everybody she called turned out! You're a hero!"

"Everybody she called, huh?" Lee repeated under his breath as he followed the boy through the house. When they approached the sunroom he looked through the expansive window and saw what his mind's eye had already created. Torchlight ringed the back deck where a crowd of thirty or more people milled in the soft dusk of the summer evening. Lee swallowed hard as Tommy drew him outside.

"Mom! Look!" the boy cried and darted into the throng.

Lee stood just outside the back door, flowers in hand, thinking that if the sentiments he had at that moment could spill over, the damn daisies would wilt right there and blow away on the breeze. He was aware of an old beach tune vibrating from a nearby stereo, a mouth-watering aroma drifting from a table spread with hors d'oeuvres, and a swirl of dark hair as Cara turned and looked his way.

She had been steeling herself all day against this specific moment, but when Cara saw Lee Powers, she found the preparations useless. Her heart leapt to her throat, and her palms went damp. Tommy deserted her, excitedly showing off the carved horse. Cara was forced to approach the man alone. He held her eyes as she walked toward him, refusing to return her fleeting smile of welcome. She was gripped by the notion that he was taller and darker than she remembered.

"What is this?" he growled as she arrived.

"Why, it's a celebration." Even to her own ears her voice sounded falsely bright. "And you're the guest of honor."

"Ah, there you are!" Jack Quincy stepped up and clapped a hand on Lee's shoulder. Lee gave him a short glance.

"Evenin', Mayor."

"And a good evening to you!" the shorter man chimed. "Ned says you did a first-rate job this week. Calls you a crack shot. I *knew* Lone Star Partners would end up being good for Walking Dune, and you're a shining example, my boy . . ."

Jack Quincy blabbered on. Lee's gaze returned to Cara. She was wearing white—a flowing dress with a high neck that bared her arms, but reached modestly to her toes . . . though the way it hung along her curves created the opposite effect of modesty. Her hair was loose and shining, curling slightly over golden brown shoulders, framing the incredible face.

Quincy was still talking, but Lee didn't hear him against the escalating roar in his ears. For a moment, it was as if he and Cara were alone in a silent meeting of eyes. She was damn breathtaking, and the thought that she should have looked this way for him alone made Lee angrier still.

"These are for you," he said, thrusting the flowers toward her.

"Why . . . thank you." Cara cradled the bouquet, a tentative smile curving her mouth. "You didn't have to do this," she added.

"I could say the same to you," Lee replied, arching a brow.

"Come on, boy," Quincy interjected, oblivious to the tension buzzing around him. "Join the party."

"Yes, do," Cara took up hurriedly. "I'll go put these in water."

She escaped to the kitchen, her thoughts churning with the ideas of how devastatingly handsome Lee Powers was, how furious he was, and how she deserved every bit of anger he cared to dish out.

Although the deck of the Chastain house was expansive, it was brimming. As soon as Quincy pulled him into the crowd, Lee found himself monopolized, congratulated, patted on the back, and generally welcomed to the bosom of Walking Dune. Hal Freemont, Nettie Wolf, Jacob Abernathy, Doc, and Ned and a host of others made it a point to seek him out. He spotted Nick, who raised a hand in greeting, but Lee had no opportunity to join his newfound buddy as a group of tittering ladies drew him into their midst.

At one point even Dahlia Dunn approached to offer her compliments. Louis Talbot kept a marked distance . . . as did Cara. Lee saw her shapely form from time to time, always on the move. She smiled, made the rounds of party guests with trays of champagne punch, and once stopped by a group of which he was the center to offer him a glass. All he had time to do was offer a glare which she seemed not to notice before slipping away. It was obvious to Lee that she was avoiding him. Nearly an hour had passed before he gained the opportunity to approach Nick.

"How ya doing, Lee?"

"I've been better," he returned curtly. "Why don't we go inside and get ourselves a real drink?"

The two of them stopped by the study, then moved toward the quieter front of the house. Lee cast a searching look through the rooms as they went, but he didn't see Cara. She was extremely adept at staying out of his line of vision. His mood soured further. They walked into the front parlor, and Nick turned to him with a curious expression.

"Why do I get the feeling you're about to explode?"

Lee gave him a look of utter frustration. "Dammit, Nick! I'm covered with mosquito bites the size of golf balls, and I haven't had a decent night's sleep in a week!"

"Is *that* what's got you in such a foul temper? Mosquito bites?"

"Hell, no!" Lee tossed down a healthy gulp of Scotch. "I *wanted* to do the paint job on the horses, all right? I felt a certain responsibility. I don't give a damn about the mosquitos!"

Nick spread his palms. "What then?"

"Your sister," Lee ground out. "She deliberately misled me. She agreed to celebrate with *me* tonight, not the whole damn town."

A look of dawning broke across Nick's face. "I see."

Lee turned his back and drained the last of the Scotch before adding, "Sometimes she makes me so mad I could throttle her!"

"Don't you *ever* lay a hand on her. *Ever!*"

Lee looked over his shoulder to find the grimmest expression he'd ever beheld on the face of Nick Malloy.

"For God's sake, Nick. It was just an expression. I've never raised a hand to a woman in my life."

"It happens," came the stiff reply. "But it will never happen to Cara again."

"Again?" Lee moved to stand directly before the other man. "What do you mean, 'again'?"

Nick scrutinized Lee Powers; his jaw was hard set, his expression ferocious. "I knew you were hot for her," Nick said, "but it's more than that, isn't it?"

Lee's scowl deepened. "I asked what you meant. Did somebody hurt Cara? Some man?"

"All right, then. Maybe you should know. Cara was sixteen, and his name was Mitch Lincoln."

Lee didn't know what was coming, but suddenly he felt as though the wind had been knocked out of him. "Hold on a minute," he said and sank into the overstuffed chair just behind him. "Tell me the whole thing from the beginning."

"The beginning?" Nick settled on a velvet-covered love seat and glanced around the antique-filled room. "Okay. To begin with, if you think Cara was born to this grandeur, you're wrong. We grew up in an ugly little mining town in western Virginia. Our father was a coal miner, our mother a schoolteacher. We both got Dad's looks. Cara got Mom's brains as well. Times were lean, but in the beginning happy enough.

"I always remember Cara being tall. She's three years older than I am, and in those days three years made a difference. I remember her being pretty, too. All the boys liked her, especially when she started growing up and filling out. But most of them kept their distance because Mitch Lincoln had set his sights on her from the time she was knee-high. He was the biggest, meanest kid in town, red-headed and hot-tempered. Nobody crossed him.

"The older Cara got, the bolder Mitch got. She kept turning him away. Finally when she was sixteen, he got fresh, and she slapped him. And then . . . she vanished."

Nick stopped talking, his gaze centering somewhere on the Oriental carpet beneath the tea table.

"What the hell do you mean she vanished?" Lee spat. His companion raised blue eyes that looked dark and tortured.

"She was locked up for nine days," Nick said.

"Locked up—"

"In a deserted mine shaft. Mitch had built a fortress around the entrance. Once he closed it off, there was no way out. She said he came by every couple of days and called through the barricade, offering to let her out if she'd give in to him. She never did."

Lee's eyes slammed shut, springing open again when the darkness offered only the image of a young Cara, penned up in a black hole.

"She dug her way out with sharp pieces of rock and walked six miles home," Nick went on quietly. "She'd been beaten, but the bruises were at least a week old, the doc said. Three of her fingers were broken, not from any effort of Mitch Lincoln's, but from banging and digging. Her hands were bandaged for weeks. And she had no voice. The doctor said she'd screamed until she caused permanent damage to her vocal cords. Eventually her voice came back, but—"

"Stop it!"

Nick looked up as Lee sprang to his feet.

"Just . . . stop it," Lee repeated. After a moment he rubbed a hand across his eyes. "What did your parents do?"

"Nothing. Dad was sick . . . dying. Mom was distraught to the point of madness, over him as well as Cara."

"What about this Mitch Lincoln?"

"He was seventeen, a minor. He was sent to reform school for a while. We heard he got out when he turned eighteen."

"You heard?"

"He never came back to town."

"Never came back?" Lee repeated in disbelief. "The authorities should have nailed him to the wall."

Nick shrugged. "A couple of mining town kids. Nobody gave a damn. Years passed before I saw Cara the way she was before it happened. Oh, she carried on, got a scholarship, went to college. Only someone who knew her well could have seen the difference. She still has nightmares. At least, I guess she still has them. It wasn't until she met Tom that the fear went out of her eyes. I guess he made her feel safe."

Jealousy welled up in Lee. He had no right to feel possessive of Cara Chastain. But he did.

"Tell me about Tom," he said and, sinking once more into the overstuffed chair, offered the false impression that he was listening very casually, when in fact he seized on every word.

Louis eavesdropped for a while—surprised and then angered by the revelations spilling from Nick Malloy's mouth. Only those closest to Cara knew about Mitch Lincoln. Outside of family, she once said, only he and Dahlia knew.

And now Lee Powers.

Making his way quietly out of the house, Louis found Cara on the back deck and drew her away from the crowd. He leveled a hostile look through the sweeping window of the sunroom, on through the dining room, into the softly lit front parlor. The two men continued to loll there, separate from the rest of the crowd.

"Did you have to invite *him?*" he demanded.

Cara followed his line of vision inside. She didn't really have to look. She knew to whom Louis was referring.

"I could hardly exclude him," she replied. "Painting the mustangs was his idea, his project."

"Is that the only reason he's here?"

Cara's gaze leapt to his. "What other reason could there be?"

"Don't play dumb, Cara. You know what I'm asking. Is something going on between you and this Powers guy?"

"First, there's nothing going on. Second, it's not your place to ask. Last week you made a similar insinuation, Louis. Please don't do it ever again." Her eyes flashed between his, releasing the anger her low-pitched voice contained. "Excuse me," she added. "I'm going to put Tommy to bed."

With that she flounced off toward the back door. Louis watched the screen slam behind her, a feeling of dread drumming in his chest like the beat of a dirge.

"But I want to say good night," Tommy complained.

Cara looked down into his fresh-scrubbed face. "To whom?"

"To Uncle Nick and Lee."

"Really, Tommy—"

"Why can't I say good night?" he asked.

"Why, indeed?" Elsa echoed from the doorway.

Cara threw an irate look in her direction. "Would you mind seeing to the guests, Elsa?"

"Hmph!" the older woman sniffed before making her exit.

Cara looked back at Tommy. "I don't want you going down there and getting all charged up again," she said. "That crowd—"

"They're not *in* the crowd. They're in the parlor, just the two of them. Didn't you see 'em when we came upstairs?"

Of course she'd seen them! Didn't she hope they were once again safely part of the crowd? Didn't she hope she could make it through the night without being cornered by the brooding Texan?

"Come on, Mom," Tommy urged. "I'll just say good night and come right back."

"All right," she allowed finally. "But you be back here inside of one minute, or you'll get no bedtime story tonight."

"Okay!" Tommy leapt out of bed and snatched the carved horse off the bedside table. "I want to thank Lee again! Isn't it great?"

Her son thrust the small piece under her nose, and Cara was forced to look at it. The lines were beautifully drawn; the luster of polished wood shone in the lamplight.

"Yes," she agreed. "It's great."

She watched her son dart out of the room and waited anxiously for his return, catching the sound of his voice and then deeper voices before she heard his footsteps once again on the stairs.

"Guess what!" he exclaimed, running into the room and vaulting onto the bed.

"Tommy!" she reprimanded. "Don't jump around that way."

He gazed at her with sparkling, unconcerned pale blue eyes as he crawled under the covers. Tom's eyes . . .

"Don't you want to know?" he challenged.

"Know what?" Cara returned, tucking the covers around him and reaching for the storybook.

"What's going to happen tomorrow?"

"Okay. What's going to happen tomorrow?"

"Uncle Nick is going to take me and Lee on the *Virgin.*"

Cara's gaze swerved to Tommy's cheerful face. *"Me and Lee?!"* She and Nick had planned to drive down to Bellehaven and surprise Tommy. Now what? Her treacherous brother had included the very man she'd been seeking to avoid all night.

"Is that a fact?" she asked. Her tone was terse. It was the best she could manage.

"Yes," Tommy chimed. "Right after breakfast. Lee's coming over, and then we'll all drive down to the boat."

"All?" Cara questioned, keeping her anger concealed.

"You're coming, too, aren't you, Mom?"

She hesitated. His sweet face, shining with hope, never failed to move her.

"Uncle Nick said you were."

"We'll see," Cara returned noncommittally.

"But—"

"We'll *see*, Tommy."

She continued reading *Treasure Island* long beyond the time she heard the even breathing announcing that Tommy slept. Finally Cara closed the volume and edged off the bed. A chorus of laughter rippled up from the deck. She glanced at her watch. Ten o'clock. Surely the party would break up soon. Leaning down, she kissed Tommy's forehead, smoothed his hair, and doused the light.

She descended the steps cautiously, listening for voices, hearing none. Accelerating her pace, she thought she'd been lucky until her name rang through the foyer. Spinning at the base of the stairs, Cara looked into the parlor and saw her fears realized. Lee Powers was standing there . . . alone.

Tall and dark, all in black but for the white V of the shirt beneath his jacket, he looked like a gunfighter, staring her down, daring her to a reckoning. The moustache hid any forgiving line there might have been to his mouth. Cara moved in his direction, halting when several safe yards remained between them.

"What are you doing in here all by yourself?" she asked with an admirable attempt at lightness.

"Waiting for you."

He walked toward her, his steps slow and deliberate. Cara could almost hear the clink of spurs, almost see the flash of a hand flipping a coattail clear of a holster. Instinct told her to back away. Pride made her stand firm as he stopped a mere foot away.

Behind Lee's steady gaze, tumultuous feelings yanked him first one way, then another. She'd played him for a fool, and he was damn mad about that. But Nick's story about the mine shaft softened his anger. Looking into her vivid eyes, Lee noted the way they slanted up at the corners; glancing at her perfect mouth, he saw her lips tremble, though he had no doubt she was doing everything in her power to stand up to him. How could any man hurt something so damn beautiful? He released a defeated breath.

"Why did you do it, Cara?"

She'd prepared a dozen glib responses to that question, but

coming as it did—in the most gentle of tones—Cara couldn't push a single riposte past her lips. Judging from the way he'd glared at her most of the night, she'd expected angry demands, hostile words—things that would have made it easy to reply in kind. But Lee Powers's searching eyes relayed only disappointment, and his features were the picture of boyish sincerity. Such a look on the face of such potent manhood knocked the wind out of her sails *and* ignited sparks of other things.

"You knew what I thought," he added.

Cara pushed a swallow down her throat. "I know."

"Well, then, why?"

She glanced aside and rubbed at her forehead. "At first I thought I was being clever . . . I didn't really mean to . . . It didn't turn out . . ." She caught her lip and put an end to the stumbling excuses. "It wasn't fair," she concluded. "I'm sorry."

Lee studied her silently, impressed by the way she 'fessed up.

"You see how ill-equipped I am for this sort of thing," she added in that throaty voice of hers.

Now he knew why it was so unusually husky. She'd screamed until she damaged her vocal cords. Conflicting emotions swirled through Lee—the urge to kill a stranger named Mitch Lincoln, the instinct to protect the woman before him, the hot drive to grab her and hold her close.

"Well," he returned with a slight smile, "at least you admit there *is* 'this sort of thing.' "

His smile broadened, and the sparks flared. It was happening again, the involuntary reaction of woman to man, and although Cara didn't move a muscle, she had the sensation of leaning toward him.

"No," she said hurriedly, "I didn't mean that. There is no *thing* between us. Nothing's changed. Tom is still the only man in my life, the only man I *want* in my life."

The words came out in a rush, too fast and desperate to ring with truth. Cara knew it, and her racing pulse raced faster at the look that came over Lee Powers. He knew it, too. Far away she heard the comforting sounds of music and people, but they were too distant to help as his dark eyes moved between hers—weaving a spell that shut out everything until the two of them were nerve-shatteringly alone.

"I have every respect for your memories," he said.

He took a step and reached for her, his hands gently catching her face and turning it up to him. Cara blinked, and after that everything seemed to freeze, including her eyes, which she was unable to divert from those directly above her.

"But I'm not going to let you pretend there's nothing going on here and now," he added in a near whisper.

His gaze dropped to her mouth. Cara's heart bucked. She knew what was coming; yet she didn't slap his hands away, which was exactly what she should have done instead of watching like a stricken bird as he bent toward her. His movements were so slow, his hold so light, that she had every opportunity to step away. Somehow the thought stalled between brain and limbs.

His breath fanned her face, and then his mouth was on hers. She experienced the prickling of a moustache, which she'd never felt before—the pressure of arousing lips, which she hadn't felt in five years—and . . . he ended it. Lifting his head a few inches, he peered down with eyes full of yearning.

A long thumb stroked her cheek. He was asking permission with those dangerous eyes, but she couldn't answer. She couldn't even breathe, although she knew that unless she said something, he'd take her silence as acquiescence. Even as Cara thought it, his hands shifted, one to the back of her head, the other around her back. He pulled her against him. This time his mouth was open as it captured hers, holding firm as his tongue moved inside—seeking admission, finding it, languidly staking claim. It was the instant of surrender.

Lee felt the change. Her mouth welcomed his kiss, and her body relaxed against him. When her hands climbed up to lock behind his neck, his senses exploded in an awareness that left him lightheaded. Her taste made him think of warm honey . . . her scent, of summer flowers . . . her hair, of black silk spilling through his fingers. He wanted to absorb her, pull her inside himself. His arm slipped down to her hips and clasped her tight against him.

Cara felt his hardness pressing against her belly, imagined it inside her. . . .

She broke away. Lee started to reach after her, but then heard the name "Tom!"—a gasping sound that fell somewhere between a whisper and a cry. Heart thundering, Lee planted his arms stiffly by his sides as Cara turned her back and walked away. Her head was bowed. Slowly it rose to its typical proud lift.

"I can't imagine how that happened," came the stilted comment.

"Can't you?"

Cara turned to face him. "No. I *can't*. It never should have occurred and will never occur again."

"Is that right?" Lee drawled.

"Yes. That is *right*," Cara flashed.

As usual, she generated feelings that clashed within Lee like stormy waves. Part of him wanted to console her; the bigger part wanted to snatch her angrily back to him. She was standing there stiff as a board, her cheeks scarlet, eyes glittering like blue jewels. The only moving thing about her was her chest, which rose and fell with a rapidity that belied her otherwise statuesque calm. Lee could read her plain as day. At least he thought he could.

"Just what exactly has got you so riled up?" he asked. "The fact that I kissed you? Or that you liked it too much?"

"I did *not*—"

"Don't say it."

The command, though spoken quietly, had the ring of authority. Cara forced herself to silent endurance as he gave her an intimate once-over that made her want to jump out of her skin.

"What were you about to claim?" Lee asked. "That you felt nothing? Forget it. I was there, too, darlin'."

She floundered for a reply, but . . . he was right. She couldn't claim she'd felt nothing. In fact, she'd never felt anything so physically overpowering, not even with—

Her hands began to shake. Cara clasped them tightly before her but couldn't prevent a chain reaction that spread like wildfire until every inch of her body seemed to be trembling.

"I want you out of this house," she whispered.

Lee Powers cocked a brow that struck her as both doubting and arrogant. Cara drew strength from that.

"I want you out of this house," she repeated. "And I don't want you back again. Not tomorrow for a boat ride. Not ever."

The dark eyes stripped her. She felt as though they were probing inside her.

"Have I made myself clear, Mr. Powers?"

"Don't call me that again. We're beyond that, and you know it."

"We're not beyond anything," Cara retorted.

Lee took long strides in her direction and saw her tense up, though she refused to back away, even when he leaned toward her with threatening nearness.

"We're beyond a first kiss, I believe. Or are you maintaining it was entirely forgettable?"

Her chin went up. *"What* kiss?"

Lee intended to chuckle at that, but when the sound emerged, it was more like a snort. Likewise, the half-formed grin that crossed his face was more of a grimace.

"I don't understand," he said after a moment. "It's good between us. Why are you dead set on ruining it?"

Cara looked pointedly away and gave no answer. Lee plunged onto forbidden ground.

"Is this what you think Tom would have wanted?"

Her gaze snapped to his. "Don't speak to me of Tom."

"Would Tom have wanted you to shut yourself off for the rest of your life?" Lee pressed.

"I told you not to speak of him!" Unlocking her clenched fingers, Cara grasped the gold band on her left hand and began twisting it in short, unconscious circles. Round and round went the ring on her finger, round and round went the images—Tom smiling at her, kissing her, making love to her. . . .

"The man is dead," Lee Powers's voice intruded.

It was as though a hidden trigger had been pulled. Before she knew what she was doing, Cara sent her right arm swinging, drawing it back in horror just before her palm would have connected with his cheek.

Lee feinted slightly, instinctively, from the approaching blow. He was surprised when she pulled back, though the thought barely made it through his mind as the realization

dawned with the blinding light of truth. Suddenly he knew.
He'd been right all along about the chemistry, or whatever
the hell it was, that flared between him and Cara every time
they looked at each other. But suddenly he knew it wasn't
enough.

Lee's vision cleared, and he saw that she was staring up
at him, wide-eyed and breathless. From what? The shock of
nearly having slapped him, or the lingering tremors of the
passion he'd ignited in her only moments ago? It didn't
matter. Such passion was no match for the ghost of Tom
Chastain.

"Now I understand," Lee said, his voice low and uncontrollably heavy. "I won't be bothering you again. Tell Tommy I'm
sorry I can't make it tomorrow."

He turned and walked out. Cara stood stock still, watching
the back of his black jacket disappear around the doorway . . .
jumping at the sound of the front door, though it was closed
so quietly, the click barely made it to her ears.

Laden with an assortment of cups and glasses, Louis had
followed Dahlia to the kitchen grudgingly—aware that she
was trying to keep him occupied, trying to draw him out of
a stormy mood that threatened to break. Setting the glass-
ware by the sink, he'd heard voices that drew him to the
doorway.

The succeeding minutes had passed in a haze, tortuous in
their sloth. Even now with the Texan gone, Louis saw him
bending to Cara, possessing her . . .

"Don't do it!" Dahlia hissed.

Louis jerked his arm free and stalked out of the kitchen.

"And just what was *that* all about?"

Cara turned and gave Louis a blank look. "What?" she
mumbled.

"I asked you what the hell's going on!" he bellowed. "You
say there's nothing between you and the Texan. Yet when
he kisses you, you plaster yourself all over him like some
dime-store floozy!"

The insult yanked her to alertness. *"What?"* Cara repeated,
this time on an incredulous note.

"You heard me, Mrs. Chastain." Louis voiced the address

with a sneer and all the emotion that had boiled up inside him.

"Stop it, Louis. You and I are friends—"

"Friends?!" he thundered. "I've been in love with you for eight years, Cara. For years I've let you pass off my feelings as nothing, let you have the respectful distance you demanded. And then Lee Powers comes along." The name twisted through Louis, provoking the memory of the man's arm slipping around Cara's hips.

"What is it, anyway?" he added, his voice harsh with loathing. "Is there so much of a rutting dog about him that you can't help responding like a bitch in heat?"

Blotches of red bloomed on Cara's cheeks. Louis knew her face so well. She was shocked and hurt. It was what he'd intended. He wanted to hurt her, wanted her to ache as he was aching.

"Get the hell out of here," she murmured.

He'd expected something like that; still, the pain intensified.

Louis gave her a snide salute and swaggered to the foyer, exiting the house just in time to see the flashy Jaguar speed past. He watched the car disappear up the highway, his eyes clouding with the most towering anger he'd ever experienced. It was a relief when the searing pain turned into cold, numbing fury.

Dahlia spun through the kitchen and hurried out the back door, her eyes scalding. She'd known it! She'd known it for eight long years; yet somehow, hearing Louis speak the words broke her heart as though it had never been prepared at all.

She virtually ran past the crowd on the porch, pausing a safe distance in the darkness of the elevated walk, swiping angrily at the tears as they spilled over. It was a moment before she caught the sound of approaching footsteps.

"Dahlia?" came the male voice. "You all right?"

Quickly straightening, she turned to peer through the darkness. Nick ambled toward her.

"Sure," she returned lightly. "Just came out for a little air."

"The way you hightailed off the deck, I thought something was wrong."

"Thanks, but no. Nothing's wrong. In fact, it's getting late. I guess I'd better collect Louis and—"

"Just what is the deal with you and Talbot?" Nick demanded. "Every time I come near you, his name is the first word out of your mouth."

Dahlia looked up. He was so tall, his face shining through the night shadows like a seductive moon. She felt it again, the entirely female excitement that had fluttered through her several times before in the presence of Nick Malloy. She stared up at him, waiting for it to pass, feeling more disconcerted by the second when it didn't.

"I've been in love with Louis since I was a child," she said, seeking steadiness from the dismal truth.

"Does he know?" came the question after a moment.

Dahlia tried for a light laugh. "He certainly doesn't act like it, does he?"

"No."

Nick took a step closer. The flutter inside Dahlia escalated to pounding.

"How long has it been?" he asked.

"Since what?"

"Since you had a man."

"Really, Nick!"

She looked away. His hand caught her chin and lifted it, the touch gentle, firm, masculine, thrilling.

"You're a fine-looking woman, Dahlia. I've always thought so."

The quiet statement hung between them, he searched her eyes, and for a shattering instant she thought he was going to kiss her. But then his hand fell away, and he stepped back.

"I'll be around," he said and—walking off toward the torch-light—left Dahlia standing in the darkness, her chin trembling with the imprint of his fingers.

Lee drove aimlessly south. The convertible top was down, a warm wind ripping through his hair, just as thoughts from the past ripped through his mind.

Marilyn. The way she looked the first day he met her, the way she looked the last time he saw her five years ago . . .

the night she walked out of his life. "You're as good as anybody, Lee."

The highway between Walking Dune and Southern Shores was dark and empty. The headlights of the Jaguar beamed across deserted wilderness that billowed from the road in mounds of sand and thicket. Lee turned on the radio, but a wailing love song failed to divert his thoughts, which turned irrevocably back, landing in a part of his life so far in the past, it seemed as though it had never happened. But it was real; he'd kept the black leather jacket all these years as a reminder.

"Caballeros!" The war cry echoed in his mind, growing stronger, clearer, until he could almost distinguish the voices—Johnny, Angel, Pete, Eduardo, Patch. . . .

They were the class gang of the East Side, at least that was how Lee had seen it. He looked up to them, envied them, emulated them. When he turned twelve, they took him in. By that time Mom was dead, his older sisters gone, and the old man too worn out with night shifts to keep up with a kid. The Caballeros became family.

It was with them that Lee learned to smoke and drink; to drive like a pro by the time he was thirteen; to fight, use a knife, shoot a gun. Most of the time they cruised the streets looking for trouble. Most of the time they found it, if not with a rival gang, then with some undeserving soul who had the rotten luck to come across the Caballeros on a slow night. Lee never joined in the beatings, though he remained behind the wheel of the hopped-up Chevy to provide a quick getaway for his "brothers," and so was just as guilty as they were.

He never shot anyone either, though he knew both Patch and Johnny had. It was Johnny, the oldest of the group, who taught him to shoot. By the age of fifteen Lee was the best shot in the gang. The following summer he left the Caballeros.

They'd driven out of the city, two cars full, and headed for a posh country club in the suburbs. It was a joy ride, designed to let off steam by jeering at the richies. Lee pulled over by the chain link fence surrounding the pool, cast a casual glance to his right, and saw her—beautiful and blond, her hair shining gold in the sunlight. The radio in the Chevy was blaring, the guys were hooting, but Lee didn't hear them. His every sense was centered on the girl walking across the pool deck in their direction.

Mindlessly he killed the ignition, got out of the car, and started toward her. Their eyes locked, and she smiled, just before some tall athletic-looking guy caught her by the arm and pulled her back . . . just before a siren split the air. Lee jumped in the back of the Chevy as Patch screeched away. The security guard stayed on their tail all the way back to the city.

The next day he slicked up, returned to the country club, and was hired on as a pool boy, thus courting the scorn of the Caballeros and eventually their ostracism.

Her name was Jennifer Blackwood, wealthy socialite, girl-friend of that big athletic type he'd seen the first day, Todd Van Camp, whose credentials were just as impressive as hers. She was out of Lee's league, but he was hopelessly smitten.

She led him on for about a month with stolen kisses, always behind the cover of a cabana or whatever else was handy. One late afternoon toward the end of summer, Todd discovered them behind the hedge lining the pool deck. Lee had pulled down the top of her bathing suit and was nuzzling her breasts. It was nothing he hadn't done before, but as soon as Jennifer became aware they weren't alone, she pushed him away and slapped his face.

"Learn your place, pool boy!" Todd had sneered. "You're not good enough to wipe her boots!"

Lee had taken an angry step forward, hands clenching into fists, ready to flatten the guy. But Jennifer stopped him, not with a word, but with the look of contempt she directed his way as she went to join Todd. Lee never saw her again, but she changed his life. Looking through her eyes, he'd seen himself as worthless. It became an obsession to be "good enough" to look down his nose at every Blackwood and Van Camp in the world.

Later, the obsession made him a success. But it cost him a wife . . . Marilyn, who never heard the story about Jennifer, but who somehow had known. "You're as good as anybody, Lee."

There were lights ahead. Lee mentally shook himself and

slowed the car as he drove through Kitty Hawk, and then Kill Devil Hills—site of the flight of the Wright Brothers, herald of the outskirts of Nags Head. He glanced at the gas gauge. Nearly empty. The fact irritated him. Everything just now irritated him, and he knew why. Cara Chastain.

He'd known her a matter of weeks; the time he'd spent with her could be measured in hours. She shouldn't be calling to mind poignant memories of Marilyn or Jennifer. But she was. And again Lee knew why. Cara had climbed under his skin just like the other two. It took no time; a single look would do—or so it seemed in the cases of Jennifer Blackwood, Marilyn Powers, and Cara Chastain. Three women . . . three devastating women.

Spotting a gas station, Lee turned in, stopped by the pumps, and climbed out of the car, his mood growing blacker by the second.

"Evenin', mister. Can I fill her up for ya?"

Lee turned to see a freckle-faced kid about twenty.

"Sure," he returned. "Fill her up."

Lee walked restlessly across the lot and back again. When the kid finished, he fished out his wallet and thumbed through his credit cards. As he withdrew one, a slip of paper fluttered to the ground. Lee handed over the card, retrieved the paper, and looked at it. There was a phone number and the name Sandy. A vision of blond hair and a sweet smile invaded his troubled mind. When the attendant got back with the credit card slab, Lee signed his name with a flourish.

"Do you know a place called RJ's?" he asked.

"RJ's?" The kid smiled. "Sure. Everybody around here knows RJ's. It's just across the causeway."

"Yeah," Lee responded. "How late does it stay open?"

"On a Saturday night? I reckon one or two in the mornin'."

"Good," Lee grunted and, climbing into the Jaguar, shot out of the station toward the bridge to the mainland.

The restaurant overlooking the Roanoke Sound was as he remembered it—sprawling, crowded, rowdy. He had a drink at the bar while he waited for a table and had been there only a short while when he spotted Sandy. Dressed in the denim skirt and white blouse that comprised RJ's waitress uniform, she, too, was as he recalled—very blond, very attractive.

He didn't end up in her section, but it didn't take her long to notice him. He'd just finished his salad when she stopped by.

"Hello, there," she said.

Lee looked up with a smile. "Hello, Sandy."

"How have you been?"

"Getting better by the minute."

Sandy beamed with tingling pleasure. She'd given up on the Texan, having decided that if he meant to call her, he would have done so by now. But here he was, more gorgeous than ever in a black suit that made him look breathtakingly sexy.

"How are things up in Walking Dune?" she asked.

"Good. But it's been a long week. I could use a break."

Sandy gave him a piercing look. "I'm very good at breaks."

Lee's gaze swept down the pert figure and returned to the face. She was in her late twenties, he'd guess—her hair sunbleached a silvery blond, her skin smooth and golden brown. She was a pretty woman, and the way she was looking at him stirred his blood.

"What's your last name?" he asked.

"Cook."

"What time do you get off, Sandy Cook?"

She had a place on the beach and a roommate who spent most nights with her boyfriend.

At 3 A.M. Sandy was contentedly asleep while Lee stared at the ceiling. With a glance at her motionless form, he left the bed and headed out back, stopping only to pick up the pack of cigarettes she'd left on the coffee table. He hadn't had one in years. Tonight he felt like a smoke. Lighting up the thing, he stepped outside into the wee hours of the summer morning.

The deck was small; the neighboring cottage mere feet away. With a fleeting thought of his nudity, Lee took a drag and found himself thinking of the Fast Break where he could have stood outside on the deck at such an hour, with nary a stitch on, and never worried about the neighbors.

Overhead the sky was pure, dark . . . shining. A path of silver moonlight shimmered on the water and streaked across the sand, just as it must have done for thousands of years. There was a feeling of eternity about the place, but . . . down the way, artificial brightness spilled from a line of beachfront motels, reminding him that he was not in Walking Dune but Nags Head.

From a distance came the sound of music, loud and pulsing. Lee thought of the silence of the untouched northern shores and knew that it would not remain silent. In months to come it would be noisy and crowded and lit up like a Christmas tree.

Walking Dune wouldn't be the same with ritzy houses scattered from here to yon, ritzy people strolling the village, ritzy shops springing up as they always did when the wealthy converged on a fashionable new spot. The town was but a few miles north. Suddenly it seemed as far away as a star, as close as a bridge soon to be crossed and left behind. Tommy's words rang in his memory. Cara was right. Lone Star *would* "castrate the town."

Below him, moonshadows shifted across the sand as nearby sea oats flirted with the breeze. Lee barely noticed, his thoughts hovering some thirty miles north. Tommy . . . Cara . . . Walking Dune. Tom Chastain's family. Tom Chastain's home.

Face it, he thought. *That's what you want—the man's wife, his son, the whole works.* But it was useless. In Cara's eyes, her husband cast a shadow no man could fill.

Lee's brows drew together in a frown. Dammit! He'd do well to forget her and put his damn mind back on his damn business! After all, that's what he was damn well here for! He was Lee Powers, CEO-incumbent for one of the most successful developers in the nation. He shouldn't be thinking of a woman, or a small boy, or some out-of-the-way place on the North Carolina coast that seemed to be seducing him.

Hell! She was probably peacefully sleeping with no more thought of him than the man in the moon. And here he was feeling lonely and rejected when a warm woman was curled up in bed just inside, waiting for him.

"Not good enough," whispered the night wind.

Grinding the cigarette into a sparkless butt, Lee sent it sailing over the rail and went back to Sandy.

She was in the kitchen when the bell rang. Don't answer it! *her mind screamed. But Cara's feet started moving, dragging*

her through the dining room, into the foyer, up to the door.
Though she sought to pull it back, her hand reached for the
knob. . . .

Cara leapt up with a scream, her hand locked around her
wrist and drawing it back. She gasped for breath, her horrified
gaze flying about the moonlit room, slowing as she saw the
shapes of the window . . . chest . . . vanity. Her grip relaxed;
her hand dropped to her heaving breast; she fell back to the
pillows.

It was one of the bad ones, maybe the worst.

Your husband is dead, the dream words rang. Only this time
the sheriff wore the face of Lee Powers.

Chapter Six

The following week, Lee threw himself into his work. Between hard days at the site and long nights with Sandy, he did an effective job of shutting out the thought of Cara Chastain . . . until Friday morning when she jogged past the site in a pair of shorts that had every man in the vicinity staring.

The construction clatter puttered to a hum as she ran by, and Lee was no less guilty of dropping what he was doing than anybody else. He was aloft on the platform near the highway. She must have known he was there. But did she even glance in his direction? Hell, no. Lee directed an angry look to the nearest group of mesmerized men.

"Is it time for a break?" he yelled down. The noisy activity launched back into gear. Lee moved to the ladder, making scant use of it as he dropped to the sand a number of feet below. Joe was standing nearby. Lee gave him a brief look and turned away without a word.

"Where you going, boss?" Joe asked.

"I'll be back," Lee returned. Stripping off his hard hat, he stalked toward the Jaguar parked on the shoulder of the highway.

Joe pulled his hat brim down to his brow, an expression of concern gathering on his face. He'd known Lee Powers a number of years. In Joe's opinion, there was no better or more likable field representative in the whole company. Most of the time Lee could be counted on for good humor and an easygoing temperament that made a job a whole lot easier.

When that temperament did a turnaround, it was obvious. And it had turned around a few days back.

Since the weekend, Lee hadn't been around the Fast Break much, and when he was there, he stayed in his room. On the site his manner was distant, his words curt, his face set hard in unsmiling lines. Joe had seen him like this only once before, and that was years ago when his marriage broke up.

The racy convertible headed north toward town. Joe turned and looked south where the bouncing figure of Cara Chastain was far in the distance. He'd been amused when the boss took a liking to the "little widow." Now it didn't seem so funny.

"Women," Joe muttered, and went to make his rounds of the site.

July came to an end with record-breaking temperatures. On the first Saturday night of August, the Wild Horse Fund met at Dahlia's tavern—minus Louis, who'd left town shortly after the celebration at the Chastain house, and of course, Lee Powers, who never had been a real part of the group anyway. At least that's what Cara told herself when she called everyone else to arrange the meeting. Still, as the group of five gathered around the tavern table, she couldn't deny that she felt his absence. The Texan had made an impact, and not just on her.

"Where's Powers tonight?" Ned asked as they took their seats.

Nick and Dahlia looked pointedly at Cara. Doc lifted curious eyes. Ned's gaze settled on her along with everyone else's.

"How am I supposed to know?" Cara responded. "The man isn't really a member of the fund, you know."

"He seemed pretty much a member when we were out shooting the mustangs," Ned insisted.

Again everyone's eyes targeted her. Cara looked down at her notebook and began scribbling trivial things like the date and location of the meeting.

"I suppose so," she said. "But we're not here to discuss Mr. Powers, rather the outcome of the painting project."

Less than three weeks had passed since the reflective paint was applied to the mustang herd, but the stuff was wearing off—or rather the horses were wearing it off by rubbing against trees, rolling in the mud, and who knew what else.

"It was a promising idea," Doc said. "No one could have predicted how clever the mustangs would prove."

"An unfortunate blessing," Dahlia responded solemnly.

Everyone agreed that something else would have to be done, but no one had any new ideas. The meeting broke up a little before ten. When the others left the inn—Nick rather reluctantly, Cara thought—she stayed to have a beer with Dahlia. One led to another, and they ended up outside, leaning against the stone fence that bordered the front drive.

Overhead a bank of clouds glowed with filtered moonlight. The night was muggy, and the cold beer tasted good. It was Cara's third, and she was a little lightheaded, but then how often did she get out with Dahlia? Besides, tonight she felt glum and guilty. The meeting had been a failure, and it was her fault. After all, she single-handedly had alienated both Louis and Lee Powers, and their absence was due expressly to her.

"Have you heard from Louis?" she asked.

"Hell, no." Dahlia took a swig from her bottle. "He's throwing one of his tantrums. When his temper wears off, he'll be back."

Cara looked off into the distance. "It's my fault."

"It's not your fault, Cara."

"You don't know, Dahlia. The night of the party—"

"Yes, I do know."

Cara glanced over with surprise. "Know what?"

"That you kissed Lee Powers, and Louis got mad as hell."

"But . . . how did you—"

"I was in the kitchen with Louis. I saw the whole thing."

"Well, why didn't you say something?"

Dahlia chuckled. "What was I supposed to say? Gee, Cara, the man really looks like he knows what he's doing . . . Does he?"

"Oh, for heaven's sake, Dahlia!" Cara took a hasty gulp of beer and pivoted to stare out over the expansive lawns stretching to the highway.

Dahlia lifted herself to a seat on the stone wall. "You're a grown woman, Cara. You can kiss anybody you want to, and if Louis doesn't like it, that's his tough luck. He has no claim on you. You're not responsible for the fact that he wants one."

Cara cast a sidelong look at her friend, who lifted a beer to her lips and proceeded to turn the bottle straight up. Dahlia had been in love with Louis for years, and Cara would have wished her a lifetime of happiness with him. It was a painful irony that she seemed to be the woman standing in Dahlia's way. Cara avoided thinking about it whenever possible, but sometimes, as now, the issue rose to the surface. The unusual thing was it never had affected their friendship. She and Dahlia had hit it off from the beginning, and through the years had grown close as sisters.

Dahlia set aside her empty bottle and leaned back to look at the sky. For all appearances, she seemed merely to be taking in the night, but Cara imagined she was thinking with longing of Louis. She deserved better.

Cara considered her a moment longer and asked, "What do you think of my brother?"

"Nick?" The name came a little shrilly. "I think Nick's a great guy," Dahlia added more casually. "You know that."

"I saw the way he watched you tonight."

"Come on, Cara."

"I can always tell when Nick's interested in someone, and he's interested in you. If he asked, would you go out with him?"

Dahlia drew an uncomfortable breath. "No."

"Why not?"

"You know why not."

A moment of silence fell.

"It's been a long time," Cara said, carefully avoiding Louis's name. "Maybe you should give yourself a chance."

"For what?"

"For something new to work out."

Dahlia tipped her head and looked Cara in the eye. "Maybe I could say the same to you."

The two women stared at each other through the luminous darkness, turning in unison when the beam of headlights swung across the lawn and a car turned up the drive.

"Expecting guests?" Cara asked.

"Not at this hour."

Leaving the stone wall, they moved to the driveway. Cara's heart skipped as the Jaguar convertible came to a stop beside them.

"Lee? Is that you?" Dahlia asked, stepping over.

"I didn't know where else to go," came the short reply.

Lee climbed out of the car and pulled the driver's seat forward. Cara stayed a few feet behind Dahlia. It didn't occur to her that she was hiding, but she was. Lee grunted as he lifted a burden from the back seat.

"I was hoping to find sanctuary for this guy," he said, turning to face them.

Dahlia caught her breath as she recognized the form of a small horse. "Damn!" she exploded. "What the hell is this?"

"A hurt foal."

"How the hell—"

"It wasn't one of my people," Lee broke in, his eyes flickering for the first time to the dark-haired woman beyond Dahlia's shoulder. Her hair was down . . . loose around the scoop neck of a white blouse. And she had on a matching skirt that seemed pretty short from what he could see in the darkness. Lee looked back at Dahlia, who reached out to the squirming animal in his arms.

"It was a bunch of kids," he went on briskly. "I was behind them most of the way from Nags Head. They were stopped when I came around the curve south of town. As soon as they saw my headlights, they scratched off."

Dahlia began to stroke the foal's face. He calmed almost immediately, whinnying softly as she murmured calming words.

"Look, I know this is a baby," Lee added on an impatient note. "But he's still a horse, and he's damn heavy. I was told you know a lot about horses. Can I put him down somewhere, or what?"

The Dunn's Lodge stables were old and sprawling and filled with the aroma of fresh hay. As Lee followed Dahlia's lead, he noticed a half dozen or so horses peeping over stall gates, snorting their complaints at the lights that had come on in the middle of the night.

"Whose are these?" he puffed to the redhead ahead of him.

"Two are mine," Dahlia threw over her shoulder. "The rest board here. Come on. Put him down in here."

Lee stepped into the vacant stall and knelt with the small horse. Dahlia dropped to her knees beside him and began an immediate inspection.

"There's blood on his foreleg," Lee offered.

"I saw that," Dahlia replied. "Looks like he was grazed, or maybe he did this to himself trying to get out of the way of the car. He seems more stunned than anything else."

"Should I call Doc?" Cara asked from behind them.

"I don't think that's necessary tonight," Dahlia answered. "I have some antiseptic in the house. You two stay with him, and I'll be right back. Cara, take my place up here by his head."

Cara had no time to think of an alternative before Dahlia was gone. Kneeling where she'd been instructed, Cara extended a hesitant hand to the foal. He sniffed at her fingers, then licked them. Cara's eyelids dropped, her gaze slipping to where Lee Powers was bent to one knee at the back of the horse. He was wearing jeans and a white shirt. About the time she caught the scent of Shalimar perfume, she spotted the lipstick on his collar. In a reflex action, Cara leapt to her feet. The horse scrambled at the sudden movement.

"What the hell are you doing?" Lee demanded quietly.

"What?"

"I asked what you're doing," he said without looking at her. "I could use some help down here."

Cara sank back to her knees and opened her palm to the foal. When he nuzzled it, she reached into a nearby bin and offered a handful of oats. He munched hesitantly at first, then with relish. Cara shifted to a sitting position that turned her back to the Texan, and willed herself not to think of the disturbing sensation that had just flashed through her. Concentrating on the dark, sculptured head bent over her hand, she thought how small the foal was. How vulnerable. Right now, but for a stroke of providence, he could have been just as dead as the two lost mares.

"I could see right off that Dahlia's good with horses," Lee commented after a few long, silent minutes. "You seem to have the touch as well."

"I don't really know what I'm doing. Just going by instinct."

"You should go by instinct more often."

The inference behind his remark wasn't lost on Cara. The image loomed before her—the two of them embracing as her instincts ran wild. She stared at the horse, grateful her stinging face was pointed away from the man.

"Right now my instincts are telling me this little guy is lucky," she said, determinedly sidetracking the issue. "He's one of two foals in the herd, and he could have been killed. Something's got to be done. We're going to have to fence them in."

From the adamant champion of horse freedom, the conclusion was a surprise. "That sort of defeats the idea of wild mustangs, doesn't it?" Lee said.

"I can't think of anything more defeating than allowing them to be slaughtered," came the husky reply.

Lee sat back on his haunches and studied her. She was turned away from him, naturally, but she made a beautiful picture sitting there—hair shining, skin glowing. He started at the sandaled feet pointing toward him and worked his way up, inch by inch. He'd been right. The skirt was short; at least it stopped above the knee. The legs curled demurely beneath her were long and smooth and golden brown against the white hemline. His pulse began to pound with familiar intensity.

"Do you think everyone else will go along with you?" he asked.

Cara shrugged. "Dahlia probably won't. Beneath that tough exterior is an idealist."

"It will take a damn big corral."

"Maybe just a fence, if positioned correctly, would be enough to persuade the mustangs to stay on safer acreage outside of town."

"It still won't be cheap."

The foal leaned into her hand as Cara reached to scratch behind his ear. "We'll just have to raise the money."

"I could help."

Her fingers went still. "How?"

"There will be a need for tools. And manpower."

"That's very generous," Cara returned slowly. "But you've done enough for us already. We'll manage."

"We?" Lee repeated, his eyes turning hard. "As in you and the others? I'd like to point out something here. I'm part of this thing. Everybody knows it. You made sure of that two weeks ago when you invited all of Walking Dune to celebrate my efforts. You can do what you want with your private life, ma'am, but there are times when you have no right to shut me out."

His drawling voice, deep and meticulously contained, echoed in Cara's ears. It was the same tone he'd used that night just before he walked out. Interminable seconds crawled by, her mind consumed with the memory of his stern expression when she all but slapped him silly. She was mortified to think how often he'd invaded her thoughts since then—especially when he showed up with lipstick on his collar, especially when her memories weren't limited to the way he looked when he left. She recalled with shameful clarity the feel of his hands, the taste of his mouth.

"I'd like to apologize," Cara said abruptly, her gaze riveted between the ears of the foal.

"For?"

"For that night at my house. I can't imagine what got into me. I'm not usually so . . . flustered."

"Maybe that's the problem," Lee returned, barely getting the words said before Dahlia rushed into the stables.

Taking swift charge, Dahlia proceeded to issue instructions like a drill sergeant. Cara was ordered to continue what she was doing; Lee to stay at the back of the horse and prevent him from moving while Dahlia applied disinfectant. She really was quite brilliant, Cara thought, watching with admiration as Dahlia bathed and bandaged the animal's leg, crooning to him all the while so that instead of panicking, the horse seemed about to fall asleep.

"There you go, little one," Dahlia said finally. Shifting beneath him, she cradled the foal's head in her lap. "You can go, Cara," she added. "You, too, Lee. I'll stay until he sleeps. You're going to be fine, aren't you, little one?" she tapered off in that crooning tone. "Just fine . . ."

Cara came to her feet and stepped away. She saw from the corner of her eye that Lee Powers did the same. As she exited the stables, she was aware that he was just behind her but couldn't bring herself to acknowledge him, much less think of anything sensible to say. She walked silently through the still and humid darkness, which was alight from the phosphorescent clouds, alive with the songs of crickets. Looking firmly ahead to the drive where both their cars were parked, Cara did her best to ignore Lee's unnerving, over-the-shoulder presence as the night enveloped them with the sensual scent of oleander.

The path from the stables stretched across fifty yards of grounds to the drive. Lee stayed several feet behind Cara, indulging himself in a blatant study of the swinging backside in the white skirt, deriving perverse pleasure from the fact that she was probably aware of his scrutiny and uncomfortable with it. She hadn't looked him in the eye since he arrived, not even when she apologized for that night.

The surly mood that had come over him since finding the foal took a turn for the worse. Two weeks had passed since the volatile confrontation with Cara. They hadn't faced each other since that night, and when she turned onto the drive and took long strides toward her car, Lee grasped the fact that she didn't plan on facing him tonight either. The realization triggered the rebellious decision that she damn well would. He followed her to the driver's side of the fancy, wood-paneled Jeep.

"The foal didn't have any paint on him," he announced when she reached for the door handle.

Cara hesitated.

"I'm sure Ned and I got him when we shot the herd," Lee added.

She turned and faced the man for the first time since he'd appeared. The glow of the sky was in his eyes. They sparkled like dark glass.

"I'm sure you *did* get him," Cara said. "Unfortunately the horses have proven themselves adept at getting rid of the paint. We had a meeting about it tonight."

"Meeting?"

"Of the Wild Horse Fund."

"Nice of you to let me know."

"It wouldn't have mattered, would it?" she challenged before she knew what she was saying. "It's obvious you've been out socializing."

"What makes you say that?"

"I used to wear Shalimar. It's a very distinctive fragrance."

Even to her own ears, the remarks sounded like jealousy. Cara bit her lip and stepped back, her behind bumping against the unyielding door of the Jeep.

Lee's mouth dipped in a wry grin as he took a corresponding step toward her. "Socializing? Is that what you call it?"

"What would *you* call it?" Cara asked with all the coolness she could muster.

The fleeting grin disappeared. Leaning forward, Lee planted a palm on the car roof near her head. "I'd call it a nice way to keep my mind off other things."

Though she looked away when he sought to catch her eyes, Cara felt his nearness like the radiance of fire.

"It's been a long night," she said and pushed away from the closeness of his outstretched arm. Taking a few steps, she turned to face him, though she failed to meet his eyes and found her gaze lighting atop the adjacent stone wall bordering the drive.

"Forgive me if I sounded as though I was chastising you," she added. "Obviously, what you do is none of my business."

"It could be," Lee returned quietly.

Cara put a hand to her brow. "Please, Mr. Powers—"

"Good night, Mrs. Chastain."

Moving swiftly to the convertible, Lee vaulted over the driver's door without opening it and sped away from Dunn's Lodge.

At five o'clock on Sunday morning, the stately halls of the Richmond Hotel were quiet. Louis walked to the elevator, pressed the down button, and closed his stinging eyes.

A royal flush! The damn Yankee had drawn a royal flush! Louis still couldn't believe it, though he had to admit it was a fitting finale to the disastrous turn his luck had taken.

The first thing he'd done upon arriving in Richmond was to get in touch with Harry Dane. Harry always had a game going somewhere, and this time he'd picked the penthouse suite of one of the city's most exclusive hotels. The first week, Louis couldn't lose. At one point he was up more than twenty thousand. But then that damn tycoon from New Jersey came into the game. From the moment he sat down at the table, Lady Luck had deserted everyone else to whisper in his ear.

The twenty thousand was gone after two nights. Harry had bankrolled him after that. Good old Harry—with his quick smile, silk suits, and musclebound "bodyguards." On the turn of a card, Louis was into him for a fortune.

"Don't let me down, Talbot," he'd said only minutes ago.

Louis turned at the door. Behind Harry stood his two faithful watchdogs—Tom, who was six-two if an inch, two hundred and twenty pounds if an ounce; and Dick, shorter than Louis at five-nine or -ten, but as broad as he was tall, and wearing a cauliflower ear that spoke of punishing time in the ring. Tom, Dick and Harry. Harry derived great pleasure from introducing the trio.

"You know I'm good for it, Harry," Louis replied.

The quick smile appeared. "Sure I do. Otherwise, I wouldn't take your marker. So, I can expect to hear from you . . . when?"

"I'm selling some land down on the coast. As soon as the deal goes through, I'll get back to you."

"The sooner the better," Harry smiled. "Interest has such a nasty habit of accruing."

Louis went to his room on the fifth floor, packed his bags, and was on the highway at daybreak. The rental car was new and flashy, but the seat wasn't comfortable, and the ride far from smooth. He missed the Mercedes. He'd told Dahlia it was in the shop. The truth was he'd sold it more than a month ago.

Louis thought ahead to Walking Dune and pictured the Lone Star crews working the Phase One site at the south end of town. How long would it be, he wondered, before the option on his Phase Three property turned into cash?

Louis's face was grim as he peered up the sunny highway. The Lone Star deal wasn't just a windfall anymore; it was his salvation.

On Sunday afternoon Sandy drove up from Nags Head. Lee gave her a tour of the site; then they went out on the beach, spread a blanket, and set up one of the old beach umbrellas stashed under the stairs to the Fast Break.

Lying back on the shaded blanket, Lee folded his arms beneath his head and closed his eyes. "God," he murmured. "I haven't done this in years."

"We'll have to make sure that doesn't happen again," Sandy replied. Settling beside him, she propped back on her elbows and looked across the strand. The sky had cleared that morning. Sunlight sparkled on the blue water and turned the sand a dazzling white. A constant breeze swept in from the ocean. It was a perfect day for the beach, and they were the only two people in sight.

"Things sure are different up here," she said. "I'll bet the beach down at Nags Head is so full of people you'd have a hard time finding a place to pitch a blanket."

"Um-hmmm."

Sandy looked over. His eyes were still closed, and he appeared to be on the point of dozing. Turning on her side, she studied him with intimate freedom—the bulge of muscle in his folded arms, the dark hair on his chest, the outline of his manhood where his gym shorts had settled provocatively. Her gaze rose to his face and traced a path along his profile.

"You're gorgeous," she said with a sigh.

Lee opened his eyes and turned his head in her direction. The blond hair was pulled up, calling attention to the heartlike shape of her face.

"You're the one who's gorgeous," he said.

She smiled, and Lee noticed once again how pretty she was when she smiled. "Come here," he added and, not moving a muscle, waited for her to lean over and kiss him. When she gave him a light peck and pulled back, Lee rolled over, caught her face in his hands and proceeded to kiss her with slow, searching thoroughness.

When it was over, Sandy opened her eyes slowly. His face was only inches above. When he smiled, a charge ran through her, reminding her how desperately in love she was with him.

"You'd better watch out," she said a bit shakily. "A girl could get addicted to that sort of thing."

Lee's smile faded. Lifting a hand, he stroked a wisp of hair from her forehead.

"In case I haven't mentioned it, I really like you, Sandy."

"I like you, too."

Lee searched her eyes. "I mean I *really* like you, and I don't want to mislead you."

"About what?"

"About . . . well, about us. I'm not going to be here forever."

Sandy willed the pounding ache within her to subside. How long had it been since he showed up at RJ's? Only three weeks? It seemed longer. The thought of going back to life without Lee filled her with dread, but even more frightening was the idea of losing him right now if she tried to cling.

"I know," she said after a moment. "I've known all along. You don't have to worry, Lee. I'm a good-time girl. I have no delusions about being anything else."

He frowned. "That's not how I think of you."

"Let's just have a good time while you're here, okay?" Sandy added and forced a cheery look to her face. "Come on. I'll race you to the water."

"What are you looking at?"

Cara yanked the binoculars from her eyes and spun around. "Good heavens, Nick! Don't sneak up on me like that!"

"I wasn't sneaking up. You were just so engrossed, you didn't hear me. What's so interesting?" he concluded, glancing out the kitchen window toward the beach.

"Tommy's out there."

"Oh?" Nick looked back at his sister, who was wearing a white shirt over a bathing suit. "You guys going for a swim?"

"I was," Cara replied, turning back to the window and raising the binoculars. "But I think I've changed my mind."

The current was northerly. In the ten minutes she'd been watching, the couple had drifted with the tide until they were now directly in front of the gazebo.

Nick followed her line of vision. "Where's Tommy?"

"On the beach right out front."

"Oh, yeah. I see him." Nick's gaze continued to the surf where he spotted a man and woman just as he lifted her and tossed her bottom-first into the waist-high water.

"Who's that?" Nick chuckled.

"Who?"

"Let me have the binoculars a minute."

"Why?"

"Come on. Hand 'em over."

Cara surrendered the things reluctantly, expecting and receiving her brother's sly look when he recognized Lee Powers.

"I see," he pronounced as though he'd uncovered a great secret.

Cara snatched the binoculars from his hand and walked over to the counter. "Would you mind going out and collecting Tommy?"

"Why don't you collect him yourself?"

She turned and gave him a warning look. "I really don't want to, Nick."

"Cara," Nick began solemnly. "I think you're making a mistake."

"About what?"

"About Lee Powers."

"I'm not interested in discussing him."

"He's a good man. You're attracted to him, and he's definitely attracted to you. What's the problem?"

"For heaven's sake!" Cara huffed. "First Elsa, Now you. Why does everybody think they have the right to delve into my private life?"

"Because we care about you." Her flashing eyes locked with his. "You've never been scared of anything, Cara," Nick added. "Don't be afraid now."

"I'm not *afraid.*"

Nick folded his arms across his chest. "Then why don't you go out there and collect Tommy yourself?"

Cara glared at him, her face growing hotter by the second. "Honestly, Nick!" she blurted and stomped off toward the kitchen door. "Sometimes you can be positively infuriating."

Nick grinned as the door banged behind her. She never could pass up a dare.

Lee looked toward the beach and spotted Tommy at the water's edge. The boy was kneeling, digging in the sand. An unconscious smile came over Lee's face.

"Excuse me a minute, will you, Sandy? There's somebody I'd like to say hello to." As he came splashing out of the breakers, Tommy looked up and rose to his feet.

"Hello!" Lee greeted enthusiastically.

"Hello," the boy returned and glanced back to the sand.

Lee's brows drew together as he took in Tommy's dejected look. "What is it, Tommy? What's the matter?"

"Nothing."

"Tell me," Lee insisted. "What's wrong?"

Tommy looked up with accusing eyes. "You didn't go on Uncle Nick's boat, and I haven't seen you since you said you would. I thought we were friends."

Lee dropped to one knee. "We *are* friends. I'm sorry, Tommy. I've been awfully busy the past couple of weeks . . ." Lee's voice trailed off as Tommy looked down at the sand once more.

"I tell you what," Lee went on after a moment. "Let me make it up to you. How would you like to go out for hamburgers with me one night this week?"

The boy's face lit up with a smile. "You mean it?"

Lee smiled back. "Sure I do. Talk to your mother and find out if Wednesday night's okay."

"I'll go find out right now!"

With that the boy sprinted away across the sand. Lee turned and saw that Cara had come out on the beach and was standing not twenty yards away. The breeze lifted her hair and flirted with the open fronts of her shirt, beneath which was a black swimsuit. He realized he was staring just as Sandy came up behind him.

"Who's the boy?" she asked curiously.

"Tommy Chastain."

Sandy watched along with Lee as Tommy ran up to a tall, elegant woman with flowing black hair and an unbelievable figure. A stream of water slipped from Sandy's hair to run down her face. She wiped it away, feeling suddenly very short and very wet.

"And the woman?" she added.

"His mother, Cara."

"So *that's* Cara Chastain."

"That's her," Lee muttered.

Sandy glanced up, and when she caught the look on his face, a sinking feeling rocked her clear to her toes. In less than a minute, the boy was galloping back in their direction. The woman remained where she was.

"Wednesday night's fine!" Tommy announced breathlessly when he arrived. "And Mom said to tell you the Wild Horse Fund is meeting tonight at Dahlia's."

"Tell your mother thanks for letting me know," Lee said, "but I have plans for tonight."

"Okay. Bye! I've got to go in now!"

"Cute kid," Sandy offered as Tommy dashed away.

"Yeah."

"Where *does* he get all that energy?"

"Good question," Lee replied, finally looking down at her with a smile. "Ready to head back and get cleaned up?"

"Sure," Sandy replied lightly, although as they walked up the beach, she felt as though her limbs were weighted with lead.

The meeting went swiftly that night. After seeing the foal, everyone was in agreement to try a fence, and everyone agreed the north end of town was the logical place to put it. When the discussion turned to fund-raising, Nick suggested a dance.

"That's what all the big groups do." He shrugged. "Throw a party, charge by the head, and donate the proceeds."

By the time everyone threw in their ideas, the thing had turned into a veritable charity ball scheduled for Saturday after next in the school gymnasium. Ned was charged with securing the proper permits and Doc with contacting a caterer friend who might donate his services for publicity.

"What about an orchestra?" Cara asked. Everyone looked at her, but no one answered. "We'll have to have an orchestra. And decorations for the gym. And bartenders . . ."

By the time she finished jotting down notes about everything that would need to be done, it was clear Cara had taken charge of the project.

"Two weeks isn't much time," she concluded. "We'll post flyers around town. And listen, everybody, be sure to get in touch with out-of-town friends and relatives. Even if they can't make it to the dance, they might send a contribution."

Nick, Cara, and Dahlia stood out front of the lodge, exchanging a few last comments as Ned and Doc drove away.

"I guess that's it," Cara said. "I'm going home to get out my Christmas list and see how many rich people I know. See you later, Dahlia." Circling around to the driver's side of the Jeep, she glanced back and saw that Nick continued to stand where she'd left him. "Coming, Nick?" she asked.

"I'll be with you in a minute."

Smiling to herself, Cara climbed in and closed the door.

Dahlia studied her toes, knowing she should smile up at Nick and say something light like "What's on your mind?" But she was miserably tongue-tied. Each time she'd found his eyes on her that night, her reaction had intensified. She knew she'd blushed on several occasions, including the last time he'd winked at her.

"Dahlia?"

"Hmmm?" Caught in the midst of reverie, she looked up unawares. Nick took a step toward her, and she was sharply reminded of how tall he was, and how handsome.

"You surprised me tonight," he said. "I thought you were dead set against fencing the mustangs."

"I was. Until the foal was hit."

"I understand. Seeing something that small get hurt kind of brings the issue home, doesn't it?"

A feeling of warmth spread through Dahlia. "Yes. It does."

Nick glanced across the dark grounds before once again meeting her eyes. "Where's Talbot hiding these days?"

"He's been out of town the past couple of weeks."

"So you're not going to tell me any minute now that you have to rush off and check on Louis?"

Dahlia released a short laugh. "No. Not this time."

"Good. Because I'd like to talk to you for a minute, and I don't want to be interrupted. First of all, I wanted to tell you I'm leaving tomorrow."

Dahlia blinked. "Leaving?"

She didn't know what she'd expected from Nick, but it hadn't been the announcement that he was leaving. The news smacked her with a shocking amount of disappointment.

"I've got two charters out of Virginia Beach. The reservations were made months ago."

"I see," Dahlia murmured. "Well, have a good—"

"The second thing is that I'll be back in time for this charity dance, and I'd like you to go with me. Will you?"

Her deflated spirits spiraled so quickly that Dahlia felt a little dizzy. "Nick, I . . . I don't know what to say."

"Say yes."

Her gaze moved between his eyes. "All right, then, yes," she replied, surprising herself as well as Nick. His smile flashed through the darkness.

"That was easy," he said.

"Yeah," Dahlia agreed with a grin. "I guess it was."

She watched the taillights of the Jeep until they disappeared, then went inside the quiet inn, amazed by the buoyant feeling that carried her up the stairs.

On Thursday Dahlia led the foal out of the stable for the first time and put him to pasture. He was getting along fine, Doc said. Soon it would be time to send him back to the herd. Dahlia propped her arms on the top rail of the fence and watched the small horse, his bay coat shining in the sunlight as he frolicked about. He was probably well enough to return even now, but it wasn't going to be easy to let him go. Here he was safe. Once back with the herd, he could fall prey to great dangers—not just from the highway, but from the herd.

There was only one leader in a mustang herd, one stud. Males who reached a certain age ended up challenging the ruling stallion's leadership. When they did so and lost, they were ostracized. "Shunned colts," they were called. Left alone to wander, they tended to find tragic ends. And the likelihood of the bay foal growing up to become a "shunned colt" was almost certain.

Dahlia's dismal thoughts were interrupted by the sound of footsteps. She turned to see Louis walking toward her. Leaning back against the fence railing, she offered a bright smile.

"Hello, kid," he said and came to stand beside her.

"Hello, stranger," she returned. He looked just the same, though a little tired. Dahlia was happy to see him, and the familiar feeling of love rose within her, but . . . somehow it lacked the old cutting edge.

"Where have you been?" she asked.

"Out of touch," Louis mumbled absently, his gaze running the length of her. "What have you done? Changed your hair or something?"

Dahlia's hand rose to the curls she'd pulled back with a ribbon.

"Not really."

"You look different," he added. "Damn good, in fact."

"Thanks," Dahlia accepted with another smile. She knew what Louis was talking about. She'd noticed it herself, and it wasn't the hair. There was a sort of glow about her that had been missing for a long time.

"So, what's been going on?" he asked.

"A lot." She told him about the foal, the fence, the fund-raiser that had been planned.

"I heard about that," Louis said. "Actually, I saw a flyer at the post office. A benefit dance for the Wild Horse Fund, huh?"

"That's right. We had to do something. The kind of fence we're talking about is going to cost about ten thousand dollars."

Louis whistled. "This thing is really going big-time, isn't it?"

"You know Cara. Once she sinks her teeth into something . . ."

Dahlia didn't bother to finish as she saw the change sweep over Louis. Straightening to tense rigidity, he cut his eyes in the direction of the foal, but not before she saw the look within them. Poor Louis. The weeks away had done nothing to relieve his pain or his anger. Dahlia reached out to place a comforting hand on his arm.

"Louis," she said gently, "please don't let this thing eat you alive."

He continued to stare out across the pasture.

"Life is too short," Dahlia added.

He looked back at her with a smile that was, at best, brittle.

"You're right," he said. "Of course, you're right. Now, about this dance. Why don't the two of us go together?"

Mere days ago, his suggestion would have shaken her to the core. Now, astonishingly, the only thing Dahlia felt was a little sad. She'd thought the recent difference in her was due to Nick, and it was to a degree. But suddenly she realized it had more to do with Louis. She was over him. Yes, miraculously, she was over him.

"Well?" he prompted. "How about it? Do we have a date?"

"I can't, Louis."

"Why not?"

"I've already got a date."

Louis almost chuckled, but her look of seriousness stopped him. "A date? With who?"

"Nick."

"Nick?" he repeated. "Nick Malloy?"

Louis stared down at her, noting the roses in her cheeks, the sparkle in her light green eyes. Suddenly he realized all the years he'd taken Dahlia for granted. Suddenly he sensed he'd lost her, along with everything else.

"Have a good time," he said gruffly and, yanking his arm from her light grasp, turned on his heel.

"Louis, wait!" Dahlia called as he strode away, but he never looked back.

Chapter Seven

On the afternoon of the dance, Cara was at the gymnasium busily putting out fires. The caterer had forgotten to bring tuxedos for the waiters, and Cara had to send a messenger all the way back to Nags Head. The decorator had put the most atrocious fake plants in every corner. The orchestra leader had called to say his pianist was sick; did she know anyone who could fill in?

Reminding herself fervently that all these people had donated their time and talents, Cara maintained impeccable grace— though by the time she headed home, her jaws ached from being forced to smile.

As she drove along and ran a mental check on things, however, she began to relax. The school gym didn't really look like a gym any longer. The bandstand monopolized one end, the bar and hors d'oeuvres stations another, and on the two flanking walls bleachers were camouflaged by tables and chairs borrowed from the church. Strings of small white lights had been strung across the ceiling, and in their flattering glow, the place was passable as a ballroom.

Inside the front door, she'd set up a station for herself. She'd offered to collect admissions and contributions, as well as solicit volunteers to help with the building. Just before she left, she'd hung Jacob Abernathy's treasured map of the island behind her table. Overlaid with transparency, the four-foot-wide map showed the intended location of the fence just north of Walking Dune.

They were being asked to pay, Cara had reasoned. They had a right to see what they were paying for.

Thinking ahead with relish to the luxury of a long, hot bath, Cara tensed up all over again when she turned into the drive and saw the black limousine. Abigail.

"Queenie is here," Elsa said when Cara came in by way of the kitchen.

Elsa didn't like Abigail and never had.

"Where is she?" Cara asked.

"In the sunroom with Tommy."

Cara walked slowly to the entrance of the room. Abigail was lounging on a couch while Tommy played at her feet. She was wearing a navy dress and matching pumps. A matching bag lay on the seat beside her. Impeccable.

"Hello, Abigail."

She looked up, her eyes cold as ever. "Good afternoon, Carolina."

"Mom! Look what Grandmother brought me!"

Tommy bounded up and held out his left arm. It was a watch, a gold watch that must have cost hundreds of dollars.

"It's very nice," Cara murmured.

"I'm glad you've finally returned, Carolina. I want a word with you before I go."

"Go? Haven't you just arrived?"

"I arrived two hours ago."

"But it's a long drive—"

"That's what chauffeurs are for," Abigail interrupted with a wave of her hand. "Besides, it was worth the ride to see my grandson. Come here, Tommy, and give me a goodbye kiss. I need to speak with your mother."

When Tommy complied and left the room, Abigail rose to her feet.

"I had hoped that with all the hullabaloo overtaking Walking Dune, you might make the sensible choice of bringing Tommy to Warrenton," she said. "Instead, I see you've planted yourself at the center of the ruckus."

Reaching into her purse, she withdrew an envelope and sent it fluttering to the floor at Cara's feet. "I received your—what shall I call it?—eloquent plea for support."

"I wrote to a number of people about the mustangs, Abigail.

I didn't expect you to attend the dance, but I thought you might consider a contribution."

"Did you? How very misguided of you, my dear."

"I have a lot to do, Abigail," Cara snapped. "If you have something to say, why don't you just say it?"

"Mustangs," she muttered on a note of loathing. "Why, if not for them, Tom . . . would . . ." Abigail raised a manicured hand to her lips and looked away.

"I don't see it that way," Cara said after a moment. "Tom loved the mustangs. He loved Walking Dune. I may not be able to stop Lone Star Partners, but at least I can intervene on behalf of the horses. Tom would have wanted it that way."

Abigail straightened at that. Raising her eyes, she gave her daughter-in-law a blatant look of doubt.

"It's true," Cara insisted. "The mustangs were very special to him. This town was very special—"

"This town is his grave!" Abigail cut in. "And those horses of yours are his executioners. If you think I'm going to put one penny toward their protection, you're sadly mistaken."

Cara gave the woman a long, steady look. "Whatever necessary funding the dance fails to raise, I intend to supply," she said. "And it will be done in loving memory of Tom Chastain."

Eyes blazing, Abigail glared for a moment, then strolled out of the room without another word.

Cara turned to watch her progress up the hallway. At the entrance to the parlor, the grand dame snapped her fingers, a chauffeur appeared, and she departed the house in typical, queenly fashion.

At twenty to eight, Dahlia was a bundle of nerves. At eight o'clock, she was a nervous wreck. Stalking the empty rooms of the ground floor, she lambasted the whole of the inn for its emptiness. The seasonal flow of guests was irritating; the late summer quiet of the place, appalling. Of course, the employees were only doors away in the west wing. But they were no help—bunch of old, wizened moles. . . .

The dance started at eight, didn't it? And it was formal, right? Right. Formal. Cara had said so. Long dress. Gloves.

The works. Dahlia paused by the floor-length mirror in the banquet room. The sheath of watermarked taffeta was simply cut—sleeveless, scoop-necked, and . . . pink. Too pink? When she bought it three years ago in Raleigh, the saleslady had assured her it was a perfect foil for her red hair. But now Dahlia wondered. She also wondered about the long gloves. Her mother's gloves.

Peering into the mirror, she remembered how her mother had always hated the tomboyish turn she'd taken. "Too much time in the stables," she'd always scolded. "Too much time in pants." God rest her soul. Dahlia nearly smiled. What would her mother think of her now? All decked out with a gentleman caller on the way? At least Dahlia *guessed* he was on his way. Glancing at the clock over the mantle, she saw it was a quarter past eight.

"God," she mumbled, barely finishing the syllable when the bell rang. Hurrying to the foyer, she patted her hair and pulled open the heavy door.

"Hello, Nick." He was in a black tuxedo that made him look like the prince of girlhood dreams. "Come in, won't you?" Dahlia added, smoothly belying her absolutely raucous state.

"Sorry I'm a little late," he said. "I docked late in Bellehaven, and I had to drop Cara . . ."

Nick stopped, his admiring gaze taking over where his words left off. "How are you?" he asked after a moment.

"Good." Dahlia smiled.

"You look more than good. You look fantastic."

"Thanks."

"Are you wearing lipstick?"

She thought of the half-dozen shades she'd tried before finding one that didn't clash with the pink dress.

"Lipstick? Yes, a little."

Bending toward her, Nick reached out to capture her chin as he had once before. When he looked in her eyes, there was no doubt of his intention.

"Do you mind?" he asked.

Dahlia could only shake her head. Seconds later, his mouth was on hers. It was the first time she'd been kissed in more years than she cared to count.

Melting against him, Dahlia murmured against his lips, "I don't mind at all."

"Thank you, Mayor."

Cara smiled as she placed his check in the cash box. Things were going exceedingly well, and she was in high spirits. Despite the absence of a pianist, the orchestra sounded wonderful. Couples were dancing, and groups mingled about the banquet tables. It wasn't even eight-thirty yet, and more than a hundred people from all over the Banks had arrived. At ten dollars a head, admissions totaled over a thousand dollars, and contributions more than that.

"You're welcome, Cara."

There was an edge to the voice. She looked up to find Jack Quincy regarding her with a less than pleasant expression.

"I only hope this will put an end to the trouble with the mustangs," he added sternly.

Cara arched a brow. "I hope so, too."

A short while later Dahlia and Nick arrived, holding hands.

"You look lovely, Dahlia," Cara said, smiling warmly at her friend.

"Yes, she does," Nick affirmed.

"Cut it out, you two," Dahlia complained, though her smile was dazzling.

Nick cast a sweeping look about the gym. "Things seem to be going well."

"Very well," Cara answered. "Better than I'd hoped."

"How about volunteers?"

"Here's the list," Cara said, pushing the pad of paper across the table. "Fifteen so far."

Releasing Dahlia's hand, Nick reached for the pen.

"Are you sure, Nick?" Cara asked, a teasing expression coming over her as she looked from him to Dahlia and back again. "We'll be at it every Saturday and Sunday for as long as it takes. Could be a month, maybe more. You sure you're going to be around?"

Nick tossed down the pen, recaptured Dahlia's hand, and looked into her eyes. "I'll be around," he said.

Cara watched them walk away together, thought of how much she loved them both, and her eyes filled with tears.

Reaching for her purse, she found a tissue and turned her back on the crowd. Moments later she heard someone come in and looked around.

Louis didn't stop, didn't even slow his pace. Dropping a ten-dollar bill by the cash box, he stalked into the gym and was quickly swallowed in the throng.

It was nearly nine when Lee parked the Jaguar outside the Walking Dune school. Sandy smoothed her skirt as she waited for him to circle around to her door.

She'd monopolized Maxine's services for the entire afternoon. Her hair was in upswept curls, her nails polished, and she was wearing her best, a full-length red satin gown that accentuated the lines of both bust and hip. Lee had said she looked beautiful, but when he ushered her into the ballroom, and Sandy saw Cara Chastain, she felt gauche.

The woman's hair was in a knot at the back of her head, and she wore black—a long, sleeveless, nondescript black dress with a choker neck, belted waist, loose skirt and . . . she looked positively smashing.

"Allow me to introduce you," Lee said. "Sandy Cook, meet Cara Chastain."

Sandy extended a hand. The beautiful woman met it.

"Miss Cook," she acknowledged, "it's a pleasure to meet you. Thank you so much for coming."

"Nice map," Lee commented, his eyes on the wall behind Cara, though what really caught his attention was the overlay showing the proposed location of the fence. It was in the shape of a right angle, one tangent stretching through the marsh to the beach, the other lining the highway north of town all the way to a forest of cedar and pine.

"That map is Jacob's pride and joy," Cara responded smoothly, although her mind was racing along with her pulse. "He loaned it to me on the threat of death if it isn't returned tomorrow."

Wasn't that the same woman from the beach? Yes. Cara was certain it was. She hadn't seen Lee Powers since then, although she'd known when he arrived to take Tommy out for hamburgers. That night he'd extended an open invitation for Tommy to come by the construction site any time, and the boy had visited him nearly every day since.

Tommy idolized Lee; Nick regarded him as a best friend. Among her family, only she was beset with muddled feelings about the Texan. Tonight he was alarmingly handsome in a black tuxedo. No less alarming was the sensation that swept over Cara as she noted the painted fingertips planted possessively on his sleeve.

"So, you're going to build on the north end," Lee said.

"That's right."

"Interesting choice," he commented enigmatically.

Dropping twenty dollars on the tabletop, he steered Sandy Cook away from the table. Cara watched as they joined the crowd on the dance floor, her heart hammering.

The evening wore on. Music played. People danced and laughed, ate and drank. Cara hung on the sidelines.

Jacob Abernathy approached and asked her to dance, and later Hal Freemont. Cara refused both with a smile, using the excuse of having to man the cash box—though she knew very well all she had to do was ask, and any number of people would have filled in for her. The truth was, she didn't want to go out on the dance floor in close proximity to Lee Powers and the woman in red.

Unable to help herself, Cara had noted their every move. When they danced, he held her close. When they strolled along the periphery, sampling the hors d'oeuvres, he seemed attentive to her every whim. Still, despite the smiling attention he devoted to the blonde, there were times when Cara caught him looking in her direction. Each time, the hammering started all over again.

At one point toward the end of the evening, Dahlia left Nick talking with a group of men by the bar and joined Cara at the gymnasium entrance.

"There's no doubt you're having a good time tonight," Cara offered as the redhead walked up. "I must say, you and Nick make an extremely handsome couple."

Dahlia's cheeks pinkened until they matched her dress. "I'm not accustomed to that term, although . . ."

"What?"

"Although when he gets back from Virginia next Friday, we're sailing away together for the weekend."

"That's wonderful!" Cara pronounced.

Dahlia lifted anxious eyes. "Is it? I don't know. Things seem to be moving awfully fast. It's kind of like being on a roller coaster—it scares you to death, but you don't want to get off."

"Nick, a roller coaster?" Cara teased with a smile. "I'll have to tell him you said so."

"Don't you dare!" Dahlia objected with horror, but joined in when Cara laughed lightheartedly.

The two of them looked across the room as the orchestra struck up "Strangers In The Night." Dahlia's gaze fell on Louis, who was standing near the bar, drink in hand, eyeing the crowd as though he'd like to strangle the lot of them.

"Have you seen Louis tonight?" she asked.

"Only from a distance."

"He's in typical foul humor—at least, typical for the past month or so."

"Um-hmmm," Cara murmured absently.

Turning her head, Dahlia followed Cara's line of vision and found it centered on Lee Powers as he led his partner onto the dance floor.

"The blonde is attractive," Dahlia commented.

"What blonde?"

"The one Lee brought tonight."

Cara pursed her lips, though she couldn't take her eyes off Lee as he wrapped both arms around Sandy Cook, and she raised hers until her wrists locked about his neck. The closeness . . . the familiarity. It seemed obvious the two were lovers.

"You're the one he wants, Cara."

Cara looked around with a start.

"He's made no secret of it since he arrived in Walking Dune. And what's more, you want him, too."

"Really, Dahlia! Just because you're in the midst of a budding romance, don't start looking for it in everyone else."

Cara's cheeks were flushed, her eyes bright—just like that night weeks ago when Dahlia first sensed the electricity between her and Lee.

"Your face is lit up like a candle," Dahlia accused gently. Cara's palms rose swiftly to her cheeks. "For goodness sake, it's nothing to be ashamed of," Dahlia added.

"I have no right to feel like this," Cara mumbled.

"Why not? Because of Tom?"

"Watch it." Cara's hands fell from her face, her fingers locking in a subconscious habit as she began twisting the wedding band round and round on her finger. The old black gown she wore was lightweight and sleeveless; nonetheless, her palms were irritatingly damp.

"You know," Dahlia began carefully, "a couple of weeks ago you gave me some advice. 'Give yourself a chance,' you said. The next night I took that advice, and I'm not sorry."

"You're in a different situation from me, Dahlia."

"Not that different."

"How can you say that? I'm a widow—"

"Locked into love for a man who's no longer around. I was a spinster, locked into an obsession for a man who will never look at me as anything but a sister. The upshot is the same. Both of us have been alone too long."

"I'm content with being alone," Cara replied.

The redhead arched a brow, her light eyes seeming to probe the darkest secrets of Cara's soul. Content? How long had it been since she'd felt truly content? Or at peace? Not since that day in the book shop when Lee Powers spoke her name, and the unfeeling armor she'd worn effortlessly for years crumbled around her.

"All right," Cara admitted in a near whisper. "You might be right. Since he showed up . . ."

She trailed off, mesmerized by the images that swept her mind—Lee standing in the shop doorway as late sunlight haloed his frame . . . Lee smiling down at her from the entrance to her very own parlor until all she could do was stare . . . Lee reaching for her with a gentle touch that contradicted the look in his eyes.

"Anyway, it doesn't matter," Cara went on briskly. "Obviously, the man has no trouble finding female companionship. Miss Cook is very attractive, as you said. I've no doubt Mr. Powers has long since forgotten any passing attraction he might have had to me."

"Sounds like you're trying to convince yourself."

"The man is here today, gone tomorrow," Cara snapped.

"What good would it do me to get involved with someone like that?"

"Gone tomorrow?" Dahlia repeated questioningly. "Funny. That's exactly what Nick is going to be—gone tomorrow."

"That's different."

"You're right. Lee Powers will still be here tomorrow."

Cara gave her friend a look of vexation. Dahlia met it with an expression of serene omniscience. The past days had been too demanding; the night, too unnerving. Cara could withstand that knowing perusal just so long.

"Dahlia," she said after a strained moment, "you seem to think our situations are the same, but they're not. When Tom . . . died . . . I ceased to live. All I needed was to be a mother to Tommy. Nothing else. Now I think I've forgotten how to be a woman. Or maybe I don't *want* to be one."

"You want to be one," Dahlia returned sagely, "or you wouldn't jump out of your skin every time Lee Powers shows his face. And you haven't forgotten anything, not as far as I could tell that night from the kitchen."

Cara's eyes widened at the careless mention of that burning memory. The orchestra ended the romantic melody with a final flourish. The dance floor crowd offered a polite sweep of applause.

"Think about it," Dahlia suggested and, with a parting wink, walked off in Nick's direction.

The crowd began to thin around eleven. At midnight when the orchestra stopped playing, only a couple of dozen people remained. Cara stood by the door and said goodbyes. A few people stopped to chat on the way out. A few more signed onto the list of volunteers. Nettie Wolf had just added her name. . . .

"Evenin', Miss Nettie," came the distinctive drawl.

Nettie turned. Cara's gaze leapt beyond her to the tall man.

"I haven't had a chance to tell you how lovely you look tonight," Lee added.

"Why, Mr. Powers," Nettie trilled. "How gallant of you to say so."

"I see you've joined the ranks of volunteers," he said.

Something red caught Cara's eye. She glanced aside to see

Sandy Cook waiting several yards away by the door . . . and staring directly at her. Cara looked quickly back at Nettie.

"Oh, yes," she was saying. "Such a worthy cause, you know. How about you, Mr. Powers? Will you be contributing to the effort?"

"Yes, Miss Nettie. I suppose I will." Lee's eyes flickered briefly to Cara as he bent to scrawl his name at the bottom of the list. "But I have a question or two for Mrs. Chastain," he added.

"Oh?" Cara returned.

Straightening away from the table, Lee gestured to the map behind Cara, though his eyes were on her. "Who decided on the north end?"

"We all did," Cara answered, noticing that the remaining people in the gym had drifted up behind him—Nick and Dahlia, Jack Quincy and his wife, Louis. . . .

"We all agreed it was the best place," she went on. "Away from town and most of the traffic. Besides, the wilderness acreage at the north end is one of the mustangs' most popular haunts."

"Wilderness acreage that's owned by the state," Lee reminded.

"We're aware of that."

"And are you aware that Lone Star is in the process of tendering a bid to the state for that very land? The parcel you've marked off comprises about half the property designated for Phase Three development."

Cara's gaze swept over the group before her. Everyone was watching, waiting for her reply.

"Perhaps the designation would change," she said after a moment, "if the state were to declare the land a sanctuary."

"What are you talking about?" Louis barked.

They were the first words he'd directed to Cara in weeks. His face was red and his eyes accusing.

"I'd like to know as well," Jack Quincy announced, stepping up beside Louis.

The mayor appeared to be just as enraged as Louis. Cara's temper flared.

"I've given this matter a great deal of thought in the past weeks, gentlemen. Two mares lost? A foal injured? It seems clear that if things go on as they are, the mustangs of Walking Dune will cease to exist. If the fence proves successful, and the horses acclimate safely to the north end, I propose we petition the governor."

The two men stared at her. Cara stared back.

"That's my sister," Nick chuckled after a moment of silence.

Dahlia gave him a swift smile before looking over her shoulder to see what was going to happen next. Marianne Quincy looked as though she'd swallowed a bug; her husband looked as though he'd inhaled an entire gymnasium's worth of air. Dahlia saw his mouth move as he dipped his head toward Louis.

"She's gone crazy with this thing," Jack muttered for Louis alone. "She's going to ruin everything."

"For once," Louis responded just as quietly, "I agree with you."

Dahlia's gaze narrowed on Louis just as he turned and strode for the door, his shoes clicking angry staccato sounds across the polished floor. Jack Quincy and his wife followed closely behind.

"A sanctuary?" Lee questioned with raised brows.

Cara met his eyes with a defiant look. "It's an idea," she said.

"And not a very popular one, judging from Talbot and Quincy."

"Well, I think it's a great idea," Dahlia chimed.

"I'm not surprised," Lee commented with a fleeting smile for the redhead. Looking back at Cara, he shook his head.

"So you're ready to battle it out with Lone Star over state lands. I've got to hand it to you, lady. When you shoot for the moon, you shoot for the moon."

Reaching inside his breast pocket, he withdrew a check and handed it to her. "I ought to have my head examined," he added quietly.

Cara lifted wide eyes. "A thousand dollars?"

"Like Nettie said, it's a worthy cause."

He started to move away. Cara took a quick step in his direction.

"Thank you, Lee," she said.

His gaze shot to her face, and in an instant determined that she knew what she'd done as well as he did. It was the first time she'd condescended to call him by his first name, and it had been intentional . . . designed to draw his attention. Maybe he should have felt honored; instead, he felt insulted, as though he'd been tossed a scrap and was expected to rise to the bait.

"Good night," Lee returned curtly. Taking long strides to Sandy, he put an arm around her shoulders.

"Come on," he muttered. "Let's go."

He hardly said a word all the way back to Nags Head. Sandy, too, was quiet.

"Sorry I wasn't very good company on the way back," Lee offered as he walked her to the door.

"It's okay," Sandy murmured. Fishing the key out of her bag, she turned the lock.

"Can I come in for a while?" Lee asked.

"I'd rather you didn't."

"Okay," he said slowly. "Then I'll call you tomorrow."

Sandy turned and looked up at him. "No," she said. "Don't."

"What's going on?" Lee demanded.

"I thought I could handle it, but I can't," she answered, her eyes stinging with the threat of tears.

"Handle what?"

"Cara Chastain. You're in love with her."

Lee stared at Sandy with disbelief. "What?"

"I guess I knew it that day at the beach. I just didn't want to believe it. But after tonight . . . You couldn't take your eyes off her, Lee."

"You're making something out of nothing, Sandy."

"I wish I were."

"I'm telling you you're wrong."

"Then why are you doing what you're doing, Lee? Cara Chastain stood there and told you she intended to fight Lone Star. And what do you do but join the fight. Are you really so concerned about a bunch of horses that you're willing to sabotage your own job?"

"Sandy, really. I—"

She put swift fingers to his lips, stifling his words. "I know what I know, Lee," she said softly. "Look. We both knew this time would come. I just never figured I'd be the one doing the breaking off. So let me do it with a little style, all right? I don't regret anything. I've had a blast, and it's lasted longer than I expected. I've known all along I wasn't good enough to—"

Capturing her hand, Lee jerked it away from his mouth. "Don't say that! You're as good as anybody, Sandy. Don't ever think you're not."

The moonshadow of a waving palm swept across his face, failing to diminish the burning look of sincerity in his eyes. Sandy's tears welled up and spilled over.

"Goodbye, Lee," she said.

Stepping quickly inside, Sandy closed the door and fell back against it. "I love you," she whispered into the empty darkness.

On Sunday afternoons Lee knew Frank liked to loll around the expansive pool at his ranch.

Lee set aside the newspaper and eyed the phone once more. After dropping Sandy off, he'd stayed up most of the night. She'd shocked him, all right—not only by ending the affair so abruptly, but also with her straightforward conclusions.

Along about three-thirty in the morning, he'd decided Sandy was right. Yes, he was genuinely concerned for the mustangs, but if it weren't for Cara, he wouldn't have been drawn so deeply into the issue. Nor would he impulsively have donated both money and allegiance to an effort that could end up jeopardizing Lone Star's position on the island.

He didn't know if what he felt for Cara was love, but it was something powerful and consuming, something he'd been trying to forget when he started seeing Sandy. It hadn't worked. No matter how much he enjoyed being with Sandy, the preoccupation with Cara had lurked in the back of his mind.

The admission made Lee feel as though he'd used Sandy. He didn't like the feeling. Nor did he like feeling that his actions of the previous night were traitorous to Lone Star. Picking up the phone, he dialed Frank's poolside number.

"Good to hear your voice, son," Frank bellowed. "How are things going out there?"

"I'm satisfied."

"Only satisfied? Not pleased?"

"All right then, pleased." Lee grinned. "We poured the foundation for the club this week. Right on schedule."

"Good, good. How do you like Walking Dune?"

"It's . . . interesting. Listen, Frank," he went on, his grin disappearing, "there's something I want to bring to your attention. Did you realize you sent Lone Star right into the middle of a hot-blooded conservation issue?"

"A what? What are you talking about?"

"Mustangs."

"Okay," Frank surrendered. "I've heard about the mustangs. Only a dozen or so in the herd, right?"

"Only a dozen," Lee responded. "Which makes the situation worse. If there were hundreds, the danger of extinction might not exist. Let me tell you something, Frank. This mustang issue looks like it's building to a fight."

"Fight? Between whom?"

"A local committee and Lone Star."

"What do they want to fight us for?" Frank boomed.

"The state land north of town. They want to turn it into a sanctuary for the horses."

"Damnation!"

"There's even been talk about petitioning the governor," Lee added. "What's the status on dealings with the state?"

"The bid's in. But, hell! Negotiations could take months. Who's on this blasted committee you're talking about?"

Lee grimaced. "A few of the townspeople . . . and me, I guess."

"You?! What the devil do you mean?"

"Frank, I've learned a few things since I've been out here. I'm not so sure the committee is wrong."

Silence. Lee rubbed a hand across his brow.

"You know I've always admired your instincts, Frank. You're right about this area. It could be a grand resort, but it's pretty grand just the way it is. The mustangs are part of the history around here. They've got no place else to go, and . . . well, I just wanted you to know how I feel about it."

"Who's head of this committee?" Frank asked after a moment.

"A woman named Chastain."

"Cara Chastain?"

"Yes," Lee answered with surprise. "Do you know her?"

"I know *of* her. So, you've thrown in with Cara Chastain's camp."

"She can be very persuasive."

"She sounds dangerous if you ask me."

"I'd have to go along with that," Lee replied.

Abigail had just returned from the gardens when the phone rang.

"Abigail? Frank Winston here."

"Oh, hello, Frank." Setting aside a basket of fresh cut flowers, she smiled. "How are things going?"

"I'm not so sure. I've got a question for you. Do you have any pull with the North Carolina governor?"

"The governor? Why, no."

"Well, then, we might be in trouble."

Her brows furrowed. "What kind of trouble?"

"It seems your daughter-in-law is gearing up to petition the governor to declare the north end of town a sanctuary for some horses."

"I should have expected something like this," Abigail muttered after a moment. "She's always been extremely stubborn."

"On top of that, she's got one of my best men behind her. I'll be straight with you, Abigail. If we lose Phase Three of this project, there's no point in continuing the kind of full-scale development we planned. The equation doesn't work."

"I'll think of something," she returned heatedly. "I am *not* going to let her win."

Frank frowned into the phone. "I didn't realize what a personal issue this is. What's going on?"

"She keeps my grandson in that wretched town, Frank, *expressly* against my wishes. I'd hoped this project might prompt her to bring Tommy here to Warrenton where he belongs."

"So, it finally comes out," Frank commented.

"What?"

"The reason you contacted me after all these years, inviting me to join you in a prime business opportunity, pressing me to be silent about your involvement."

"You agreed it was a good idea," Abigail pointed out.

"Yes, but I didn't know we'd end up with a fight on our hands. That makes it a risky investment, Abigail."

"I don't mean to sound unfeeling where you and Lone Star are concerned," she replied. "But frankly, I'd invest anything for my grandson. He's all I have left."

Frank leaned back in his chair, picturing her and carefully choosing his words.

"You have yourself, Abigail," he said finally. "When I saw you last fall, I was astonished at how little you've changed. Thirty years must have passed since those golfing days with the Judge, but you're the same—elegant and lovely."

A flustered hand flew to Abigail's throat. "Why . . . thank you, Frank. But I have changed, you know. I'm a grandmother now. And that's *all* I am."

"You're still a damn attractive woman, Abigail. And I don't have any problem telling you so."

"Really, Frank—"

"All right, all right," he broke in, deciding he'd gone as far as he should . . . for now. Thinking once more of Lee, he added, "Let me ask you something before you go. This daughter-in-law of yours . . . what does she look like?"

"Some call her a beauty," Abigail admitted.

A few minutes later, Frank was staring unseeingly across the sparkling surface of the pool, his mind's eye trying to picture the raven-haired woman Abigail had described.

Sure, he wanted to see an end to the restlessness that bristled about Lee these days. He wanted Lee happy, fulfilled, settled down . . . but not—God forbid—with a woman so firmly entrenched on the North Carolina coast that she was willing to fight Lone Star for a piece of it.

To have turned Lee's head the way she had, Cara Chastain must be something pretty damn special. And dangerous, Frank thought once more, his bushy brows settling in a scowl.

During the last week of August it rained nearly every night in Richmond. Turning up his collar, Mitch started out the back door of the smelly kitchen.

"Hold on a minute, Lincoln," the fat man said.

He had a name, but he was only the fat man to Mitch. Waddling over, he pointed a spoon in Mitch's face.

"You were late tonight, Lincoln. Parolees ain't supposed to be late. Don't get sloppy just because you're short. I know you've only got one more day, but that's one more day you've got to show gainful employment. Don't be late tomorrow."

One more day, Mitch repeated to himself. Drawing strength from the idea, he refrained from punching the fat man's face in, and merely stepped into the rain.

It was two in the morning. Other parts of the city were quiet, but here in the slums music spilled from late-night dives, and hookers called from alleyways.

"Gainful employment," Mitch said with a sneer. What a laugh. He was a busboy in a greasy spoon, taking home barely enough each week to pay for a room in the fleabag hotel up the street.

One more day, he thought again. One more day, and he'd be out from under the yoke that had strangled him the past three years.

The irony sucked. When he was nineteen, he'd run a taxi cab rip-off scheme that yielded thousands; by the age of twenty-five, he'd gained a reputation as one of the best breaking-and-entering men around, and one of the more deadly. A target who surprised him in the middle of a heist had gotten his throat slit; a partner who tried to pad his share of the take had met the same fate.

Mitch had, quite literally, gotten away with murder. Then a few years back he'd run short on cash, knocked off a convenience store, and been caught. Eighty-two dollars. Eighty-two damn dollars, and they'd made him pay for three years.

Soon it would be over. In twenty-four hours he could go anywhere he wanted, do anything he wanted.

Trotting up the steps to the hotel, he walked through the small, dingy lobby without looking at the man behind the counter.

"Where's my money, Lincoln?"

Mitch stopped and glanced over. "You'll get it tomorrow, Brady."

"You sure about that?"

"I said you'll get it. I get paid tomorrow."

"Okay, then. Here. This came for you."

Brady waved a letter at him. Mitch stuffed it in his hip pocket without looking at it and climbed the three flights to his room. A blinking neon light from across the street flashed alternating red and white through the interior. Mitch closed the blinds and stripped off his shirt. It might be raining, but it was damn hot.

The room contained a single bed, sink and toilet, a scarred dresser, and a straight-backed chair. Walking over to the dresser, Mitch snatched up the bottle of whiskey and took a long gulp.

"Parolees ain't supposed to have booze, are they, fat man?" he muttered, and took another swig.

A while later, he stretched out on the bed and pulled the letter from his pocket. Holding it up before him, he saw that his name and address were typewritten. Mitch tore it open, and a series of bills fluttered down to his chest.

"What the hell!" he sputtered, pushing swiftly up to a sitting position. Shocked and leery, he gathered the money. Five bills. Five one-hundred-dollar bills.

Mitch turned the envelope upside down. A key fell out, along with a note. Grabbing it up, he read the typewritten words:

If you're interested in doing a job, there's more of the same and further instructions in Post Office Box 210. Nags Head, North Carolina.

Mitch looked at the money, then at the note, then picked up the key, then looked at the money again. Fanning the bills like a hand of cards, he buried his face in them, and fell back on the bed.

On the first Saturday when work began on the fence, there were more than two dozen volunteers. The following weekend the number shrank by half, and when the news came out that Nettie Wolf had contracted Lyme disease, Cara suspected no one would show up the third weekend.

Poor Nettie. All she'd done was steady a post while the next was driven in line. But then, everyone knew that ticks and mosquitos, not to mention snakes, were abundant in the marsh bordering the wilderness acreage. The grass was tall and concealing, the pockets of water shallow but dangerous. Ned had killed a cottonmouth the first day; since then, both he and Lee had worn pistols.

With so many hands pitching in, the group had made good progress the first couple of weeks. The length of fence stretching across the marsh to the beach was almost complete. After that the work along the highway would be relatively easy.

On the fourth Saturday, Doc was on an emergency call, and the number of workers dwindled to a faithful five—Nick, Dahlia, Ned, Lee, and Cara. It was late September. Summer was technically over, but the sun was scalding, the marsh stifling. Everyone wore shorts, but also boots and gloves, a bane in the heat but a necessity. Working in teams, they talked little and concentrated on what they were doing. All of them were anxious to work their way out of the damnable marsh.

By midafternoon, they'd nearly succeeded. Ned left to report for duty; Nick and Dahlia—who had become a positively radiant couple since their sailing weekend—made a run into town to pick up cold drinks. Paired with Lee, Cara stood aside as he wielded the post-hole-digger with admirable expertise.

He'd taken off his shirt a while back. Studying him from beneath lowered lids, she noted the breadth of his sunburned shoulders and back. It was the first time she'd been alone with him since that night in Dahlia's stables. So much had changed since then.

Setting aside the digger, Lee reached for a nearby sledge hammer. Cara steadied the post as he shook her with rhythmic blows to the flat head.

She was tired and hot and miserable, but not just physically miserable. More than anything, she felt the need to push accolades past her parched lips. Lee Powers had proved himself beyond measure. She supposed it had started with the painting of the mustangs. After that, there was his generous contribution, not only of money, but of himself. Cara had no doubt the group would be only half as far in their goal if not for him. In addition to much-needed tools, he'd provided a leadership she once would have resented, but now gratefully relied on.

In the past few weekends of silent teamwork, he'd said nothing to her—nothing personal, at any rate. His few words had been addressed to the task. Cara, as chairperson of the project, had merely assessed them and passed on his suggestions when they turned out to be invariably brilliant.

Setting aside the hammer, he drew a bandanna from his pocket and wiped it across his forehead. Cara's gaze rose to his, meeting it briefly before the awestruck, tongue-tied sensation overtook her once more.

"I'll get the rails," she said, and turned away.

Watching her step as she plodded through the marshy wetness, she headed for the dry ground near the highway where the rails were stored. As she arrived, a car pulled over. Cara glanced up, expecting to see Nick and Dahlia. What she saw stopped her breath.

The red hair. The face. The smile. Years had passed, and he was sitting in the shadows of a car, but Cara knew him instantly. *Mitch!* her mind shrieked. *Mitch!*

Her feet began backing away as she continued to stare in horror. He turned the car back on the highway and drove slowly out of sight. Still Cara could do nothing more than back away, splashing heedlessly into the marsh, until her frozen state was shattered by a piercing pain in her right leg. She looked down and screamed.

Several yards away, Lee pivoted and, in a heart-stopping instant, saw the cottonmouth hanging from her bare calf. A split second later, the snake disengaged. Cara fell, then started scrambling away, more on her knees than her feet.

"Don't move!" Lee yelled, whipping the pistol from its holster as he charged into a gallop. She didn't appear to have heard him. He cast a quick look in the direction of the snake, spotted it, and killed it with a single shot on the run. Looking back at Cara, he saw she was maintaining a frantic, stumbling pace. She'd reached dry ground when Lee tackled her, pinning her body with his weight. Cara looked up with wide, terror-stricken eyes.

"I said, Don't move!" Lee commanded. When he was convinced she had listened, he quickly shifted, grabbing up her leg and spotting the two oozing punctures left by the fangs of the snake. Already a nasty inflammation was swelling around the marks, blaspheming the otherwise perfect calf.

Instinct took over. Tossing the unholstered pistol on nearby ground, Lee tore the bandanna from his pocket and cinched it just below her knee. Cara gasped when he withdrew the pocketknife and snapped it open, but he barely heard. Securing her leg with iron fingers, he slashed the flesh between the two marks and, discarding the knife in the near vicinity of the pistol, applied his mouth and began to suck.

After the third or fourth mouthful of blood and venom, Lee spat, glanced up, and saw that Cara had swooned. With grim determination he carried on until there was no more reddish swell, only a deepening bruise the shape of his open mouth.

With a power born of desperation, he swept Cara up and made his way to the Jaguar at a near run. Piling her into the passenger side, he jumped in and sped toward town. He didn't know where a hospital was. He didn't even know where a damn doctor was! Lee glanced over at her. She was out cold.

He was nearly to the town limits when he spotted her Wagoneer coming toward them. Nick and Dahlia.

Lee laid on the horn and screeched to a stop in the middle of the road. Nick halted the Jeep almost as quickly.

"What is it?" he shouted out the window. "What's wrong?"

"Cottonmouth got her!" Lee shouted back.

"Oh, my God." Leaning over Nick, Dahlia yelled, "Take her to my place! I have antidote!"

The Jaguar gunned away. For a quick moment, Nick regarded Dahlia with wonder.

"You're really something, you know that?" he said, and pulling a fast U-turn, took off toward town.

Cara began to stir as Lee pulled up in front of the lodge. Nick and Dahlia arrived just as she came to with a scream. Leaping out of the car, Lee circled around, opened the door, and bent to her.

"It's all right, Cara," he said. "We're at Dahlia's."

Nick bolted for the Jaguar as Dahlia ran to unlock the door.

"I've got her," Lee said, sweeping Cara swiftly up in his arms.

Cara turned hysterical eyes to her brother. "Nick, I saw him! Mitch! He's here!"

"Come on, Cara," Nick replied, hurrying along beside Lee. "Let's just get you inside."

"But he's here!"

"Follow me," Dahlia directed and led the way to a back room outfitted with medical trappings including a cot, a sink, and shelves of medicines and bandages.

Nick and Lee looked around in surprise.

"First aid for the lodgers," Dahlia explained quickly. "Put Cara over here on the cot."

"Oh, Dahlia," she wailed as Lee deposited her on the small bed.

"Everything's going to be all right," Dahlia soothed. "Where's the bite, Lee?"

"Right leg."

Shifting along the cot, Dahlia spotted the trail of blood on her calf.

"You cut it?" she asked.

"It seemed the thing to do," Lee replied.

"You're right. It was."

"Will somebody listen to me?" Cara shrieked. "I saw Mitch Lincoln! He was watching me!"

"I'm listening, Cara," Dahlia said calmly. "But right now, that's not the top priority."

Cara turned her face to the wall, but not before Lee saw the tears sliding down her cheeks.

Stepping over to the sink, Dahlia began washing her hands. "The first thing to do is get that wound cleaned up. Why don't you boys wait outside in the receiving room?"

Long minutes ticked by. Nick and Lee spotted a bottle of brandy on the sideboard.

"What the hell happened?" Nick demanded.

"Damned if I know." Lee set aside his glass and pulled a T-shirt over his head before continuing. "I was waiting at the post we just sank while she went to get the rails. I heard a scream, turned around, and . . . the cottonmouth had already struck."

"Did you see anything?"

"Just a snake hanging from her leg."

"I mean Mitch Lincoln."

Lee hesitated as he reached for the snifter. "No," he said, taking a healthy gulp before he met Nick's searching gaze.

"You didn't see anything? Not even a car?"

"I told you, Nick. I didn't see anybody."

Nick drained his glass. Lee reached for the bottle.

"That doesn't mean he wasn't there," Lee added, carefully pouring amber liquid into Nick's glass.

"Right," Nick returned with a nod, and turned his back.

"What is it, Nick? You seem more concerned about Mitch Lincoln than the cottonmouth."

Nick turned around slowly. "I am. There's a cure for snake bites."

"Meaning?"

"Meaning, my sister is not the hysterical type. There's no doubt of her strength, her constitution, but . . . there's also no doubt of her nightmares. This has happened once before."

Lee felt a chill. "When?"

"Years ago. Before Tom—while she was in her first year of college. She thought she saw Mitch. Thought he was following her."

"And?"

"And it turned out to be somebody who only looked like him. The man haunts her, Lee. I'd hoped it was over, but . . ."

Their eyes met, and a look of concern passed between them—Nick's, old and weary; Lee's, new and sharp. A half hour had elapsed when Dahlia came out to join them.

"How is she?" Lee asked quickly.

"She'll be fine," Dahlia returned. "I didn't have to administer any antidote. From what I could see, you did a good job of getting out the poison. I did give her something to calm her down, though. The best thing is for her to sleep a while if she can. She's a little groggy, but . . . she wants to see you."

Putting aside his glass, Lee walked into the small room and bent to one knee beside the cot. Cara looked at him with heavy-lidded eyes. He placed a light hand on hers.

"How are you feeling?" he asked.

"Fit as a fiddle," she returned thickly.

Lee smiled. "You gave me quite a scare."

"I wanted to tell you . . ." she began, her lashes dropping. "I wanted you to know . . ."

Trailing off, Cara raised his hand to her lips and kissed his fingers. "Thank you," she murmured.

A moment later her hand drifted back to her side as her eyelids closed. Lee rose to his feet, his heart thundering until he could have sworn the sound of it filled the room.

So Sandy was right, he thought, gazing down on Cara's sleeping form. It *was* love after all.

PART TWO

He who has a thousand friends
        has not a friend to spare,
And he who has one enemy
        shall meet him everywhere.
              –Ali Ibn-Abi-Talib
               (7th century)

Chapter Eight

It was nearly seven when Lee joined Nick and Dahlia outside the first aid room.

"She's sleeping," he announced, his voice low and gruff.

Dahlia insisted on preparing a light supper for the three of them. Nick went to call Elsa; Lee followed the redhead to the inn's sprawling kitchen where she began pulling platters and containers out of the refrigerator.

"How long will she sleep?" he asked.

"All night if she's lucky."

Lee moved to a large table in the center of the room, pulled out a chair and sank into it.

"Are you sure she's going to be all right?" he added after a moment. Dahlia turned and approached the table, bearing a plate of cold cuts and a warm smile.

"She'll be fine, Lee," she said. "Rest your mind."

The "light supper" turned out to be a spread of ham and turkey, potato salad, deviled eggs, cheese and fruit. Lee should have been hungry, but he had little appetite. In fact, all three of them ended up picking absentmindedly at the food as they reconstructed the events of the afternoon. Eventually the conversation lapsed, and Lee rose to his feet.

"I appreciate your hospitality, Dahlia," he said. "It's been a long day. I think I'll head on out."

Nick stood and extended a hand. "Thanks, buddy," he said simply. Lee returned the handshake and nodded silently.

"Can I show you out, Lee?" Dahlia asked.

"That's okay. I can find my way."

Leaving behind the cheerily lit kitchen, he entered the dark corridor that crooked along the rear of the inn. There was no question of where he was going. He opened the door, greeted by the dim glow of a night light and the whispering sound of Cara's breathing. She lay on her side, curled in the fetal position, her hands clasped to her chest as though to protect herself. A lump of emotion rose to Lee's throat and stayed there all the way back to the Fast Break.

The house was empty, the boys presumably having taken off on a Saturday night ramble. Lee climbed the stairs with a weary step. He was hot and dirty and felt as though every ounce of his strength had been sapped. He wanted nothing more than to shower and crawl between cool sheets. Yet when he did so, he found his thoughts buzzing in a way that kept him awake most of the night.

Over and over, the scenes raced through his mind—the striking snake extended full-length from Cara's leg, her frantic eyes as he pinned her to the ground, her look of terror as she released the name of Mitch Lincoln in a shrill, uncharacteristic shriek. Lee thought of Nick's questions and the unspoken worry that lay behind them. Closing his eyes, he brought forth the memory and once again was running toward Cara as she scrambled up the bank. Trying his best to freeze the image, Lee forced a scanning eye to the blurred background of the highway beyond her and found it empty of everything but the brilliance of afternoon sunlight.

"There's no question of her strength," Nick had said. Lee agreed. In addition to being highly intelligent, Cara possessed an iron will. It was difficult to picture the woman he'd come to know letting her imagination run away with her . . . but then until today, he never could have pictured her hysterical, either.

And so his thoughts went, leaping from one image to another, until they finally settled on one that drowned out all others—the dark lashes falling to hide her eyes as she kissed his hand. Even now, the memory of the touch sizzled up his arm and straight into his heart, fanning to flame the feeling that had overtaken him at that moment, and continued to smolder within him ever since. There was no doubt about it.

He was in love with Tom Chastain's widow, a woman who'd told him from the first she wanted no man but her husband.

"In the eyes of the world I may be a free woman," she'd once said. "But in my heart, I am not."

Lee knew better than to think a kiss of gratitude to the back of his hand had changed anything. The certainty drove him from bed, and he was still pacing the shadows of his bedroom when he heard the crew return in the wee hours of morning.

The first of them showed his face downstairs at around eleven and headed wordlessly for the coffee urn. Lee had already consumed three cups and was wired, not only by caffeine and a sleepless night, but also by the conclusion he'd reached sometime around daybreak. He was dressed and ready to go. But it remained to be seen whether or not he was going to have any help. Forcing himself to be patient, he waited at the poker table and made a pretense of reading the Sunday paper.

By noon, a half dozen of the crew had straggled in. They were quiet and red-eyed, obviously hung over. Lee grimaced, his hopes dwindling. When Joe appeared, got a cup of coffee, and sat down with the others, Lee rose from his chair.

"I'd like to talk to you, boys," he began. They raised squinting eyes. "Though from the looks of you, I doubt I'll be able to count on much. I'm sure you're aware of the fence going up north of town. Well, something happened yesterday—something that shows very clearly that it's not a job for amateurs, however dedicated they might be. Cara Chastain was bitten by a cottonmouth."

The men turned to each other with murmurs of surprise.

"How is she?" Joe asked.

"She'll be all right," Lee answered. "But like I said, that wilderness is no place for beginners. It's a place for professionals who can put the damn fence up in a hurry."

Joe rubbed his chin. "Are you saying *we're* gonna do it?"

"I'm asking you to think about it." Lee looked around the group of men. Most of them turned their eyes to the tabletop.

"Reckon I'll say what's on our minds," Joe said after a moment. "Everybody's sorry about the horses that got killed, but everybody knows that fence is going up on Lone Star land.

Seems kind of funny for us to build it."

"It isn't Lone Star land yet, Joe." Silence. "Look," Lee added impatiently. "These people are stubborn. They've raised the money, and the fence is damn well going up. It's just a matter of who's going to build it—women like Cara Chastain or us."

"How long do you reckon it'll take?" Joe asked.

"With an experienced crew, maybe a few days."

"What about the site?"

"I figured you could run things for a while, Joe. Production might slow down, but not to the extent we couldn't make it up."

Joe leaned back in his chair and looked up. "Reckon I'll say what else is on our minds. None of us is happy to hear about 'the little widow' getting hurt, but all of us are wondering just how far this thing is gonna go."

"What are you implying, Joe?"

"It ain't no secret, boss. What's doing your thinking for you these days? Your head, or something else?"

Lee frowned, his hands forming quick fists at his sides as he prepared to light into Joe—the impertinent old codger! But then, pair by pair, the men's eyes lifted. Beneath their silent scrutiny, Lee realized he couldn't brush off the issue. Joe's question was in the mind of every man there, and Lee could give nothing less than an honest reply—not if he wanted their help.

"All right, I admit it," he said finally. "However pointless it may be, the woman gets to me. I probably wouldn't have gotten so involved in this thing if not for her."

Everyone but Joe looked away.

"But I'm not so besotted that I can't think straight," Lee went on. "The longer this mustang issue drags out, the more it's going to cost Lone Star in the long run. If we're going to war over Phase Three, let's find out about it sooner instead of later. The faster decisions are made, the faster we can finish off this development and head back to Texas."

This time when the men raised their eyes, Lee perceived a few friendlier looks, though no one offered any comment.

"I propose we start today and go at it tooth and nail until the damn fence is finished," he concluded. "Anyone who's with me will be on my personal payroll with a twenty percent bonus."

An enthusiastic mumble broke out at that. One by one, the men came to their feet.

"Get your boots and gloves," Lee instructed. "I'll meet you outside at the trucks."

While the others headed for the stairs, Joe followed him to the door. Lee gave him a searching look.

"What about you, Joe? Are you with me?"

"Reckon so."

"Good, but just for today. I need you at the site."

"And then?"

"Then we go full-steam. I'd like to be out of here by the end of next month, at least where Phase One is concerned."

Joe cocked his head to one side. The boss was wearing the familiar grim expression he'd worn for the past month or so.

"Since when did you get so anxious to clear out of Walking Dune?" Joe asked. The younger man's face turned downright fierce.

"Since I got sick of lost causes," Lee replied and turned away.

The sun was high and scorching when the Lone Star trucks pulled off the highway north of town. Lee's heart skipped as he saw Cara's Wagoneer parked ahead, then calmed when he spotted Nick and Dahlia down the bank, turning wide-eyed stares in their direction as the men climbed down from the trucks.

Nick joined exuberantly with the work crew; Dahlia assumed the role of caretaker, fetching cold drinks, supplies, tools, whatever was needed. The team worked together with the purring rhythm of a machine, their rate of progress astonishing. Segments rose from the ground with an almost eerie precision, and the fence was done in two and a half days, complete with a latching gate that swung wide enough to admit a galloping herd.

On Tuesday evening the boys loaded up and headed back to the Fast Break while Lee stayed behind to tie the gate securely open. His one concern was that the mustangs might come across the fence at night, unawares, and plow into it; though he sensed that Star was too shrewd to allow such a thing to happen. More than likely, the stallion was well aware of the structure, though there had been no sightings of him during the construction.

Lee finished tying off the gate and paused for a moment. The slatted fence streaked into the distance in dark, perpendicular lines—one to the beach, the other to the forest—bordering but not infringing upon the wilderness acreage owned by the state. Cara's vision had been realized. He would always think of it as *her* fence.

The sun had set, leaving behind a soft gray dusk, as Lee walked south along the highway. Looking ahead, he saw an unfamiliar car parked on the shoulder, and a man leaning against the passenger door of the Jaguar. As he got closer, he recognized Louis Talbot. Stepping up to the driver's side with no more than a passing glance, Lee stripped off his shirt and tossed it in the back seat.

"Can I do something for you, Talbot?"

"Just came out to see this thing with my own eyes," Louis answered. "Amazing, isn't it?"

Lee glanced beyond the other man to the fence. "It's a solid job. A lot of good people worked hard at it."

"I didn't mean the fence. I meant the power of a woman."

Lee's gaze narrowed as it shifted. "You got something to say to me, Talbot? If so, spit it out. I'm tired."

Louis straightened away from the convertible, folding his arms across his chest as he eyed the Texan. "I'm immensely curious about Lone Star. Do your superiors know what you've been up to?"

"I have one superior," Lee snapped, "and he's well aware of the mustang issue and its ramifications."

"The mustang issue," Louis repeated with a sneering smile. "Do you really think anyone believes that's the reason for this fence? Or particularly your dedication to it?"

Lee's jaw set hard as he swung open the car door and climbed wordlessly inside.

"She's like a fever, isn't she?" Louis taunted. "She makes you delirious. And then one day you wake up and find yourself doing the most extraordinary things . . . things of which you never would have thought yourself capable."

Lee started the engine with a gunning roar.

"I thought *I* had it bad," Louis jeered, raising his voice. "But you beat me by a long shot!"

Lee would have liked to laugh in Talbot's face, to tell him *he* was the one who was delirious. Instead he shifted into gear and pulled away, his expression deepening to a scowl as he drove through the sultry twilight toward town.

Cara was putting Tommy down for the night. Nick strolled into the deserted master bedroom, propping himself listlessly against an antique chifforobe as he waited for her. He was due in Virginia Beach day after tomorrow, but there were two very good reasons why he didn't want to leave—Dahlia and Cara.

His thoughts were still hovering between the two of them when his sister walked in. She was wearing a light robe that reached her ankles, but he could detect a slight limp.

"How's the leg?" he asked.

"I hardly feel the pain anymore," she answered with a smile. "What's up?"

"We finished the fence today."

"Oh, Nick, that's great. I can't tell you how much I appreciate everything—"

"I'm not the one you should be thanking," he interrupted. "Lee handled it. You know that."

"Yes," Cara replied pensively. "I know that."

Nick ambled toward the bed. "Come here a minute," he said. "Sit down with me."

"What is it?" she asked, settling herself beside him.

"I need to leave day after tomorrow, Cara." Her quick look of fright was gone almost before he could be sure it had been there. Still, it stoked his worries.

"Maybe I can get out of it," he added.

"Why would you want . . . Aha!" Cara broke off with a knowing grin. "Dahlia."

"She's part of it," Nick replied, his sober expression unchanging. "But I'm concerned about you, too."

"Why? I already told you. I hardly feel a bit of pain in my leg anymore."

"I'm not talking about your leg. I'm talking about Mitch."

Just the sound of the name chilled her. Cara's expression turned hard, a rebellious though superficial response to the

terror that boiled up inside her . . . the same terror that had
plagued her for years at the mere thought of Mitch Lincoln.
Since returning from Dahlia's Sunday morning, she hadn't so
much as stuck her nose out the door. Everyone assumed she
simply needed a few days to recover from the snake bite. That
wasn't it.

"What about him?" Cara asked tersely.

Nick sighed. "Tell me again what happened the other day."

"Don't patronize me, Nick."

"I'm not patronizing you."

"Okay. Then *you* tell *me* what happened."

Glancing down, Nick took her hand. "You saw a man in a
car, a man you thought was Mitch."

"It *was* Mitch."

Nick looked up, his eyes betraying his troubled thoughts.
"You said yourself you saw him for only a few seconds, Cara.
After all these years, how can you be sure it was him?"

"How can you doubt I'd recognize him no matter how many
years have passed?"

"Because you did before," Nick returned gently.

Cara stiffened. "So, you're still holding that over my head."

"I don't mean to hold it over you. I just wish you could
see things as they really are. I just . . ." Nick caught her up
in a sudden, rough hug. "I love you," he finished softly.

"I know you do. I also know you'd never leave me if you
thought I was in danger . . . *real* danger. What is it you're
truly afraid of, Nick? That I might be going out of my
mind?"

He shifted, putting a hand's breadth of distance between
them as he frowned down at her. "You're one of the most
sane people I know, Cara. I've looked up to you all my life.
All I'm saying is that the kind of thing you went through can
affect a person—"

"Shhh," Cara broke in, her fingertips against his lips. Dredg-
ing up a smile, she looked into her brother's eyes. "Go on your
charter and hurry back. I'll be fine. I promise."

But when Nick left, she slumped against the bedroom
door, imagining the house without his comforting presence,
drawing ragged breaths, feeling the familiar claustrophobia
of fear.

*   *   *

Thursday afternoon the mustangs were spotted in the vicinity of the fence. It was after six before Lee could get away from the site and drive north. A truck and horse trailer bearing the Dunn's Lodge emblem was parked by the highway. Lee pulled up behind it, got out, and spotted Dahlia down the bank. A hundred yards north, the herd meandered outside the fence, not far from the open gate.

"Hi, Lee," Dahlia offered as he arrived.

"Where's Nick?"

"He left this morning on a charter."

Lee nodded, his gaze shifting north. "Anything happening with the mustangs?"

"Not much." Dahlia sighed. "I got here about an hour ago, and they haven't wandered far from where they are right now. Once the stud ventured toward the gate, but when the others followed, he chased them back."

Lee leaned against the fence, propping an elbow on the top rail as he looked up the highway.

"Maybe it will just take some time," he suggested.

"Maybe," Dahlia agreed.

A half hour passed, a fiery sun sinking low in the west as the horses maintained their position. Often they seemed to look over the fence, sniffing and assessing the lush meadow grass bordering the forest on the other side. But never did they move toward the gateway that would have admitted them.

"Who have you got in the trailer?" Lee asked.

"A mare of mine. I thought maybe I might be able to herd them toward the gate, but so far I haven't figured out how to get close without spooking them."

"Mind if I give it a try?"

Dahlia raised a brow. "You ride?"

"I used to. Have you got a rope?"

"A rope? Yes. There's one in the trailer, but what do you want—Wait a minute," Dahlia said, her expression turning incredulous. "Are you thinking what I think you're thinking?"

"It might be worth a try."

"But those mustangs have never had a rope on them," she objected. "You're liable to start a stampede."

"I'll go slowly," Lee replied. "Or . . . if you think it's a bad idea, we could just wait it out."

Dahlia scrutinized the man. "Are you sure you know what you're doing?"

"There's one way to find out."

"Hell," she said after a moment, "let's give it a shot before the mosquitos get here and eat us alive. You want a saddle?"

"Oh, yeah," Lee chuckled. "I most definitely want a saddle."

A short while later, he was mounted and headed north at a slow walk. Cradling the reins loosely in his left hand, he rested his right on the rope coiled about the saddlehorn. The closer he drew to the gate opening, the closer he got to the mustangs. When he was maybe twenty yards away, the stallion separated from the herd and moved forward, coming to a proud stance as he eyed the approaching stranger. Adrenaline pumped through Lee in a way he remembered from rodeo days.

"Hello, Star," he said quietly.

The stud's ears pricked as he caught the softspoken words. Tossing his head, he snorted and sidled an anxious step. Lee took note of Star's powerful build along with the defiant look in his eye. Put a rope on one of *his* mustangs? Not likely.

"Listen, buddy," Lee added in the same quiet tone. "I'm sure you don't like me worth a damn, but watch what I do anyway."

Arriving at the gate some ten yards south of the herd, Lee turned the mare through and proceeded into the meadowland that rolled up to the nearby forest. Circling the mare in a slow, unthreatening walk, he directed her back the way they'd come. Up ahead, Star stood at the open gate. The others were gathered behind him. Lee reined in the mare and let her drop her head to graze. The mustangs watched, swishing their tails but otherwise motionless. Going purely on instinct, Lee waited and let the mare chomp away to her heart's content.

Perhaps ten minutes had passed when Star stepped forward and moved just inside the gate. Raising his head high, he appeared to smell the air, as if searching it for some threatening quality. Then he turned and looked directly at Lee. Not for the first time, Lee felt the impact of something more than he would expect from a horse. Just as he was thinking it, the stallion reared and launched into a gallop, his mane and tail flying.

The mare's head came up, and she sidestepped nervously. Lee grabbed the reins and held her at a prancing standstill as the herd plunged to follow their leader hell-bent across the field stretching to the beach. Lee watched them go, his pulse thundering like the sound of their hoofbeats. They were small shapes in the distance when he turned the mare toward the gate and saw that Dahlia was waiting there, her truck and trailer nearby. Lee trotted the mare through the gate, pulled up, and dismounted.

"Well, that was pretty incredible," Dahlia greeted. Coming around, she took the reins. "I thought you planned on roping one of them."

"It didn't seem like a good idea once I got there."

They walked toward the trailer, Dahlia leading the mare.

"Let's see," she began with a grin. "You're a whiz with a pistol, a knife, horses. Is there anything you *can't* do?"

The beginnings of an answering smile died as Lee's thoughts took a turn. "Yeah. There are things I can't do." Looking ahead to the trailer, he added, "How's Cara getting along?"

"She's doing well. She ran a temperature for a couple of days. I've no doubt the wound is still painful, but she doesn't let it show." Dahlia cocked her head to one side, boldly studying the man's rigid profile. "I'd have thought you'd stop by the house to see for yourself," she added.

Lee continued to gaze straight ahead. "I consider Nick and Tommy good friends of mine, but as for Cara . . . Well, I was told a while back I wasn't welcome in her house."

"I know. The night of the party." He looked over with surprise. "I heard what she said," Dahlia went on. "But that was weeks ago. Don't you think things have changed since then?"

"Have they?" Lee returned stonily. "I don't see any difference."

In the past few days he'd done a lot of thinking. The whole time they worked together on her damnable fence, Cara had kept her distance like always . . . she'd worn her wedding band like always. He could only assume she remained wholly committed to Tom Chastain, and since discovering that he was in love with her—mind, body, and soul—Lee didn't think he could handle being confronted with that.

Picking up the man's brooding mood, Dahlia held her tongue until they reached the trailer.

"Want a ride back to your car?" she then asked.

"No. I'll walk it."

"You could be wrong," she challenged as Lee turned away.

Hesitating, he looked over his shoulder.

"For heaven's sake, you virtually saved her life!" Dahlia added. "Don't you think that changes anything?"

"Not really. I don't want her gratitude."

"What *do* you want?"

Lee barked a short laugh. "You just come right out and say what's on your mind, don't you?"

"Where Cara is concerned, I do," Dahlia responded. "I care about her. I thought you did, too."

The semblance of a smile drained from Lee's face. "I care about her," he said. "That's the problem."

"She just needs time."

"Time? Like the kind of time Talbot has given her?" Lee shook his head. "I'm no Louis Talbot, Dahlia. I don't intend to follow Cara around like a puppy hoping for a pat on the head. She's in love with her husband. She wants no other man. She's told me so many times, and I believe her."

"I still say you're wrong."

Lee grimaced. "You know, Dahlia," he said, "after burning his fingers a few times, even a fool learns not to stick his hand in the fire."

This time when he turned, Lee took long strides toward the Jaguar and didn't looked back.

Late sunlight poured through the west-facing windows, creating golden rectangles that stretched through the room to warm Cara's back and limn the reflection in the mirror. She was wearing white walking shorts and sandals. Her hair was loose and shining about her shoulders; her blouse was a rich blue that repeated the color of her eyes—which seemed rather wide, as though she'd been caught by surprise.

In fact, she *was* startled by the raucous emotions, which—during the past five days—had careened between cold terror and a mercurial warmth that would sweep suddenly over her like the scorch of a fire. Since that terrifying Saturday, it hadn't stopped—back and forth, day and night.

Even sleep failed to interrupt the pattern. There had been the expected nightmares in which Mitch loomed, face sneering, hands grasping. But on Wednesday night, or rather Thursday morning, there had been a good dream. All Cara remembered was Lee putting his arm around her, pulling her close, but the *feeling* . . . God, the feeling. She'd awakened with it, and it had stayed with her throughout the day.

That morning Nick had left, that afternoon Tommy and Elsa had brought her a get-well bouquet, and that evening Cara had gone downstairs for supper for the first time since the weekend. Through it all, she'd maintained the heady sensation of floating just above whatever was happening around her.

Shortly after supper, Dahlia had stopped by with the news that the mustangs were inside the fence . . . courtesy of Lee Powers.

"However did he manage it?" Cara asked.

"Rode one of my mares inside and let her graze. Simple as that—like a pied piper or something. After a few minutes the herd galloped in and headed for the beach."

"He's really something, isn't he?" Cara added a bit dreamily.

"The man has pride," Dahlia replied with a stern look. "If you don't do something, you've lost him."

Not even twenty-four hours had passed since then, but it seemed longer, for Cara had been unable to think of anything but Lee. She'd retraced it all—their meeting at the Lone Star picnic, the day in the book shop when she first looked at him with the eyes of a woman, the night she infuriated him by inviting half the town to their private celebration. She thought of the time he showed up with the injured foal, of the dance when he appeared in a dashing tuxedo with Sandy Cook on his arm, of sweltering days in the marsh and the way the muscles in his bare back moved as he worked. She remembered his laugh, his smile, the smoldering look in his eyes when he'd kissed her.

Round and round the memories had whirled, flashing snapshot images of Lee across her mind's eye. And then imagination took over, creating the scene Nick had described when Lee arrived at the fence with a crew of Lone Star men . . . and the way he must have looked astride Dahlia's mare, luring the mustangs to safety.

By daybreak, the feelings that engulfed Cara were like the swelling waters of a flood. There was no stemming them, or denying them. What started that day at the book shop had grown into something quite different.

She couldn't put a name to it—indeed, could scarcely take it all in, much less categorize it. She looked up to Lee, took pride in him, trusted him . . . was drawn to him in a way that shook her with its intensity.

And yet she'd hurt him. Looking back with newly opened eyes, Cara saw clearly that she had, and the urge to go to him became overpowering. Even the nervousness that had her stomach tied in knots failed to curb the compulsion.

Now the sun was sinking in the west. He'd have finished at the site and returned to the beach house. There was no reason for further delay. Turning from the mirror, Cara went downstairs and headed for the kitchen. Nick had mentioned Lee drank Scotch. It had been Tom's drink as well, and there was a case of the best in the cellar.

Scanning the house for Tommy as she walked along the hall, she spotted him in the sunroom where he'd constructed an enormous tower of building blocks.

"Wow!" he exclaimed as she walked up. "You look pretty!"

"Do I?" Cara asked with a smile. Bending down, she planted a kiss on the top of his head. "Thanks. I needed that."

"Look at my building, Mom."

"It's terrific."

"When I grow up, I'm going to build things like Lee."

Cara straightened slowly, her fingers lingering to run through his hair. "I have to go out, Tommy. Be a good boy for Elsa, okay?"

"Okay." He shrugged and went back to his blocks.

Cara walked on to the kitchen and found Elsa puttering about the stove. "Something smells good," Cara announced as she passed.

"Broiled grouper, just the way you like it." Elsa looked up as Cara opened the door to the basement. "Ready in ten minutes."

"I'm sure it's wonderful, Elsa, but you'll have to save mine for me. I need to go out for a while."

Flipping on the overhead light, Cara started down the narrow stairs, the sound of Elsa's complaints pelting her from above. The dark bottles were stored respectfully in a rack along the north wall. Cara made a selection and returned to the kitchen. Elsa made no effort to hide her pique.

"I've made your favorite dish. Did you say you're going out?"

"Yes, Elsa. I'm afraid I did." Striding to the sink, Cara picked up a cloth and began wiping the dusty bottle. "I don't mean to sound ungrateful, but I haven't got much of an appetite just now."

Elsa moved up behind her and peered around her shoulder. "Since when do you drink Scotch?" she asked.

"I don't." Setting aside the cloth, Cara headed for the door.

"Then what the devil are you doing?" Elsa trilled.

Cara hesitated at the doorway. "I have absolutely no idea," she replied, and continued determinedly out of the house.

Nonetheless, Elsa's question rang in her ears as she backed the Jeep down the drive. What, indeed, *was* she doing? With a flash of cowardice, Cara found herself hoping he wasn't home. But when she pulled off the road near the Fast Break, the first thing her gaze lit upon was the distinctive convertible parked out front.

Lee hunched forward on the couch as he examined the blueprints spread over the coffee table. Across the room, a bunch of the guys were playing poker, as they did most evenings. When a knock sounded at the door, Joe went to answer it.

Lee glanced up, then shot to his feet as Cara walked into the room. Her presence had the same effect on the other men, who scrambled up from the table, noisily scraping their chairs across the floor in the process. Cara smiled beneficently as she moved in their direction. Like a queen, Lee thought.

"Please, gentlemen," she said. "Take your seats. I don't mean to interrupt your game. I just came by to extend my thanks to all of you who helped in building the fence north of town. I was astonished when I heard what you'd done. A great many of the townspeople were. Thank you on behalf of all of Walking Dune."

Never had Lee seen such a red-faced, speechless group of men.

"Mighty nice of you to come by and say so, Miz Chastain," Joe said, heralding a gush of similar remarks from the other men, which was followed by a round of questions about the snake bite.

Cara glanced down her leg, where the only evidence of her injury was a small bandage. "It's healed remarkably quickly." Turning her head, she looked at Lee. "Due, I'm told, to the quick action taken by your boss."

He continued to stand some distance across the room, wearing jeans and a black, short-sleeved shirt that was open at the collar and recalled a night long ago in her own house.

Lifting the bottle, Cara added, "I brought you a token of appreciation."

Lee's gaze dropped to the bottle and returned to her face. But he said nothing, and an awkward silence fell as Cara wondered if her decision to come here had been a mistake after all.

"Me and the boys were just getting ready to go out," Joe spoke up, his face taking on a warning look as the men turned to him with blatant surprise.

"Don't leave on my account," Cara objected.

"Not at all, ma'am," the man returned smoothly. "Me and the boys drive down to Nags Head most every Friday night. Don't we, boys?"

This time the men jostled each other in their hurry toward the door. Cara saw the sheepish grins that encompassed herself and Lee. In under a minute the front door closed, and they were alone.

She waited, hoping Lee would say something . . . anything. But he only took a single step away from the couch and halted, the distance of a room's breadth remaining between them.

Clearly, if any approaching was to be done, she would have to do it.

"Well, well," he offered finally. "This is a surprise."

She started toward him, and Lee's eyes devoured her in a way he wouldn't have stopped if he could. As always, Cara was more striking than he remembered; the physical charge at seeing her stronger than he'd convinced himself it could be. He'd conjured up her image so often, and now out of the blue here she was in the flesh, shocking the hell out of him with this sudden appearance.

She stopped a few feet before him, their eyes met, and love welled up in Lee until he was swamped with it—the sensation both mellow and sharp, sweet and bitter.

"It occurred to me that I still owe you a drink," she said.

Lee caught her inference immediately. Oh yes, he well remembered the night he'd gone to the Chastain house with such naive hopes.

"I figured that debt was paid," he drawled, "considering the surprise party you threw for me."

So, he was going to be difficult. Cara supposed she deserved it.

"Do you have glasses?" she returned obstinately.

His eyes flickered over her as he walked past, returning in short order with two shot glasses. Handing one to her, he took the bottle in exchange and removed the stopper. He didn't look at her as he poured the stuff and set the bottle heedlessly aside. When he lifted his eyes, the unreadable darkness of them set her nerves jumping like live wires.

"What are you doing here, Cara?"

She drew a quick, deep breath and raised her glass. "Getting ready to propose a toast. To you, Lee. In grateful appreciation of all you've done for the mustangs . . . and me."

"And to you," he returned, his gaze darting to the bandage on her leg. "With congratulations on your speedy recovery."

Eyeing each other as they drank, Cara took a small sip, Lee a healthy gulp.

"Quite a few people came by the house after they heard about the snake," she said. "Doc and Ned, Nettie, Jacob. I kept thinking you'd be curious to see how your handiwork turned out."

"Nick kept me posted."

"Then today it came to me," Cara continued briskly. "Instead of expecting you to call on me, it was I who should call on you."

His silent comment was the arching of a brow.

"And express my thanks in person," she added.

"Very prettily done, too." Finishing off his drink, Lee reached for the bottle and splashed more into his glass.

"You know," Cara said quietly, "it took some courage to come here tonight. I would appreciate a less offhanded manner."

Lee spread his arms. "What do you want me to say, Cara? You're welcome? Okay. I was happy to do what I could for you. Anyone in my position would have done the same."

She shook her head. "I don't think so. I've done a lot of thinking about you lately. You're quite a remarkable man."

He halted in the midst of raising his glass, a look of amazement forming on his face. Cara finished her drink in a gulp and let the liquid burn its way to a warm puddle in her stomach as she considered what to say next. She'd rehearsed several approaches, but at the moment they all seemed contrived.

"May I ask how things are going with Miss Cook?"

"I haven't seen Sandy for weeks."

"So things between the two of you—"

"It's over, Cara. Why do you ask?"

"Well, I . . . Can you spare a little more?" she added, and offered her empty glass.

Lee retrieved the bottle, his pulse racing in a way that made it difficult to pour with a steady hand. *What the hell is going on?* he wondered as Cara tipped her head to do away with the shot in one fell swoop. After that, she set her glass on the table with a clink and looked at him with the defiance he remembered from the first time he laid eyes on her.

"I can't abide coy women. I refuse to be one of them."

Setting down his own glass, Lee stuffed his hands in the pockets of his jeans. "Of all the adjectives I might use to describe you, coy isn't among them."

Cara squared her shoulders. "I said I'd thought a lot about

you. I didn't say how much I've come to admire you."

A sense of elation flashed over Lee, followed closely by the quelling doubt that he had heard her right.

"I'm not quite sure what I'm hearing," he said after a moment. "Are you saying you admire me as a friend . . . or as a man?"

Cara's gaze darted between his eyes. "Both," she admitted softly and watched a telling flush of crimson streak across his cheekbones. "I'm sure you must see my actions as conflicting," she went on in the same low tone. "But they really aren't. The whole time I've known you, I've behaved true to my feelings. The fact is they've changed."

"How?" Lee rasped.

She stepped forward and raised a hand. He flinched as her palm cupped his jaw.

"Like I said," Cara whispered, rising on tiptoe, "you're a remarkable man."

She kissed him fleetingly and sank back on her heels, though her palm remained on his face. Lee stood there with his hands in his pockets, still as stone, eyes glittering like polished onyx.

"Don't do that again," he warned eventually. "I won't be content with it."

In flagrant disobedience, Cara lifted her mouth and pressed her lips to his in another chaste kiss. This time she stepped back and let her arm fall to her side. Lee's eyes opened only slightly, their lowered lids hiding any clue of what he might be thinking. Silence crackled in the air between them.

"I think this is the part where you compliment me in return," Cara suggested huskily. "Or else you say, 'Thank you very much,' and send me on my merry way."

He did neither, but only very slowly took his hands out of his pockets—so slowly, in fact, that she thought she'd lose her mind before she found out what he intended to do with them. What would he do? What would he say? In a matter of seconds, Cara's mind raced over a dozen possibilities—none of them coming close to his ultimate response.

"Will you come to my room?" Lee asked in a voice so low it barely rumbled past his throat.

Holding his breath, he watched for her reaction. The lovely

face flamed red; the incredible eyes went wide. Her surprise was obvious, as was her uncertainty. Acting on impulse, he stepped forward, his hands closing lightly on her arms, holding her no more demandingly than a dinner guest who might be thanking her for a pleasant evening. He had no control over the look in his eye—which was nothing like that of a casual guest—nor the longing that expressed itself with wordless eloquence as he kissed her.

Lee took his time and made it as seductive as he knew how—sandwiching each of her lips between his own, filling her with his tongue, making love with her mouth as he longed to do with the entire woman. When he lifted his head, she looked up with glowing eyes. Lee hesitated no longer. Stretching an arm about her shoulders, he propelled her toward the stairs.

As his arm went around Cara, there was the fleeting recurrence of that wonderful feeling from the dream. But along with the dreamlike effect of his kiss, it gave way to alarm as she climbed the stairs to the second floor, each step sealing the meaning of their destination more unnervingly in her brain. In under a minute, she was ushered into a spacious bedroom that smelled of sea salt and the provocative remembrance of Lee's after-shave.

He left her and backed away—retracing his steps, Cara gathered, to close the door. As he did so, she looked around, noting two low-slung chairs at a small table, a rag rug, and most absorbingly, a bed—big and accommodating, though covered with a plaid bedspread that appeared immediately masculine and scratchy. There were walls of knotty pine like the study at home, pictures of sea gulls, and—

Her mind convulsed as she felt his hands on her shoulders.

"Second thoughts?" came the whispering question at her ear.

Cara tried to voice an answer but couldn't.

"If you have them, tell me now," Lee demanded.

"I hadn't thought of this," she mumbled after a moment. "I suppose I should have."

The fingers on her shoulders tightened. "What *had* you thought of, then?"

Could she tell him he was virtually all that had been on her mind for days?

"Of last weekend," she said instead. "The snake, and the way you saved me. Of all the things you've done, not just in completing the fence, but ever since you came to Walking Dune."

There was a quick, spasmodic squeeze before his fingers released her. Cara heard him move away, though it took a moment to gather the nerve to turn and see that he'd walked to the window.

The blinds were drawn. Lee pulled them aside and peered into the falling darkness.

"Your gratitude has already been duly noted, Mrs. Chastain. You didn't have to come to my bedroom to confirm it."

Cara straightened. "I haven't."

Lee turned and leaned back against the wall. His expression was nothing short of furious; his voice, soft as silk.

"Then what the hell are you doing here? You said before I might see your signals as conflicting. Well, damn right. I do."

"You haven't given me much time to digest this," Cara replied defensively.

Lee's brows knitted over narrowed eyes. "I realize I engineered this little trek up the stairs, but you could have spoken up if you didn't want to come."

"I didn't say I didn't want to come."

"What the hell *are* you saying, then?" he thundered.

"Hell if I know!" Cara returned in kind.

Her hand flew to her brow as she spun around. Time passed. She was aware of the muffled sound of the tide slapping against the shore beyond the window . . . and the closer rhythm of labored breathing as Lee apparently fought to control his rage. The room grew more ominously silent with each dying second. Eventually, as Cara stared unseeingly at the knotty pine wall, her hand dropped to clasp the other in an unconscious death grip.

"I'm sorry," she said quietly. "We both know I'm no virginal little debutante, but somehow I feel like one right now."

Her words seared the murky cloud that had formed about Lee, opening holes of light that swiftly spread and joined each other until there was nothing left but a golden glow. Suddenly, instead of his own chaotic feelings, he felt hers. Suddenly he saw her standing there, staring at the wall . . . Walking slowly up to her, he took her by the shoulders and turned her around.

"Do you want me, Cara?" he asked gently. "Can you at least tell me that?" She lifted her gaze, beholding once more the dark handsomeness of the face above her, studying the lines of chin, mouth, and brow before looking deep into the eyes. She'd seen those eyes sparkling with laughter, clouded with disappointment, black with anger. Now they were alight with rays of red and gold, like windows to a fire in the night.

Cara could feel the blaze of his desire, though Lee regarded her with the stillness of absolute restraint. Did she want him?

"Yes," she whispered, shocked as the admission escaped the privacy of her mind to slip through her lips.

Lee's first impulse was to crush her to him. Instead, he reached up with painful slowness and began unbuttoning his shirt.

Cara's gaze fastened on his long fingers. Bit by bit, the fronts of the black shirt parted, and with each freed button, it seemed another tendon locked about her chest until it was all she could do to breathe. Eyes glued to his hands, she watched them pull the shirttail free, then fall to his sides where they remained expectantly, nerve-shatteringly still.

He stood before her, his shirt open in an invitation Cara recognized but could do nothing about. Her gaze traveled up his arms and stopped; she couldn't force it to his face, and so was helplessly focused on the shoulders outlined in black as he shrugged out of the shirt and let it fall to the floor behind him.

Cara had seen him shirtless, but not this close and not under such circumstances. At intimate range his shoulders were broader than she'd imagined, his arms more muscular, his chest more powerful, its strength clearly defined in a series of tensile ridges. His skin was bronze from the sun and appeared so smooth that it called her to touch it. The thought had the contradictory effect of sapping her capability for even the slightest movement.

Despite Cara's rigid features, her gaze took in the breadth of his shoulders, the contrast of dark hair against sun-bronzed chest, and traced that dark hair unforgivably downward as it narrowed to an erotic column. Her eyes stopped at his jeans, and at that moment Lee reached to pop the snap so that the waistband stood open.

Again, the invitation; again, her breath stopping in her lungs, she could do nothing.

"Look at me, Cara."

His voice was deep and melodious . . . urging her to lift her eyes, though she found they remained riveted on the open waistband of his jeans.

"I don't think I can," she managed.

Lee reached out and closed a hand about her tightly clasped fingers. They were freezing. Applying his other hand, he parted hers—which curled immediately into fists—and brought them to rest against the warmth of his chest.

"It's okay," he said softly.

Her gaze rose, and Lee was treated to the sapphire eyes that had conquered him at first glance. Only now they brimmed with such emotion that it brought his own to the surface.

"Don't you know how much I want you?" he added in a near growl. "How *long* I've wanted you?"

The knotted fists relaxed until her nails rested on his skin, then opened all the way, her fingers fanning across the breadth of skin just below his nipples. Lee thought of the way he'd imagined her touching him with those slender fingers, and when she rubbed them through the hair on his chest, passion flared so strongly that his eyes slammed shut, his grip stiffening uncontrollably on her wrists.

"God, woman," he muttered. "What you do to me . . ."

The rasping words had a startling effect—their raggedness making Cara steady; their need precipitating the urge to satisfy. It had been a long time since a man's hunger had whetted her own. Yet when it happened, it occurred so swiftly—so consumingly—that it was as though the ungovernable drive had waited, all these years, just below the surface.

Beneath her fingers she felt Lee's flesh, his rapid heartbeat, his heat. He'd managed to wake the woman in her when no other man could; perhaps Cara shouldn't have been surprised

when her own heat flared to life, but she was . . . at least for
a few seconds, before nearly forgotten instincts surged forth
to overtake everything else.

Her hands, no longer hesitant, twisted out of his hold to
rise and lock behind his neck. Her eyes, no longer avoiding,
rose to his. Her lips parted as she lifted her mouth.

Lee met her open mouth with his own, his hands cupping
her face, gliding down her throat, drifting along her shoulders.
His thumbs caressed her collarbone and stretched to brush
across the tops of her breasts, confirming the fullness of them,
and the firmness that allowed her to go without a bra. All that
barred his touch was the fabric of her blouse.

The realization stalled him for only a moment before he
moved a hand boldly down to surround a breast, gather it
up, and run a thumb over its taut nipple. At the touch, he
thought she caught her breath, but the idea dissolved as she
met his tongue and pushed it confidently aside to plunge her
own into his mouth.

What had begun in painstaking slowness escalated with
riotous speed. Stripping off his pants as they continued to
kiss, Lee returned his hands to find she'd unbuttoned her
blouse. Lifting it impatiently off her shoulders, he brought
her to him and reeled with the impact of her bare breasts
against his chest. His embrace tightened, his kiss turning
hard and urgent. He was unaware of her stepping out of
her sandals, unfastening her shorts, letting them drop to the
floor. Minutes must have passed before he realized her naked
legs were against his own.

His hand slipped instinctively down, his fingers brushing
the silk of her panties. Sweeping her up, he moved to the
bed, holding her with a single arm of unconscionable strength
while he tore back the covers.

They fell onto the cool sheet, both their bodies shining
with perspiration, Lee taking the top position by an instinct
that was driving him like a maddened jockey. Her long legs
enfolded him, wrapping around his hips. Lee secured a hand
in her hair, knotting his fingers in the black mass as he went
on kissing her. The other strayed to her left thigh, finding it
tense and straining as every muscle in his body seemed to be.
He pressed against her, desperate and throbbing in a way he

hadn't felt since adolescence. His very blood burned as he captured her hands, planting his forearms on each side of her as he lifted his head.

"Cara . . ."

The name escaped him, a sound both pleading and triumphant. Her expression seemed to mirror the sentiments as she pried a hand between them to begin the dissolution of the final barrier. What she started, he completed—flinging the flimsy panties backward over his shoulder, then stripping his own underwear down his legs to let it drop who-cared-where off his toes.

Lee stretched full-length on top of her, his manhood hard against the softness of her belly. Her arms encircled him, her hands moving down his back. He realized he was shaking when he lowered his head to press trembling kisses to her eyelids, her cheeks, the corner of her mouth. She turned into the kiss, freeing a leg from beneath him to curl it across the backs of his own. Lee groaned a mindless sound of passion, his thighs pushing insistently along the inside of hers as he shifted down her body.

When the first touch came, it was as though lightning struck the spot and bolted through the length of his body. Halting just inside her, Lee tore away from her mouth and gasped for breath, his wild eyes searching the woman beneath him. Her hair spilled across the pillow, and her nostrils flared with ragged breaths. Her lashes parted, and she looked at him with eyes the deep color of desire. She was more beautiful than he ever could have imagined.

Lee raised a trembling hand to trail along the smoothness of her cheek. Every inch of his body pounded with desire for her as his brain exploded with the same phrase over and over again—*God, I love you! . . . God, I love you! . . . God, I—*

Piercing the chant came a shocking afterthought—Tom Chastain, how he must have loved this woman . . . how she must have loved him.

Lee recaptured Cara's mouth in a fierce kiss and drove deep inside her, swearing with his last shreds of sanity that she'd never think of the man again.

Chapter Nine

Cara lay perfectly still. Her limbs were limp, her eyes sealed, her nerves vibrating with aftershocks that were now dim and cooling . . . though they called to mind the shattering climax that had blasted through the length of her only moments ago.

A blanket of languor closed over her, rendering her motionless, though her senses sprang to life—reporting the solid weight and length of Lee's body upon her . . . the bristle of his moustache against her cheek . . . the sound of his breathing . . . his scent, mixed with her own . . . most notably, the pressure of his manhood still inside her.

Cara's mind reeled. She hadn't anticipated such a union when she crossed his threshold, and wouldn't have expected such ecstasy if she had. She'd always thought it took practice and familiarity before lovemaking could be so fulfilling—that one couldn't expect the first time to be good.

She would have smiled if she could. Hell, if it had been any better, she couldn't have stood it—would have died right there, her death mask etched in lines of delirious pleasure.

He moved then, and although his withdrawal was smooth and slow, Cara caught her lip. He shifted off her, fanning a cool breeze across her dampened skin before the sheet billowed down upon it. Closing her thighs, Cara turned on her side. When she managed to lift her eyelids, she found Lee propped on an elbow beside her, his gaze directed in the vicinity of her toes. Behind him, a single bedside lamp glowed in the otherwise dark room, spilling golden highlights across his hair, along his shoulder and arm.

God, he was so perfectly formed—like a classic statue. That was one aspect of Lee Powers's appeal; another—which radiated from bedroom eyes, a sexy moustache, and a flashing smile—had to do with the quintessence of maleness that caused dreamy-eyed girls to both quake and quiver. As Cara thought such things, his gaze traveled slowly up her body, finally reaching her face.

"Hello," he said.

The greeting brought a smile to her lips. "Hello."

He smiled back, his gaze roaming, then returning to her eyes.

"What are you thinking?" Cara asked, her voice a husky sigh.

"How clear and sharp everything looks right now," Lee replied in a similar husky tone. "How black your hair is against the pillow, how your skin shines in the light of the lamp, how blue your eyes are in that light. I was thinking I've never seen eyes the color of yours. It's something I would have thought reserved for . . . the throat of a violet, maybe . . . or the deep sea when the sun is bright above it."

A lump rose to her throat. Swallowing it down, Cara lifted a hand and ran her fingertips along the dark hairline stretching from temple to cheek.

"I knew you were good with words," she managed after a moment, "but I hadn't realized you're a poet."

"Only when I'm inspired."

Suddenly an image returned from the past. Lee glanced up at the ceiling, recreating the memory, searching for the words. The haze cleared, and he saw her sitting cross-legged on the floor, reciting to a group of mesmerized children.

"Thus departed Hiawatha," he began slowly. "Hiawatha the beloved, In the glory of the sunset, In the purple mists of evening—"

"What?" Cara interrupted, her eyes flying wide.

Lee flashed her a smile. "Longfellow, right? A week or so after I got here, I happened across the tail end of one of your performances in the book shop. You were wearing buckskin, and your hair was in braids. It was the damnedest thing I ever saw."

"You're kidding!"

"No. I watched from the doorway." Lee's smile drifted as he recalled the bewildering weeks that had followed. "I thought a lot about the way you were with those children," he concluded.

"What way?"

"Soft and warm, your eyes shining, your face lit up with a smile. I used to wonder why you couldn't be that way with me."

Capturing her hand, Lee raised her palm to his mouth. "Now I know you can," he added.

Beneath the brush of moustache, his tongue caressed the cup of her hand. A tingling started at the spot and traipsed up Cara's arm, reminding her once again of the startling effect he had on her body.

"You have an amazing touch," she said.

Lee twined his fingers through hers and brought their clasped hands to rest between them. "So do you. Beyond anything I ever imagined, and believe me, I've imagined quite a bit."

"Did you find what just happened . . ." Cara's gaze dropped to the sheet, tracing the shape of his hip beneath it. "Did you find it somewhat out of the ordinary?"

Lee chuckled. "I think that's an understated way of putting it, don't you?"

She raised searching eyes. His expression of amusement faded.

"I've never experienced anything quite like that," he said. "With anyone. Ever."

She smiled.

"Oh, you like that, do you?" Lee added. "Being able to drive a man clear out of his mind?"

"Yes," Cara admitted, her smile broadening. "I like that."

Lee glanced at their hands, dark interlocking shapes against the white sheet. "You know, I used to fantasize about you, but I always knew it was just fantasy. Never in my wildest dreams did I think you'd actually end up here in this bed."

"Neither did I."

"Then why?" he asked. "Why tonight?"

Cara shifted up, positioning an arm beneath her head as she gave him a long, steady look.

"I couldn't stay away any longer," she answered simply. "I've thought about it so much, pictured it over and over again—you chasing me down, cutting my leg, bending over me, saving me. The last thing I recall about that day is you kneeling by my bedside."

Lee stiffened. She could see it in his face.

"What's wrong?" she asked.

"I hope you're not saying this was out of gratitude."

"No, Lee," Cara replied softly. "You were right about us from the start. It just took me a little time to catch up, although . . ." Her gaze darted beyond his shoulder. "Gratitude does figure in, I suppose. That was, after all, one of the most frightening afternoons I can remember."

A chill raced over Lee, the same kind that had danced over him that afternoon at Dunn's Lodge . . . the afternoon Cara had been so terrified . . . the afternoon Nick had made him wonder if the source of her terror was real or a creation of her mind.

"What exactly do you remember?" he asked.

"The snake. But before that . . ."

"Yes?"

She answered the question with one of her own. "Did you see a car pull off the highway just above me?"

Lee sensed how much it would mean to her if he could say that he had. He expelled a heavy breath.

"No, Cara. I didn't."

"It was blue. A long sedan like they used to make years ago."

"I didn't see a car, blue or otherwise. But then I wasn't looking in your direction until you screamed."

"I saw a car and a man inside it."

"Mitch Lincoln," Lee supplied, drawing her eyes back to his.

"Yes."

"Are you sure?"

"I'm sure. You don't know what this man did, Lee. You don't realize why I would remember every inch of his face, even though years have passed."

"Yes, I do."

"What?"

"Nick told me everything. About Mitch Lincoln, the mine shaft . . . everything."

"No one knows everything," Cara returned somberly.

"I'd like to," Lee said. "If you feel like telling me."

She looked at him and thought of dark days that knew no beginning or end because the sunlight was blocked. She thought of dank water, and the smell of sulphur, and the eighth day when a noise had drawn her attention, and she'd pounced like an animal on a beetle . . . cramming it into her mouth with grimy hands, then spitting it out and turning to vomit, though there was nothing in her stomach to spit up, and so she ended in dry heaves that shook her until she was certain she was going to die.

"Some things are best left alone," she said.

"There are times when it's sensible to confide in someone," Lee suggested. "If the man really is here—"

"If?" Cara broke in on a sharp note. He had the grace to blush. "You've been talking to Nick," she added. "I know where he stands. Nick thinks I imagined the whole thing."

"Is that possible?" Lee asked gently.

She tugged at her imprisoned hand. Lee held onto it.

"Do you think I'm the type to imagine things?" she demanded. "To concoct something out of nothing?"

"No, I don't."

"Then why would you ask such a thing?"

"Because stranger things have happened than someone having a mirage on a long, sweltering day. Because, like Nick said, you still have nightmares about Mitch Lincoln."

"And like *I* said, Nick doesn't know everything!"

"I'd like to know," Lee reiterated quietly. "Tell me."

Gradually Cara's fierce expression settled into something Lee could only describe as haunted.

"It's not a pretty story," she said.

"I don't expect it to be. But it involves you, and I find that I want to know everything that involves you."

A small smile appeared on her mouth, but dropped quickly away. "It might change your opinion of me."

"Do you really believe that?"

Looking into his face, Cara found herself tempted to reveal the secret she'd never told a soul; to share the burden she'd carried alone so long. Quelling the impulse, she glanced sharply away.

"Do you think *I'm* lily white?" Lee asked.

"Few people are."

"Hell, Cara, I spent the better part of my youth a member of a street gang that mugged old people for a good time."

Her eyes turned to him at that. "I was trash, Cara, and when I was sixteen, the girl I loved made sure I knew it."

In a deep, rumbling tone, Lee told her—all about the Caballeros and Jennifer Blackwood . . . how the obsession to be good enough had made him a success and lost him a wife.

"Marilyn wasn't out of line," he said. "I was. I couldn't give it up—the money, the life, the glory. And so I sold out my marriage for something that happened when I was sixteen."

Lee smiled bitterly. "Poetic justice, huh? Retribution for the hell I raised with the Caballeros."

Hearing his pain, Cara felt shards of it herself. "I think you're being too hard on yourself."

"Do you?"

"You were a kid . . . sixteen." She took a deep, shuddering breath. "Things happen when you're sixteen."

Feeling the tremor in her fingers, Lee clasped them more firmly. "What things, Cara?"

Her gaze darted between his eyes, so dark, so warm. Surprise washed through her as her lips parted, and she realized the confession was coming.

"I let him have me," she whispered. "Mitch said he'd let me out if I would, so . . . I did."

The emotion that bolted through Lee started as remorse and ended as rage. "He raped you."

She shook her head. "No. I told you. I let him."

"It was rape, Cara."

"Nick has always thought I dug my way out," she said woodenly. "I tried, but I never made it. Mitch let me out. He had a knife, but he only showed it to me, laughed, and tossed it aside. He knew he didn't need it."

Tears started to her eyes, but she kept them stalwartly on Lee, whose face had turned a flaming red.

"Once he got started, it didn't take long," she concluded.

"It was rape," Lee insisted, his tone quietly murderous.

"No—"

"Now who's being hard on herself?" His eyes raced over her face, his heart thudding at the sight of her on the brink of crying. "I hope to hell the bastard *is* here. I'd like the chance to tear his damn head off."

A sense of joy broke unexpectedly through Cara, scattering the darkness that always enclosed her at the thought of Mitch. She smiled through a sheen of tears.

"My knight in shining armor?" she asked.

"If you'll have me," Lee replied.

"I think I already have," she quipped.

His brows rose, and he laughed. Cara studied him, a look of bemusement forming on her face.

"I've never told anyone the whole truth," she said eventually. "I can't imagine why I told you."

"I'd like to think I know why," Lee returned.

His voice poured over her, deep and stirring. Cara looked into his eyes, her heart swelling with emotion.

"Did you love her very much?" she asked.

"Who?"

"Marilyn. I suppose you were very much in love with her."

Lee raised Cara's hand once more. "Yes," he mumbled against the back of it. "There were times when I thought I'd never get over losing her."

Lee nuzzled Cara's fingers, his lips coming suddenly across the cool metal of a gold band. Raising his head with a start, he looked at the thing as though he'd never seen it before. It had no place on her hand now—at least, he wanted to think it didn't.

As Lee's attention shifted to her wedding ring, so did Cara's. An icy feeling washed over her, the thought of Tom returning so urgently that she broke out in chills.

Shifting his hand, Lee grasped the ring and twisted it lightly about her finger, as he'd seen her do many a time.

"What's past is past, Cara," he rumbled. "For both of us."

"Is it?"

Lee glanced up to find her looking altogether different from a moment ago, her face tense, her eyes opaque.

"Yes, it is," he answered firmly.

"I'm sure it's getting late," she said. "Do you mind if I use your shower?"

She started to turn, pulling her hand as she went. Lee held onto the ring. It slipped to her knuckle. Cara's gaze flew to his.

"I think it's time you took this off," he said.

Cara searched his face, and the amazing new feelings swamped her once again, clashing with the old loyalty, the old love. Drawing a deep breath, she drew her hand from Lee's unresisting grasp and climbed out of bed, taking the sheet with her. Tucking it across her breasts, she turned to look at him where he lay in all his naked splendor, still and watching, waiting for her response.

"I need time, Lee."

Staring up at her, Lee was struck with the notion of how beautiful she was—the hair like a dark cloud, the magnificent body showcased by the draping sheet.

"Is an hour enough?" he asked.

She smiled, but he thought it a sad smile. It was gone before she'd fully turned toward the bathroom, gathering her clothes along the way. The door closed, and a moment later came the sound of the shower.

"Dammit," Lee muttered and, rolling off the bed, reached for his jeans. When she emerged a scant ten minutes later, fully dressed, he was in the process of pulling on his boots.

"I'd better be going," she said.

Lee rose to his feet, tucking in his shirttail as he straightened. "I'd like to drive you home."

"That doesn't make sense. I have my car."

"Then I'll follow you home, and we'll go for a drive."

"No. I—"

"Come on, Cara," he broke in and took swift strides up to her. Lifting his hands, he smoothed the hair back from her face. "Let's not end it like this."

Grasping one of his hands, Cara turned into it and placed a warm kiss in his palm.

"I need time, Lee," she murmured. "Please. Give me some time."

They walked down the stairs silently, side by side, without touching but for the occasional brush of their arms. Lee felt the battle going on inside her but had no idea of how to help her fight it. When they reached the door, he started out with her.

"Good night," Cara said.

"I'll walk you to your car."

"No. Let's just say good night here."

"For God's sake, Cara—"

She stopped him by rising quickly on tiptoe and kissing him. Lee's arms went around her, but within an instant she was backing out of them . . . stepping through the doorway.

"Can I see you tomorrow?" he asked.

She hesitated, though she didn't look back. "Call me," she said and was gone.

Lee watched her shape blend into the moonlit darkness, watching long after she passed from view. He had the eerie feeling any hope of a future with Cara was riding on this very night—that she was about to draw some monumental conclusion that would either admit him to her life . . . or shut him out forever.

She'd made love to him, confided in him, trusted him. But, Lee had realized at the end, the big question hadn't been answered.

"Tom Chastain," he murmured.

Stepping inside, Lee crossed to the table, poured himself a Scotch, and tossed it down. The frustrating truth was, it was Cara's decision . . . Cara's battle. There wasn't a damn thing he could do about it.

Snatching up the bottle, Lee headed for the back porch. It was going to be a long night.

The coastal highway was dark. Even if she'd looked in his direction as she hurried to her Jeep, she wouldn't have noticed him. And she didn't look.

Mitch's eyes narrowed on the white shorts. They glowed in the moonlight, gilding her hips' undulating movements as she walked to the driver's door. An old tightening gripped his stomach, spreading to his loins as he pictured her from the other day—the black hair shining, bare legs gleaming. She always did have a body that made a man's mouth water, and from what he'd seen, she'd only gotten better with time.

His gaze flickered beyond a copse of trees to the Fast Break. The door was closed, but he pictured it as it had been only moments ago—open . . . the lamps from inside backlighting the couple as Cara rose to kiss him. Jealousy flared in Mitch as he pictured the man's dark head bending to her. He knew who it was—the same guy he'd spotted at the marsh that day, the same guy he'd heard snatches of conversation about ever since arriving on the coast some two weeks back. Lee Powers. Development boss. Architect extraordinaire. Son of a bitch . . .

She started the car and pulled away. Mitch grinned as he watched the taillights disappear up the highway, a delicious taste of anticipation filling his mouth.

"Cara Malloy," he muttered into the darkness. "I broke you once. I can do it again."

As Cara let herself in the back door, the grandfather clock began to chime. She absentmindedly counted the bells as she turned off lights on her way to the hall. Eleven. It seemed later than eleven. It seemed she'd been in Lee's bed much longer than a couple of hours . . . and away from home a lifetime.

The house was quiet, as it typically was at this hour of night. Tommy was asleep, and Elsa, who rose with the chickens, presumably the same. There was nothing to interfere with Cara's careening thoughts as she walked into the study and moved unerringly through the darkness to Tom's desk. Sitting down in his chair, she reached for the ornate switch of the Tiffany lamp. Soft light encircled the spot, leaving the rest of the room in shadow.

Her fingers strayed to her wedding band, and despite the fact that she was in Tom's domain, it was Lee's voice that returned to her: *It's time you took this off.*

Never before had anyone presumed to suggest such a thing; but then no one had ever had the right. It occurred to Cara that she'd given Lee the right. *It's time* . . . The memory of his words sent her pulse racing, for she knew what Lee was

saying. It wasn't just the ring he was asking her to leave
behind. Once again Cara thought, he had the right.

Propping her elbows on the desktop, she formed a temple
with her hands, resting her chin on her fingertips as her gaze
traveled across the surface. Tom's papers, pictures, memen-
tos . . . the belongings of her husband, her beloved.

Cara took a deep breath. For a long time after he died, she'd
been able to catch his scent at this desk. Now there was only
the aroma of polished wood. Pain shot through her with the
sensation that she was losing him all over again.

She began going through the desk, picking up his things,
searching for the feeling of closeness that had never died.
She came across the manuscript in the bottom drawer. She'd
seen it countless times, of course, but always had respected
his wishes to keep it private. Covered with a blank sheet, the
pages were bound with a single rubber band. Cara stared at
it for a full minute before transferring it to the desktop.

Carefully removing the band, she set aside the cover sheet.
"One Love," read the title page. "By Tom Chastain." Cara ran
a caressing fingertip over his name, then flipped the page.

*It was raining the first time he saw her—a dark angel with
hair like the night and eyes the blue of autumn skies.*

Tears came to her eyes as she read on—immersing herself
in the golden memories of the day they met, their first kiss,
the first time they made love. Time ceased to register as she
turned through the pages. An hour passed, and then another.
Cara was oblivious. He wrote of their wedding, and moving
to the Outer Banks, and countless moments between them
she'd all but forgotten. Tears streamed down her face. She
was oblivious to that, too.

Their love story lived within the pages . . . *Tom* lived within
them! And by the time she forced her blurred vision through
the final lines, Cara was weeping uncontrollably. Pushing
aside the manuscript, she buried her face in her arms and
surrendered to the sobs, allowing them to rack her until she
gasped for breath.

A long time later her body quieted out of sheer exhaustion.
Stretched across Tom's desk in a pool of tears, Cara stared,
dry-eyed, at the facing wall. Memories of Tom, revived and
vibrant, filled her mind, until without warning, the image of

Lee appeared to overpower them.

She thought of Lee's smile, his kiss, his touch. The radiant feeling rose within her, and there in the crystalline aftermath of blinding sorrow, Cara saw it quite clearly for what it was. She loved the man. She loved *two* men. And Lee Powers deserved more than half a woman.

Rising from the chair, Cara walked purposefully from the room. When Tommy woke up the next morning, she'd already packed for both of them. They were on the highway before nine.

Having polished off nearly an entire bottle of Scotch, Lee woke late in the morning with a hangover. After a shower and coffee, he felt better. Checking his watch, he saw that it was nearly noon, and wondered if it was too early to call Cara. He waited almost another hour before reaching for the phone. Elsa answered.

"She isn't here, Lee."

"When do you expect her back?"

Elsa released a heavy breath. "I don't."

"What do you mean?" Lee asked, his stomach sinking.

"She and Tommy left town early this morning. She did leave something for you, though. A note."

Hopping in the Jaguar, Lee sped the short distance to the Chastain house. Elsa opened the door, letter in hand. He turned his back and took a few steps across the porch as he tore open the envelope and withdrew a sheet of elegant stationery embossed with the initials, CMC.

Lee, I ask your understanding. I thought I knew my mind, but I don't. I thought I could leave the past behind, but I can't. Forgive me. Cara.

Lee read the delicately scrawled words again, finding them once more exceedingly brief . . . and final. His arm fell to his side, his fingers crumpling the fine paper.

"Where is she?" he asked, his back still turned to Elsa.

"I was instructed not to say."

The Texan turned, and when Elsa saw the look on his face, it was all she could do to blink back the tears. She'd wanted the right man for Cara for so long, and here he was. But she was throwing him away.

"Did I ever happen to mention that Tommy's grandmother lives in Warrenton?" Elsa asked.

"Warrenton?"

"A rich little city in Virginia. A couple of hours' drive northwest of here."

Lee stepped forward and shook the woman's hand. "Thank you, Elsa," he said and turned away.

"What are you going to do?"

He paused halfway down the steps. "I really don't know. But it helps to have an idea of where she is. Thanks again."

Elsa stepped out on the porch and lifted a hand to shield her eyes against the bright afternoon sun. The man walked straight and tall, but she sensed a slump about his shoulders.

"Good luck," she murmured, and returned to the empty house.

Saturday night, Louis mused.

Drink in hand, he meandered through the dark rooms of the homeplace, remembering Saturday nights when the place had blazed with light, when music had overflowed the ballroom and fashionable guests had strolled the halls . . . times when the Talbots held an honored place in society.

Tonight the only lights in the house were the silvery moonbeams spilling through the windows, and it had been months since the place had seen a guest. It was silent and deserted but for himself, as it had been ever since the family's ancient housekeeper passed away in the spring. He was alone. On this particular night, the fact struck Louis as poignantly ironic.

He, who had been named Most Popular by his college frat house . . . who had been regarded the most eligible bachelor in Walking Dune . . . who once had roamed the seaboard and dropped in on any parlor, any club, any poker game, always sure to be welcomed with gracious deference. *He . . .* was alone. And not just for tonight. He was alone, period. In the weeks since he retreated to the sanctum of the old house, Louis had sought out no one, and no one had sought him out. Not even Dahlia. The one saving grace of such solitude was that no one had learned his secret . . . not yet.

Louis retraced a path to the dining room sideboard. Charitable shadows hid the changes in the room, walls with light marks where paintings once had hung, a cabinet stripped of heirloom china, a table bereft of the silver candelabra that had been his mother's pride and joy. Treasures sold discreetly out of town.

Louis snatched up the prized bottle of wine, one of the last from his father's cellar, and poured a healthy amount into his glass. Taking a large, disrespectful gulp of the vintage Beaujolais, he peered into the darkness.

He'd done the best he could, dammit! One of these days he'd replace it all . . . one of these days when Lone Star Partners forked over a fortune for that worthless land at the north end.

Louis scowled as he remembered the damnable fence that had sprung up across the highway. Seeing it with his own eyes a few days back, he'd felt ominously threatened. Somehow he'd never really thought it would come to pass. Now he realized he never should have doubted Cara. She'd said a fence would be built, and it had been—the project aided and abetted by her Texas lover.

The pain that overtook Louis was familiar. He took a long draught of wine, but the burning continued, rising within him until it reached his eyes. He remembered bright mornings in her kitchen, sunset walks along the beach, long talks on quiet nights when Tommy had gone to sleep. He remembered kissing her on New Year's Eve, reveling for a sweet instant as she seemed to respond, despairing as she pushed him away.

Louis rubbed a hand across his eyes, but the despised, alternate image materialized anyway—Cara lifting her arms to Lee Powers . . . kissing him with a passion Louis had dreamed of for years.

"God," he moaned aloud. He'd loved her for so long. How could she do it to him? *How?* Since that night when she kicked him out of her house, everything had gone to hell.

The bell rang. Louis jumped. Setting aside his drink, he walked to the door and peeped through the side pane. Despite the darkness of the porch outside, he recognized them instantly—Tom and Dick, Harry Dane's goons.

"Shit," Louis muttered and, running quick fingers through his uncombed hair, plastered what he hoped was a convincing smile on his face.

"Evenin', boys," he greeted. "What brings *you* here?"

They stepped in, and Dick closed the door behind them.

"I figure you got an idea of why we're here," he said. "Why the hell don't you turn on some lights, Talbot?"

The gigantic Tom remained silent, though he started cracking his knuckles.

"I was just about to," Louis replied. Backing away, he turned on the nearby floor lamp. Its effect reached no farther than the doorway, but it afforded enough light for him to clearly see their faces—which were rock hard. This time, despite his best efforts, the smile Louis produced was shaky.

"Can I offer you a drink?" he asked.

"This ain't a social call," Dick replied. "Mr. Dane wants to know what's going on. It's been a long time since he heard from you, and you ain't been answering your phone. Mr. Dane don't like people who don't answer their phones."

"I've been away," Louis stumbled. "I've had to be out of town on business the past few months."

"Mr. Dane figures you got unfinished business with *him*. How about it, Talbot? You got something I can take back with me?"

"Not yet. Like I told Harry, as soon as my land sells, I'll pay him back in full . . . with interest."

"Mr. Dane wants something on account now."

"I don't have it now."

Dick scowled. "I saw a fancy car parked out front."

"It's rented."

"You got a bank account?"

"Yes. With just enough in it to meet expenses until the sale comes through," Louis answered.

"Seems to me you've forgotten your biggest expense."

Dick gave a quick nod to Tom, and before Louis knew what was happening, the man had grabbed his hand. Louis's forefinger snapped like a twig.

"Dammit!" he shrieked, hugging the injured hand to his chest. "You didn't have to do that! Harry's going to get his money!"

"You're damn right he is," Dick commented. "And he'll get something on account within the month. If he don't hear from you, you'll be hearing from us."

The man opened the door, and Tom stepped out.

"One last piece of advice, Talbot," Dick tossed. "Start answering your phone."

Clutching his throbbing hand, Louis slammed the door behind them with a violent shove of his hip.

The next morning he showered and shaved—cutting himself mercilessly with his left-handed efforts—and set off on a hated errand. He had to have some answers, and like it or not, the man to ask was Lee Powers.

Louis found him at the construction site, bent over a set of papers he'd spread across a wooden crate. He was alone, the rest of the Lone Star crew far in the distance and apparently hard at work on one of the towering houses that had risen near the dunes. There was no better opportunity. Louis walked up to him.

"Could I have a word with you, Powers?" he asked stiffly.

"Depends on what it's about."

"Lone Star."

Lee folded his arms across his chest. "Okay. Shoot."

"How's the development coming along?"

"On schedule."

Louis glanced toward the shoreline. "Looks like you're nearly through here."

"Nearly. It'll take a few more weeks."

"Then what?"

"Then Phase One will be complete. What are you getting around to, Talbot?"

Louis caught his lip, then released it with a heavy breath. "When do you think Lone Star might exercise the other options?"

Lee arched a brow. "You mean the options on Phase Three?"

"I'm sure you know what I mean," Louis returned.

"I can't help you, Talbot."

"Can't? Or won't?"

"If I had an answer, I'd give it to you. The fact is I don't know what's going to happen with Phase Three. At the moment its future seems to be in the hands of the state."

Fear spiraled through Louis. "Its future? Surely you don't

mean there's a chance Lone Star won't go forward with their plans."

"It's not for me to say. But more than half the land proposed for Phase Three is state land. And right now the mustangs are sitting smack in the middle of it. It figures that Lone Star will wait to hear from the state before going forward."

"How long?"

"Before we hear from the state?" Lee questioned.

There was no love lost between them, and never had been. But there was an air of desperation about Louis Talbot that piqued Lee's curiosity. Tipping up the brim of his hard hat, he gave the man a searching look.

"I don't know, Talbot. I really don't."

Louis nodded and turned away, barely aware that the Texan continued to watch inquisitively as he walked back to the car. Climbing in, Louis gripped the steering wheel, grimacing as his bandaged finger sought to bend.

"Mustangs," he muttered, his heart plummeting until he could swear it throbbed in the soles of his feet. "Cara and her damn mustangs."

Pulling away from the site, he drove the short distance to the Chastain house. Louis killed the engine and slouched back in the seat, staring across the grounds to the familiar door, remembering the years he'd passed through it on a daily basis.

It had been months since he darkened that doorway. It seemed more like years; so much had happened. Since the night he stormed off that porch, luck had turned on him, pushed him to the brink of disaster where only a single lifeline remained. Then came the cruel twist that threatened to snatch even that out of his grasp.

The cold anger returned as Louis sat there outside Cara's house, reviewing the seemingly disparate events that had linked up to pit him against her. The woman he'd worshipped had become his enemy.

"They're not here, Louis."

He looked around with a start to find Elsa standing by the car, peering at him from over a bag of groceries.

"They're not?"

"She and Tommy left town yesterday—liable to be gone quite a while," she said.

"How long is quite a while?" he asked.

"She wouldn't say, but she was in a dadblamed hurry to get out of here, I can tell you that."

Cara gone? And in a hurry? She never left Walking Dune . . . hardly ever anyway. Could it mean—

"I haven't seen you in a month of Sundays, Louis. Where you been keeping yourself?"

Louis smiled into the curious face. "Just around. I'll be seeing you, Elsa."

Starting up the car, he headed home, a glimmer of hope lighting his dark thoughts for the first time in days.

Cara was in bed reading when the tap came on her door.

"Yes?" she called. Abigail stepped inside.

"May I have a moment, Carolina?"

She moved forward, obviously taking the moment no matter what Cara might have said.

"I've held my tongue for a week," she went on as she arrived at the bedside. "You offered no explanation when you arrived, and I asked for none."

Cara set the book aside and folded her hands. "I was under the impression you'd be delighted to see Tommy whenever possible."

"I *am* delighted. But I must say I didn't expect you to enroll him in kindergarten today."

"Does that displease you? You've always said the school here is superior to the one we have in Walking Dune."

"It doesn't displease me. It puzzles me. What are your plans, Carolina? Exactly how long do you intend to stay?"

Cara shifted up against the pillows. "I thought it might be nice for us to spend the holidays together."

"Christmas?" Abigail voiced on an incredulous note.

"Elsa will be gone for several weeks. She always spends the season with her sister in Florida. Besides, it would make sense to take Tommy back to Walking Dune during the school break at the end of the year."

"But that's two-and-a-half months away!"

"Is that a problem, Abigail?"

"Of course it's not a problem. I'm simply shocked. You've never brought Tommy for longer than a weekend, and even then you were always anxious to return to the coast." Abigail's expression turned shrewd. "Has something happened to make your beloved Walking Dune lose its appeal?"

"No. But things there are rather complicated right now."

"In what way?"

"I told you about the developers, the mustangs. Everything is in an uproar."

"Are you sure that's all there is to it?"

Cara gave the woman a shrewd look of her own. "I'm sure that's all I'm going to say about it."

Abigail pursed her lips. "The years have done nothing to curb your tongue."

"Nor your misplaced interest in my private affairs."

"Well!"

"We are not confidants, Abigail, and never have been. Tommy is here. That's what you wanted. Isn't it enough?"

"Quite enough, Carolina. You're right. Tommy is all I care about, and I *do* mean all."

With that, Abigail turned on her heel and left.

Cara sank back against the pillows, her gaze moving disinterestedly about the opulent guest room. Heavy antiques, velvet drapes, the furnishings of the Chastain mansion were splendorous, but she'd always found them stifling. She longed for the airy rooms of the beach house, the smells of cedar and sea salt. She ached for home, but . . . the mere thought of it brought the thought of Lee.

Cara turned off the bedside lamp and closed her eyes against his forming image. Yet its seductive presence remained through the night, chasing away nightmares of Mitch, wrapping its arms about her in the bed of her husband's childhood home.

The past weeks had been hard. Back-to-back charters had made them the most lucrative of Nick's career, but they had seemed interminable. He was worried about Cara, who had taken off without warning for Warrenton; and he missed Dahlia. Since they'd started seeing each other, it was the longest time they'd been apart.

Now October was at an end, the waters of the Virginia harbor cold and murky, reflecting a temperature and cloud-laden sky that promised the onset of winter. Nick gave the *Virgin* a last assessing look. The hatches were battened, every nut and bolt in order. Satisfied, he walked away from the docks toward the beat-up station wagon.

As he approached, he gave the car a long look. That paint job last spring had helped, but all in all, it still looked like a wreck—the taillights mismatched, the driver's door sagging in its hinge, both courtesy of accidents that probably should have totaled the thing long before Nick ever bought it five years ago.

He climbed in, reflecting that the old wagon had served its purpose when he was getting started and needed to haul tackle and equipment. But now? Now he had enough of a nest egg to think about something new. Now he had enough to think about a whole new life.

Starting up the engine, he reached into his jacket pocket and felt for the black velvet box. A whole new life . . . with Dahlia at its center.

It was the time at sea that had done it, Nick thought. After a rain, the ocean's color was close to that of her eyes; at sunset, the sky was streaked with the shade of her hair. This time, as never before when he left Walking Dune, the image of Dahlia had stayed with him. Everything had reminded him of her.

Nick turned on the highway and headed south, smiling as he thought of the way he was going to surprise her. He'd called her only two nights ago but hadn't said a word about coming down.

It was dusk when he turned into the lodge, his heart skipping as he spotted her outside the front doors. She was kneeling . . . lighting a candle inside a jack-o-lantern. It was only then that Nick remembered it was Halloween. The thought disintegrated as he stopped the car beside her, and she looked up.

She straightened slowly, her gaze searching through the gathering darkness to see who sat behind the wheel of the unfamiliar wagon. Nick climbed out and closed the door, watching the emotions that shifted across her face—curiosity, amazement . . . joy. His own rose to match hers. And then she was moving toward him, trotting at first, then breaking into a full-fledged run. Catching her in open arms, Nick lifted her up against him.

"I love you," he said.

"I love—"

His seeking mouth covered hers and found it just as hungry as his own.

Lee stepped onto the balcony and looked out to sea. It was the first day of November, and the autumn sky was absolutely clear, the water sparkling with morning sunlight. The view alone was worth a half million, he decided, not to mention the other luxuries offered by the three-story villa.

Crossing the master bedroom, he went out on the south-facing balcony and took a sweeping look across the development. Phase One construction was complete. Subcontractors would work on the interiors through the winter, but his work was done. The mansions and clubhouse were beautiful, carefully nestled into the rolling landscape so that scarcely a hill or tree had been lost. Lee was proud of it, but beneath that pride rang the solemn note that what he was doing would change Walking Dune forever.

He took a last look about the rooms and went outside, where dozers were clattering and truck engines humming. The clean-up crew was making good progress. When they finished, there was nothing else to be done. Within the week, they'd be packing up and heading back to Houston.

Lee's solemn mood deepened as he left the house and walked back toward the highway. Thanksgiving was coming up, with Christmas just around the corner. The men were excited about returning home to their families; all he felt was a mounting sense of dread.

He could stay behind, of course. There was nothing for him in Texas, and he sure as hell didn't want to leave Walking Dune. He'd fallen in love with it just as surely as he'd fallen for Cara. But there was the rub. She and Walking Dune were as one. Everywhere Lee looked, he saw her, remembered her. As long as he stayed, there was no hope of getting over her. She and Tommy had been gone a month, but he still thought about them day in, day out . . . still searched the road for any sign of her car. It was driving him crazy.

"Hello, Lee."

Looking up, Lee broke into a smile. "How are you, Nick?" he asked, offering a hand.

"Good."

"What are you doing out here?"

"Just thought I'd drop by and take a closer look at your handiwork." Nick cast an appreciative look toward the newly constructed buildings beyond Lee. "Very impressive. I don't think I've seen anything nicer."

"Thanks. I'm pretty happy with it. What have you been up to? I haven't seen you in weeks."

"The fall season is my biggest of the year. Business is booming, and I've been away a lot. When I get to town . . . well, I spend most of my time with Dahlia."

Lee's smile broadened. "I haven't seen her in weeks either. How is she?"

"Fine, but busy. The fall season's a big one for the inn, too. Speaking of Dahlia, she said you guys are going back to Houston."

Lee nodded. "For a few months. Phase One is in. It could be a while before things get going again."

"How long will you be gone?" Nick asked.

"I don't know yet. Why?"

"Because I'm dead set on asking Dahlia to marry me, and I'd like you to be best man at the wedding if you're around."

Lee clapped his friend on the shoulder. "I'll be around," he said. "You just tell me when. Congratulations."

Nick smiled ruefully. "She hasn't said yes yet."

"She will."

"The ring's burning a hole in my pocket. I was thinking of Christmas . . . if she says yes."

Lee grinned. "Sounds good," he said. "Very romantic."

Nick's face turned a little red.

"I remember the way you watched her that night at the Chastain house," Lee added teasingly. "Who would have thought it would end up like this?"

"Not me," came the brisk reply.

They laughed, Nick's merry expression gradually turning to one of curiosity.

"That was a fateful night, all right," he said. "As I recall, you were keeping an eye on a certain lady yourself."

The swift way Lee's face changed reminded Nick of the sun being suddenly covered by clouds.

"Come on," he said. "Walk with me to the car. I have to drive into town for a few supplies."

Nick fell in step beside him. "I thought you might ask about Cara."

"I'm making it a point not to."

"Don't you want to know how she's doing?"

Lee walked along, his gaze fixed ahead. "I have no doubt your sister is doing just fine."

"You sure about that?"

"As sure as I can be about anything to do with Cara."

"I talked to her this weekend. She asked about you."

Lee's head snapped around at that.

"I told her you're leaving," Nick added.

"And?" Lee questioned after a moment.

"And she said to give you her best."

"Her best." Lee's expression darkened as he looked ahead once more. "Interesting choice of words."

"What do you mean?"

"What I mean is that your sister is *unable* to give her best— to me, at any rate."

"What the hell happened between you two?" Nick demanded.

"That's my business."

Nick scrutinized the Texan's hard profile. "When I heard she left for Warrenton, I thought it was because of this Mitch Lincoln thing. But it wasn't, was it? It was because of you."

"I really don't know, Nick."

"What did you do to her?"

"What did I—" Lee released a brusque laugh that ended as abruptly as it began. "I didn't do anything to her, except invest more time and effort and energy in trying to get close to her than with any woman I've known."

Nick arched a brow. "I'd say she's worth all that."

"I'd say I agree with you."

"Well, then?"

Lee gave him an openly frustrated look. "Well, then, what? It hasn't done a damn bit of good. There's something between us, yeah. But not enough to make her forget Tom Chastain."

"How do you know?"

They arrived at the Jaguar. Lee whipped off his hard hat and tossed it in the back. "For God's sake, Nick," he growled, "she wrote me a Dear John and skipped town."

"Where was I during all this?"

"On a charter, I guess. Why?"

"Because I would have seen it."

"Seen what, dammit?"

"The change in Cara."

"She hasn't changed, Nick."

"Listen to me, buddy. Cara hasn't so much as *looked* at a man in five years. If anything happened between you— anything at all!—it's a *major* change. Are you sure you want to go back to Houston without seeing her?"

"Take a look around," Lee replied with a derisive sweep of his hand. "She ain't here."

"No. She's a piddlin' two-hour drive away."

Lee frowned. "Like I said," he muttered after a moment, "I've already invested more effort in Cara than any woman I've known."

"Like I said," Nick countered, "she's worth it."

Having changed out of her riding gear, Dahlia was about to go downstairs when a knock sounded at her bedroom door. She opened it and gasped.

"Louis!" His jaw was swollen, his eye black. "What on earth has happened to you?"

Louis stepped in and tried to smile. "It's not that bad, is it?"

Dahlia lifted a hand to his face, wincing and withdrawing before she touched it. "It's terrible," she said. "What happened?"

Louis walked past her into the room, his attempted smile draining away. "I'm in trouble, kid."

"What kind of trouble?"

"Real trouble." Louis turned and gave her a desolate look. "I owe a guy some money. He's being rather unpleasant about it."

"He did this to you?"

"His hired hands did."

"Well, then, let's call Ned—"

"I can't call Ned," Louis interrupted, running a weary hand through his hair.

"Why not?"

"I just *can't,* Dahlia! All right?!"

His voice rang harshly in the room. Dahlia looked away. Louis stepped quickly forward and took her by the shoulders.

"I can't bring in the police," he added quietly. "Believe me."

Dahlia met his eyes and saw the desperation within them.

"What can I do?" she asked.

Louis swallowed hard. "The goons are still in town. If I don't give them something tonight, I'll get a repeat of last night. I need some money, Dahlia. Just enough to get them off my back."

"You can have whatever you need, Louis. You know that."

Relief flooded Louis, leaving him weak in the knees. "Thanks, kid. I knew I could count on you." His gaze moved between her eyes, and unexpected tears sprang to his own.

"Everything's so messed up, Dahlia," he added thickly. "I don't know how everything got so messed up."

She opened her arms. Louis sank into them. He said nothing more, and his breathing remained staunchly even. But Dahlia could feel the wetness against her neck where his tears flowed.

The lodge was different with guests roaming about it. There were about a dozen, mostly elderly folk who'd been coming to the inn each fall for years, Dahlia had explained. They walked the grounds, played bridge in the card room, reminisced about days gone by when husbands and friends had spent the day hunting duck.

Nick smilingly greeted a couple of silver-haired ladies on his way up the stairs to Dahlia's room. Knocking lightly, he stepped inside without waiting for an answer. His face fell as he took in the sight of Dahlia embracing Louis Talbot.

"Forgive me," Nick stated, his face flooding with heat.

"Guess I should have knocked louder."

Talbot straightened and turned, surprising Nick with the battered condition of his face.

"Good God, man," Nick mumbled. "What happened to you?"

"A little accident," he said. "I was just leaving."

The sight of his injuries may have touched Nick, but not to the extent that it erased his jealousy.

"Good," he replied shortly.

Louis smiled a dismal little smile as he looked back to Dahlia. "Goodbye, kid. And thanks."

Nick thought Louis straightened as he walked past.

"See ya, Malloy," he offered.

"Right," Nick returned.

Talbot left the door standing open. With a stormy glance at Dahlia, Nick stepped over and pulled it shut.

"What was that about?" he demanded.

Dahlia walked in Nick's direction, her face a picture of sincerity. "He needed a friend."

Nick stuffed his hands in his jacket pockets, his fingers colliding with the velvet box. "How good a friend?"

"A friend. That's all. He wanted only friendship, and that was all I had to give."

"Are you sure?"

Nick's eyes were still troubled. Dahlia reached up and looped her arms around his neck.

"I don't love him anymore, Nick."

He said nothing, though he put his arms around her and pulled her fully against him.

"You're the one I love," Dahlia whispered.

Nick smiled, "Yeah?"

"Yeah."

"Then prove it."

He kissed her, his hands roving over her back, under her blouse. Suddenly Dahlia grasped what he meant.

"You mean now?" she gasped. "In the middle of the day?"

"I want you, Dahlia," Nick returned, his expression one of deadly earnest. "Right now."

She gazed up at him with wide green eyes.

"Is that okay?" he added.

Dahlia slipped out of his arms. "Give me a minute," she said.

Nick stepped back and locked the door as she walked off toward the bathroom.

Dahlia was trembling as she closed the door and gazed at the negligee hanging on the back of it. The fabric was the pale green of her eyes, and sheer as gauze. It had hung there since before Nick left some weeks ago, and she hadn't yet had the nerve to put it on.

She adored Nick, but having a lover was still a new experience. Each time, she felt a moment of unnerving modesty she could only describe as bridelike jitters. Eyeing the shimmery negligee, Dahlia finally discarded her clothes, pulled it on, and looked in the mirror above the sink.

Cords of pale green silk tied over her shoulders and trimmed the dipping neckline, which hovered lightly atop the crest of her breasts. But for those silken cords, the rest was as pale and light as a cloud. The merest pass of a hand would shift the neckline below nipples, which in their current state protruded like rosebuds. The creation was a mere veil over her body, an invitation to touch what was clearly visible beneath.

With a deep breath Dahlia opened the door and stepped out. Nick was in bed, covered to the waist.

"God in heaven," he muttered huskily. "Come here."

Dahlia's desire for him overpowered her nervousness. He pulled back the covers. She climbed in, and he bent immediately over her, his arm encircling her shoulders as he kissed her.

"I have something to ask you," he eventually murmured against her lips.

"Now?" she asked dreamily.

"I don't think I can wait any longer."

"What is it?"

He took her hand, and she felt a pressure on her finger that was unmistakably a ring. Dahlia's eyes flew open.

"Will you marry me?" Nick asked.

Her gaze leapt from the ring to the handsome face above her. With a squeal Dahlia threw her arms about his neck and drew him down to her. Nick chuckled into her mouth.

"I take it that's a yes," he said after a moment.

"A resounding yes." Dahlia beamed, flashing her left hand behind his head and watching the diamond sparkle.

"What do you think of a Christmas wedding?"

"Christmas?" Dahlia repeated with a start. "That's only a matter of weeks, Nick. I don't know if I can arrange a whole wedding in a matter of weeks."

"A whole wedding? You want a big shebang?"

"Did you ever hear of a bride who didn't?"

"So . . . do you want to wait?" Nick asked.

Dahlia studied the look of concern on his face, then broke into a smile.

"How about New Year's Eve?" she asked.

"Sure!" Nick agreed wholeheartedly.

Dahlia clasped him to her once more. "I'll get the church, the florist, the caterer—"

"I'll get the *Virgin* ready for a cruise to the Bahamas. Or would you prefer someplace else?"

"The *Virgin*," Dahlia repeated thoughtfully. "Guess you know you'll have to change the name of your boat."

"Oh, really?" Nick grinned.

"Really. I don't intend to have a virgin in the family."

"No?"

"No."

"How about the *Mrs. Malloy*, then?"

Dahlia sank back on the pillows, a bright smile on her face. "I like it," she said.

"I'll need to go to Virginia Beach sometime soon," Nick commented. "Lease my apartment, trade my car—"

"Trade your car?" Dahlia repeated, suddenly alert. "You mean the station wagon?"

Nick trailed a palm over her fiery curls. "I already decided before I came down, Dahlia. It's time I got something new. Something we can both use."

Dahlia jumped up in the bed. "Let me do it!"

"Do what?"

"Trade the car for something new. It'll be my wedding present."

"A new car?" Nick questioned doubtfully. "I was already thinking you'd want to live here at the inn. That's okay with me. I can run my business out of Bellehaven. But a new car?

That's a little extravagant, don't you think?"

"No. I can afford it. I *am* rich, you know."

Nick's smiling expression went momentarily sober. "Rich?"

"Of course. The Dunns are one of the first families of Walking Dune. Didn't you know?"

"No."

Dahlia's lively gaze swept his face. "Good," she pronounced.

"Why?"

"Now I know you aren't just after me for my money."

Nick settled into a grin as a devilish gleam came to his eyes.

"You're right about that," he said, and reaching swiftly out for her, pulled her beneath him.

Late afternoon sunlight filtered through the stained glass windows. The pub was deserted but for an irritating blonde who kept plugging quarters into the juke box. Mitch sat in a corner booth, nursing a beer and brooding.

The typewritten note he'd just opened lay beside him on the scarred table. Like the others, it was short and to the point.

"Good work," it said. "Your services are no longer required." Another five bills had been enclosed. Severance pay from a boss who remained a mystery.

Mitch scowled. He didn't like mysteries, and right now his life was full of them. As near as he could tell, Cara had taken off some three weeks back, her brat in tow. Mitch couldn't risk asking anyone where they'd gone, and so he was completely in the dark as to their whereabouts.

He would have tailed good old Nick, but he was gone, too, having left Walking Dune some days before his sister. So Mitch had kept an eye on Lee Powers, the last person he'd seen with Cara, the man who'd kissed her that night in the doorway. But Powers had only reported to the construction site each morning and returned to the beach house each night. It made Mitch wonder if the lot of them were in cahoots to place Cara outside his reach.

He took a long gulp of the brew. He detested the idea of being on the butt end of a scheme, particularly where the

Malloys were concerned. But clearly at the moment they had him over a barrel.

He simply hadn't expected Cara to jackrabbit, not yet anyway. Mitch was virtually certain she'd spotted him only once—that day shortly after he arrived on the coast, when he'd carefully engineered an appearance, and she'd stared with such breathless horror that his blood had raced. He'd looked forward to a few more such occasions before making his move.

His expression turned murderous. But Cara had thrown him a curve. He'd underestimated the situation, and she'd taken advantage—whether by chance or by design made no difference to him. The game was on.

Folding the hundred-dollar notes, Mitch tucked them in his boot. It wasn't a fortune, but he'd scraped back enough from other payments to tide him over. With a sneering glance for the anonymous note, he crumpled it and dropped it in the ashtray.

"Good work," Mitch repeated to himself with a snort. If his mysterious benefactor thought scaring the bitch out of town was good work, he had no imagination.

Draining the last of his beer, Mitch left the pub, climbed into the blue rattletrap, and pointed it north toward Walking Dune.

Now he was on his own time. And playing by his own rules.

Chapter Ten

The sun was going down as Lee drove through the Virginia countryside, the sky aglow above rolling pastureland interrupted by stands of timber, bordered for the most part by white-railed fencing announcing yet another elegant farm.

It was horse country, *fine* horse country, home of the hunt and the steeplechase. One could almost hear the baying of the hounds, almost see the flash of shining coats as thoroughbreds thundered across the countryside. The atmosphere of refinement was overwhelming, and though none of the horses were out on this cool November evening, Lee imagined their well-groomed lines. He thought contrastingly of the mustangs, whose coats had never been touched by a brush, whose manes and tails were as likely to be matted with burrs as not. Still, there was a majesty in their wildness their aristocratic counterparts couldn't match.

It wasn't long before his musings about the mustangs melted into the thought of Cara. Lee's jaw tightened. He still wasn't sure what he was doing, much less what to expect. But for the past few days Nick's comments had been ringing in his ears, pushing him to a point where he felt compelled to come. He was leaving for Houston in two days. At the least, Lee figured grimly, he deserved a face-to-face goodbye.

The sense of refinement intensified as he drove into Warrenton. The place reeked of money—old money, the kind a newcomer simply wouldn't have enough of.

White-columned mansions sat back on acres of carefully landscaped lawn; water oaks the size of buildings shaded quiet avenues. There was no poor side of town. From the time Lee passed the city limits sign, he saw only a parade of wealthy neighborhoods.

Finally he came across a shopping center with a gas station and phone booth. There was only one Chastain listed in the book. Lee asked directions and found his way to the address just as darkness fell, and the front lamps came on outside an immense iron gate at the head of the drive. Turning in, he nosed the Jaguar to a stop mere inches before the barrier. A uniformed security officer stepped forward, an unpleasant look on his face.

"Can I help you, mister?"

"I'd like to see Cara."

The officer's expression settled into blatant disapproval. "Cara?"

"Mrs. Chastain," Lee supplied.

"Who may I say is calling?"

"Lee Powers."

"Is she expecting you?"

Damn, this guy was getting on his nerves. "No," Lee replied shortly. "Do I need an appointment?"

The guard straightened at that and walked to a side post where he lifted a mike and presumably contacted the house. A minute passed. Lee shifted in the seat and ran an irritable hand over his hair. He hadn't considered this. It seemed he'd driven all this way and might not even be admitted.

"Dammit," he muttered under his breath.

But when the guard stepped away from his post, it was to open the gate. Lee hit the gas and scratched off. Glancing aside, he saw that the guard gave him a gratifying glare. But when Lee looked back at his surroundings, the grandeur of the estate drive reduced him to a respectful speed.

Considering the places he'd been, the things he'd seen, he'd have thought wealth would cease to impress him. It still did. Lee's eyes conveyed the message of magnolias and oaks centuries old, and the towering brick house just ahead. They all meant the same thing. So *this* was what Tom Chastain grew up in. A memory of his own humble homeplace darted to mind. Lee did his best not to draw any further comparisons as he stopped beneath the sheltered drive outside double doors trimmed with shining brass. Climbing out of the car, he turned to find those doors opening.

Lee walked around the front of the Jaguar, his eyes on the woman who stood in the doorway. She was silver-haired and slight, nonetheless imparting the impression of stature. Barring the way, she didn't move an inch but to lift her chin as he stepped up to tower above her.

"I'm Abigail Chastain," she announced. "May I help you?"

Now that he stood only a foot away, Lee detected the hard look in her eyes. She was decked out in a dark dress, thousands of dollars worth of pearls, and an unmistakable air of superiority. Southern aristocracy—wealthy, cultured, arrogant.

"I don't think so," he returned bluntly. "I realize this is your house, Mrs. Chastain. But it isn't you I've come to see."

Only by virtue of the door lanterns was Lee able to catch a glimpse of the annoyance that marred her carefully arched brow.

"As I told your security guard," Lee added, "I've come to see Cara. Is she here?"

"My daughter-in-law is upstairs," Abigail answered, "preparing for supper. I'd ask you to join us, but—"

"I'm not here to wangle an invitation for supper, Mrs. Chastain. All I'd like is a few minutes of Cara's time."

"And all I'd like is an explanation of your uninvited appearance on my doorstep, young man."

In spite of himself, Lee was taken aback.

"Excuse me?" he managed.

"I hope you haven't come here with the purpose of talking my daughter-in-law into returning to Walking Dune."

"I doubt anyone could talk her into much of anything."

"Well, then, why have you come?"

Lee gritted his teeth. "With all due respect, Mrs. Chastain, my reasons for coming are my business. But if you're afraid I've come here to spirit your daughter-in-law away, I haven't."

The woman gave him an imperious look of doubt.

"May I come in?" Lee demanded.

"Oh, all right," she huffed after a moment and moved aside.

Lee stepped into a huge, tiled foyer that was embraced by a flying staircase, presided over by a chandelier, graced by a center table with a vase of magnificent gladiolas. A butler in formal livery stood a respectful distance behind his mistress.

"I suppose I'll go up and notify Carolina," she said.

Carolina? Lee glanced down at the woman.

"I'd appreciate it," he rumbled.

A side door opened, and Tommy bolted across the floor.

"Lee!" he shrieked.

Running up, he leapt at Lee, who caught him under the arms and swung him around with a light laugh.

"That's quite enough, Tommy," Abigail chastised. "Mr. Powers has come to see your mother."

With a sharp look for the woman, Lee set the boy on his feet. "And Tommy," he responded in a deep tone. Smiling once more, he dropped to one knee. "I brought you something," he added, fishing in his back pocket and producing the small carving he'd finished the previous night.

"Wow!" Tommy exclaimed. "It's a colt!"

"One of Star's colts, do you think?" Lee asked.

"Yeah! One of Star's! Thanks, Lee!"

Lee reached out and tousled his fair hair. "You're welcome, Tommy. Glad you like it."

"Do you think you might go up to your mother's room and tell her she has a visitor?" Abigail interrupted.

"Sure. And I'll show her this!" Tommy added, waving the carving as he bounded toward the staircase.

"Slow down, Tommy!" his grandmother admonished, though Lee was glad to see her rebuke had little if any effect on the boy.

The woman put a manicured hand to her temple as though the weight of the world rested there, then flourished the same hand in a graceful gesture that ended in an extended palm.

"If you'll follow me, Mr. Powers? I'm sure Tommy will bring his mother to the drawing room straightaway."

She led the way to an anteroom that was cozier, if no less grandiose, than the foyer. Drapes of crimson velvet framed the windows, the color repeated in a plush carpet patterned with blue roses. Scattered about in tasteful groupings, overstuffed chairs and settees carried on the varying shades of blue.

Looking around as he followed the woman, Lee was a fair distance into the room before he noted the marble fireplace on the facing wall. Above it hung a gigantic portrait of a young man who looked so like Tommy that Lee knew immediately he was looking at Tom Chastain. He came to an abrupt halt.

"I'd prefer to meet Cara in the foyer, if you don't mind."

Abigail turned. "Yes. I do mind. We're not in the habit of receiving callers in the foyer."

"Perhaps I could ask your indulgence on this occasion," Lee returned with a bow.

Abigail arched a brow. "You surprise me, Mr. Powers," she remarked. "I'd heard you're from Texas."

"So I am."

"Are all Texans so courtly?"

Lee slipped into a charming smile. "I can't speak for all of us, Mrs. Chastain. But I will say we tend to cater to our callers' wishes when they turn up—however *unannounced* they might be."

Catching the reproach, Abigail sucked in her cheeks as she assessed the man from head to toe. He was wearing denim jeans, a white shirt, and a tweed jacket—acceptable enough for the afternoon, but disrespectfully casual for the supper hour. His hair, dipping to his brow in front and below his collar in back, deserved a thorough cutting; below his black moustache, the shadow of a beard called for a shave.

"I'd say you western folk carry hospitality to a fault," she remarked drily.

"Maybe so, ma'am," Lee replied in an exaggerated drawl, "but I'd still prefer to meet Cara someplace else."

Abigail drew herself up. "And I'd still prefer we abide by the rules of propriety long established in this house. What is it about this room that doesn't suit you, Mr. Powers?"

Before he could stop them, Lee's eyes shifted to the portrait.

Abigail followed his line of vision. "I see."

Lee looked back to find the most infuriatingly smug expression he'd ever seen.

"There's an old saying, Mr. Powers," she went on. "True love never dies. If you have in mind that you might be able to take the place of my son, you're sadly mistaken. Carolina remains entirely devoted to him, as well she should."

"As well she should?"

"My son was an extraordinary man."

Lee's face turned to stone. "So I understand. But he's been gone five years. Isn't that enough time for a widow to grieve?"

"So you don't deny that it's a matter of the heart that has brought you here tonight."

"I'm not denying or acknowledging anything . . . to you. I told you before. My reasons for coming here are private."

"But hardly inscrutable," Abigail pointed out. "Perhaps you should be apprised of the fact that many men have tried their wiles on Carolina since my son's demise—all to no avail. I wager your luck will prove no better than theirs."

"I can speak for myself, Abigail."

Lee spun around. She was standing a few yards behind him, just inside the doorway. Tommy was beside her, beaming, and still holding onto the wooden likeness of the colt. Although Lee managed a wink for the boy, he couldn't prevent his gaze from returning to Cara and fastening there. Disconcertingly beautiful as always, she was wearing a white sweater and slim matching skirt, her hair pinned up in a smooth twist— every inch the refined lady who belonged in such a drawing room. Yet as Lee stood there helplessly staring, the vision he saw more clearly was that of her standing by his bed, clad in a sheet, her hair wild and loose.

"Hello, Lee," she said. "This is a surprise."

"Turnabout is fair play," he retorted quietly. "Seems I remember you surprising me about a month ago."

Cara's cheeks colored as she looked beyond him. "I'll thank you for a moment of privacy, Abigail."

"Very well," the older woman pronounced, her icy look darting from Cara to Lee and back again. "But I hope this intrusion won't delay supper. Cook has prepared coq au vin."

"You may begin without me if it comes to that," Cara said.

"Hardly a good example to set for Tommy."

"I'm sure he'll take it in stride." Cara looped a fond arm about Tommy's shoulders as she looked down at him. "Won't you, Tommy?"

"Are you going to eat with us, Lee?" the boy chirped.

Lee smiled. "I'll take a rain check."

"What's a rain check?"

"That means we'll do it another time. Okay?"

"Okay." The boy sighed with obvious disappointment.

"I *promise* we'll do it another time."

"Come along, Tommy," Abigail intervened and walked swiftly to her grandson. "I've been informed these two have *private* business to discuss."

Shuttling Tommy out, the woman drew the doors—a courtesy Lee wouldn't have expected. The boy gave him a last wistful look before the doors fully closed. Lee smiled again, the expression slowly draining as he turned his eyes to Cara.

"I've missed Tommy," he announced. "Things at the site haven't been the same without him dropping around every day."

The deep voice reached across the distance between them, embracing Cara with a shivering touch. She stood silently rooted, still feeling the shock of his appearance, her mind swelling with impressions—how tall he was, how handsome, how the mere sound of his voice stole her breath. Being here with him, in this particular room, was a situation she never would have imagined—his darkness thrown into relief by the fair-haired portrait behind him. Tom and Lee . . . Lee and Tom. Her single gaze beheld the two of them, and Cara thought no woman ever could have been more torn.

"Tommy's missed you, too," she managed finally.

Lee took a few steps in her direction, his glance traveling about the room before landing squarely on her once more.

"This is quite a castle," he said. "Guard at the gate, butler at the door, the whole works. I can see why you've settled in."

"I haven't settled in."

Lee lifted a brow. "No?"

"No."

"Sure looks that way from Walking Dune."

She appeared to straighten, though she didn't move an inch beneath his piercing scrutiny. Lee was reminded of all the times she'd stood up to him, to the town . . . hell, to Lone Star.

"Cara Chastain," he murmured. "Community leader . . . champion of causes . . . crusader against the odds." He shook his head. "I never would have expected it of you, running like that."

Though spoken in that quiet drawl of his, the words cut. Cara's chin rose another notch.

"Maybe there's something in all of us that will run," she replied, "if given reason."

"Okay. What was your reason? Mitch Lincoln or me?"

The name sent the old chill shuddering over her. Cara's gaze shifted beyond Lee's shoulder.

"It was a lot of things," she said. "Me, you, the town. All of a sudden, everything seemed to be spinning out of control."

"So you turned your back on it all."

She met his eyes once more but said nothing.

"Even the mustangs," Lee added.

"I did *not* turn my back on the town or the mustangs. I've stayed in touch with Dahlia, and I intend to write the governor. I can do that just as well here as I could in Walking Dune."

"Excuse me. Then it seems I'm the only one you ran out on after all."

Though the low-pitched timber of his voice never changed, the look on his face spoke volumes of contained fury.

"I was afraid you'd see it that way," Cara said after a moment.

"How else could I see it?"

"I left you a letter."

"Thank you very much. I gather you didn't think it necessary to talk to me face-to-face."

"What good would it have done?"

"Some," Lee answered sternly. "It would have done some good."

The planes of his cheeks were bright with color, his brows furled over eyes flashing with accusation.

"I asked for your understanding," Cara said a bit vehemently.

"I'd like to give it, but you're asking me to understand an awful lot."

"Am I?"

"I'd say so."

She walked stiffly past, her hands clenched before her as he'd seen her do many a time. If Lee had to guess, he'd say they were bonded like sheet metal.

"Your letter was a little vague," he added. "What exactly is it you want me to understand?" After an excruciating moment, she turned to face him.

"That I'm not free."

The huskily spoken words echoed in Lee's ears. "You said that before," he commented. "But you never ran."

"Things are different now."

"Are they?"

"Of course they are. That night we . . . were together, you said it was time to take off my ring. That's not what you meant." Cara spread her palms. "You expect me to forget him, Lee, and I just . . . can't."

Lee's gaze dropped to her left hand, searching for and spotting the gold band on her finger. Bitterness closed in on him, clouding his vision until he could barely see.

"I thought you needed time," he muttered. "How is it you managed to make a decision and be on your way out of town by daybreak the next morning?"

"It was all the time I needed," Cara responded solemnly.

He released a quick laugh. "Not very complimentary."

"Don't be flip, Lee. This isn't easy for either of us."

"It isn't easy for me. That's for sure."

"I'm . . . sorry."

"Not half as sorry as I am, darlin'."

Cara stiffened. "You used that term once before and in the same sneering tone. I don't like it."

"Pardon me," Lee returned shortly.

"You know," she went on with a challenging look, "it was when Lone Star came to town that everything changed. Before that, Walking Dune was peaceful, content, safe . . . and so was I."

"Safe from what? Living life as any kind of normal woman?"

She stared at him a few long seconds, reminding Lee of a wounded doe, making him wish he could take back the words.

"Did you drive all this way to hurt me?" she asked. "Is that why you've come?"

"No. I . . ."

"Why *did* you come, then?" she demanded, her sharp tone stirring the coals of his anger.

"Looks like I came to say goodbye," Lee snapped.

That stopped her. It stopped them both. Suddenly the inevitability hung between them like an impassable curtain. Like the phantom of Tom Chastain, Lee thought.

"I'm leaving for Houston day after tomorrow," he added.

She'd walked out of his life weeks ago, and she'd known for days that he was going away. Still, it shook Cara to hear him say it.

"Nick told me you were leaving, but he didn't say for how long."

"There's no telling, not with this mustang issue up in the air."

Lee's gaze roamed her face—the high cheeks set off by upswept hair, the blue eyes regarding him so steadily from between lashes as dark as the slanted brows above them. Little by little, his temper drizzled away as he was engulfed with other feelings.

"You've really stirred things up, you know," he went on. "I never would have thought it possible, but I get the feeling that all of Lone Star is waiting to see what Cara Chastain will do next. If I were in charge, I'd can the whole thing. But I'm not . . . not yet anyway."

"Not yet?" Cara repeated with a note of surprise.

"Don't suppose I ever told you I'm practically locked in to succeed Frank Winston at Lone Star."

"What does that mean?"

"CEO. Chief executive officer. Considering the ambitions I told you about some weeks back, I guess you can see what an appointment like that would mean to me."

"Yes. I guess I can." Cara looked down, absently tracing the blue roses twining across the carpet, trying to digest the image of Lee as some high-powered executive sitting behind a desk thousands of miles away. Suddenly her eyes began to fill with ungovernable tears.

"So you'll be living in Houston permanently," she said.

"It's where I've lived the past fifteen years."

"I see," Cara acknowledged. The blue roses were blurring, drifting, swimming on a crimson tide. "But somehow I find it difficult to picture you anywhere but Walking Dune, doing anything but shouting orders from a platform."

The dejected tilt of her head made him long to reach out to her, touch her, hold her. Flipping back the open fronts of his jacket, Lee buried his hands in his pockets.

"It's tempting," he said. "The idea of staying in Walking Dune, making it my home."

She looked up slowly. Lee drew a long, heavy breath.

"But I can't do it," he added. "Not unless I have you. I'm in love with you, Cara."

The statement resounded in the quiet room, calling for a response she'd already said she couldn't give. She gazed at him speechlessly, her eyes wide and glistening, wanting but rejecting.

"I can see that makes no difference," Lee concluded.

"It makes a difference."

"Not enough."

A tear spilled down her cheek.

"Don't do that," he commanded.

"I can't help it." Cara swallowed hard but couldn't control the ache in her throat, nor the hot moisture flooding her lashes.

"You're special to me, Lee," she added, her voice whispering like a reed in the wind. "No matter what happens, you'll always be very special to me."

"Nice. But once again, not enough."

A second tear joined the first, slipping down her cheek in a shining path that caught the light from a nearby lamp. Lee couldn't stand the sight of her that way. Yanking his hands from his pockets, he took a few swift steps, captured her face in his fingers, and bent to her.

He'd had in mind only a brief kiss—hell, who knew what he'd had in mind?—but when her trembling lips parted, Lee found himself unable to break away . . . until he tasted the salt of her tears. Raising his head, he peered into the brimming eyes and caressed the wet cheeks with a parting stroke of his thumbs.

"Goodbye, Cara," he said, turning away before the words were fully out of his mouth.

He left her standing there in that damnable room with that damnable portrait and stalked through the foyer to find Abigail Chastain waiting at the door.

"Sorry to have interrupted your evening, Mrs. Chastain."

"Quite all right." She pulled open one of the double doors. "It was worth it to meet you. After all, we are comrades of a sort."

Lee stepped outside, paused, and glared over his shoulder, his explosive emotions finding a target he couldn't pass up.

"What the hell do you mean, lady?"

"Why, Mr. Powers, I've been trying to bring about their move from Walking Dune for years. It seems you've managed to accomplish the feat in a mere matter of months. My compliments, sir."

Before it fully registered on Lee that she must have eavesdropped on his exchange with Cara, Abigail Chastain had smiled sweetly and closed the door in his face.

The Jaguar shot through the gate as though it had been launched from a cannon. Parked by the curb in discreet shadow, Mitch merely settled back in his seat. There was no need to follow any farther. Mr. Powers had served his purpose.

Lighting up a cigarette, Mitch blew a long drag out the window. The Virginia night was brisk, the air stinging his cheeks as he sat alone in the darkness. He didn't give a damn; his brain was lit up with an idea that warmed him inside and out.

Mitch squinted as he took another look at the impressive gate, far beyond which loomed the massive shape of a mansion with lights in most of the windows. The engraved marker at the street said Chastain. Mitch rolled the name in his mind, savoring it the way he would a cool drink on a hot day. He'd seen the towering house in Walking Dune. Even so, he now realized, he'd thought of Cara only as Cara Malloy . . . until tonight.

Tonight he saw what she'd become. Cara Chastain of the Warrenton Chastains. She must be so damn rich. Mitch grinned. And Cara was *so good* at sharing.

He'd always known he'd cross paths with her again some day. It was inevitable. His fate was linked with hers. He'd just never realized how profitable the situation would prove.

Starting up the engine, Mitch cast a parting look at the iron bars closing off the Chastain drive. The place reminded him of a damn fortress; he had no thoughts of approaching her there. But that was okay. She'd left that old housekeeper of hers tending the house and shop in Walking Dune. Cara would return, and circumstances on the isolated Outer Banks island were much more conducive to the plan taking shape in his mind.

She'll be back, Mitch thought, pulling away from the curb. *One of these days, she'll be back.*

And after all, he had nothing but time.

On the sunny morning Lee was to leave for Houston, his mood was black, his thoughts stormy.

The crew was gone, having driven north the previous day and flown out of Norfolk International. Lee had postponed his flight a day, staying behind on the excuse of closing up the Fast Break. Now the water was turned off and the windows secured. His packed bags were in the car. There was nothing else to be done, but the closer the time came to lock the door and walk away, the more Lee recoiled from doing so.

Stepping out on the back porch, he welcomed the chill of the November morning, the sting of the salty breeze. The beach was deserted, beautiful—the sea oats waving above blinding white sand bordered by deep blue water. He could almost think it was the same as it had been four months ago, but for knowing that to the south, the villas he'd built for the ultra rich overlooked the same beach.

Dammit! He didn't want to leave, didn't want to turn in the Jaguar, didn't want to do anything that smacked of cutting his ties with Walking Dune. Finally he stalked inside to the phone. Frank answered his private line on the first ring.

"Who the thunder is it?"

"That's a nice way to greet somebody."

"Lee? Sorry. I just walked into the office, and the first thing I see are the proposed plans for that Alaska deal. What the hell's the matter with that division of yours? I wouldn't wish these houses on a pack of hound dogs!"

"Come on. I'll bet they're not that bad."

"They're not that good," Frank growled. "What's up with you? You're due back today, right?"

"I'm due back, but . . . I'm going to cancel my flight, Frank."

"Has something gone wrong?" came the quick demand.

"No. Everything's pinned down. I just want some time to myself. Maybe a month or so."

"What?!"

"You don't need me back in Houston right now, Frank."

"How the hell do *you* know?"

"Because I do," Lee said with a brief laugh.

"Didn't I just tell you these Alaska plans stink like manure on a hot day? I could use a hand—"

"I need a break, Frank. Don't give me a hard time about it."

Frank sank back in his chair and rubbed a hand across his brow. "Are you staying in Walking Dune?"

"No. I'd like to be footloose a while—keep the Jaguar, drive across country, take my time."

"Are you all right, son?"

"I'm fine," Lee answered. "Don't read something into this that isn't there. I'll see you in about a month, okay?"

Frank slowly replaced the receiver, eyeing the phone as though it were a dangerous snake poised to strike down all his plans. An instant later, he picked up the direct line to his secretary.

"Sophie? I want you to get me an Austin number. The name?"

Frank's gaze settled on the mirrorlike surface of his giant desk, seeing his own reflection and imagining Lee's in its place.

"Marilyn Powers," he replied decisively.

Dahlia hurried out of Wolf's Fabric and Notions, her bundle draped across her arms, the smile on her face as bright as the wintry sunset.

"See that you mind what I said, Dahlia Dunn!" Nettie called. "Hang it up the first instant you get home!"

She did, hanging it on the eave of her closet door, unveiling it as though it were a prized work of art. And so it was. Her mother's wedding dress was ivory satin with long sleeves and a sweetheart neck, the bodice patterned with seed pearls, the train stretching a full two gowns' lengths in back.

Dahlia had rescued it from the attic some weeks ago, viewing it with dismay after all the years of storage, fearing that the yellow cast was permanent. But Nettie had taken care of it. Dear Nettie! Now the satin shone like candlelight, and the pearls gleamed. All that remained was to take it in a little at the waist.

She couldn't wait until Nick saw it. He was in Virginia Beach, trading the damn station wagon, refusing to take her wedding gift to heart. Nick . . . the mere thought of him made her insides swell until she thought she'd burst.

Crossing to the dresser, Dahlia retrieved the engraved invitation she'd tucked in the edge of the mirror. She'd sent them out only yesterday, the first of December, a mere four weeks before the wedding date. She'd flouted etiquette on that point; wedding invitations should be received six weeks in advance. Nonetheless, she expected relatives and friends to turn out from miles away and had already cleared the dining table for the traditional display of gifts.

"Miss Dahlia Marie Dunn requests the honor of your presence . . ."

Dahlia caught her lip as she read the invitation. She'd thought a great deal about her parents in the past few weeks, and she thought of them now. They'd passed away years ago—Dad, while she was away at college, Mom shortly after she returned to Walking Dune. But the idea of getting married made Dahlia miss them with new intensity. As she raced around making arrangements for invitations and flowers, she thought how her mother would have preened; as she considered walking down the aisle, she thought how proud her father would have been.

Dahlia's eyes began to sting with the tearful emotions that tended to swamp her these days.

"For heaven's sake," she scolded herself. Replacing the invitation, she drew a decisive breath and shrugged into her jacket. There was one detail of the wedding she'd yet to confirm, and there was no time like the present.

The sun melted into the sound, December darkness falling on the coast with a swift, chilling hand. But as she drove along, Dahlia's warming smile returned with thoughts of the life that lay ahead—one of falling asleep in Nick's arms, waking up in Nick's arms. Turning down the familiar drive, she stopped in front of the old house, climbed out, and skipped the few steps to the door. Oblivious to the fact that everything about the place was dark, she rang the bell.

With a panicky look down the sloppy front of himself, which was no less dismal than the house, Louis crept cautiously to the door and peeped through the window. He jumped back when Dahlia's curious eyes appeared on the other side of the glass.

"Go away, Dahlia," he called. "I'm sick."

"I knew something was wrong. You haven't been around in weeks. In fact you haven't been yourself in months. What's the matter with you, Louis?"

He cringed as a truthful answer rolled through his mind. "Just the flu," he lied.

"Are you sure that's all it is?" Dahlia demanded.

"What do you mean?"

"You haven't had another visit from those goons, have you?"

"No. Listen, if you're worried about the money—"

"Money?" Dahlia laughed. "Who cares about money? Did you get your invitation?"

"What invitation?"

"You haven't gotten it yet. Well, then, you don't know. I have something to tell you, Louis. You won't believe it."

"What?"

"I'm getting married."

Of all the feelings that swamped Louis, the one he felt most urgently was loss. "Married?"

"On New Year's Eve. Me and Nick."

"You and Nick," he murmured.

"Aren't you happy for me?"

"Sure I am, kid."

Dahlia ran a finger along the old brick framing the window. On the other side was Louis, sweetheart of her childhood, prince of her girlhood dreams.

"I'd like you to give me away," she said.

Leaning back against the closed door between them, Louis closed his eyes—remembering Dahlia as a child chasing after him and Tom, a girl gazing at him from across a crowded room, a woman probing him with questioning eyes he could never answer.

"Give you away?" he repeated, thinking that the phrase had never been so appropriate. "I'd consider it an honor."

"All you have to do is escort me down the aisle of the church, and when the reverend asks who gives this woman, you say 'I do'."

"I think I can handle that."

"You'll have to wear a tux, of course, but it will be worth it. After the wedding the reception at the inn is likely to go on till sunup."

"Sounds like a good time."

Dahlia's brows drew together. "Are you sure you're all right, Louis? Open the door for a minute."

"No, really." Blinking back tears that came from nowhere, Louis peered into the dingy shadows that had become boundaries of life. "You've got no business coming in, risking the flu, especially now that you're a bride. I'll be in prime shape for the wedding. I promise."

"Okay," she answered slowly. "Are you sure I can't do something for you? Get something for you?"

Once again, Louis's eyes slammed shut. "Dahlia," he said, once he'd breathed the name, wondering if it had carried beyond the breadth of the door.

"Yes?" came her concerned voice.

"Nick Malloy's a damn lucky man," Louis answered, a tear seeping through his tightly closed lids to roll down his stubbled cheek.

Instead of four weeks, Lee took six, returning through nameless cowpoke towns to a Houston dressed in Christmas greenery and bustling with shoppers. The city was sleek and shining in the winter sunlight, and he felt no more connection to it than he had to any of the dozens he'd driven through in the past weeks. The feeling persisted even when he pulled into his space outside the apartment house.

Lee turned off the engine and glanced in the mirror. A creased, ten-gallon hat sat low on his brow, and the bottom half of his face was shadowed by a full beard. He'd let it grow since he hit the road. It seemed to suit his temperament. The apartment manager looked up as he walked in, then did a double take.

"May I help you, sir?" the foppish man asked, stepping from behind the elegant counter. "This is a security building. May I call someone for you?"

"No thanks, Jeffries."

"Why, Mr. Powers! I didn't recognize you. Welcome home."

Lee gave him a short smile. "Thanks. Everything all right?"

"Fine, sir. Your mail is just inside the door."

"Thanks again," Lee said, and on the way to the elevator mused that he must look worse than he thought.

The apartment was the same—clean, empty, seemingly uninhabited. The refrigerator was bare; a forgotten plant stood dead on the window sill. Collecting the mail, Lee sank down on the couch and began thumbing through the envelopes, stopping when he came across one postmarked Walking Dune. Tearing it open, he found a short note from Nick.

"I've tried calling," it said. "Don't you ever go home? Dahlia said yes. The wedding's on for New Year's Eve. I'm counting on you to be here, buddy. Give me a call."

Lee smiled at the scrawl, his hand rising to stroke his bristled chin. He was going back. Suddenly he felt like a shave.

Christmas Eve night it snowed in Warrenton, filling Tommy with excitement, though he still worried that Santa Claus might not know the way to his grandmother's house.

"Don't you worry," Cara smiled as she tucked him in. "Santa Claus knows everything. Besides, he used to leave toys here for your daddy when he was a little boy, you know."

Tommy's expression brightened at that. "Do you think Santa Claus remembers about the robot that walks and talks?

"I think Santa Claus is wonderful at remembering what good little boys ask for."

"I've been good, haven't I, Mom?"

Cara bent and kissed him on the cheek. "You've been very good."

"So do you think he'll bring the robot?"

"I'd bet my last nickel on it," she said and brought a smile to his face. With a light tousle of his hair, Cara rose, turned off the bedside lamp, and walked to the door.

"I love you, Mom."

She peered through the darkness where the glow of a night light haloed his hair. "I love you, too, sweetie." Wagging a finger, she added, "Now off to dreamland with you. The faster you go to sleep, the faster Santa Claus will get here."

Tommy turned swiftly on his side and pulled the covers up to his ears. Smiling as she thought of the three-foot robot she'd barely been able to fit under her bed, Cara pulled the door softly closed and started down the stairs.

The great house was beautiful with Christmas splendor, long strands of garland draping the staircase, a huge fir in the foyer sparkling with hundreds of tiny lights, and candles in the windows. Cara meandered toward the front doors and looked through the side pane. All was quiet, the Christmas feast having long since been cleared away, the servants returned home to their families. And outside, the hush of falling snow. On impulse, she opened the door and stepped out.

The night was freezing cold, the air biting and filled with the smell of snow. Hugging herself, Cara looked through frosty clouds of breath to gaze across the grounds. Blanketed in white, they gleamed in the muted light of the gray sky. It was very pretty, but as she stood there in the lee of the Chastain mansion, she yearned for the dunes and the sea. She'd never been away so long from Walking Dune, and missed it terribly. Even so, she didn't regret following the instinct that had made her leave.

Scared out of her wits by Mitch, shaken to the core by Lee . . . Looking back, Cara saw herself then as a jangled mess, not at all like her normal self. Time and distance had cleared her head.

The sighting of Mitch seemed long ago and hazy, almost like one of her dreams. Now she could think of him—even picture him—without the jabbing terror that had returned to her that day in the marsh. She hadn't exactly come around to Nick's way of thinking, but one thing was certain—the fear that once gripped her had ebbed. She hadn't had a nightmare in weeks.

As for Lee, she still thought of him, but the memories were not so sharp. Time had a way of chasing things into the shadows, and with each day of knowing he was halfway across the country, Cara's tempestuous feelings had calmed.

Coming to Warrenton was the right decision, she thought once again. Tommy had made new friends and had been given a chance to spend time with a grandmother who adored him and loved showing him off to all her friends at the museum, the symphony, the theater. Astonishingly enough, even her own relationship with Abigail seemed to have improved, though Cara was leery of putting much credence in the idea just yet. All in all, she and Tommy had enjoyed the stay in Warrenton more than she would have thought possible. But Cara knew he was just as excited as she to be returning home in a few days.

Nick and Dahlia's wedding was only a week away. Tommy was ring bearer, and she the matron of honor. The best man, Nick had informed her yesterday, was Lee Powers.

It had happened then, and now it happened once more—the thrill of the man fluttering through her, making Cara realize she'd been kidding herself these past weeks. With Lee so far away, it had been relatively easy to cram her feelings in a dark corner of her mind, block them off, tell herself he was gone—almost in the same irrevocable way as Tom.

But now she would be facing him in a matter of days. Now she felt the guilt-ridden excitement all over again—part of her longing to see Lee, another springing to crush the longing. It had been so since that day months ago in the book shop, and on this freezing Christmas Eve night, Cara saw that nothing had changed.

With a last shivering look at the snow, she went inside to the front closet and took out the dress she'd bought just the day before. The wedding was at seven and the reception at the inn scheduled to last into the night and double as a New Year's celebration. Since she was the only attendant, Dahlia had given her a free hand in selecting a bridesmaid's gown, but Cara had been unable to find anything and was beginning to get desperate—until yesterday when she spotted the dress in the shop window. Stripping off the garment cover, she walked across the foyer to the huge gilded mirror and held it up before her.

It was blue velvet, the shade nearly navy but with a royal sheen. Long-sleeved and high-necked, it fit close to the body until reaching the hipline, where it fell in full-skirted folds to the floor. Cara looked down and ran a caressing hand over the velvet, remembering how elegant it had made her feel when she tried it on, and how well it fit, which was lucky since she had no time for alterations.

"It's very pretty."

Her gaze darting back to the mirror, Cara saw that Abigail was standing some few feet behind her.

"Unfortunately," she added, "all I can think as I look at that dress is that you and Tommy are leaving. Must you go?"

Cara turned and rested the gown over her arm. "Nick is my brother. Of course we must go."

"Of course," Abigail mumbled, her troubled gaze dropping to the package in her hands, then rising slowly to the eyes of her daughter-in-law. "I'd like to say something to you, Carolina."

"Yes?"

"This isn't particularly easy to put into words. But I've done some thinking lately, and there are certain things in the past that I regret. I had no idea when you showed up here that . . . Well, whatever your motives, these have been some of the happiest weeks I can remember. Merry Christmas."

She handed over a small package wrapped in silver paper. Cara looked up with surprise.

"Thank you, Abigail. I'm afraid I haven't wrapped yours yet. I was thinking we'd exchange gifts tomorrow."

Abigail waved an uncaring hand. "Fiddle faddle. Go ahead. Open it. I'd like to see how it looks against that new gown of yours."

Beneath the silver paper was a black velvet box. Cara lifted the lid and withdrew a gold locket on a long, glimmering chain.

"It's lovely," she breathed. Laying it against the blue velvet, she added, "And it's perfect with the dress."

"I've put something inside."

Cara released the catch and opened the locket to find a smiling portrait of Tom, a miniature of one of her favorite pictures of him. She'd taken it herself six or seven years ago and given a print to Abigail. Cara's vision clouded as she traced the lines of his face.

"Now you can have him close to your heart."

Cara looked up with shining eyes. "He's always close to my heart, Abigail. You know that."

"Yes, child. I know that."

It was the closest thing to an endearment Cara had ever heard from Abigail's lips. For a split second, she almost thought they might embrace, but . . . that was too much after all. Each of them looked uncomfortably away.

"It's getting late," Cara said. "I suppose I'd better put these things away and start thinking like Santa Claus."

Abigail trailed behind her as Cara returned to the closet and hung up the gown.

"Do you think I might help?" she asked finally. "With Tommy's presents, I mean."

"Sure." Cara smiled. "You know, all he's been talking about for months is this walking, talking robot. Wait till you see it. The thing is at least three feet tall."

Whispering excitedly, the two of them climbed the stairs.

Clouds had hung over Houston all day, the temperature dipping into the forties as night fell. Now a cold rain pelted Lee as he ran for the apartment house, his progress impeded by the bulky package he was trying his best to shelter under his coat.

"Dammit," he muttered, hurrying through the glass doors and swiping at the raindrops spattering the ribbon. The woman at the shop had wrapped it special, in paper with pictures of horse-drawn sleighs and a voluminous red bow. Lee's frown eased as he saw the package was none the worse for wear.

Running a hand over his wet hair, he glanced around the lobby. It was deserted and quiet, except for the strains of piped-in Christmas carols, peacefully dim but for the lights on the tree by the elevator. On the way up Lee examined the gift once more, his sense of pleasure returning.

The construction set had been expensive, but it had hundreds of finely crafted pieces, the most intricate he'd ever seen. Tommy could create elaborate structures with arching windows, peaked roofs, even turrets. The only limit was the kid's imagination, and he had a vivid one. Shifting the package under one arm, Lee stepped off the elevator, unlocked the door, and let himself into the apartment, his thoughts still lingering on the boy.

"Pretty dismal, Lee."

Whirling around, he peered into the dark room and saw her rise from the armchair.

"No wreath. No tree. Where's your Christmas spirit?"

Lee fumbled behind himself for the switch. When light flooded the area, he squinted in disbelief.

"Marilyn?"

She strolled toward him, swinging her hips in the remembered way, smiling the remembered smile.

"What are you doing here?"

"Is that all you have to say after all this time?" she returned, arching a brow. "Don't I look pretty?"

Executing a graceful turn as she moved forward, Marilyn gave him the opportunity to view her slim figure in a suit of plum silk, her legs shown off by heels and a short skirt.

"You look great," Lee mumbled, noting that her fair hair was shorter, curlier, her face pretty as ever. "How the devil did you get in?"

She lifted polished fingertips from which dangled a silver key. "I never gave this back, remember?"

Lee rubbed his forehead, trying to pull his wits together. "This is quite a shock."

"I'd prefer you thought of it as a pleasant surprise."

"Where did you come from?"

"Austin. A couple of weeks ago."

"What the hell are you doing here?"

Marilyn stopped a few feet away, her eyes traveling the length of him. Rain glistened on his hair, which was still coal black, as was the gunfighter's moustache. A gaily wrapped package pulled aside the front of a long topcoat, beneath which he wore a dark turtleneck and jeans. His shoulders appeared just as broad, his body just as muscular and well-toned. And that sexy air? Only more intense. The old thrill overtook her. How had she ever walked away from this man?

"Who's the present for?" she replied, ignoring his question.

"A friend of mine." Setting the package aside, Lee shrugged out of his coat and tossed it on a chair, his expression still a mask of surprise.

"You look good, Lee."

Walking up to him, Marilyn looped her arms about his neck. "I think I'd forgotten just how good you can look."

Lee's hands found her waist, his eyes searching her face. "You mean you've moved back to Houston?"

"That's what I mean." Her gaze falling to his mouth, she lifted her own mouth invitingly.

Lee raised a hand, his fingers closing on her chin, gently halting her. "Why, Marilyn? Why now?"

"Must we talk?" she purred.

"I haven't seen you since you walked out of here," Lee answered huskily. "I'd like some answers."

"After a hello kiss."

He kissed her gently, his tongue barely teasing hers before he pulled away. "Okay?" he said.

"It'll do." Marilyn grinned. "For a start."

Lee smiled, although he reached up and disengaged her wrists. "Still as straightforward as ever, I see. So, how about some answers. Why are you here after all this time?"

"Would you believe that I simply missed you?"

Lee gave her a doubting look.

"Oh, all right." Marilyn sighed, taking a few steps away before she went on. "I suppose you should know. It was Frank."

"Frank?"

"You know he never forgave me. Not for leaving you, but for making you choose between Lone Star and me. I've come to know that he was terrified you might choose *me*. Anyway, a few weeks ago Frank tracked me down in Austin and offered me a job I couldn't refuse. All I had to do was move to Houston—into a luxury apartment of my own choosing, I might add—and be available should you decide you want to see me. Just my cup of tea, don't you know? Getting paid for having a good time."

"I don't understand," Lee muttered with a look of bewilderment.

"It's your dream come true. Frank wants you to succeed him as CEO—to head up one of the most powerful companies in the nation. But he's afraid your heart has wandered from Texas."

Pausing for a moment, Marilyn gave him a sexy smile. "I'm here to entice you back where you belong."

"I don't believe this," Lee rumbled with a frown. "You're telling me Frank is playing some kind of game with our lives, and you regard it as a joke?"

Her smile evaporated. "It isn't a joke, Lee. I was *glad* he called me, *glad* to have another chance. It's been almost six years, time enough to look at things from a distance, see them more clearly. I've learned something in the past six years. Love isn't something that comes along every day, or even every lifetime."

Her gaze danced between his dark eyes. "I made a mistake," she concluded softly.

"Mistake?" he echoed. "You call ending our lives together a *mistake?*"

"What do you feel, Lee?" Marilyn challenged. "Do you blame me, resent me . . . love me? What?"

Lee released a long shaky breath. "I don't blame you, Marilyn. I've known it was my fault all along. I couldn't expect you to wait around for me while I was gallavanting all over the country."

"It wouldn't be like that if you were CEO."

His eyes snapped to hers.

"It's what you've always wanted, isn't it?" she added.

"Yes," Lee responded slowly.

"Then what's the matter? You hardly look joyful."

"No. I guess I don't feel joyful."

"Why?" Marilyn demanded, a dawning look breaking across her face. "Frank was right," she breathed. "Your heart *has* wandered. Who is she?"

"It isn't just a she." Lee's grimace took on a wistful cast

as thoughts of Tommy and Cara whirled through his mind, followed by memories of Nick and Dahlia, Ned and Doc . . . the smell of pine permeating the tree-lined boardwalk . . . the way the sun shone through the sea oats on the dunes.

"It's a whole way of life," he added pensively.

"The Walking Dune way?"

Lee looked up abruptly. "What do you know about Walking Dune?"

"Frank mentioned—"

"Frank again!" Lee's expression softened along with his tone as he added, "The old man said it was another world. He was right. I've touched it, but it's slipping through my fingers."

"Things turn out the way they're supposed to," she said with a shrug. "Walking Dune may have its appeal, but it's not where you belong."

"How do you know, Marilyn? We haven't seen each other in six years. How can you know where I belong *or* what's best?"

"I know *you,* Lee. You wouldn't be happy stuck somewhere in the North Carolina boondocks."

Lee cocked a brow. "Maybe I've changed."

"Not that much."

"Would you still say that if I turned down Frank's offer?"

Marilyn gave him a shocked look. "Is that what you want to do?"

Lee ran his fingers through his hair. "I don't know what I want. With you showing up here out of the blue, I don't seem to be able to think very clearly."

Stepping smoothly forward, Marilyn lifted a hand to cup his jaw. "That's more like it," she said. "It's nice to know I can still blow your mind."

"It's blown, all right."

Her index finger strayed to his moustache, her nail tracing his upper lip. "I want to see you, Lee. I've wanted it for a long time. How about you? How do you feel?"

"I . . ." Lee's shoulders rose and fell as he tried to think. "All these years, I—"

"Shhh," she broke in, her finger lightly blocking his mouth. "Just think about it. Think about the good times we had, days

when we laughed in the sun, nights when we made love by
the light of the moon."

Her words performed their task. Lee's mind was flooded
with memories, her peachy gold body beneath him, atop him,
responding no more wildly to his touch than he responded
to hers.

"You'll find my number on the bedside table, Lee." With
a gentle caress of his chin, she walked past.

Dumbfounded, he turned and watched as she stopped by
the closet, retrieving a coat and handbag from its depths as
though it had never stopped being her own. She opened the
door and turned, the light from the hall silhouetting her shape
on the threshold.

"Merry Christmas," she said just before the door closed.

Long after she left, the scent of her perfume filled the
apartment.

The day after Christmas, Lee stormed into Frank's office.

"Sit down, Lee. Glad to see you."

"Sorry I can't say I'm glad to be here. What the hell's
gotten into you, Frank? I haven't really minded your match-
making up to now, but this time you've gone too far."

"Have I?"

"Damn right you have."

Frank leaned back in his chair. "You always cared a great
deal for Marilyn. I thought you'd be happy to see her."

"That's not the point. You're trying to manipulate me,
Frank."

"Only for your own good."

"Who the hell gave you the right to decide about my own
good?"

Frank folded his hands. "I look on you as a son, Lee. And
an heir. Don't begrudge an old man the impulse to safeguard
his son's future."

"And is mine in danger?" Lee demanded.

"I believe it is. Yes."

With an incredulous look, Lee opened his hands. "From
what?"

"Walking Dune."

"You don't know what you're talking about, Frank."

"You're going back in a few days, aren't you?"

"For a friend's wedding."

"And what else? Perhaps the chance to see Cara Chastain?"

Lee stared at the older man, unable to deny that the thought of seeing her again had him aching with anticipation.

Frank selected a letter from the pile of mail on his desk. "I just received an interesting note from the governor of North Carolina. It seems your Mrs. Chastain wrote to him some time around the first of the month. He's taking her proposal about the mustangs 'under serious advisement' and thought it 'appropriate' to let me know."

"So she did it," Lee muttered. "She said she would."

"Of course, I could sweeten the offer to the state. I'm sure that's what they expect. But I wonder about Cara Chastain. The governor writes that she's offered to meet with him in Raleigh. Just how far does she intend to go with this horse fight?"

"Pretty far, I'd say."

"Seems it's time for me to meet the lady head-on."

Lee took on a look of surprise. "You're going to Walking Dune?"

"Nope. Can't. I'm leaving for Alaska next week, and I've got too much to do. But she could come here. She could fly back with you from Walking Dune. I'll put the company jet at your disposal."

Lee considered the idea, surprise giving way to a fast-rising thrill. Time with her. A legitimate excuse for more time with her. He shouldn't feel so elated, but he did.

"What makes you think she'll do it?" he asked.

"Don't you have any influence with her?"

"Not much."

Frank leaned forward, resting his forearms on the desk as he gave Lee a piercing look. "Convince her. Tell her what she wants to hear. Tell her I'm thinking about pulling Lone Star out of Walking Dune."

Lee's brows shot up. "And are you?"

Frank smiled slyly. "Bring Cara Chastain back with you and find out."

Chapter Eleven

Cara turned the Wagoneer onto the seaside highway. It was December thirtieth, cold but clear as a bell. The afternoon sun was brilliant, lighting up the deserted road, warming the cab of the car, making one forget it was a brisk forty degrees outside.

"With a moo-moo here and a moo-moo there, a bow-wow here and a bow-wow there, a cluck-cluck here and a cluck-cluck there . . ."

Cara collapsed into laughter, and Tommy did the same. Glancing in his direction, she reached out and fondled his shoulder. The robot sat on his lap and had hardly been out of a clutching grasp since Tommy saw him Christmas morning.

"We're almost there, aren't we, Mom?" he asked.

Turning back to the road, Cara smiled. "Yep," she replied. "Almost there."

She slowed the car as they passed the timberland north of town, then downshifted to a crawl when they broached the fence. Both she and Tommy stared across the sunlit marsh.

"Lee's the one who finished building it, isn't he, Mom?" Tommy asked with a note of pride.

"He sure is. Oh, look, Tommy! There they are! The mustangs!"

"Where?"

Pulling onto the shoulder of the road, Cara stopped the car and pointed.

"Right there. See? In the meadowland near the trees." On impulse, she killed the engine. "Put on your jacket," she added. "Let's take a closer look."

Holding hands, they trotted across the highway, climbed down the bank, and moved to the fence. Tommy stepped up on the bottom rail and propped himself beside Cara, the two of them shading their eyes as they peered across the sunny expanse.

The mustangs were grazing some hundred yards away. Their winter coats were shaggy, but they looked fat and happy. Cara counted them—the stallion, the mares, and a dark colt nearly as tall as Star though half as broad. With a jolt of surprise, Cara realized it must be the foal Lee brought to Dahlia's that summer night.

"They're all there," she murmured. "Dahlia wasn't exaggerating. They're doing exceptionally well out here. If they can't roam free in safety, then I suppose this is the next best thing."

"Lee did a good job on the fence, didn't he, Mom?"

Once again noting the pride in his voice, Cara felt a thrill of it herself. "A very good job," she answered, running a hand over his shining hair. "Come on. Let's get going."

As they drove into town, Cara found she couldn't look at everything fast enough—the tree-lined street, the familiar buildings. She honked the horn and waved as she saw Nettie scurrying along the boardwalk, and again as Jacob stepped out of the post office. It was wonderful to be home.

The house was in perfect order. Elsa wouldn't have had it any other way. A trailing note that had been added to over a period of time was taped to the refrigerator—explaining the various meals that were tucked in the freezer, a listing of her sister's address and phone number (though Cara had had the same statistics the past four years), an agenda of her family's holiday plans, and so on.

"Merry Christmas and Happy New Year," the epistle concluded. "See you in February. Love, Elsa."

Cara turned as Tommy skipped into the kitchen.

"Can I go out on the beach, Mom?"

"Have you brought in all your presents?"

"Yes. They're up in my room."

"All right, then," Cara allowed. "But see that you don't go far!" she added as the door banged behind him.

Cara took her time unloading the luggage, reveling in the smell of the ocean, the bite of the salty air, not even minding when her legs began to complain after endless trips up and down the stairs. When she finished, she sank onto her bed, reached for the phone on the night table, and dialed the number of the inn.

"Is this the bride-to-be?" she asked when Dahlia answered.

"Cara! Are you back?"

"We're back," Cara answered, noting the noise in the background. "What's going on? Sounds like you're in the middle of a party over there."

"I guess we are," Dahlia agreed with a laugh. "People have been showing up all day, family from all over the Carolinas, friends from up and down the Banks. Nick is tending bar. I must say, he's making quite a hit. Instead of congratulating *him,* they're all telling me how lucky *I* am. Get your butt over here, girl, and take up for me."

Cara chuckled. "I do want to come by. I have a little something for you." The sudden thought of Lee slammed into her mind. "Who all did you say is there?" she added quickly.

"Family, friends. Some of them you've met, I'm sure. Oh—" Dahlia broke off in sudden understanding. "No. He's due tomorrow around noon. The word is he's being flown in on a company jet."

"I see. Well, I just wanted to make sure . . . you know . . . Forget it," Cara finished lamely. "I'll see you soon."

Lee's image flooded her mind. Tomorrow at noon. Steering her thoughts determinedly toward Dahlia, Cara rose from the bed and searched through the array of bags until she found the package wrapped in bridal white. She'd come across the peignoir in Warrenton, a beautiful, lacy thing with a sheer, lace-trimmed robe. Tucking the box under her arm, she went downstairs, passed through the parlor and glanced absently out the window.

And there it was—a blue sedan cruising slowly past the house.

Cara halted, chills erupting on her arms and racing over her body. The car passed from view within seconds, and for a moment she was unable to move. As soon as she could, Cara dashed to the door, fumbled with the lock, and lunged onto the porch, her panicked gaze sweeping the road and finding it empty. The car was gone without a trace, its only legacy the sense of danger pounding within her.

Tommy, she thought. *Tommy!*

Cara ran through the house, out the kitchen door, and all the way to the gazebo, spotting him a short distance away on the beach and feeling such relief that she grasped the railing for support.

"Tommy!" she called. "Come on! We're going to Dahlia's!"

Strapping him into the car with swift hands, Cara drove to the inn in record time.

The milling crowd inside the lodge was a comfort, as was the absolute joy radiating from Nick and Dahlia. Little by little, Cara's pounding heartbeat slowed, the feeling of fear receding in the face of their jubilance. The happy couple showed off the booty of silver and china and crystal displayed in the dining room, then made the rounds with introductions to family and friends who'd driven miles to attend the next day's nuptials.

"Never has the adage been more true," Dahlia joked. "There truly *is* no room in the inn."

An hour passed before Cara found the opportunity to draw her aside. Nick took charge of Tommy as they climbed the stairs to the privacy of Dahlia's room, where Cara exclaimed over the wedding gown hanging outside her closet, the train trailing across a length of cellophane.

"It's gorgeous," Cara murmured. "You're going to be breathtaking, Dahlia."

"Don't forget, you're going to help me dress tomorrow. First we have the rehearsal at two, then you pick up your dress and come over. I have a feeling my hands are going to be shaking so, I won't be able to fasten a single button."

"The indomitable Dahlia Dunn nervous?" Cara questioned with the lift of a brow. "I don't believe it."

"Are you kidding?" Dahlia countered. "I've never been so nervous in my life."

"It doesn't show. You just look very happy . . . very pretty . . . Come here, Dahlia."

They sat down on the bed, and Cara gave her the package.

"Cara," Dahlia murmured scoldingly, "you've already given us so much, a place setting of china, that lovely tablecloth—"

"This is just for you," Cara interrupted.

"All right, then." Tearing off the paper with swift fingers, Dahlia pulled out the lacy peignoir.

"It's beautiful!" she exclaimed. "I'll wear it tomorrow night."

"I hoped you might, or at least your first night on the *Virgin.*"

"You mean the *Mrs. Malloy.*"

"Oh, really?" Cara voiced with a smile.

"It was part of Nick's wedding present. When he brought the boat from Virginia Beach, he'd already changed the name."

"So you'll sail off into the sunset on New Year's Day."

"Um-hmmm. South down the waterway, maybe all the way to the Keys. Nick says we can go where we want, come back when we want." Dahlia's beaming expression settled into a soft smile. "I'm getting married to Nick. Sometimes I can't believe it's really happening. It's like a fairy tale."

"And they lived happily ever after," Cara supplied. Reaching out, she placed a light hand on Dahlia's. "I suppose you know there's no one in the world I'd rather have for a sister."

A sheen came to the lime green eyes. Clutching the peignoir over one arm, Dahlia leaned forward and gave Cara a hug with the other.

"Come on now," she said, backing away with a quick swipe at her lashes. "It won't do for the bride to have swollen eyes. Let's get back to the party."

"I think Tommy and I will head on home," Cara said. "I'd like to be there before dark."

"Why?" Dahlia asked curiously.

The thought of the blue sedan swept Cara's mind. "It's been a long day," she replied simply.

Downstairs they joined up with Nick and Tommy, and the four of them moved to the door.

"I guess I'll be seeing you later, Nick," Cara said, her passing glance stopping and returning when he gave her a puzzled look. "You *are* staying at the house, aren't you?"

Nick's cheeks turned a telltale red. "Well, no. I hadn't planned on it. I've kind of moved in . . . Why? Do you want me to?"

"No," she replied with a quick smile. "Of course not. I should have realized . . ." Cara stepped up to her brother and kissed him on the cheek. "Sleep well," she added with a wink for Dahlia.

She'd managed a graceful exit, but Cara couldn't control the sinking feeling that overtook her as she drove home, passing the Lone Star site where luxurious villas stood tall and empty, the deserted Fast Break that once had buzzed with activity.

Lee was gone. Elsa was gone. Nick was gone. And she'd seen a blue car on the road.

Cara tried to tell herself not to be ridiculous, but as she pulled into the familiar drive, the sense of alarm intensified. In direct contrast to her caution, as soon as she opened the door, Tommy bounded in and headed for the stairs. She almost called him back and then caught herself. What was she going to do? Tell him to wait outside while she looked under the beds?

Cara locked the door, double-checked it, and moved swiftly through the downstairs rooms, lighting every lamp she passed.

Ridiculous or not, the seaside house she'd always loved seemed suddenly isolated, vulnerable, almost sinister. And before the sun was fully down, she'd checked every nook and cranny in it.

Lee was packing when the bell rang. Tucking his shirt in his jeans as he walked through the apartment, he opened the door carelessly, then did a double take.

She was wearing a strapless black dress that clung all the way down to her ankles, except for a side split in the skirt that reached halfway up her thigh. Draped over her arm was the black cloak he'd given her some years back, and in her hand, a bottle of champagne.

"I hear you're leaving tomorrow," Marilyn said. "Thought maybe I could persuade you to toast the New Year with me tonight."

She followed him into the kitchen. Lee withdrew a couple of glasses from the cabinet, his gaze flicking over her.

"You're making quite a fashion statement tonight."

Marilyn smiled as she lifted her palms. "Do you like it?"

"Yeah," he said. "I like it."

Turning his attention to the champagne, Lee held the bottle over the sink and popped the cork. Marilyn laughed lightly as the bubbly liquid spewed and he hurried to catch it in the glasses. A moment later when they touched rims, she was still smiling. Lee would have had to be blind not to notice how lovely she was.

"Happy New Year," she said.

"Happy New Year," Lee repeated. As they drank, his memory darted back to the many New Year's nights he'd spent alone, often thinking of her, wondering where she was, how she was.

"So," he said, his gaze tracing the lines of the black gown. "Are you going to a party?"

"Only with you."

Lee took another drink. "How did you know I was leaving?" he asked.

"Frank, of course."

"Of course," Lee replied with a frown.

"Well, if I waited to hear from you, I wouldn't know a blasted thing, would I?"

Lee drained his glass, glancing away as he set it on the table.

"It's been six days, Lee. Why haven't you called?"

"I've been thinking."

"Exactly what have you been thinking?"

"I'm not sure. That's why I haven't called."

"It's not so complicated, Lee. Wouldn't you like to go out for a nice dinner with me? Drink some good wine? Have some good laughs?"

"Sounds great," Lee said with a brief smile. "But it wouldn't end up just for laughs, not with you and me."

"What's so bad about that?"

Stepping forward, Lee lifted a hand to cup her cheek. She leaned into the touch, her lashes drifting.

"You're a beautiful woman, Marilyn. Any man alive would desire you."

"Well, then," she murmured.

Lee withdrew his hand and tucked it in his pocket. "But there are a lot of things knocking around inside me. I don't think I'd be good for you right now."

She arched a brow. "You've always been better than good."

"I'm serious."

"I can see that." Stepping back, Marilyn leaned against the counter and gave him a sweeping look. "Tell me about her."

"Who?"

"Cara Chastain."

A muscle in his jaw twitched angrily. "Frank's really working overtime on this one."

"He says you're bringing her back with you."

"For business purposes. And there's no telling whether she'll come or not."

"How long have you been involved with her, Lee?"

"I'm not involved with her."

"But you want to be."

"What I want is an end to this discussion."

Taking a sip of champagne, Marilyn studied him over the rim of the glass. His cheeks were flushed, his eyes glittering. He was angry as hell—and frustrated. She knew the look. It came over him when he couldn't make things turn out the way he wanted.

"Let me tell you what *I* want," she said quietly. "You, Lee."

She paused for a moment as he glanced self-consciously away.

"I've thought it for years," Marilyn went on. "And I knew it for sure when I saw you the other night. What we have is special, the kind of thing other people only dream of."

"What we *had*, Marilyn. Past tense."

"We could have it again, if you gave us half a chance."

"I can't give us anything right now. That's what I'm trying to tell you."

The words hit hard. "Yes. I guess you are." Marilyn set her glass aside, a slow smile coming to her lips. "Well, *this* certainly didn't turn out the way I hoped."

"Look, Marilyn. I'm sorry—"

"Don't apologize, for God's sake. You'll make me feel even worse. Come on. See me to the door."

Handing him the cloak, she turned her back. Lee helped her on with the wrap, searching for something to say and coming up with nothing. On impulse, he bent and kissed the top of her head. Marilyn took a deep breath and stepped into the hall.

"Don't let that champagne go to waste," she said, turning to face him. "And don't get me wrong. I'm walking away for right now, not for good. You'll come to your senses one of these days."

"Will I?" Lee mumbled.

"She must really be something," Marilyn replied testily. "But then I'm not the type to give up until I'm soundly beaten."

Turning in a swirl of black, she sacheted to the elevator, pushed the button, and stepped in. Lee was still watching when she blew him a kiss just before the elevator doors closed.

He went back to his packing, memories of his ex-wife dancing through his mind. Marilyn looked good, damn good. But it wasn't long before her image dissolved into one of Cara—the way she'd looked the last time he saw her, with tears in her eyes.

The wedding was less than twenty-four hours away. By now, she must be out of that damn mansion in Warrenton and back in Walking Dune. Tomorrow night he, the best man, would be escorting her, the matron of honor, up the aisle of the old whitewashed church.

Had she thought about that? Lee wondered. Had she thought of him at all in the past two months?

Suddenly aware that he was staring into space, a stack of T-shirts in his hands, Lee stuffed them in the bag and grimaced.

Come to his senses? Not yet, apparently—for the vision of Cara stayed with him long after he stretched out on the bed and closed his eyes.

Moonlight filtered through the blinds in silver slivers. Cara came awake with a start, momentarily disoriented to find herself still in the rocking chair by Tommy's bed. Something had roused her, some sound that didn't fit with the groans of the old house, the moans of winter wind.

She shifted forward. The rocker creaked. Cursing it silently, Cara stared about the room, her ears pricked. All was as it should be—the shapes of dresser, shelves, and chest . . . the glow of the night light across the way. All was quiet, but for the rhythmic whisper of Tommy's breathing in the bed beside her. Stretching stiff legs before her, Cara yawned as she peered through the shadows at her toes.

That was when she noticed.

Beneath the door to Tommy's room was a strip of light—courtesy of the lamps she'd left on all over the house. But as she watched, the strip dimmed . . . and then dimmed again. Someone was turning off the lights. Someone was in the house.

Springing up in a fluid motion that drew nary a creak from the rocker, Cara crept to Tommy's bedroom door. It was still locked, still secure. She breathed a shallow sigh of relief—cut short as yet another light went off, and the room she was standing in grew infinitesimally darker.

Cara spun at the door, bracing her back against it, straining to hear the dreaded sound that finally came—footsteps moving up the stairs, halting at the top mere feet from Tommy's door. She stopped breathing, feeling the presence on the other side, picturing a man with flaming hair, narrow eyes, a slit for a mouth. She remembered that mouth, the lips so thin that when he grinned they disappeared. Cara broke out in a cold sweat, her fingers fanning on the surface of the door, nails digging into the wood. Such a barrier was nothing . . . not to Mitch.

The footsteps started up once more. She peered into the darkness, releasing her breath in a shuddering whisper as they moved past Tommy's room in the direction of the master chamber. Once again, her relief was short-lived. No sooner had the footsteps faded into the distance than they returned again. No doubt he'd looked in her room and found it empty.

Her blinded eyes spinning into focus, Cara scanned the room, little realizing that she was looking for a weapon until her gaze fell on something shiny at the foot of Tommy's bed.

The robot! He was made of hard silver plastic and weighed a considerable few pounds. If brandished smack in the face . . .

She didn't bother to complete the thought. Lunging for the thing, Cara propped it on her shoulder like a baseball bat and resumed her place by the door. No sooner had she looked at the knob than it began to turn. She tightened her grip on the robot's legs. The knob reversed its motion, turning counterclockwise, once again encountering the lock. It sprang back to position as if released by an impatient hand.

There was a shattering instant of stillness. Cara imagined the door bursting open and took a backward step, catching her lip in her teeth, listening for the horrific noise that would announce his crashing entry.

There was a soft knock and then, "Cara? Are you in there?"

Nick! In her haste to open the door, Cara forgot the robot. Rushing out of Tommy's room, she grabbed her brother in a one-armed hug. Nick slowly enfolded her.

"What's the matter?" he asked.

"I thought you were . . ." Cara began. Embracing the solid strength of Nick, she felt suddenly, scaldingly foolish.

"You thought I was what?"

"Never mind," she mumbled.

Backing out of the embrace, Nick cut his eyes to the robot. "Cute," he murmured with a smile.

Cara set the thing down and, leaning back, pulled Tommy's door closed. "What are you doing here, Nick?" she demanded quietly. "I thought you said you weren't coming tonight."

"Got kicked out," he replied unabashedly. "Dahlia started thinking about it, and all of a sudden it wasn't right that I should stay at the inn the night before the wedding."

Cara produced a shaky smile. "Unconventional, go-to-hell Dahlia. Who would have thought she'd become a victim of tradition?"

"I guess I can wait one more night. But not any more than that."

Cara's gaze danced between her brother's eyes, her thoughts briefly spirited away from a private state of alarm.

"Do you know how happy I am for you, Nick?"

He grinned. "Yeah. I know."

"Do you know how much I love you?" Cara added thickly.

There was a shifting sparkle in her eyes, something that looked like tears. Nick's grin faded.

"Are you all right, Cara?"

"Sure I am," she mustered. "Just a little nostalgic before the big day."

"Women," Nick murmured, his grin reappearing. "Okay if I bed down in my old room?"

He ambled away, and Cara watched him go—filled with the feelings of how much she loved him, how glad she was he was here, how strange it was that she should have been triggered into near hysteria by the sound of his footsteps.

It all stemmed back to the blue car. Had it been there? And even if it had, was Mitch inside it? Or . . .

Cara's fingers rose to massage her aching forehead. Was she losing her mind?

Lee sat up front with the pilot, a friendly guy named Pete who'd been flying for "Mr. Winston" the past ten years.

"Guess you're picking up a pretty bonus for this one," Lee said. "It being New Year's."

"Mr. Winston was generous about it, I must admit. Seems this flight is pretty important to him."

They landed at a private air strip a few miles north of Kitty Hawk. Nick was supposed to be waiting to drive him to Walking Dune. As the plane taxied down the runway, Lee spotted him standing across the field. The whirring sound of the plane wound to a standstill. Lee unstrapped himself and reached for his bag.

"What time tomorrow do you want me back?" Pete asked.

Lee considered the question. Either Cara would go along, or she wouldn't. If he couldn't talk her into it overnight, he wouldn't be able to talk her into it at all.

"How about twenty-four hours?"

"Right, boss. See you at noon."

Hoisting Tommy's Christmas present under one arm, his bag under the other, Lee descended the narrow steps off the jet, lengthening his stride as he crossed the distance to Nick.

"How's the groom?" Lee asked, shifting his bag so he could join Nick in a handshake.

"Great. I really appreciate your coming all this way."

"You and the redheaded terror getting married?" Lee returned with a smile. "I wouldn't miss it for the world."

When they arrived at the old sedentary lodge Lee remembered, he could scarcely recognize it. The drive was filled with vehicles, the place buzzing with wedding day activity, the foyer filled with well-wishers who called congratulations to the groom as Nick led the way up the stairs to a guest room set aside for Lee's use.

"Quite a crowd," Lee commented.

"Tell me about it." Nick opened the bedroom door. "I had to guard your room with my life."

"I didn't see the bride. Where is she?"

"In her room," Nick answered with a grin. "It seems the bride is taking all this very seriously. I'm not allowed to lay eyes on her today until she walks down the aisle."

Lee stashed his bag, hung up his tux, and he and Nick joined the downstairs crowd. The hour before they were due at the church for rehearsal raced by. The booming tones of an organ greeted them as they stepped into the sanctuary and moved down front to the altar.

The minister, a silver-haired man who introduced himself as Reverend Stowe, was waiting there . . . and Nettie Wolf, who was standing in for the bride. A few minutes after Lee and Nick arrived, Louis Talbot came in, though he kept a distance from the rest of the group as they waited for the last of the wedding party—Tommy and Cara.

Lee told himself to be calm, patient. But he couldn't help glancing toward the door every few minutes. When it finally swung open and they stepped inside, his heart seemed to leap.

"Sorry we're late, folks," she called from the back of the church. "I suppose we'd better get started."

Lee devoured the sight of her from a distance as everyone took their places. Slim jeans, a bulky fisherman knit sweater, her hair pulled up in a ponytail. Beautiful. His gaze shifted to Tommy, who waved happily. Lee raised an answering hand,

and as the rehearsal got underway he did his best to keep his eyes on the boy.

It hurt too much to look at Cara.

Assuming his position at the rear of the sanctuary, Louis offered Nettie Wolf his arm, his gaze settling on the back of Cara's head. Suddenly she turned.

"Hello, Louis," she said.

"Hello."

"It's been a long time. I'm glad to see you."

"It's good to see you, too," he replied hesitantly.

She smiled, and the sight of it speared Louis like a shaft of sunshine on a summer's day.

It had been a long time since Cara smiled at him, since the previous summer, in fact. Now as he gazed on her, he remembered odd disjointed images—the way she looked the first time he saw her, when Tom brought her home to Walking Dune . . . how she looked running along the roadside, her hair like a dark banner . . . how radiant she was when she smiled at Tommy, all soft and glowing. In that passing instant he thought of mornings in her kitchen, evenings on the beachfront deck, long hours talking, laughing, just passing the time. It seemed a lifetime ago.

The bridal march began, and she turned to face the front. Even so, Louis continued to feel the warmth of her smile.

God . . . he still loved her.

During the brief rehearsal, Lee glanced toward Cara a number of times. As she came down the aisle she gave him a fleeting smile, but since then hadn't so much as looked in his direction. In fact, she seemed dead set on giving her attention to everyone *but* him—the minister, Nick, Tommy, Nettie.

When the mock ceremony came to an end, however, she could avoid him no longer. The joyous notes of the recessional reverberated through the sanctuary. Nick started down the aisle with Nettie. Tommy followed. Stepping up, Lee offered her his arm.

"Hello, Cara."

Taking the arm he proffered, she looked up.

"Hello, Lee."

The rasping voice reached inside him as it always had. Lee met her eyes, felt the urge to clasp her to him as if there were no tomorrow, and looked abruptly away. Descending the few steps from the altar, they started up the aisle.

"I need to talk to you," he said.

"About what?"

"Business."

Lee glanced down and found her classic features a picture of curiosity. He slowed his step.

"I'm just the messenger boy," he added. "Actually, the proposition is from Frank Winston. He's inviting you to Houston and has put the company jet at your disposal."

Cara blinked. "He wants me to come to Houston? When?"

"Tomorrow."

"What in the world for?"

"A party."

The curiosity turned to skepticism.

"He *is* having a small get-together at his ranch," Lee went on. "And he *is* inviting you. Frank heard about your letter to the governor. It must have been a good one. It seems the governor is seriously considering your proposal."

"And Mr. Winston wants to talk to me about it?"

"Yes."

"Why in Houston? Why can't we just talk over the phone?"

"The matter is a little more complex than that, Cara. I told you once before, we're talking about millions. And Frank Winston isn't the type to make a multimillion-dollar decision without sizing up his adversary."

"I'm not his adversary."

"The hell you're not."

She looked wounded, as though he'd said something unexpected, something she hadn't known from the first moment they'd tilted swords over the mustangs.

"For God's sake, Cara," he said in a huff, "you're not stupid. This thing's been brewing for months, and now it's come to a showdown. It's you against Lone Star."

By the time they reached the back of the church, the others had moved outside. Letting the things Lee had said sink in, it took Cara a minute to realize they'd stopped walking and were standing intimately close, her hand still tucked in the crook of his arm. A sudden awareness of him flooded her, and she stepped away.

Lee's arm fell as she withdrew her hand. All it took to see how they were together was a moment alone, an instant of nearness. The fact that it wasn't enough stung him anew.

"If Mr. Winston wants to talk, why can't he come here?" she asked.

"He's leaving on an extended trip to Alaska and was hoping to settle this matter first. He told me to tell you he's considering pulling Lone Star out of Walking Dune."

Cara's face mirrored her surprise. "Well, I can't just pull up roots and take off on a moment's notice."

"Why not?" Lee challenged. "As I recall, you're pretty good at it."

Cara gave him a stunned look and turned on her heel. Frowning to himself, Lee followed her out of the church.

"Cara, wait."

He caught up to her as she walked down the front steps, staring straight ahead.

"I'm sorry, okay?" he said.

She looked up and their eyes met, the moment coming to a swift end as Tommy ran up and wrapped himself around Lee's leg in a bear hug. With a laugh Lee reached down and patted him on the back, dropping to one knee when Tommy backed off.

"I've got something for you, Tommy. A Christmas present I found in Houston."

"What is it?" the boy demanded eagerly.

"Well, now, you'll just have to open it up and find out."

"Can I open it now?"

Lee rose to his feet. "I'm afraid I didn't bring it with me. It's back at the inn."

"Oh." Tommy sighed.

"We're going to the inn in a little while, Tommy," Cara said. "Maybe you could open it then."

"Okay," the boy replied, his smile quickly returning. "Can I open it then, Lee? It's way past Christmas, you know."

Lee laughed again. "You're right about that. Sure, you can open it. As soon as you get to the inn."

Cara took Tommy by the hand. "That was sweet of you, Lee."

The easy smile he had for Tommy faded as Lee looked at her. "Don't mention it."

"Well, then," she said, beginning to turn. "I guess we'll see you at the inn."

"Guess so . . . and Cara."

She looked around, the vivid eyes lifting.

"Think about what I said," Lee concluded.

She said nothing, only regarded him silently for a moment before walking away with Tommy. Sometimes her eyes betrayed her feelings, but not this time. Lee had no inkling of what her decision would be, but if he had to lay odds at the moment, he'd say she wasn't going to budge an inch toward Houston.

Laden with bundles, Cara nudged her way through the bedroom door, closing it with a shove of her elbow.

"Have you got everything?" Dahlia chirped.

"Let's see—Tommy's tux, and pajamas for later. My dress, slip, hose, shoes, jewelry, makeup . . ."

Cara glanced up and laughed. Dahlia's eyes were wide as saucers.

"What's so funny?"

"You look as though you're about to be led to the guillotine instead of down the aisle. Relax, Dahlia. Everything's going to be fine. Take a few deep breaths."

Dahlia followed the advice, diligently inhaling and exhaling as Cara put aside her things, hanging her gown next to the ivory satin wedding dress.

"That helps," Dahlia murmured. "Show me your dress."

Cara unzipped the protective cover.

"I love it," Dahlia breathed. "It's perfect."

"Here's something else that might be perfect," Cara said. Retrieving her purse, she withdrew a small box, removed the pearl earrings, and held them up against Dahlia's gown.

"Something borrowed?" she questioned with a smile. "When I saw your dress yesterday, I thought these might do. I wore them on my wedding day."

The green eyes filled with tears.

"None of that, now," Cara scolded. "Let's get busy."

The hours flew. All that remained was for Dahlia to step into her gown when Cara called below for Tommy and helped him into his little-boy tuxedo, a miniature of the black-and-white formal wear Nick and Lee would be wearing.

"Hold still now," she instructed as she straightened Tommy's tie and stood back to look at him.

"Gorgeous," she pronounced. "Positively gorgeous."

"Guys aren't gorgeous, Mom," Tommy complained.

"No?"

"No. We're handsome."

"Oh, I see. Well, why don't you go downstairs and find your uncle, handsome one? I need some time to get dressed myself."

"Maybe I could play with the construction set Lee gave me!" he suggested buoyantly.

"For a few minutes," Cara replied. "As long as you don't get yourself wrinkled. Dahlia's cousin is going to drive us to the church, and we need to leave in fifteen minutes. No later."

"I've never had blocks like those before. It's a great Christmas present, isn't it, Mom?"

"Yes. From what you tell me, it is."

Tommy opened the door and turned.

"I like a Lee a lot," he said.

Cara looked up and met her son's eyes. "I know you do, Tommy." The door closed.

"So do I," she added in a murmur and, turning briskly away, reached for the blue velvet gown.

Pale sunlight streamed into the church through arched windows lining the north and south walls, filling the sanctuary with a glow enhanced by two tall stands of candelabra on the altar. Between them was a huge spray of long-stemmed scarlet roses, baby's breath, and palmy fronds of greenery.

Peeking through an inch-wide gap in the doorway, Cara saw that the pews were full, the guests nodding to each other and whispering respectfully against the organ music, a romantic ballad that ended as Cara watched. A moment of silence ensued before a side door opened and the men filed out, Reverend Stowe in long white robes, Nick and Lee

in their tuxedos—both tall and dark, strikingly handsome.
Taking their places to the right of the aisle, they turned and
faced the congregation.

The organist began the processional, a stirring prelude to
the bridal march that filled the sanctuary and sifted into the
foyer where the group of four waited.

Cara drew open the door and reached down to smooth
Tommy's hair. He didn't look up, his eyes glued to the ring
cushioned in the center of the frilly pillow he was holding.

"Be good, son."

"I will," he whispered.

With a slight turn, Cara glanced over her shoulder. Handsome in black-and-white formality, Louis had Dahlia's hand
anchored firmly in the crook of his arm. She still wore that
wide-eyed look, but was radiant.

"You're beautiful," Cara murmured. And indeed she was—
the slim figure perfect in the satin gown, the fiery curls tucked
under a pearl-studded veil.

Gaining a tremulous smile from the bride, Cara turned and
walked into the sanctuary at a reverent pace, her eyes on the
tall spray of roses ahead, her fingers tightening on the single
long-stemmed bud she carried.

For Lee time seemed to stop when Cara started down the
aisle. The light was soft, just enough to gleam on the raven
hair coiled on her head, the long velvet gown that shone
with the color of her eyes. Never had he seen anything more
stunning.

It seemed to be the consensus of the crowd. A hush fell on
the congregation, interrupted only when Tommy came down,
and a smiling murmur made the rounds. Following Tommy's
progression, the chords of the bridal march intervened, and
Dahlia made her entrance.

The bride was beautiful in white satin and lace, but . . .

As Louis Talbot brought Dahlia to stand beside Nick and
himself, Lee only had eyes for Cara.

"Dearly beloved, we are gathered together here in the sight
of God, and in the presence of these witnesses to join together
this man and this woman."

Dahlia had heard the words hundreds of times before, but as Reverend Stowe spoke them, they struck her as new and shocking.

But then everything at the moment struck her that way—the flicker of candles was particularly bright, the scent of roses amazingly pungent, the hushed sanctuary positively crackling with expectation. Beads of moisture broke out on her lip, her pulse racing like a runaway horse over which she'd lost control. Within her trembling grasp, the bridal bouquet began to shake.

"Nicholas, wilt thou have this woman to be thy wedded wife, to live together in the holy estate of matrimony? Wilt thou love her, comfort her, honor and keep her, in sickness and in health, and forsaking all others, keep thee only unto her, so long as you both shall live?"

"I will," Nick responded firmly.

Looking beyond Louis, Dahlia met Nick's gaze for the first time since arriving at the altar. He winked. . . .

And she was transported in time, back to the night of the meeting at the inn when he winked at her from across the table and later asked her to the charity dance. Even then she'd sensed her life was about to change. But as she peered into his deep blue eyes, Dahlia realized she hadn't known how much. How *could* she have known? Until Nick, she'd had no idea how a woman could love a man.

The shining emotion rose within her, stilling the shakiness of her limbs, quieting her nerves, overpowering all in a flood of serene happiness. She was so lucky . . . so wonderfully, miraculously lucky.

"Dahlia, wilt thou have this man to be thy wedded husband, to live together in the holy estate of matrimony? Wilt thou love him, comfort him, honor and keep him, in sickness and in health, and forsaking all others, keep thee only unto him, so long as you both shall live?"

"I sure will," came the clear, cocksure voice of the old Dahlia.

Nick gave her a dazzling smile as a chuckle rippled through the congregation.

"Who giveth this woman to be married to this man?"

"I do," Louis answered and, after pressing a kiss on Dahlia's cheek, retired to the front pew.

Cara followed his progress, catching Louis's eye and exchanging a brief smile with him before returning her gaze to the bride and groom, her eyes settling on her brother as he began repeating after the minister.

"I, Nick, take thee, Dahlia, to be my wedded wife, to have and to hold, from this day forward, for better, for worse, for richer, for poorer, in sickness and in health, to love and to cherish, till death us do part . . ."

Love and happiness welled up in Cara. As her brother spoke the beautiful promises, she thought of her own wedding and for a moment heard Tom's voice in Nick's. Ironically, at the same time, her gaze drifted to Lee, who was looking squarely at her, his dark eyes gleaming with more than candlelight.

You're beautiful, he mouthed silently.

You, too, she responded in the same way.

Lee smiled, and Cara found herself caught up in the sight of him, barely hearing Dahlia as she began her vows.

"I, Dahlia, take thee, Nick, to be my wedded husband, to have and to hold, from this day forward, for better, for worse . . ."

Some flashing movement beyond Lee drew Cara's gaze to the window. And there was a man, his palms pressed against the pane as he peered into the church. *Mitch!*

Cara went rigid, her fingers straightening spasmodically so that the forgotten rose fell to the floor. Even in the dim light of dusk, the red hair was unmistakable, as was the silhouette framed in the tall window. Though she couldn't make out his features, she sensed he was grinning.

"Here, Mom."

Cara glanced down with glazed eyes, scarcely seeing Tommy, scarcely realizing she reached out to take the rose he offered. When she looked back to the window, Mitch was gone.

The remainder of the ceremony passed in a haze. Nick and Dahlia exchanged rings, completed their vows, and knelt to receive the blessing. Cara performed her part with a numbness that seemed to slow her movements. Through it all she kept a covert watch on the window, which remained vacant of all but the dying winter light.

But Mitch had been there . . . hadn't he? A clammy hand of doubt clutched her, chilling Cara beneath the warmth of the velvet gown.

She had no way of knowing that another pair of eyes in the church had also fixed on that desolate window.

"The Lord bless you and keep you. The Lord make his face to shine upon you. The Lord lift up his countenance upon you, and give you peace. Amen."

Nick and Dahlia rose and turned.

"Ladies and gentlemen," Reverend Stowe announced, "allow me to present Mr. and Mrs. Nick Malloy."

There was a round of applause from the congregation as the organist launched a jubilant recessional.

Still feeling as though she were a great distance from everything taking place around her, Cara bent to arrange the train of Dahlia's gown, then gave Tommy his cue when the bridal couple had moved halfway up the aisle. Taking Lee's arm, she turned mechanically to face the onlookers.

"What's the matter with you?" he whispered as they started down the altar steps.

Cara glanced up.

"Halfway through the ceremony, your face turned white as a sheet," Lee added. "It still is."

Neglecting to reply, Cara looked ahead once more, her gaze traveling beyond Nick and Dahlia, through the foyer, and on to the door. Was Mitch out there? Watching from the shadows? Waiting for the moment to catch her alone? Part of her longed to dash out that door, scour the churchyard until she found him, and force him to confront her. Another part questioned her sanity.

Lee waited until they passed through the threshold at the rear of the sanctuary. Drawing her aside, he placed his hand over the fingers clutching his arm. They were cold as ice.

"What is it, Cara?"

She looked up quickly, as if startled—as though she'd been in another world.

"What the hell is wrong?" Lee added.

"Nothing," Cara replied, "except that I've decided."

"Decided about what?"

"Houston. When do we leave?"

"You mean you're going?" he asked with blatant surprise.

"As long as Tommy can come along, too."

"Done," Lee responded, his wondering eyes watching her produce a stiff smile as the crowd poured out of the church to engulf them.

By eleven o'clock, the Nags Head Pub was so crowded with New Year's Eve revelers that Mitch couldn't hear himself think. And he wanted to think. He wanted to savor every detail of Cara's expression of terror when she looked up and saw him at the window.

Tucking a few beers under his coat, he crossed the street to the motel. The night was cold and dark, a mere sliver of a moon overhead. Unlocking the door, Mitch stepped into the darkness of his room and flipped the light switch.

"Hello, Mitch."

The beers fell clattering to the floor as Mitch spun around, whipping the knife out of his boot and switching it open in one swift motion. In a matter of seconds, the blade was pointing squarely in the direction from which the voice had come.

"There's no need for that."

Squinting against the light, Mitch peered at the one chair the room had to offer. In it was a slick-looking stranger decked out in a tuxedo.

"How the hell did you get in here?" Mitch demanded.

"An obliging clerk."

"What do you want?"

"Not to rob you. Why don't you put the knife away?"

Mitch replaced the blade, though he continued to palm the weapon. "Do I know you?"

"Only through the mail," Louis replied slowly, his gaze racing over the man.

Mitch Lincoln was bigger than he'd expected, taller, heftier, though he moved with the speed of a lithe animal. The unruly mop of curling hair was bright red against a pale face, its spatter of freckles failing to lessen the severity of a sharp chin and nose, eyes so narrow Louis couldn't tell their color. If he had to picture the devil, he could do no better than the hard face before him. In that instant, Louis sensed the man had no scruples, no limits. Instinct whispered he'd been a fool to come. But he was here. All he could do was try and carry things off.

"Through the mail," Mitch repeated. "Are you saying what I think you're saying?"

Louis nodded.

"So, it's been you all along." Mitch gave him a swift once-over, gauging him as a rich dandy who'd never dirtied his hands with a fight in his life. Tucking the knife in his boot, he added, "I saw you tonight, didn't I? At the church in Walking Dune."

"That's why I'm here, to ask what you were doing at the church."

"Just looking around."

"I figured you would have left the Banks by now. Our business is completed."

Mitch shrugged. "You hired me to keep the lady's mind off those horses."

"It seems you did. She nearly ran out of town."

"But now she's back. What if she starts up where she left off?"

"If she does, she does," Louis said on a tired note.

"What's the matter, buddy? Lose your taste for the kill?"

Louis's expression turned sharp at that. "There was never to be any violence. I made that clear from the start. And now that our business is over, I'd like you to leave the Banks."

"You'd like me to leave the Banks," Mitch repeated with an unflattering chuckle. "Who the hell are you, anyway?"

"My name doesn't matter. What should be of interest to you is the final sum I'm prepared to offer if you agree to leave."

"Okay," Mitch surrendered. "I'm interested."

Rising out of the chair, Louis held up three one-hundred-dollar bills. "But I insist on having your word that you'll be on your way out of here by tomorrow."

"My word?" Mitch stifled a sneering laugh. "Sure. Why not? There's nothing to keep me in these parts."

Retrieving his overcoat from the back of the chair, Louis walked toward the door, slapping the bills in Mitch's ready palm as he passed.

"What is this, anyway?" Mitch called after him. "A little conscience money?"

Louis hesitated in the midst of stepping outside. "Maybe," he said without looking back. "Maybe it is."

The door closed, and Mitch stuffed the bills in his pocket. "Sucker," he muttered.

The reception was in full swing, the old banquet room of the lodge having been transformed into a flower-decked ballroom with a champagne fountain at one end, a nine-piece orchestra at the other, and a dance floor in between. At the moment the band was playing "In The Mood," a rousing tune from the forties full of blaring brass. In the center of a crowd of onlookers shouting encouragement, Nick whirled Dahlia in circles so that she threw back her head and laughed in delight.

Propped against the wall near the door to the entrance hall, Lee watched them and chuckled. No one in this crowd was feeling any pain. Champagne was flowing like water, and the noisy laughter swelled as the hands of a giant clock over the bandstand moved ever closer to the enchanted hour of midnight.

Lee glanced around the doorjamb to the deserted hors d'oeuvres tables. After the wedding a sizable portion of the congregation had converged on the lodge to a spread of chicken wings, Swedish meat balls, liver wrapped in bacon, and finger sandwiches of every description . . . not to mention the wedding cake, which had been eight elegant tiers standing five feet high on a table of honor.

Enough to feed two towns the size of Walking Dune, Lee had thought, though to his surprise most of the food had been consumed before the guests followed a beckoning call of trumpets to the ballroom. Now the crowd had thinned, but only to a small degree. The place was still filled with celebrants dedicated to toasting in the New Year with the bride and groom.

Lee checked the clock against his watch. 11:10. His left hand swung back to his side as he took a sip of champagne from the glass in his right. During the past few hours he'd mingled with the guests, meeting new people and reacquainting himself with friends he hadn't seen in months.

Ned: "Hey, Powers. How's the gun arm these days?"

Doc: "Good to see you, boy. Nice job finishing that fence at the north end . . ."

Miss Nettie: "It seems mighty quiet around here since you boys went back to Texas . . ."

Dahlia, following a swift kiss to his cheek: "Thank you for coming all this way, Lee. It means a lot to both of us . . ."

Lee was reflecting on the way he'd missed them all, the way his willful heart seemed to have sunk roots in Walking Dune despite his own internal warnings, when Jack Quincy approached.

"Good evening, Lee. I've been looking for a chance to speak with you. It's a matter of some importance."

"Oh?"

Leaning closer, Quincy took on a conspiratorial look.

"I tried to get some information from your company a month back. I was told you were incommunicado somewhere, and your boss was unavailable for comment on the Walking Dune project."

"Yes?" Lee replied absently, his gaze sifting through the crowd, searching for Cara, though she and Tommy had been conspicuously absent the past hour. Prior to their disappearance up the lodge stairs toward the bedrooms, Cara had kept her distance, chaperoning Tommy through the crowd, lavishing attendance on Nick and Dahlia, wearing the same frozen smile she'd dredged up just after the wedding. Something was wrong.

"Has something gone wrong?" Quincy asked.

Lee turned his head and focused on the shorter man. "What did you say?"

"I asked if something's gone wrong with the plans for the development here in Walking Dune."

"I guess you could put it that way."

"Well!" Jack blustered. "Forgive me for being bold, but I'd like to know if something's happened to jeopardize the future of this development. After all, I *am* the mayor."

Lee studied the flushed face. Of all the people he'd come to know in Walking Dune, Quincy was his least favorite—except maybe for Louis Talbot, who hadn't so much as shown his face at the wedding reception.

"Nothing new has happened, Mayor. The mustangs are on

state land. Lone Star wants the same land. If Phase Three folds, then I imagine Phase Two will follow suit."

"You mean the whole damn thing could come to an end?"

Losing interest, Lee glanced again across the crowd. "Who knows?" he tossed.

"This is worse than I thought."

"What's the matter with things as they are?" Lee asked. "Before Lone Star turned up, you were happy with Walking Dune as it was, weren't you?"

"Before I knew what it *could* be!" Jack's face went dark with the disappointment of shattered dreams.

"Damn those horses," he muttered. "And damn Cara Chastain for putting everyone's future at the mercy of theirs."

Lee's head swiveled, his gaze and mind suddenly sharp. For a few seconds, he merely peered at the irritating man, telling himself to back off, to bite his tongue. He lost the battle.

"Listen to me, you greedy little bastard," he said ultimately. "What Walking Dune is—as it is—is a hell of a lot better than what you're giving it credit for. Don't you have any idea how special it is? Don't you have any regrets at turning it into just another playground for the idle rich?"

"None whatever," Jack Quincy snapped and, moving briskly away, merged with the crowd.

"Jerk," Lee muttered under his breath. Checking his watch again, he saw that it was eleven-twenty. He started to raise the champagne glass to his mouth, then stalled as he glanced aside and saw Cara.

She was standing in the entrance to the ballroom—her typical, regal self—though somehow when Lee looked at her, he thought of a richly gowned waif, her eyes dazed and searching, her arms filled with the shape of a sleeping child. Setting his glass on the floor, he stepped swiftly forward.

"Let me take him," he said, extending his hands.

The wide eyes turned to him, swallowed him.

"Thank you, Lee," Cara murmured, surrendering her son to his strong arms. "Please, may I ask you two favors? Could you drive us home? And . . . could you stay with us tonight?"

*   *   *

Leading the way to Tommy's room, Cara turned down the covers and waited as Lee deposited him gently on the bed. They tucked him in together.

"Night, Mom. Night, Lee," Tommy mumbled sleepily.

Their eyes met across the bed. Turning away, Cara bent to kiss Tommy and left the room. When Lee came down the stairs a moment later, he found her at the hall closet.

"I think Nick and Dahlia were a little disappointed we didn't stay until midnight," he commented as she reached up to the shelf.

"They seemed okay about it when we said we'd stop by and wish them bon voyage tomorrow."

Lee watched silently as she unloaded a Christmas wreath, picnic basket, a stack of mufflers and caps . . .

"What the devil are you doing?" he asked when he could no longer contain his curiosity.

Rising on tiptoe, Cara felt to the back of the shelf, her fingers coming upon a wooden case. "Here it is."

"Here *what* is?"

Cradling it cautiously in both hands, as though it might leap out of her grasp at any moment, Cara stared down at the box. "I was always against having this in the house, but somehow, after Tom died, I couldn't bring myself to give it away."

"Looks like a fancy pistol case," Lee observed.

Cara released the latch, lifting the walnut lid to reveal an ivory-handled pistol resting against red velvet. In two dozen notches lining the oblong box were a collection of bullets, only two of which were missing.

"This belonged to the judge," she said. "Tom's father."

Lee reached out and picked up the weapon, weighing it in his palm before shifting it to a ready position.

"Forty-five Colt single-action revolver," he murmured. "Very expensive nowadays. They say there's nothing better than a Colt."

"Looks like I'm talking to the right man."

"Right man for what?"

"Teach me, Lee. Teach me how to shoot."

"To shoot?" he repeated incredulously. "What's happening, Cara? First you ask me to stay over. Now you want me to teach you to shoot. What the hell's going on?"

"I don't want to tell you."

"Why not?"

"Because I know what you'll think."

"What will I think?"

"That I'm imagining things."

Lee studied her closely. "Is this about Mitch Lincoln?"

Cara's chin went up.

"Is it?" Lee demanded.

"I saw him tonight."

"Where?"

"At the church."

"He was at the wedding?"

Cara shook her head. "Outside the church. One minute he was there, watching through the window. The next, he was gone."

A look of dawning broke across Lee's face. "And that's when you looked as though you'd seen a ghost."

"I suppose so."

"Cara, it was dark," Lee said gently. "Are you sure?"

"I knew you'd ask me that. I'm aware of what you think, Lee. You and Nick. But if I've come to any conclusion tonight, it's that I have to proceed according to what *I* think. Now, will you teach me to handle the damn gun?"

Her voice never rose, but Lee had seen that look of determination before. It was a welcome break from the trancelike expression she'd worn all night.

"Okay," he agreed finally. "This is a fairly heavy pistol. Here. Feel the weight."

Twirling it expertly around his finger, Lee offered it to her, handle first. Cara regarded him for a moment. Despite the formal tuxedo, he looked for all the world like a gunslinger. It wasn't the first time she'd thought of him that way.

"Take it," Lee prodded. "You can't learn to handle it without handling it. Or have you changed your mind?"

Cara took the thing briskly from his hand, surprised at its weight, though he'd warned her.

"If you're going to have a gun around," Lee went on, "you should know everything you can about it. The range on that pistol is somewhere between fifty and seventy-five feet. It's single-action, which means you have to cock the hammer manually each time before pulling the trigger. And it's a .45, which means it fires .45 caliber bullets. The loading gate is on the side. Go ahead. Open it up."

Cara turned the thing gingerly in her hand, keeping the barrel carefully pointed away as she looked for what he described, found it, and unlatched it.

"That's right. Now, roll the cylinder. Hear the clicks?" Reaching into the box, Lee withdrew a bullet and handed it to her. "When a hole comes up in the gate, you load the bullet. Try it."

Cara slipped the bullet in the slot.

"Turn the chamber until you hear the click. Okay. Now you've got one round in the chamber. It will accommodate six, but it's a good safety precaution to load only five. A pistol with a full chamber could misfire if the hammer were dropped. Always leave the one under the hammer empty. So that leaves you with five rounds, right? After all five have been fired, the spent cartridges, or brass, have to be removed the same way they were loaded. Open the gate, and bring them out one at a time. Any questions?"

"No," Cara murmured, staring at the pistol as if mesmerized.

"Okay, then. Take the bullet out, and I'll show you the stance."

"Take it out?"

Lee raised a brow. "You're not planning on shooting anyone tonight, I presume?"

They moved to the head of the hall where Lee positioned her in front of him, facing her toward the study.

"That doorway down there is your target. Plant your feet a shoulder's width apart, evenly distributing your weight. You're right-handed?"

Cara nodded.

"Okay. Holding the pistol in your right hand, fold your left on top of it around the handle. Good. Now, raise your arms, keeping your elbows straight, and point the barrel at the target."

Taking a step closer, Lee reached around her and lightly grasped her wrists, lowering her aim by a few inches.

"Straight like this," he said, "your arms forming an isosceles triangle with your body. Now, lift your left hand and cock the hammer . . . Okay, grip the handle again. Looking straight at what you want to hit, squeeze the trigger. Don't pull or yank it. Squeeze it."

Click! The hammer closed down with a sharp smack.

"Good," Lee pronounced. "Now, to fire again, you have to cock the hammer again."

Cara repeated the procedure, then once again with more speed.

"Now, don't go thinking you're Billy the Kid or somebody," Lee said. "It takes a while to learn how to fan a hammer."

His arms remained around her, his hands supplying a support she didn't need as Cara squeezed off a few more mock shots. Lee closed his eyes as the scent of her filled his head, the nearness of her firing his blood.

"That's all there is to it," he murmured.

"It doesn't seem so hard, after all," she replied in a similar breathy tone.

"You can't really know what it's like to shoot until you've fired a live round, Cara. We'll be going to Frank's ranch tomorrow, and he has a shooting range. If you're serious about this, we could take some target practice."

"I'm serious."

"So am I," Lee said, his palms traveling up the velvet sleeves to her shoulders. He thought he heard Cara catch her breath as his hands continued down her sides, his fingers brushing the swell of her breasts before closing on her waist.

His touch was at once gentle and provocative, drawing the strength from Cara's arms so that they drifted slowly down, the pistol dangling from listless hands. He wrapped his arms around her and pressed close, the warmth of his body sifting through the back of her gown, his breath stirring her hair.

It felt so good to lean on him. Cara couldn't bring herself to break away. Resting her head against Lee's shoulder, she absorbed the strength of him, the feel of him. And at that moment the grandfather clock began chiming the hour of midnight. Turning her head, she glanced up.

"Happy—" The single word was all that passed her lips before his mouth covered hers.

Shifting around, Lee gathered her close, holding her tightly, desperately, as he went on kissing her. He'd wanted her so long, and as Cara kissed him back with passion, he lost his senses. All he could hear was the thunder of racing blood; all he could feel was an aching need that pounded from the very core of him. He shifted a hand to the back of her head, holding her steady as his mouth slanted across hers. He wasn't even aware of the arm that slipped down to her hips and drew her urgently against him.

With a swift turn of her head, Cara tore her mouth away. "Please, Lee," she mumbled breathlessly.

Just as swiftly, he pulled her back to face him. "Please what?"

"We've got to stop."

"Why?"

"Because we're getting carried away."

"I don't call that a reason to stop," Lee said, his voice uncontrollably ragged. "I want to make love to you, Cara. I *need* to make love to you."

She shook her head. "No. We shouldn't—"

"We *should!*" he thundered, jerking away and glaring down at her. "Dammit, Cara! Doesn't it make any difference at all that I love you?"

Lee endured her silent, shimmering stare as long as he could.

"Stay out of my range, then," he ordered, and stalked off toward the bar in the study.

Chapter Twelve

The first day of the year was cool and clear, but for billowing mountains of white clouds that only made the Texas sky seem bluer.

Marilyn stood on the porch of the ranch house, staring across the lawn milling with party guests, beyond the fenced-in pasture where horses grazed, on to the open acres of mesquite-covered plain. It was a beautiful panorama, but she had no eye for it. Her thoughts were locked in the memory of that disappointing night.

Once again she saw herself showing up in the sexy black gown. Once again she saw Lee's haunted face, heard his stern refusal. It had been a rude awakening. Despite the fact that she'd ended the marriage—or perhaps *because* she'd ended it—Marilyn had always thought of herself as his one true love . . . always pictured him longing for her . . . believed no woman could take her place.

In one telling stroke, Lee had proved her wrong. She'd stood right in front of him, champagne in hand, invitation in her eyes. And from thousands of miles away, Cara Chastain had maintained a hold she couldn't break.

Now Lee was bringing her here. At any moment the Jaguar could appear in the drive. The anticipation was making Marilyn crazy.

She checked her watch. Two-thirty. She'd arrived at noon, the first of fifty or so guests now congregated in front of the house. The "small New Year's get-together" Frank had described had turned out to be a lavish barbecue catered by Houston's finest. The lawns, a rich green from winter rain, were dotted with white tea tables and chairs. And banking the party area, a striped cabana presided over tables laden with brisket and links, chicken and ribs, as well as a fully stocked bar. A Mexican string ballad lilted on the air, courtesy of a trio of troubadours strolling among the guests.

Marilyn's gaze drifted through the crowd, a wealthy crew adorned in leathers and jeans, boots and hats—a style reminiscent of the rugged Old West that now cost thousands in stylish shops. She was a bit overdressed in the emerald suede suit. But the slim pants and jacket showed off her figure, the shade did wonders for her coloring, and today she wanted to look her best.

Spotting Frank in the center of a group of guests across the way, Marilyn felt a flash of irritation. His crop of snowy hair shone as he threw back his head and laughed, as though he hadn't a care in the world. Her own nerves were tied in knots at the thought of what the afternoon might hold in store. It could very well mark a turning point in Lee's life. Would he stay in Texas or return to North Carolina? Frank knew the question hung over them like a cloud. Was he such an adept actor? Or didn't he care as much as she'd thought?

Turning away, Marilyn went inside the house. A short while later, Frank wandered in and found her checking her makeup in the hall mirror.

"You look fine, Marilyn," he said. "Stop primping."

"I have to do something."

"Why don't you go outside? Mingle. Have a good time."

Marilyn turned to face him. "You must be joking," she said. "It's nearly three o'clock. Where the devil are they?"

"They'll be here," Frank returned placidly. "They were going to see the newlyweds off on their honeymoon and meet up with Pete sometime after noon. The flight takes several hours, the drive out here at least an hour. They couldn't have arrived by now if they'd sprouted wings. Relax, Marilyn."

"Relax?" she questioned with a tight smile. "Obviously I'm taking this thing a lot more seriously than you."

The bushy, salt-and-pepper brows drew together in a forbidding line. "I'm taking it seriously," Frank uttered in a

rumbling tone. "I've thought everything through, noted every
detail, every nuance. Like this morning, for instance, when
Lee called. He was short-tempered and sharp-tongued. Something's wrong, and I'll wager it's the Widow Chastain. He was
the same way when *you* walked out on him."

Marilyn's gaze moved between the frowning eyes. "Don't
rub it in, Frank," she said eventually. "Just . . . don't rub it
in."

Approaching Houston, the jet descended to an altitude
affording a view of the city. In the compact but luxurious
passenger compartment, Cara was sitting behind Lee, who
had Tommy on his lap by the window.

"Wow! It's big!" Tommy exclaimed.

"Kind of pretty, too, isn't it?" Lee asked.

Glancing out, Cara had to agree. The big city wasn't her
cup of tea, but she had to admire the sight below. Patches
of green were crisscrossed with white roadways. Monumental
buildings reflected the sun.

"Look, Tommy," Lee went on, pressing a finger to the glass.
"There's the Astrodome where the big games are played—
football, baseball, all kinds of things. It's huge. Some of
the players call it the 'House of Pain.' And there's Transco
Tower. See? It's the really tall building of black glass."

As she listened, Cara experienced the warm feeling that had
sprung to being that first day she saw them laughing together
on the beach. But soon the preoccupation that had gripped her
hours ago took over. Lee and Tommy's voices faded into the
background as she retreated once more to private reflection.

It seemed no one could stand between her and Mitch.
Despite Lee's protective presence in the house the previous
night, she'd had a nightmare—one that broke the pattern, for
rather than replaying the past, it previewed things to come.

In the dream, she was standing in the hallway when Mitch
opened the front door with ease, as though it hadn't been
securely locked against him. He swaggered up to her, Cara
raised the pistol, and he laughed in her face.

She'd wakened with that laughter ringing in her ears, and
something inside her snapped. Rising at dawn, she'd paced the
room, peering out the window overlooking the road, searching

for a blue sedan. He was out there somewhere. She knew it—
knew it in the way a hare sensed a mountain lion hiding in
the trees.

Why had she questioned herself the past months, crippled
herself with doubts that went against her most basic instincts?
Lee and Nick would think her crazier than they already did if
she told them she and Mitch were connected. But it was true.
Cara could feel his presence; sometimes she could feel him
thinking of her. For years it had been like being caged with
a demon.

Gradually, miraculously, as she walked to and fro, to and
fro, the old pounding fears stilled in a blanketing sense of
purpose. Mitch came to her dreams whenever he wanted,
terrorized her whenever he wanted, and . . . it was going to
end.

Once made, the realization seemed so simple, like a corner
that merely needed turning. Cara made herself recall the
worst—the blackness of the mine shaft, the smell of Mitch's
breath as he grabbed her, even the feel of his flesh ripping hers
apart. None of the memories managed to start up the pounding
again, though they stoked a consuming blaze of hate.

She was out of the cage—free—and all by the grace of her
own will. So simple. So profound.

Lee said it had come to a showdown between her and Lone
Star. Cara knew a more primal one was brewing. Mitch would
come for her—next week, next month. Reaching for the purse
in her lap, she felt the unfamiliar weight of the pistol within it
and fancied herself a warrior preparing for battle. For the first
time since the age of sixteen, she welcomed the fight.

The plane landed, interrupting Cara's thoughts, but not the
feeling of grim serenity that enveloped her.

Insisting on carrying all their bags, Lee escorted them
through the busy airport and into the bright chill of the Houston
afternoon. Tommy, who was having a great adventure, broke
into a run as they approached the parking lot and he spotted
the Jaguar.

"I *always* wanted to ride in your car, Lee!" he called out.

"Did you, now?" Lee asked with a smile. Loading the luggage in the trunk, he opened the passenger door and pulled
the seat forward. "You'll have to sit back here, Tommy.

I'm afraid there's not much room. Actually, the car is built for two."

As Tommy scrambled in, Lee's attention settled on Cara. She met his gaze. It was the first time that day they'd really looked at each other, and Cara could see how angry and disappointed he still was. It showed clearly in his black eyes as he silently offered a hand and helped her into the low-slung sports car.

They drove away from the airport, and Lee resumed the role of tour guide, pointing out a variety of landmarks to Tommy's eager eyes. "And there's the Lone Star building," he said ultimately.

This time it was Cara who turned to look. Tall and impressive, its glass walls mirroring the city, the Lone Star Partners building was bigger than she would have expected. So, Lee would be head of all that. As they drove past, Cara traced his profile from beneath discreetly lowered lids, remembering the way he looked on the site in Walking Dune, imagining him in the penthouse atop all that shining glass . . . feeling the unmistakable ache of loss.

As they left the downtown area behind, Tommy pivoted to peer out the rear window. The three occupants settled into silence.

"Where are we going?" Cara asked after a few minutes.

"My place," Lee replied. Glancing aside, he noted her look of surprise. "I thought you might like to catch your breath before we head on to Frank's."

"That's a nice thought, but actually I'd prefer to find a place, check in . . . you know."

Lee flicked a piercing look her way. "I've got plenty of room. Since it's just for one night, I planned on you staying with me."

"I don't think that's a good idea, Lee."

"Why doesn't that surprise me?"

They drove on in silence. After a few minutes Lee turned on the radio and glanced in the rearview mirror to make sure Tommy was still peering out the back.

"Rest your mind, Cara," he then said, his voice low against the music. "You'd be perfectly safe. Believe me, you've made it perfectly clear you don't want me to touch you."

She glanced down at her clenched hands. "Even so, I think it would be more appropriate—"

"A hotel, then?" Lee cut in.

"Yes," Cara confirmed, her gaze still on her lap. "A hotel."

"The Ritz-Carlton is on the West Side not far from my place."

"Fine."

"Fine," Lee snapped.

Perhaps if he hadn't been so tall it would have seemed less like a dark, silent mountain sat beside her.

It was after five o'clock. Many of the party guests had taken their leave and headed home to prepare for the supper hour. Marilyn sat alone at one of the lawn tables, watching the front drive and growing more impatient by the minute.

Where the devil are they? she wondered for the hundredth time. She'd barely completed the thought when the Jaguar rolled to a stop directly across from her.

Marilyn straightened in her chair as Lee climbed out and then pushed the seat forward to help a fair-haired boy. The passenger door opened, and a woman emerged. Marilyn's gaze closed on her as she moved around the front of the car.

She was tall and shapely, dressed casually in jeans, a white turtleneck, and tweed jacket . . . though the way she carried herself evoked an impression of formality. The dark hair curling about her shoulders was black as a raven's wing and gleaming in the sun. Even from a distance Marilyn could make out a face with high cheekbones and dark, slanting brows.

"Oh, shit," she muttered. Rising from the chair, she walked gracefully across the lawn to meet them, noting that Lee halted in midstride as he saw her.

"What the hell are you doing here?" he mumbled as she stepped up to them.

"Don't be rude, Lee," Marilyn drawled sweetly. "Introduce me."

"Cara Chastain," he succumbed slowly. "Allow me to present Marilyn Powers."

"Marilyn . . . Powers," Cara repeated slowly as she met the woman's extended hand. "How do you do? This is my son, Tommy."

"Hello there," Marilyn greeted.

"Hello," Tommy replied with a puzzled look. "Did you know you've got the same last name as Lee?"

"Yes," Marilyn answered with a laugh. "I guess I do, don't I?"

Lee cleared his throat. "Excuse me for a minute. I'll see if I can find Frank."

With that, he strode off in the direction of the house.

"Poor Lee," Marilyn murmured, looking after him. "In terms of business, he's one of the best diplomats around. But in his personal life? I'm afraid he never *was* very good with confrontations."

"Is there going to be a confrontation?" Cara asked.

Turning back, Marilyn met eyes so deep a blue they seemed to leap from the sun-burnished face—the kind of eyes that haunted a man.

"I imagine so." The longer Marilyn studied her, the more beautiful she became. "So, you're Cara," she added.

The blonde had reminded Cara instantly of Sandy Cook, though Marilyn Powers was prettier—the perfect features framed by perfect hair, the slim figure shown off in a stylish suit. There was an air of class about her, as well as an unmistakable flair for directness. Cara met her steady gaze.

"So, you're Marilyn," she replied.

Lee strode into the ranch house and headed straight for Frank's study. He should have realized the old buzzard would have Marilyn here, but it hadn't occurred to him. Doubtless, Frank relished the idea of throwing them all together just to see the fireworks. Without knocking, Lee pushed the door open, walked in, and found him on the phone.

Frank looked up, his craggy face breaking into a smile. "Hold on a second, Bud . . . Lee! Welcome back. Have a good trip?"

"I need to talk to you, Frank."

"Did everything go according to plan? Are Mrs. Chastain and the boy with you?"

"They're here. I said I need to talk."

"Not now, Lee." Frank held up the phone. "I'm on with Bud Finley in Alaska. Go out and get yourself a drink. Join the party."

"We'll be at the shooting range," Lee announced as Frank replaced the receiver at his ear. Moving straightforwardly to the gun cabinet on the south wall, Lee removed a box of forty-five cartridges, stuffed them in his jacket pocket, and turned.

"Letting off steam," he added with the sharp arch of a brow. Frank merely waved a hand and went on with his conversation.

It took a few minutes to round up a hired hand who agreed to set the targets. Lee hurried out front and spotted the group just where he'd left them on the grassy lawn—the woman he was in love with, her son, and his ex-wife. Never would he have imagined such a trio.

"Frank's tied up," Lee said as he arrived, his gaze shifting from Cara to Marilyn and back again. "The light will be fading soon. If you want to go to the shooting range, we should go now."

"Oh, yes, let's!" Marilyn put in with a triumphant glance for Cara. "Lee is an excellent marksman, you know. That's how we met. He was giving exhibitions on the rodeo circuit, and my girlfriends dared me to go down to the arena and introduce myself."

"I'm not the one who's going to be shooting," Lee said, his gaze still on Cara. "She is."

"Who?" Tommy questioned. "*Mom?*"

Suddenly, Cara had all three pairs of eyes drilling into her.

"She's learning how to shoot," Lee said.

"How thrilling," Marilyn remarked drily.

"You *are?*" Tommy trilled.

"Yes, Tommy," Cara mustered. "I'm learning to shoot your grandfather's pistol."

"Why?"

"Because with Elsa and Uncle Nick gone, it's occurred to me it would be a good idea to have some means of protection."

"Against who?"

"Whom."

"Against whom, then?"

"Against . . ." Cara's gaze rose to Lee. "Against anyone bad who might ever try to bother us."

"Let's go, then," Lee said briskly. "The range is out back."

Circling the east wing, the four of them proceeded down a terraced walk to the rear of the house. Cara knew little of ranches, but Frank Winston's seemed exceedingly grand, the white house sprawling in three directions, the back lawns landscaped with rock gardens and meandering paths, cactus, yucca, and a few rare oaks. Against the lush green of the grounds, the shooting range was a barren plot with a high dirt bank built up behind it.

Marilyn took Tommy by the hand and drew him back as Cara and Lee moved to the firing line.

"That's Slim over there," Lee said, gesturing to a cowboy standing on the sidelines. "He set up the silhouette at fifty feet. After you've fired all your rounds, he'll bring us the target and we'll check your shots."

Cara looked across the field. The target was a slab of cardboard with the black imprint of a man's torso. "That's fifty feet? It looks farther than that."

"Where's the gun?" Lee asked.

Withdrawing the pistol, Cara set down her purse and turned to find him offering a box of bullets. For a fleeting instant, her gaze became riveted on the things—lead death in brass casings—and her stomach coiled in a knot. All she had to do was remember Mitch, and the sick feeling passed. Selecting five bullets, Cara loaded the chambers, leaving the slot under the hammer empty.

"That was pretty smooth," Lee remarked.

"I practiced."

"When did you have time to practice?"

"Last night," she replied with a flickering glance. "While you were brooding in the study."

Planting her feet a shoulder's width apart, Cara assumed the stance he'd taught her, took aim, and fired. The pistol recoiled, jerking her arms so that the barrel spun skyward. Lee started to reach around and correct her grip. At the last instant he stuffed his hands in the pockets of his jacket.

"Relax," he said. "Don't fight it when it bucks. Ride with it."

Cara nodded. Drawing a new bead, she eyed the target and focused all her concentration on the distant outline of a man. Once again she thought of Mitch, and suddenly the faceless silhouette had narrow eyes and a mouth she'd never been able to forget. In smooth fluid motion, she cocked the hammer, reestablished her grip, and squeezed the trigger . . . again . . . again . . . again. The four shots split the air in rhythmic cadence.

"Damn, Cara," Lee sputtered.

"It's quite a sense of power, isn't it?" she asked, turning her eyes to the pistol and opening the chamber. As she extracted the cartridges one by one, Slim came running up with the target.

"Damn!" Lee exclaimed once more.

Her first shot had been wild, probably embedding someplace in the dirt well beyond the target. But all four rounds she just fired had struck within a six-inch circumference smack in the middle of the silhouette's face.

Lee looked up with wondering eyes. "What were you aiming for?"

"His nose," Cara replied, extending her palm. "Could I have some more bullets, please?"

Frank peered out the rear window of the study, watching the man he'd dispatched approach the group at the shooting range. A moment later, the lot of them started walking toward the house. Frank's gaze fastened on the tall, dark woman in the tweed jacket. She didn't fit Lee's usual preference for petite blondes, but then from what Frank had determined in the past weeks, Cara Chastain *wasn't* usual.

Never would he have imagined that a solitary woman could pose a double threat to his plans, his goals, his very dreams. Frank Winston had wheeled and dealed with the best of them and come out on top, called shots that affected thousands of lives, made millions that made more millions. And now a young widow had him cornered on two scores—Walking Dune and Lee. If Frank had to sacrifice one of them, it would be Walking Dune.

Moving to the front of his desk, he rested his hips against it and watched the door. Minutes later, not bothering to knock, Lee pushed the door open, and they walked in. Frank nearly caught his breath. Hair black as night, eyes blue as sapphires, Cara Chastain had the face of a goddess, the body of a temptress. More than likely, she was the most beautiful woman he'd ever seen.

"We're here," Lee announced bluntly.

Frank's gaze darted to Lee. No wonder he was smitten, and there was no doubt that he was. The dark look on his face might fool others, but not Frank. Turning on a smile, he stepped forward, shook the lady's hand, and made a decision then and there.

"I appreciate your coming, Mrs. Chastain," he said when the three of them were seated by the fireplace. With a quick, sly look at Lee, he added, "Where are you staying, by the way? I'd be happy to offer you—"

"My son and I are at the Ritz-Carlton," Cara broke in. "Thanks just the same."

"As I said," Frank took up smoothly, "thank *you* for making the trip. Distance can be such an impediment at times."

"Impediment to what, Mr. Winston?"

The lovely face was calm and composed, the voice provocative.

"Understanding," he replied. "I'd like to know what's on your mind, Mrs. Chastain."

"I was told you'd heard from the governor of North Carolina."

"Yes."

"That's what's on my mind," Cara added.

Frank raised a brow. She was shrewd, too.

"Okay," he said. "No beating around the bush. I know who you are, and you know who I am. Why do your damn horses have to camp on *my* land?"

Cara cast a quick look at Lee, but he offered no support, only continued staring at his boss with an inscrutable expression.

"That acreage wasn't selected out of maliciousness," she said. "It's the only logical place. There's beach and fresh water, timberland where the mustangs can take shade in the summer, refuge in the winter."

"Sounds like a regular Garden of Eden," Frank quipped.

"For them, it's home," Cara replied quietly. "Besides, the north end is safer. Development has been creeping up on us from the south for years. Every mustang that's been killed or injured has been hit on the highway south of town."

"Why can't they settle on the west strip?" Frank questioned. "Somewhere along the sound?"

"There's no place," Lee put in. "Every plot of habitable ground near Walking Dune has been slated for development."

Frank sat back in his chair, eyeing the raven-haired beauty over a temple of fingertips. "One prize. Two contenders. What do you propose we do?"

"I'm not sure there's anything we *can* do. I feel very strongly about my position, Mr. Winston. I'm sure you do as well."

"Yes, but there's a difference between us, Mrs. Chastain. We've got different things on the line. You've got a cause, I've got an investment. When an investment stops making sense, I tend to stand back and take a good look at it. Just how far are you prepared to go in championing those mustangs of yours?"

"As far as Raleigh, for one," Cara answered slowly. "I wrote the governor that if he agreed to see me, I'd bring a petition."

"And if that doesn't work?"

Her gaze moved between Frank Winston's probing eyes. "Then I'll think of something else," she replied succinctly.

The heavy brows rose to a cheery level as he smiled, though to Cara's way of thinking, the man still looked as crafty as a silver-haired fox.

"You talk a good game, little lady," he said. "And you've made my decision for me. Lone Star Partners is out of Walking Dune . . . as of now."

Lee snapped to sudden alertness. "Just like that?"

"It makes no sense to do otherwise, Lee. What if we proceed with Phase Two—the golf course, the marina, all the amenities—and Mrs. Chastain, here, ends up winning Phase Three for her mustangs? We wouldn't have enough residences to come *close* to clearing a profit. It's over."

Getting to his feet, Frank looked once more at Cara and extended a hand. "Guess you didn't realize you'd be pulling off such a coup when you boarded my jet for Houston."

Feeling a little dazed, Cara rose and joined him in a handshake. "No, I didn't," she said. "Thank you, Mr. Winston."

"You don't thank a runner you've just outdistanced, Mrs. Chastain. It was a pleasure meeting you."

As she turned away, Lee sprang from his chair. "I'll be out in a minute, Cara," he said curtly. When she closed the door, Lee took a stiff step in Frank's direction.

"I'd call that a damn weak effort," he accused.

"Would you?"

Lee's glare was unfaltering. "Any other time you'd have fought local issues, given concessions, raised the ante—whatever it took. Why not this time?"

"I think you know the answer to that."

"You're yanking my chain, Frank. I don't like it."

Despite the fear that he'd gone too far at last, Frank grinned. "Just think of it as a love tug. Besides, aren't you the one who said Walking Dune should stay as it is? Untouched? Unspoiled?"

Lee gave him a look of frustration. Yes, he'd said it, and yes, he believed it. But now that Lone Star was out of the picture, so was he. Turning abruptly, Lee walked across the room and turned troubled eyes out the window. Marilyn and Tommy were sitting at a lawn table, the late sun shining on their fair hair.

Frank ambled up beside Lee and followed his line of vision. As they watched, Cara joined the table. Giving the boy a light hug, she sat down across from Marilyn.

"So, that's her boy?" Frank asked.

Lee nodded. "Tommy. He's a good kid."

Abigail's grandson, Frank mused silently. "I'd like to meet him. I've got an idea. Why don't we use the limousine to take them back to the hotel?"

"No."

"Come on, Lee. The boy might like it."

"For God's sake, Frank!" Lee exploded. "You've fixed it so I have no reason to go back. Let me at least have tonight."

Frank watched him stalk out of the study, still worried but certain he'd taken the only course he could. He didn't even mind the financial loss he would undoubtedly incur from a deserted, Phase One project. It was worth it. After meeting Cara Chastain, he didn't want Lee returning to Walking Dune . . . ever.

Stepping out on the porch, Lee glanced across the lawn to the pasture, where several of Frank's horses were grazing. On impulse, he stopped by the cabana and loaded a plate with apple slices and carrot sticks. As he arrived at the lawn table, the group of three looked up. Lee kept his eyes on Tommy.

"How would you like to visit the horses before it gets dark?" he asked.

"Could we?" Tommy chortled, leaping to his feet.

"Sure. They're tame enough. We'll be back soon," Lee tossed in the direction of the ladies before walking off with the boy.

Both Cara and Marilyn watched them go, the long-legged man shortening his stride so Tommy could keep up.

"I never pictured Lee behaving so . . . fatherly," Marilyn commented.

"They're great pals."

"And what about you? Are the two of you great pals, too?"

Cara looked swiftly across the table. "I think a great deal of Lee," she said. "If that answers your question."

"Not entirely," Marilyn drawled. "I'm glad we have a chance for a little chat, Cara. I'll be straight with you. Lee, and Lee alone, is the reason I'm in Houston. I want him back."

"I gathered that."

"Is it so easy to see?"

"It isn't too difficult," Cara replied.

Marilyn glanced back at the corral where Lee and the boy were passing through the gate. "He loved me once," she said.

"I know."

"I may have left him, but I never stopped loving him."

"I don't believe he stopped loving you either," Cara said slowly. "Lee once told me there were times he thought he'd never get over losing you."

Marilyn looked at the beautiful woman with the remarkable eyes. "But apparently he did . . . enough to be able to fall in love with you."

Cara regarded her steadily. "How do you know that?"

"I can see it. Now I know why Frank's running scared. He's counting on Lee to step into his shoes when he retires. Within the year Lee would become head of Lone Star Partners, one of the most powerful men in Texas. It's the bonanza he's wanted all his life."

"But . . ." Cara prodded as the blonde's eyes bored into her.

"But now he seems drawn to turn his back on the whole thing," Marilyn went on without hesitation. "It would be the biggest mistake Lee could possibly make. And, frankly, he'd be making it because of you. What exactly are your intentions, anyway?"

"I don't intend to fight you for him, Marilyn."

"Why the hell not?"

Looking into the blatantly curious face, Cara suddenly saw an aura of humor in the situation.

"It's a long story," she said with a smile, "and hardly one I would have expected to discuss with his ex-wife."

"You love him, don't you?" Marilyn pressed.

Cara's smile faded. "Whatever I feel, I can't be what he wants or deserves. Like you, I want only the best for Lee, and I can't give it to him. Not now anyway."

Marilyn's gaze roamed over the elegant features. Behind Cara Chastain, the sun was melting into the plain, spilling red highlights on the ebony hair, shadows across the haunting eyes.

"Oh boy, am I in trouble," she murmured after a moment.

"What do you mean?" Cara asked.

"I actually like you," Marilyn replied.

The corridor of the Ritz-Carlton was hushed and dimly lit. As Cara applied the key to the lock, the muted light of lanterns shimmered on Tommy's hair, sparkled in his glistening eyes.

"No, Tommy," Lee replied firmly. "You'll fly back with Pilot Pete. I won't be going this time."

"But I thought you said we were making the trip together!"

"I did . . . we did. And now the trip is over for me. Houston is my home."

The door swung open. Tommy ran through the elegant receiving room and into one of the two bedrooms afforded by the hotel suite. Though he didn't slam the door, he closed it with a bang.

Stepping inside, Cara dropped her purse on a side table and put a hand to her forehead. "I'm sorry, Lee. He's upset right now. And tired. He'll be all right after a good night's sleep."

Following her in, Lee closed the door behind him. "I'll meet you in the morning, then. Take you to the airport."

Cara shook her head. "No. You see how Tommy is. Let's not put him through another goodbye."

Lee's hands were in his pockets. When he spread them, his jacket flared like a pair of wings.

"What are you saying, Cara? I won't see you tomorrow?"

"I think it's for the best."

Lee cocked his jaw. "You think it's for the best."

Cara started at his boots and worked her way up . . . the long legs and narrow hips so at home in faded jeans . . . the crew-necked sweater and leather jacket, both black as the ace of spades . . . the incredibly handsome face with the moustache draping sexily over his mouth. She would remember the way he looked at this moment for always.

"It wouldn't be easy for me either, Lee," she said. "I think you mean more to me than you know."

"If it's so hard for us to say goodbye," he murmured after a moment, "then why are we saying it?"

"Maybe the old line holds true. We live in two different worlds—you the rising mogul of a big-city corporation, me the librarian of a small, secluded town."

"Which you've just made sure will stay small and secluded. Do you realize you've won, Cara? You went up against Frank

Winston and backed him down. Walking Dune is going to stay the way it is, just like you always wanted."

"Perhaps," she allowed. "Until another Lone Star comes along."

"I have a feeling you're safe."

"Do you?" Cara asked, the thought of Mitch returning. "There are things more terrifying than Lone Star stalking the Banks."

"Like what?" Lee's eyes narrowed as he studied her. "Like what, Cara? Mitch Lincoln? He's there, isn't he?"

Cara looked at him with surprise. "You almost sound as if you believe it."

"I believe it if you believe it."

She stiffened. "I'm entirely aware of what I believe, and of the truth. They're one and the same, though I don't expect you to accept that."

"If I do," Lee replied, "then I should go back with you."

Cara's chin went up. "I can take care of myself, Lee. After this afternoon on the range, you should know that."

"Why? Because you were a crack shot against a cardboard target? It's different when you're up against a live man, Cara."

"I'll be fine," she returned spiritedly. "I had a good teacher."

Silence fell as their eyes locked. Lee caught his upper lip as he considered her, the smooth cheeks he knew the feel of, the mouth he knew the taste of.

"What do you expect me to do now?" he asked in a rumbling tone. "Turn around? Walk out? I don't know if I can."

Cara glanced away as her eyes began to sting.

"Okay, then," he murmured after a moment. "I guess I can." Fishing in his pocket, Lee withdrew a business card and held it out. "Here. I put my home number on there. If you ever need me, just call."

Taking the card, Cara looked up and met his eyes. Lee shook his head in frustration.

"So, this is it," he said. "The end of the line. I feel there's so much mixed up between us, Cara, so much I'd set straight if only I knew how."

"It isn't something that's within your control, Lee. You were never the problem. We both know that."

Lee's gaze darted between her eyes. Stepping swiftly forward, he caught her face in none-too-gentle hands. "God, I wish I could just shake some things out of your head, you know that?"

Pressing a quick kiss on her lips, he spun around and walked out. Taking a few stiff, lurching steps after him, Cara pressed her forehead and palms against the door. On the other side, Lee trailed an open hand along its surface as—unknowingly—they reached for each other through the barrier.

The first two weeks of January passed. Days on the Banks were brilliant and brisk, the Atlantic whipped into lively blue waves frothed with white. Sometimes in the afternoons Cara and Tommy went for a walk on the beach. But most of the time they stayed in. All of Walking Dune tended to take cover when winter set in—the air was too piercing, the salty wind too biting, to go out for a frivolous cause.

Cara had an additional reason. Although she hadn't spotted him since returning from Houston, she occasionally got the eerie feeling that Mitch was nearby. She kept the loaded pistol on the top shelf of the china cabinet, out of Tommy's reach. Most nights she stayed awake into the wee hours of morning.

Nights in the old house were long, the covers clammy with uncontrollable dampness, the rafters rattling with the keening wind that howled across the dunes throughout winter. Many evenings Tommy played with the construction set Lee gave him for Christmas. And Cara allowed him to watch more TV than usual. Januaries had never seemed lonely before. This one did.

On the evening of the fifteenth, Cara was in the kitchen fixing supper when a knock sounded on the door. She jumped, her thoughts darting to the pistol in the next room before she peered through the sheers and recognized Louis. Wiping her hands quickly on a towel, she moved to the door.

"Louis," she greeted with a note of surprise. "Come in."

"I'll only stay for a minute."

"Stay as long as you like. It's been a long time."

"Yeah. I guess we established that at Dahlia's wedding."

Their eyes met, and a host of memories flooded between them.

"Yes," Cara agreed. "I guess we did. Would you like some coffee? I just made a pot."

"No, thanks. I just came by to tell you I'm leaving Walking Dune."

"For how long?"

"For good."

"What are you talking about, Louis? This is your home. The Talbots have been here for generations."

"I can't do anything else. I owe a dangerous man a lot of money."

"Money? But you've always had plenty . . ."

Her voice trailed off as Louis raised a quelling hand.

"I'm ruined, Cara. The announcement came from Lone Star yesterday. They're canceling all the options, closing down the development. All I have left is the house, and it's mortgaged to the hilt."

"I don't understand."

Louis rubbed a tired hand across his brow. "I did it to myself. I've gambled for years. For a while, I won. For a long while, I haven't."

"But if all you need is money, I can come up with—"

"I've borrowed for the last time, Cara. My number's up, and I know it. Besides, you're the last person I'd take money from, considering the jeopardy in which I may have placed you."

"What jeopardy?"

"Mitch Lincoln."

Cara's eyes went wide.

"I saw him today. At least, I saw his car cruising past your place so slowly that I got the impression he was scoping it out. I'm certain he's up to no good."

"You saw him?" she asked woodenly. "You saw Mitch?"

"Yes. And it's my fault he's here."

"How can it be your fault?"

Turning away from the searching, violet eyes, Louis peered unseeingly across the familiar kitchen.

"I guess it was a year ago," he murmured. "I spent a fair amount of time in Richmond, and one night at a poker game his name came up. He was on parole after a few years in prison, working in some greasy spoon as a busboy. I made the connection between him and you and forgot about it . . . until last summer, when everything went to pieces."

Louis drew a long, shuddering breath. "I brought him here. I paid him to come to the Banks. I told myself I was protecting my interests, that if you kept on stirring up things about the mustangs you were endangering my sale to Lone Star. That turned out to be right, but now I know it wasn't my true motive."

He turned and looked at her, almost welcoming the punishment of the beautiful face marred with unspeakable sadness.

"I wanted to hurt you, Cara. I think I lost my mind last summer along with everything else. Now, as I look at you, I picture you with Tom, me with Dahlia. We were so close."

His voice broke. Cara stepped quickly forward and put her arms around him.

"Weeks ago," Louis whispered, "I went to Mitch's motel room in Nags Head, gave him a few hundred bucks, and told him it was over, told him to leave. He took the money and gave me his word. I must have been crazy to believe him. He hasn't left, Cara. I feel as though I've opened Pandora's box. The devil's loose . . . and on a mission of his own."

Louis pulled away from the sweet embrace that filled him with such guilt he couldn't bear it.

"This afternoon," he went on, "after I saw his car, I went back to the motel. He checked out New Year's Day, the clerk said. I'm afraid for you, but what can I do? I have no idea where Mitch is, and if I don't clear out of town, I'm a dead man."

"It's all right," Cara murmured. "You've warned me. Thank you."

"Thank you?" Louis repeated. "After what I've told you, you're thanking me?"

"All these months, I couldn't be sure he was real. Now I know. You have no idea what that means to me, Louis."

He shook his head. "You're really something, Cara Chastain, you know that?"

Disregarding the comment, she studied her old friend with a look of concern. "What will you do?" she asked.

Louis shrugged as though the matter were of little consequence.

"Disappear for a while. Put the house on the market. Hope I can elude the hired guns until I sell it."

"But really, Louis. If all you need is money—"

"What I need," he broke in, "is to feel like a man again. Goodbye, Cara."

She followed him to the door, watched him start down the steps.

"Good luck," Cara called softly.

Louis looked over his shoulder. "Luck?" he questioned with a bitter smile. "Now there's a lady I haven't kept company with in quite some time."

An hour later he was loading a bag in the rented car when a dark sedan sped up the drive, the tires kicking up sprays of sand.

"Evenin', boys," Louis said as Tom and Dick climbed out of the car. "I've been expecting you."

The next windy morning, beneath a cloud-banked sky that threatened a northeaster, John and Amos Wilkes found his body washed up on the beach, a half-mile south of the old Talbot homeplace overlooking the sound.

Chapter Thirteen

It was late afternoon when the bell rang. Peeping through the side pane, Cara smiled. A chilling blast of wind shot in as she opened the door.

"Well, hello, Ned. Come on in," she said, hastily closing the door behind him as he stepped inside. "It's a nasty day. Looks like a northeaster brewing."

"Yep. We'll see it break some time before the night is through."

"Want some coffee?"

"No thanks, Cara."

He stood there with his hat in his hands, looking entirely ill at ease. Cara's cheery expression changed to one of concern.

"What is it, Ned? What's wrong?"

"Bad news," he replied, his troubled eyes searching hers. "It's Louis."

"What about him?"

"He's dead," Ned replied quietly.

A cold hand gripped Cara's heart. For a moment it seemed to stop beating.

"Louis?" she managed.

Ned's chin drifted to his chest in affirmation.

"How?"

"I'm not a medical examiner, but it looks like a plain and simple drowning. John and Amos Wilkes found him washed up on the sound."

"Where is he?"

"The Talbot place."

Bundling Tommy up in a hooded jacket, Cara followed Ned to the white-columned house, noting as she stepped inside how drastically the place had changed. It was stripped of so many things she remembered—paintings, carpets, furniture. Remembering the things Louis had revealed only the previous day, her heart ached all the more.

"He's upstairs in his room," Ned said. "Reverend Stowe is with him."

"Tommy, I want you to stay down here with Ned," Cara said and climbed the stairs with a heavy step.

Reverend Stowe looked up from a chair by the bed where Louis was stretched out, dressed in a blue suit, his hands folded peacefully on his chest as though he were merely sleeping.

"I'm sorry, Cara," the minister murmured as she walked up.

She barely heard. Louis's face was uncharacteristically puffy, the color of life having succumbed to the ashen gray of death. Unable to bear the sight, Cara swung her head around, her stinging eyes passing the bedside table, returning when she caught sight of a deck of cards. Her gaze froze on the fancy red pattern covering the back of the top card, as her memory turned back time and Louis was once again standing before her.

I did it to myself, Cara. . . . I've gambled for years . . . gambled for years . . .

"Oh, Louis," she said and sighed raggedly.

"I baptized this boy," Reverend Stowe commented. "I can't believe I've lived to see this."

Reaching down, Cara smoothed the hair from Louis's brow. "He's so cold." After a moment, she added, "I'll have to call Dahlia."

"It's a shame to cast a pall on the honeymoon, but I'm sure she'd want to know."

Cara stood there, staring at Louis, smoothing his hair.

"I'm going to stay with him," Reverend Stowe said. "He won't be left alone. Make the call to Dahlia and go on home, Cara. There's a bad storm coming."

Nodding wordlessly, Cara gave Louis's cheek a parting caress, turned away from the sight of his motionless form, and went downstairs. It took a half hour to patch through to the *Mrs. Malloy*, which was docked near Beaufort, South Carolina. Cara tried to break the news as gently as she could; still, Dahlia broke into tears. Nick came on the line.

"We can be there in two days," he said. "We'll start back right away."

When Cara hung up the phone, Ned walked in with Tommy.

"Tommy and I have closed all the shutters around the place," Ned announced. "It's going to be a bad one, Cara. Do you need any help buttoning things down at your house?"

She put an arm around Tommy's shoulders. "No thanks, Ned. We can manage."

"Then let's get going," Ned suggested. "We've all got things to do. I'd like to get back to Corolla before the storm breaks."

With her mind filled with memories of Louis, Cara drove home, parked the car, and went inside by way of the kitchen door.

"Let me have your jacket, Tommy."

Hanging their wraps on the pegs by the door, Cara turned and put an arm around Tommy's shoulders, still sorrowfully preoccupied as they walked together into the dining room.

"Well, well . . . Home at last."

She looked up, and for an unforgiveable instant, she froze. Mitch was sitting at the dining table, an arm slung casually about the back of a formal chair. As she peered at him speechlessly, his gaze moved from her to Tommy and back again.

"This your boy?" he asked.

"Sure I am," Tommy replied boldly. "Who are you?"

"An old friend of your mother's."

Cara snapped to alertness. "Go upstairs, Tommy."

"But—"

"Go!" she commanded with a light swat to his bottom.

Mitch grinned as Tommy disappeared obediently up the stairs. Cara peered across the dining table, meeting the narrow eyes, willing the hatred she felt to fill her gaze.

"So, you show your face at last," she said.

"You knew I would sooner or later."

"Yes, I knew. But I still don't know what you want."

He rose to his feet. The face was the same, but he was bigger than before, filled out with the huskiness of a full-grown man.

"Just to renew an old friendship," he said, starting around the end of the table between them.

"Don't come near me, Mitch," she cautioned.

"And what will you do if I do?" he taunted. "Stop me like you did the last time?"

He kept on walking, moving closer with every step. Cara began to back away, her mind blazing with the image of the pistol in the china cabinet mere paces behind her. Mitch kept on coming, backing her up until she bumped against the wall. He reached up as if to touch her hair.

"Don't touch me!" Cara commanded, slapping his hand away.

"Or what?"

"Or I'll kill you," she promised quietly.

"You and what army?" he laughed.

Cara made a sidelong lunge for the china cabinet, but he grabbed her, his hands closing about her upper arms, pinning them to her sides, shoving her back against the wall.

"Don't make any sudden moves, Cara," he warned.

The smell of stale beer was on his breath. Cara turned her head quickly aside. Even so, she saw the flash of a blade as he pulled a knife and pointed it at her.

"I hadn't planned on this being a close encounter," he added. "But it can go that way if you want."

"Get your hands off me, Mitch."

"Sure," he replied after a moment and released her. "For now."

Facing him once more, Cara gave him a look of loathing. "Get out," she said.

"When I'm ready," he returned, the sneering grin dropping away as he tucked the knife in his boot. "I have a little proposition for you. An exchange, you might call it."

"What kind of exchange?"

"You get peace and quiet. I get a hundred thousand dollars."

Cara released a sharp laugh. "What are you talking about?"

"I'm talking about you, Mrs. High-and-Mighty Chastain. You've come a long way since the old days."

"Money," Cara muttered. Suddenly Mitch's appearance took on a whole new light. Pushing away from him, she moved around in front of the china cabinet.

"This is about money?" she added.

"You've got it, baby. And I want it."

"You're insane," she said. "I don't have a hundred thousand dollars."

"You can get it. I've seen the Chastain mansion in Warrenton. I know what kind of dough your dead husband was worth."

"Even if I *could* get it," Cara returned coldly, "what makes you think I'd give it to you?"

"Because I'll make life hell for you if you don't. I know all the right buttons to push. Or have you forgotten?"

He moved forward, once again on the prowl. Cara thought of reaching for the pistol but knew she couldn't get to it before he could pull the knife once more.

"Stop right there," she commanded. "I'll call the police on you, Mitch. I swear I will. Like you said, things are different now."

In a lightning move, he stepped up and grabbed her by the chin, jerking her face cruelly close to his.

"Don't do something you'll regret. Nobody can stop me, Cara. Not when it comes to you. We're all tied up together, and you know it the same as me."

"Let go of me," she rasped.

Mitch pushed her roughly away. "I can get to you any time I want."

Sweeping her with a lurid examination that made Cara's skin crawl, he walked past and purposely brushed his arm across her breasts.

"Stop it!" she hissed. He chuckled and continued across the room, where he turned in the arched doorway.

"How much is it worth to you, baby? Do you want to see the last of me? Or would you like me to stick around and become an *intimate* part of your life?"

"Go to hell," Cara retorted.

He grinned. "Maybe. But if I do, you can be damn sure I'm taking you with me."

With that, he walked out. Hurrying to lock the door behind him, Cara heard him laugh from the other side.

The storm held off until eight o'clock, when it struck with fury in the black of the winter night. By then Cara's nerves had settled from the brush with Mitch, though the eerie feeling of his nearness lingered. As she'd gone about the business of locking windows and shutters, she'd half-expected to run into him each time she rounded a corner. Beneath the cover of a bulky sweater, the loaded pistol was tucked in her belt.

The house was closed up tight as a tomb. Even so, it groaned in the high winds, echoed with the pound of driving rain. In Tommy's room, the northeast window began to leak, a stream being driven beneath the frame despite the shutter. Mopping up the puddle with one towel, Cara began stuffing another along the sill.

"We'll be all right, won't we, Mom?" Tommy asked.

"Of course we will, sweetie. This old house is the best place in the world to be. It's stood up to a hundred storms like this one."

"Can I have something to drink?" he asked after a moment.

"Sure," Cara replied, reaching for another towel and dabbing at the wallpaper.

Tommy had been gone mere minutes when the icy chill swept over her. Turning as she straightened, Cara looked across the room to the open doorway.

"Tommy?" she mumbled.

Hurrying to the landing, she peered below.

"Tommy?" she called shrilly.

Flying down the stairs, Cara leapt down the last few and ran through the house. Even before she reached the kitchen, she heard the unobstructed roar of the storm. The back door was open, the storm raging freely into the room, the wind whipping the curtains, the rain blasting across the floor in sheets. Cara's wild eyes searched the room, noting first that Tommy's jacket was missing from the peg by the door, then lighting on a piece of paper nailed to the cupboard.

"Just a little insurance," it said in big, scrawling letters. "Want him back? Keep your mouth shut and get the money."

Moving closer, Cara read the words again, her mouth opening though no sound would emerge. Lunging through the back door, she was engulfed in howling, stinging blackness. Shielding her face with her arm, she peered across the deck she knew was there, though she could see no farther than the end of her nose. Horror welled up until it exploded from her throat.

"No!" Cara screamed, the cry of anguish swallowed in the shriek of the wind.

Stumbling back inside, she coursed mindlessly through the deserted house, ending up in the study where she peered about the room that had been Tom's sanctuary, straining to find some strength or comfort that failed to come until . . . like a glorious light, Lee's image burst into her mind.

Racing up the stairs, Cara searched through her purse, snatched out the business card, and suddenly was plunged into blackness as the power failed and the lights went out. Feeling across the bedside table, she found the book of matches, lit the candle, and grabbed the phone. There was static on the line. Soon the phones would be out, too.

It didn't occur to her to call Ned, who was probably embroiled in fighting the storm in Corolla . . . or Doc, who was only a half hour away in Nags Head . . . or Reverend Stowe, who was keeping watch over Louis's lifeless body . . . or Jacob, or the Wilkes brothers, or any man near Walking Dune.

The only man—the only person in the world—she trusted to help her was Lee. Staring at the card in the flickering light of the candle, Cara dialed his number with shaking fingers.

Marilyn moved about her old kitchen, the familiar aroma of Texas chili flavored the air, and she almost believed the years had never passed . . . until she glanced in the living room and saw Lee, once again staring moodily out the window.

With a spirited lift of her chin, Marilyn went back to stirring the chili. There had been less of that brooding distance the past few days. She was sure of it. Time was all he needed.

Hands buried in his pockets, Lee leaned against the window frame and peered outside. The sun was low, the sky streaked with red and gold, the city shining in the distance. It was pretty, but he just damn well plain and simple didn't want to be there. Each night he'd hoped that on the dawn he'd miss them less. But it hadn't worked that way. Memories of Cara and Tommy that should have grown cloudy were clear as glass, and just as sharp.

He'd been foul to be around the past couple of weeks and wondered why Marilyn had put up with him at all, much less sought him out so insistently—drinks here . . . supper there. . . .

The phone rang. Lee picked it up listlessly, frowning as crackling burst of static met his ear.

"Hello?"

"Lee, it's me."

The voice was barely audible, but he recognized it at once. Lee's every sense sprang to alertness.

"Cara? Cara, speak up. I can barely hear you."

"We're in the middle of a northeaster. We could lose the lines any second. Please, Lee—"

A wave of static drowned her out, breaking up her voice. "Help me," he heard after a nerve-shattering few seconds.

"What is it?" Lee yelled into the phone.

"It's Mitch. He's real, and he's got Tommy."

"I'll be there—" There was a distinct click, and then a dial tone. "Cara?" Lee boomed.

Hanging up the phone, he spun around. "Son of a bitch!"

"What's the matter?" Marilyn asked.

Lee looked up, remembering with a start that she was even within a hundred-mile radius.

"That was Cara," he answered tightly. "The son of a bitch has taken Tommy. I've got to get out there. Maybe the jet . . . No, Frank has that in Alaska. He won't be back until tomorrow. It'll have to be the airport. Intercontinental's a little farther than Hobby, but it's got more flights . . . Where's the phone book? Dammit! Where's the damn phone book?"

Walking calmly forward, Marilyn retrieved the phone book from the place on the bureau where it had sat for years and handed it to him. He began thumbing through the pages in such a frenzy that several of them fluttered to the floor. The first carrier he called had no flights until morning. Lee hung up on the reservationist and dialed again.

"You have an eight-fifteen flight but it's delayed?" He checked his watch. "Fine. That will give me time to get there. And I want a car. What? Transfer? Don't transfer me, lady!"

Lee yanked the phone away and stared at it in disgust. "Dammit!" Planting it back at his ear, he tapped his foot impatiently.

"Hello?" he said after a moment. "Yeah, I want a car waiting for me in Norfolk . . . I don't *care* if they've got bad weather!" he barked. "Get me a damn car! The name's Powers. There's a hundred in it for whoever's waiting for me with a key!"

Slamming down the phone, Lee stalked to the coat rack, grabbed a hat, and crammed it on his head. He was in the midst of reaching for the doorknob when he spun around and headed for the bedroom. Yanking a duffle bag out of the closet, he started stuffing things into it. When he emerged minutes later, Marilyn was standing by the door, her coat over her arm.

"The stove's off, the chili a memory in the garbage disposal. Take care of yourself, Lee. I won't be here when you get back . . . *if* you get back."

Hesitating, Lee peered across the room. "Where are you going?"

"Back to Austin. You were right, Lee. You *have* changed. Once, no one could challenge Lone Star, the power, the glory. Now you don't even want it anymore."

"It isn't that exactly—"

"I know exactly what it is, or should I say whom." Marilyn shook her head. "I once told you I wouldn't give up until I was beaten. Remember?"

"I remember," Lee mumbled.

"Well, I have been. And you know what's funny? She never even had to throw a punch. Give her my regards, okay? And beat the hell out of whoever's got Tommy."

With that, Marilyn stepped out and closed the door. Lee stood for a stunned second, a feeling of sadness passing over

him. He'd watched her walk out once before, but this time
was different. This time, Marilyn was part of the past, and he
knew he'd never lay eyes on her again.

Launching back into motion, he grabbed a few things out
of the bathroom, hurried down to the Jaguar, and headed for
the airport.

He spent a frustrating hour and a half pacing Intercontinental, picking up news tips about the winter storm mauling
the southeastern coast, wondering if the only connection he
had was going to be cancelled after all. He tried calling Cara
several times, but the lines were down. Finally at 10:11 P.M.
Eastern Standard Time—Lee boarded for Norfolk International.

Strong head winds demanded an extra half hour from the
flight. He arrived at two-thirty in the morning, startling the
young black who stood in the rain outside the airport holding
the keys to a maroon Monte Carlo.

"They said a hundred was in it," he challenged.

Lee fished out his wallet and pealed off the bills. Throwing
his bag in the back, he leapt into the driver's seat.

"Where you heading, man?" the guy asked, leaning around
the open door as Lee reached to close it.

"South."

"They got a big mama-jama storm going on down there,"
he warned. "Watch yourself."

"Thanks, kid," Lee tossed and, starting up the engine,
roared away toward the coastal highway.

The farther south he drove, the worse the storm became.
Rain came down in swirling sheets; high winds grabbed at
the car. Visibility was next to nil, and in some spots water
covered the road. The only benefit of the northeaster was that
nobody else was crazy enough to be out in it. Lee had the road
to himself; nonetheless, the trip that should have taken slightly
over an hour took more than two.

Just north of the timberland bordering Walking Dune, storm
tides had pushed the dunes clear across the highway. Lee had to
slow to a crawl to skirt around. Praying he wouldn't get stuck,
he strained to see through the stormy darkness and noted the
debris littering the shifting sand—driftwood, tree branches,
pieces of docks and piers washed from who-knew-where.

His anxiety rose to a fevered pitch for both Cara and Tommy. Clearing the mountain of sand, he scratched back onto the highway, deriving small solace from the fact that the storm's fury had lessened by the time he crossed the town limits.

Part of the boardwalk had collapsed. A piece of roof lay in the street, along with a couple of fallen trees. Lee took no time to notice more in his haste to reach the Chastain house. Screeching to a stop out front, he ran through the freezing rain to the porch. The door was unlocked. He rushed inside, his pulse racing along with his gaze.

Illuminated by the flickering light of a single candle, Cara was sitting dead still on the couch in the parlor, her eyes fixed on the window. In that instant, Lee got the impression she'd been in that exact position for hours.

The house was cold and damp, but she was wearing nothing more than jeans and a long-sleeved shirt. Her hair was wild about her shoulders, glinting in the light of the candle, as was the pistol tucked in her belt. Putting a tight rein on his stride, Lee walked slowly up to her.

"Cara?" he said. She looked up, though Lee had the feeling she didn't really see him.

"I should have known," she mumbled.

Lee sat down beside her. "Known what, darlin'?"

This time there was nothing but warmth in the endearment. Cara knew it from a bleary distance just as she knew Lee was next to her, wearing a sheepskin jacket and cowboy hat that made him look all the more like the western desperado she'd always pictured.

"Mitch was here yesterday," she said dully. "I told him to go to hell. I should have known he'd do this."

Opening his jacket, Lee extended its warmth as he stretched an arm around her. She was rigid as stone.

"How could you have known?" he asked gently.

"He did the same thing to me, didn't he? But Tommy—"

Cara's voice cracked as she spoke the name. Settling numbly into the shelter of Lee's shoulder, she squeezed her eyes tightly shut.

"I can't bear it," she whispered.

"Yes, you can."

"No."

"Listen to me, Cara. Don't you realize this is exactly what Mitch wants?"

After a moment she pulled back and met his gaze, some of the dazed look having left her eyes.

"If you fall apart," Lee went on, "he's got you exactly where he wants you—just like before—so you're no good to yourself or the boy. Pull yourself together, Cara. Your son needs you."

Cara blinked, the world suddenly spinning into focus. Lifting a hand, she touched Lee's face. He needed a shave and looked as though he'd been up all night. Even so, the dark eyes blazed with determination.

"What do we do first?" she asked.

Taking her hand, Lee kissed it and met her eyes once more. "First, we get a big question out of the way. The storm seems to be letting up. Do you want to try to get to the police?"

Cara pictured a bunch of troopers like Ned bursting in on Mitch. "No," she replied. "Mitch told me I'd regret it if I did, and now that he's got Tommy—"

"It'll be you and me then."

Her gaze raced over the handsome, firmly set features.

"Yes," Cara answered, a sense of relief washing over her. "You and me."

"Then tell me every last detail about the bastard. He's been here all along, hasn't he? Ever since last summer." When Cara nodded, Lee added, "After all these years, why did he show up out of the blue?"

"Someone paid him to come—to frighten me off the mustang issue, among other things."

"The mustangs again?" Lee scowled. "Who paid him?"

"Louis."

"Talbot? That little weasel. I ought to—"

"Don't, Lee," Cara interrupted quietly. "He's dead."

"Damn! . . . I'm sorry," Lee added gruffly. "When?"

"He was found yesterday. Drowned. God, has it been only a day since then? It seems like years have passed."

Lee's eyes narrowed. "Do you think Mitch might have done it?"

"No. Two days ago, Louis came to see me. He said he was in debt to a dangerous man and couldn't pay. He was going

to leave town and wanted to warn me about Mitch. Louis
regretted what he'd done and tried to call it off. Weeks ago
he paid Mitch to leave the Banks but then spotted him near
my house."

"Mitch never left?"

"Apparently not. And Louis had no idea where to look
for him. He'd left the motel in Nags Head where he'd been
staying."

"He could be anywhere, then."

"I have the feeling he's close by," Cara remarked, her
expression brightening. "Finally, for once, maybe this hellish sixth-sense relationship I have with Mitch can work for
the good. He's close, Lee. Somewhere on the island. I can
feel it."

"Go on," Lee prodded. "You said you saw Mitch yesterday."

"He was in the house when Tommy and I got back from
Louis's. He said he wanted a hundred thousand dollars to get
out of my life. I told him to forget it, and so . . ." Cara paused
for a moment, her eyes filling with tears.

"The storm had broken, and we were upstairs," she went
on in a thick voice. "Tommy said he wanted something to
drink. When I came down to the kitchen, he was gone. Mitch
left a note saying he'd taken Tommy for insurance, that if I
wanted him back I should keep my mouth shut and get the
money."

"So, he needs a little boy for insurance," Lee muttered.
"Son of a bitch."

"Mitch is more than that," Cara said. "He's evil. And
cunning. He said he knew the right buttons to push, and he
was right. He took Tommy for ransom, yes. But most of all,
he took him to exert control. Money isn't all Mitch wants. He
wants me, too, just the way he had me before . . . beaten and
groveling."

Lee studied her. "That's not going to happen, Cara. Believe
me. We're going to beat this bastard, once and for all. What
do you think he's expecting you to do?"

"Probably sit tight, follow his instructions to the letter."

"Let's throw him a curve then. We'll find him, surprise
him . . . take the control out of his hands."

"How can we find him, Lee? I have no idea where he's gone."

"You said he's somewhere on the island. That makes sense to me. Last night when he took Tommy, it was in the middle of a raging storm. Mitch probably didn't travel far. Where would he hide?"

"I don't know. A vacant house, maybe?"

"Exactly," Lee agreed. "All we have to do is pinpoint which one, without him spotting us in the process."

"And then what?"

"Then we take him."

"You mean fight him?"

"Damn right."

"But Tommy—"

"We'll be careful."

Cara shook her head. "You make it sound simple. There's nothing simple about going up against Mitch Lincoln. Don't underestimate him, Lee. He's big, mean, ruthless, and . . . he's got a knife."

Lee's gaze moved between her eyes. "So do I," he replied. "Get your jacket."

They drove south to the tip of the island where they discovered the narrow roadway to the mainland had been washed out. That fact seemed to confirm that Tommy was still somewhere in Walking Dune, and their hopes rose.

As Lee turned the car around, the blackness of night began to lift, dissolving in the watery first light of dawn. Although rain continued to fall, it was clear the storm had passed. They were just south of town when Lee spotted a spiral of smoke coming from one of the chimneys at the Lone Star site.

"Damnation," he exclaimed, pulling off the road and killing the engine. "Nobody's supposed to be out there."

A thrill raced through Cara. "That's him," she breathed. "I'm sure of it."

Leaving the car by the highway, they skirted through the rain to the lofty villa, plastering themselves against the wall of the double garage as they arrived. Inching quietly along the wall, they peered around the rear corner. An old blue sedan was parked behind it, half-buried in sand that had been hurled by the storm from the neighboring dune.

Cara looked quickly to Lee. "That's his car," she whispered. "What do we do now?"

"I designed this house, remember? Inside the garage there's a stairwell leading up to a kitchen entrance. From the inside, unless you know what you're looking at, it appears to be a cupboard door. Ten-to-one, he hasn't locked it. Come on."

Creeping through the dark shelter of the garage, they moved silently up the stairs. The door opened noiselessly, and they stepped into the shadows of the kitchen. Beyond a breakfast bar was a firelit den, the room an odd mix of elegant and raw. Hardwood floors were littered with boards and discarded building materials. Sculpted windows showed naked light bulbs hanging from the ceiling. Before a graceful hearth of stone, Mitch crouched by the fire like a beast in its den.

The urge to kill swept over Lee. He walked straightforwardly into the room, scarcely aware Cara moved with him.

"Hello, asshole," he said.

Mitch spun and was on his feet in seconds.

"Pretty sure of yourself, aren't you?" Lee added. "Building a fire? Sending up smoke signals?"

Mitch grinned. "I wasn't expecting company."

The grin faded as he looked at Cara. "This is between you and me. It always has been. I told you to keep your mouth shut. I don't think you're going to like what happens to stoolies."

He made a threatening move in Cara's direction. Lee sidestepped in front of her.

"No, no," he chided as if scolding an errant child. "You'll have to go through me first."

Mitch's beady eyes narrowed to slits. "With pleasure," he grunted, and in a swift, practiced move, pulled the knife from his boot and switched open the blade.

A split second behind him, Lee had palmed the pocket knife. Keeping his eyes glued on the man, he nodded in Cara's direction.

"Find the boy," he said.

"I'll save you the trouble of looking," Mitch taunted. "He's upstairs, baby. Go ahead. Get him. After I finish here, I'll be along for both of you."

"I wouldn't make any extended plans," Lee growled. "Go on, Cara."

As she moved toward the curving staircase, Lee slipped out of his jacket and flipped it around his left wrist in a makeshift arm guard, keeping the knife trained and ever ready all the while. Mitch Lincoln looked just as Nick and Cara had described—big, redheaded . . . mean.

"I been wanting a piece of you, Powers."

"Come and get it," Lee invited. "Let's see how you do when you're up against something besides women and children."

With a bestial snarl, Mitch lunged.

Caballeros! The old cry rang in his ears as Lee fended the thrust and wielded a slashing swipe of his own.

Mitch looked down with surprise at his left arm, where a line of blood showed red against the rendered shirtsleeve. He looked back with murder in his eyes.

"You son of a bitch!"

"Cut the small talk, Lincoln," Lee said, a hard grin curling his lips. "Time to pay your dues."

Starting up the curving staircase, Cara cast a quick look below. The two men were faced off, silhouetted warriors in the dancing light of the fire. Peering into the darkness above, she scaled the steps with barreling speed.

"Tommy?" she called.

"Mom?" came a muffled voice. "Mom?!"

Spinning around, Cara saw a flicker of light across the landing. Swiftly unlocking the door, she burst inside and nearly knocked Tommy down before she could grab him up in eager arms.

For a few seconds she couldn't speak, could only hold him close. He began to cry. Turning his face to her, Cara studied him in the meager light of the lantern sitting nearby.

"Are you hurt?" she demanded.

"No," Tommy returned tearfully. "But he locked me in here."

"I know, sweetie."

Cara clasped him to her and scanned the room. It was cold and bare, but for a pile of blankets on the floor near the lantern. Hatred closed on her like the fall of night.

"Hold on tight," she said. "We're getting out."

Tommy's arms locked around her neck, his legs around her waist. Cara raced down the stairs, her wary gaze searching for Lee. The two men were circling in the center of the den. Streaks of blood stained the shirts of both.

"Lee!" Tommy shrilled.

He didn't look around as he ordered, "Get him out of here, Cara! . . . Now!"

The final word blasted through the room like a cannon shot. Cara dashed to the front door, threw it open and, yanking the hood of Tommy's jacket over his head, plunged outside.

Though the rain had diminished to a drizzle, the January dawn was bitterly cold, piercingly wet. Mindless of Tommy's weight, Cara ran the full two hundred meters to the car. Climbing into the back with Tommy, she quickly shut the door behind them.

"Are you all right, darlin'?" she asked breathlessly, absently using the endearment she'd heard from Lee's lips alone.

"I'm okay," Tommy replied.

"Are you cold?"

"Just a little."

"Here . . . let me see."

Cara pressed an anxious palm to Tommy's cheeks and forehead. Despite the night of terror, he appeared to have no symptoms—no feverish skin, no cough. Her alarm receded for only a moment. Now that Tommy was safe, it swerved to Lee. Looking over her shoulder, she stared across the expanse they'd just traversed.

"I have to go back, Tommy."

"Please don't leave me alone, Mom!"

She turned and looked into his distraught face. "I have to. Just for a little while."

"Why?!"

"Because of Lee."

The pale blue eyes studied her, their terrified look gradually replaced by one of determination.

"Yes," Tommy said. "You have to help Lee."

Cara grabbed Tommy's face and kissed him. "You're the bravest boy in the whole world, do you know that?"

Stripping off her jacket, she tucked it swiftly around him.

"It's hardly raining anymore, and the sun is up. You can see the house over there quite clearly. Keep a sharp watch, Tommy," she cautioned, her hands gripping his shoulders. "Watch it every minute, and if by some chance, Mitch should come out, you get out of this car and run straight to Miss Nettie's. You hear?"

"I hear."

Waiting no longer, Cara climbed out, hearing Tommy's "Good luck!" just before she closed the car door. Blowing him a kiss, she turned and faced the distance she'd just run with her son in her arms.

Her legs felt like Jell-O, but as she began to move, the strength of long-term conditioning returned, taking her to the euphoric plane where muscles performed on their own. The rhythmic trot stretched into a long, sailing stride, her breath coming, going . . . coming, going . . . the sound of it filling her ears until she heard nothing else, and was one with the cold mist sweeping across the dunes.

Her eyes were trained on the house looming ahead, but in the back of her mind she saw Lee, a streak of blood trailing down his shirtsleeve. How long had it been since she left him? She had no concept of time. Minutes seemed like hours. She was barely aware of bolting into the garage and up the stairwell. With her heart thundering, chest heaving, she stepped into the kitchen.

Gray light flooded through the tall windows of the den, spotlighting the two men who continued to fight, now crouching and circling . . . now lunging at each other with flashing blades. Both were bloody, though Cara decided in a fleeting comparison that Mitch looked the worse. Even so, he didn't appear anywhere near the point of giving up. As she watched, he made a lightning jab at Lee's chest so that Lee was forced to leap back, where he stumbled against a pile of discarded timber. Mitch advanced, his knife like a lance before him.

Whipping the pistol from beneath her sweater, Cara ran forward.

"Drop it, Mitch!"

Lee whirled. "I told you to get the hell out of here!"

Cara's gaze darted from Mitch long enough to see the

trickle of blood trailing from Lee's brow to his jaw.

Looking back to Mitch, she screeched, "Lee! Watch out!"

But she was too late. In the few seconds Lee's back was turned, Mitch had grabbed a two-by-four from the pile at his feet and swung. Lee was turning when the plank connected with his rib cage. Cara cringed as she heard the cracking sound of wood against bone, gasped as she saw Lee fall to his knees, his knife clattering to the floor as he grasped at his chest.

In a flash, Mitch grabbed him under the arms and pulled him up, positioning Lee in front of himself like a shield. Lee could do nothing to prevent it. He drew a breath, a hot pain scalded his lungs, and it occurred to him that he was about to die.

Cara raised the pistol and took aim.

"And just what do you plan to do with that thing?" Mitch sneered.

"Blow your damn head off if you don't drop that knife."

"Don't make me laugh. Do you even know how to fire a gun?"

"What are you willing to risk to find out?"

"Maybe the blood in this one's jugular vein," Mitch replied, grabbing Lee's hair, yanking his head back, pitting the point of the knife squarely against his throat.

Cara heard Lee groan, and her fear congealed in icy calm. She cocked the hammer, her shaking hands suddenly steady.

"Don't do it, Mitch."

He grinned the old grin, his lips disappearing, baring teeth that reminded her of fangs.

"You never could stand up to me, Cara Malloy. You've always tried—that's part of your appeal. But in the end I always win."

"Not anymore," she replied, tears of sincerity starting to her eyes and spilling swiftly over. "Not ever again. I told you to drop it, Mitch. Don't make me kill you."

"Kill me? You couldn't make the shot, even if you had it in you. Get ready for a reunion, baby. As soon as he's dead, I plan to celebrate with you."

His gaze shifted to Lee's neck, and everything went into slow motion. Cara heard Mitch laugh as though from the depths of a tunnel, saw him extend the knife so the blade flashed just below Lee's ear.

"Stop, Mitch!" she cried, her voice like slow-unfolding thunder in her ears. Her gaze lifted as he turned back to her—his eyes dark, narrow, glinting with evil purpose.

"Say goodbye to this Texas son of a—"

The gunshot rang out with a deafening crack. A red hole appeared in the center of Mitch's forehead. His death gaze fixed on Cara, the grin disappearing as his knees buckled. Both men crumpled to the floor.

"Lee," she whispered. Dropping the pistol, Cara scurried across the room, sank beside him, and gathered him onto her lap.

Lee looked up into her tear-streaked face.

"Nice shootin', pardner," he mumbled just before his eyes closed and his head lolled in her cradling hands.

Chapter Fourteen

"What the hell's going on?" Frank exploded.

Lee held the phone away and still could hear the tirade clearly.

"Four days you've been gone! Four damn days! I get back from Alaska, and you're missing without a trace! I try to get in touch with Marilyn to see if she knows anything, and *she's* gone, too!"

There was a pause. Lee put the receiver back to his ear.

"Are you finished?" he asked.

"Where the hell are you, Lee?"

Lee shifted beneath the stiff, white sheet, flinching as, beneath constricting layers of bandage, his rib cage moved.

"At the moment I'm in a hospital just outside Nags Head."

"What?!" Frank's voice changed abruptly as he added, "What's wrong, son? Are you all right?"

"Yeah, except for a few cracked ribs. They're letting me out of here this afternoon."

"What happened?"

"It's a long story, Frank. Let's just say I tangled with a bronco that had a mean kick."

Reverting to his earlier tone, Frank demanded, "What the hell are you doing back in North Carolina, anyway?"

"I had to come. Tommy Chastain was kidnapped."

"Damn! Is the boy okay?"

"He is now." Lee frowned, his gaze drifting absently across the room. "I need to talk to you, Frank," he added.

Frank had sprung out of his chair at the sound of Lee's voice. Now he sank back into it, a chilling wave of premonition closing over him.

"About what?" he asked.

"The past couple of days I've had a lot of time to think, and . . . I know you're counting on me, Frank. I know you want me to walk into your office and pick up where you leave off, but—well—I'm going to have to turn you down."

There was a moment of silence.

"Think about what you're saying, Lee."

"Like I said, I *have* thought about it."

"Why?" Frank asked. "Why are you throwing away the kind of power you've craved as long as I've known you?"

"Because I crave something else more."

"Cara Chastain."

"Not just Cara," Lee replied. "It's Tommy, too . . . and friends I've made. Even if things never work out between me and Cara, the people I want in my life are in Walking Dune. I tried to leave it before, tried to come back to Houston. It's just no good, Frank. Walking Dune is where I need to be."

Another tense moment passed.

"What are your plans?" Frank asked ultimately.

"Doc, a friend of mine who lives nearby, is going to drive me up there today. I'll be at Dunn's Lodge the next few days."

"And then?"

"As soon as I can tolerate the trip, I'll fly back to Houston, but only to get my affairs in order so I can leave for good."

"What the devil are you going to do, Lee, stuck out there in the middle of nowhere?"

Lee shrugged. "Free-lance. Maybe do some renovations around town. I don't know yet."

"Are you absolutely sure about this?"

"I'm sure, Frank. I've never been more sure of anything. Now that I've stopped fighting it, I feel as though a giant weight has been lifted off my shoulders."

Frank rubbed a rough hand across his brow. "I was afraid this might happen, but I guess I didn't want to believe it really could. I don't know what to say, Lee."

"Maybe you could say you wish me well."

"I do, son. You know I do." Frank sighed heavily. "Walking Dune . . . A year ago, it looked so peaceful and innocent. Little did I know how much the damn place would end up costing me."

Lee smiled. "Look on the bright side. Maybe I'll take one of those expensive Phase One beauties off your hands, *if* you're willing to let it go at a steal."

"You've got nerve, boy. You're the reason I'll have to let them *all* go at a steal."

Lee started to laugh and caught himself.

"Don't make me laugh," he complained, ending on a chuckling note in spite of himself. "It hurts like hell."

Leaning back in the plush, leather chair, Frank surrendered a grin. "I must say, you're in a damn good mood for a racked-up wrangler who's fresh out of a job."

Most of the town turned out for Louis's funeral. Afterward Cara settled with Nick and Dahlia in the deserted tavern of the inn. Dressed in the black of mourning, they were a somber trio, their conversation hushed and sporadic.

"Ned said the coroner found signs of a struggle," Nick remarked. "It was murder, but the police haven't got a clue who did it."

"Probably the same hoods who beat him up," Dahlia said. "Though I guess no one will ever prove it."

"Poor Louis," Cara murmured, her gaze dropping to her clasped fingers. "Who would have thought Walking Dune would ever be the scene of such violence? The past few days have been filled with death. First Louis, then Mitch. I killed a man. I can't believe I killed a man."

"You killed an animal," Nick corrected.

"It's so strange," Cara went on, "as if I didn't really do it. I don't remember pulling the trigger or hearing the shot. All I remember is Lee falling to the floor."

She raised a hand and covered her eyes. "God, I never even liked guns. Now I've killed with one."

"Don't you dare feel ashamed," Dahlia objected.

"No, don't," Nick put in sternly. "You saved Lee's life. That's what he told us yesterday. It was either him or Mitch. He said you gave the son of a bitch every chance, warned him to drop the knife, and then at the last possible instant took him out like a regular Annie Oakley with one shot."

"Then dragged Lee to the car and drove like a bat out of hell to the hospital," Dahlia said, reciting the rest of the tale. "Sounds downright heroic, if you ask me."

Cara sat back in her chair and gave the two of them a fleeting smile. "I don't feel like much of a hero. Anyway, I owed Lee. He saved my life once, remember?"

They drifted into silence, all three of them recalling memories from that fateful September afternoon.

"Anybody want a beer?" Nick asked eventually and, when Dahlia and Cara declined, ambled away toward the bar.

Cara's eyes rose to the bright ones across the table. "How did Lee look yesterday at the hospital?"

"He's got some bruises, and his chest is bound, but he'll be all right. He was disappointed you didn't come with us, Cara."

"Did he say that?"

"Not in so many words. The look on his face when he asked about you said it for him."

"I imagine he'll be going back to Texas soon."

"Dammit, Cara. If you want him to stay, tell him so."

Cara glanced away. "I don't think I should."

"Why in the world not?"

"Maybe I love him too much."

"You're making no sense at all," Dahlia announced with obvious exasperation.

"Yes, I am. The prize Lee has worked for all his life is about to become his, Dahlia. But he has to stay in Houston to keep it." Cara's voice dropped until it was barely audible. "It's ironic, isn't it? Now that all my walls have come tumbling down, an insurmountable one seems to have sprung up around *him*. I want to reach out for Lee, but I'm afraid I'll hurt him if I do."

Nick wandered back to the table. "What are you ladies whispering about?" he teased.

"Bullshit," Dahlia replied.

Cara grimaced at her. Dahlia lifted her shoulders.

"That's how I feel about it," she stated simply.

"And I told you how *I* feel about it," Cara returned, a willful hint of a grin flickering about her lips as she came to her feet

"I need some fresh air, you guys. As long as Nettie's watching Tommy, I think I'll drive out and take a look at the fence."

"What's the matter with it?" Nick asked.

"The northeaster dragged off a section. I guess that land was never meant to be fenced in. Just like the mustangs."

"Just like feelings," Dahlia challenged, and received a scolding glare before Cara turned and walked away.

The afternoon sun was bright but hardly warming. The temperature had hovered at freezing most of the day, and icy marsh grass crunched beneath Cara's boots as she walked toward the beach. Having changed clothes after leaving the inn, she was bundled in warm pants, a down-filled jacket, mittens, and a red woolen scarf wrapped twice around her neck so that it reached up to her nose. Even so, her cheeks stung from the windy cold.

The northeaster had crushed the section of fence nearest the beach. Splintered rails littered the ground; a half-dozen jagged posts pointed to the sky—apt symbols for the folly of trying to cage the Banks. Having passed through the breach, the mustangs were frolicking some distance down the beach.

Leaning back against a fractured post, Cara tucked her hands in her pockets and watched, taking a moment for the first time to relish the fact that they were free once more . . . free to roam Walking Dune as their ancestors had for hundreds of years. The highway was still a danger—the twentieth century was still a danger—but the threat of Lone Star was gone.

Tom would be proud . . . *was* proud, Cara thought, her gaze lifting to the heavens. Sometimes she sensed his spirit still. She'd felt it at Louis's funeral, and she felt it now—though it was nothing like the tangible presence she'd tried to keep alive for years, but more like the unchained wind sweeping across the dunes.

Drawing her left hand from her pocket, Cara removed the mitten and studied the gold band. Tom was of the air; she was of the earth. Without hesitation or doubt, she slipped the ring off her finger and turned her eyes once more to the horses.

Their freedom seemed to suggest that everything had gone back to the way it had always been. But Cara knew it wasn't so. Since Lone Star came to Walking Dune, irrevocable events had transpired—the death of mustangs, the murder of a friend, the killing of an enemy. And, somewhere along the line, her own rebirth. Now she felt with the keenness of the living all the magic of being in love, all the dread that it was not to be.

Staring up the shining beach, Cara visualized Houston, the Lone Star Partners building, Marilyn Powers . . . and imagined Lee returning to all three. Turning briskly away from the picture, she started back through the marsh and was nearly across when she looked up and saw him standing at the top of the bank.

Cara came to an abrupt standstill, her pulse lunging into a gallop as her gaze moved over him. Feet planted firmly apart, he was wearing boots, jeans, a sheepskin jacket, and ten-gallon hat. Never had a man looked so like a man. As she stood spellbound, he took a hand out of his pocket and beckoned. Digging her steps firmly into the slope, Cara scaled the slippery bank.

"How are you?" he asked when she stopped before him.

"How am *I?* The question is, how are your ribs?"

"Taped up tight as a hat band, but I'll live. Thanks to you."

Glancing beyond him, Cara surveyed the deserted highway. "How did you get here?"

"Nick dropped me off. I thought I could ride back with you. Are you avoiding me, Cara?"

Her gaze leapt to his eyes. Shadowed by the brim of his hat, they were black and inscrutable.

"I expected to see you at the hospital," he added. "When I didn't, I got worried. The other morning was hard on both of us. It isn't easy to kill a man, even one like Mitch Lincoln. How do you feel?"

"I've thought a lot about it," Cara admitted, her voice soft against the woolen muffler. "I don't take it lightly, but I can't regret it. Mitch was a curse I'd carried around for sixteen years. Now he seems like one of my nightmares—long ago and unreal."

"No more nightmares?" Lee asked.

"No. I have the feeling I'll never have them again. It's as if Mitch has been exorcised from my life."

A freezing wind whistled by as Lee's expression settled in a frown. "So, you're all right," he said. "Then why didn't you come to see me with Nick and Dahlia?"

"I kept in touch with the hospital," Cara replied. "I knew you were doing well."

"But you didn't feel the need to see me?"

But for a suffocating sense of misery, she almost could have laughed.

"Or bring Tommy to see me?" Lee added sharply. "Dammit, Cara. When you called, I dropped everything to get to you. *Everything!*"

"I know."

"And you couldn't even make a thirty-minute drive?"

"It wasn't that I couldn't . . . No, I guess I couldn't."

"Why the hell not?"

Cara looked sharply away, her gaze falling to the frozen tundra as she searched for an answer. *Because I love you,* her mind whispered. *Because you're going away, and knowing it I can hardly bear to look at you.*

"I'll be leaving for Houston in a few days," Lee said finally.

Cara swallowed hard. "That's what I figured."

"Would you consider coming with me?"

It never crossed her mind that he would ask such a thing. She looked up as clashing images stormed her mind—sunlit dunes and sparkling skyscrapers . . . faces of friends and faceless strangers . . . the newly recovered peace of Walking Dune, the bustle of the big city.

"What would I do in Houston, Lee?" she asked quietly.

"Help me pack."

"Help you *what?*"

"I'm coming back, Cara. I'm going to make my home here in Walking Dune."

The vivid eyes peered at him. Lee reached out to the red scarf hiding her face.

"What's going on behind there?" he asked, tugging the thing to her chin and unveiling a brilliant smile. "You like the idea?"

"Oh, yeah," Cara whispered, the smile disappearing as a sudden thought came to mind. "But . . ."

"But?"

"What about all your plans? Taking over for Frank Winston, becoming one of the most powerful men in Texas? Marilyn said it's what you've wanted all your life."

"What I *needed*," Lee corrected. "I don't anymore. You're not the only one around here who's won a battle with the past, Cara. I think I've known ever since I first came to Walking Dune. I fell in love with this place almost as fast as I did with you. I can't say it's going to be easy, living here, seeing you, not having you the way I want. But I know it's impossible for me to leave."

Cara searched his face, love rising within her like a sparkling fountain, filling her until it spilled from her eyes.

"There's no need for that," Lee reprimanded gruffly. "I know how you feel. I'm not going to push you. Or maybe in days to come I will. I can't promise—"

"Shhh. Don't say any more."

Cara wiped her tears away and gazed up into the dark, beautiful face, thinking back to the night she almost lost Tommy, the night she almost lost Lee as well.

"I have something to tell you," she began slowly. "That night, when I realized Mitch had taken Tommy, I went crazy."

The revelation took shape in her mind, and Cara picked up speed as she went on. "I remember racing through the house, running into Tom's study, searching for some kind of aid, some kind of support. But there was nothing—nothing but a dark, empty room. I didn't stop to think about it at the time, but it was then that it struck me. No matter how much we'd loved each other, Tom was gone."

Lee shivered, not from the cold, but the tremor of hope that raced through him. "Go on," he prompted.

"You asked how I felt about shooting Mitch. Except for Tommy, I don't think I could have done it for anyone else, not even myself. But there you were," she said, lifting her mittened hands, "hanging in his grip."

Cara's arms fell to her sides. "I'd lost one man I loved. I couldn't stand to lose another. That's what pulled the trigger, Lee—the fear of losing you."

Lee's breath froze in his lungs. He stared at her, wanting to accept what he thought he'd heard, afraid to believe she was saying what she seemed to be—even though she was looking up at him with that unwavering gaze that had so often relayed unbending purpose, iron conviction.

"You said 'love,' " he mumbled.

"Yes. I did."

"You love me?" Lee asked.

"With all my heart," Cara replied steadily. "Without reservation."

"Say it, then."

"I love you, Lee."

"Say it again."

Cara broke once more into a dazzling smile. "I love you, Lee."

He stepped forward, catching her chin in his fingers, lifting her face to his. His open mouth took hers, gentle but commanding, his tongue moving boldly inside. Cara met it with her own, willing her mouth to communicate all the passion that sprang to life at his slightest touch, his merest glance. No one had ever kissed her the way Lee did, aroused her the way he did. She was losing herself in the feeling when he pulled away.

"It took you long enough to wake up," he murmured.

"Thanks for waiting."

"Does this mean you'll marry me?"

The dark brows rose, the blue eyes flew wide. "Will I marry you?" she questioned in that unforgettable, husky voice. "Hell, yes, I'll marry you."

Lee winced as she caught him in a fierce embrace that threatened to crush his punished ribs. Throwing his head back, he took the pain, folded his arms about Cara, and drew her closer still.

March 2, 1992

Cara ran her fingers across the desktop, her gaze lighting on the silver-framed picture of herself. She'd been happy then, but it was an old photograph. Opening her hand, she looked once more at the gold locket, placed it lovingly atop Tom's manuscript, and closed the drawer.

When Elsa bustled in moments later, she found Cara looking pensively about the study.

"Come now," she scolded. "Let's not have you getting maudlin on your wedding day."

"I'm not," Cara replied with a wistful smile. "A little nostalgic, perhaps. It's hard to believe I'll be walking out of here today."

"You can't blame Lee for wanting to make a fresh start in a home of his own."

"I don't. I want it, too. But I'll miss this house. It was the first place I ever felt really safe, really happy. I'll miss you, too, Elsa. Are you sure you won't reconsider and move with us?"

"I'm too old to be making fresh starts," Elsa said with a twinkle in her eyes. "Things won't change that much. I'll be available to watch Tommy any time. Between his grandmother and me, the boy is going to wind up with two homes. Besides, she needs me. Can you picture Abigail Chastain living anywhere without some hired help to order around? Or *try* to order around, I should say."

Cara smiled. "The two of you are going to give each other a run for the money, that's for sure. Never in a million years would I have imagined Abigail moving to Walking Dune, nor the two of you living under the same roof."

As if summoned by their words, Abigail came flying into the room. "Honestly!" she exclaimed. "What are the two of you standing around for? Neither of you has even dressed. Miss Nettie is coming by with the bouquet in a half hour. Mr. Wilkes bringing the limousine in forty-five minutes. For heaven's sake, do I have to arrange everything myself?"

"Yourself?" Elsa objected. "Who prepared the hors d'oeuvres? Who set up the tables at the new house?"

"Calm down, you two," Cara interjected.

"Calm down?" Abigail repeated on a shrill note. "Really Carolina, I should think you'd want to give yourself time to make everything just so. After all, you don't prepare yourself as a bride every day!"

With that, Abigail turned on her heel. "Tommy?" she called, exiting the room at the same speed with which she'd entered. "Don't you go getting yourself mussed up!"

Folding her arms across her breasts, Cara gave Elsa a look of amusement. "Things are going to be lively around here."

"No doubt about that," Elsa replied with a smile. "Although Queenie does seem to have changed for the better over the past few months."

"Yes, she does, doesn't she?" Cara mused. "Now, if only I could get her to stop calling me Carolina."

The day was cool but sunny. After a small ceremony at the church, the wedding crowd met at the bridal couple's new home. The three-story villa overlooking the beach was not the largest of the development, but it was Lee's favorite. As he took a few of the men on a tour, most of the guests gathered 'round the hors d'oeuvres tables Elsa had set up in the expansive dining room.

Having helped themselves to glasses of champagne, Cara, Dahlia, and Nettie stood by the marble fireplace in the great room. With a cathedral ceiling, and a wall of windows facing the sea, it was light, airy, elegant. Although only a few pieces of furniture had arrived in time for the wedding celebration, it was clear the house was on its way toward becoming a showplace.

"It's going to be beautiful," Dahlia said, her gaze sweeping about the room, then turning to Cara. *"You're* beautiful," she added.

Cara glanced down herself. The long-sleeved suit was of champagne silk, tailored and reserved. "It's hardly as grand as your wedding gown," she replied with a smile, "but thanks."

"We go a dozen years without a single wedding in Walking Dune," Nettie commented. "And now in a matter of months, we have two. My sense of romance is positively glowing!"

Lee came into the room, followed by Nick and Jack Quincy. Cara's gaze settled on her husband. He was so incredibly handsome in the dark suit. But then, she supposed she'd find him so in tatters.

"Marble countertops?" Nick was saying. "A whirlpool built for two? What did you do, Lee? Install all these luxuries just in case you decided to move in?"

Lee chuckled. "Maybe. In the back of my mind, I always thought this wouldn't be a bad place to hang my hat."

"I hardly see this as a laughing matter," Jack put in. "What's going to happen to the rest of this development now that Lone

Star has deserted it? For that matter, Lee, what are *you* going to do now that you've transplanted yourself?"

"Who knows?" Lee returned with a devilish grin. "After I finish fixing up the house, maybe I'll run for mayor."

Overhearing him, Cara laughed lightly, her gaze drifting across the room, lighting on Frank Winston. The distinguished man was standing with Abigail by the door to the deck, and it occurred to Cara that she hadn't seen the two of them apart since everyone arrived. Excusing herself from Dahlia and Nettie, she moved to join them.

"I have to thank you, Frank," she said. "Lee told me you insist on giving us this house as a wedding present. A lovely gesture, but terribly extravagant."

"It was mine to give," Frank replied gruffly. "I still look on the boy as a son, you know, even though you *have* stolen him away from me."

"Tsk, tsk," Abigail put in. "You always did have a tendency to exaggerate, Frank."

"Always did?" Cara repeated with a note of surprise. "You two know each other?"

Hesitating, Abigail looked at Frank. He shrugged, as if to say "it's your call." At that moment Lee stepped up and put a light hand on Cara's back.

"What's going on?" he asked.

"I don't know," Cara replied, looking from Abigail to Frank and back again.

Abigail drew a deep breath. "Frank and I have known each other for decades," she said. "And we've been partners for over a year."

"Partners?" Cara echoed.

"The Walking Dune development was my idea, Carolina. I had in mind to drive you and Tommy to Warrenton."

Cara could only gaze in astonishment.

"Well, well," Lee murmured. "So *you* were the silent partner."

"I told you there were things I regretted," Abigail added to Cara. "Can you forgive me?"

Never in her life would Cara have imagined Abigail Chastain begging forgiveness of anyone. "Of course I can, Abigail."

The solemn moment abruptly ended as Tommy ran up beside them.

"Look!" he squealed, swiftly drawing open the door and darting outside.

"Slow down, Tommy," Abigail admonished.

"But the mustangs are on the beach, Grandmother!"

The four adults moved out behind him. The sea air was brisk, although the warmth of the sun made it seem like a spring day. In the distance, the mustangs mosied about the edge of the shining tide directly in front of the house.

"Let's go down and see them!" Tommy suggested buoyantly.

Turning to Cara, Lee offered a hand. "Feel like a walk?"

With a smile, Cara twined her fingers through his. "Don't mind if I do."

"I'll take this one," Tommy announced, grabbing Lee's free hand.

Abigail and Frank watched as the three of them walked off together.

"They make a nice-looking family," Frank said.

"Yes," she admitted softly. "I wish it could be my own boy out there, but . . . it can't."

"I was shocked when you told me you'd moved here, Abigail. I thought you hated Walking Dune. You once told me you thought of it as Tom's grave."

"I did. But I nearly lost my grandson. Something like that tends to put things in perspective. It's wrong to dwell in the past. One never knows just how little future there may be."

"It's cost us a pretty penny, but I guess we've both learned the same lesson," Frank commented, his thoughtful gaze shifting along the walkway to Lee. "Lives aren't meant to be controlled by anybody except the people living them."

"That's very profound, Frank."

Turning back to Abigail, he studied her upturned face and thought once again what a pretty woman she was. He'd always admired her, and at this moment he did so more than ever.

"Unlike you, I've always liked Walking Dune," Frank commented. "Not a bad place to retire to, now that I think of it. Come here, Abigail."

"Why, Frank!" she sputtered, her eyes flying wide as h[e]
bent to kiss her.

Cara glanced over her shoulder and came to an abrup[t]
halt.

"Lee? Do you see what I see?"

They stared for a moment at the silver-haired couple embrac[-]
ing on the deck. Then they broke into surprised laughter an[d]
continued on with Tommy. Stopping on the bottom step jus[t]
above the sand, they watched the mustangs milling freely o[n]
the shore.

"As far as I know, they haven't ventured this far south sinc[e]
the fence went up," Cara said.

"Maybe they came to give us their blessing," Lee suggeste[d]
with a smile, though the fanciful notion seemed to ring true a[s]
Star separated from the herd and walked toward them, haltin[g]
mere yards away from the stairs.

"Hello, Star," Lee said quietly.

Eyeing the man with an uncanny semblance of recognition[,]
the stallion tossed his head and whinnied, almost as if he wer[e]
returning the greeting.

"That's amazing," Cara breathed. "I never saw him do tha[t]
with anyone except—"

"Can I call Lee 'Dad' now?" Tommy interrupted.

Glancing down at the boy with a start, Lee looked swiftl[y]
to Cara, wondering what he'd find on her face, almost fearin[g]
it. When she met his gaze, he could see it was filled wit[h]
emotion, but he couldn't tell what kind.

"Sure you can, Tommy," she answered. "That's who h[e]
is."

Star turned then, trotted back to his herd, and rounded the[m]
into a canter up the beach.

"Can I follow them?" Tommy asked, already springing ont[o]
the sand in his brand new Sunday shoes.

"Don't go too far!" Lee and Cara called in unison, thoug[h]
their eyes remained on each other.

Lee stared into the blue depths that had conquered him a[t]
first glance, wondering at the feelings that seemed to gro[w]
and keep on growing, with no end, no bounds.

"We love you," Cara whispered.

Lee couldn't speak. Leaning down, he pressed a kiss to her temple and pulled her close.

Settling against him, Cara stretched an answering arm about Lee's waist, and as she looked up the sunlit beach, felt that heaven itself was smiling down on them all.

Afterword

As much as I feel that I know them, Cara and Lee—and all of Walking Dune—are fiction. The Outer Banks mustangs are not.

They roam Corolla, North Carolina, as they wish . . . as their ancestors have done for centuries. Only now it's different. Now only a dozen or so wild horses ramble where hundreds once did, and they do so at perilous risk.

N.C. Highway 12 used to end some miles south of Corolla. The land beyond was private, consisting of wild forest and dune, the road passing through made only of sand. Then the state gained permission to extend N.C. 12, completing the construction in the late 1980s. In August and September of 1989, six mustangs were killed when cars crashed into them.

Amplifying the danger is the unprecedented development taking place in this heretofore isolated area of the Outer Banks. As lush golf courses, posh inns, and elegant resort homes draw increased traffic, the mustang fatalities continue. One might think the horses would flee. Instead they stay on their oddly changing home turf—presented with a banquet of sodded, planted, grazing land . . . and a tab to pay.

The Corolla Wild Horse Fund has tried a variety of protective measures—reflective paint (which the horses rubbed off), herding dogs (whom the stallion challenged), and a fence at the north end (which the mustangs walk blithely around). "Horse Crossing" and "Reduce Speed" signs pepper the highway. Still, people drive too fast. Ordinance notices posted all over town prohibit coming within fifty yards of the mustangs. Still, people approach them.

The state of North Carolina remains staunch in its refusal to recognize the mustangs as wildlife. As of this writing, the horses are receiving no state protection.

One day in June, 1990, I opened a newspaper, saw a picture of the real-life Star, read about the mustangs, and was captivated. A month later I stood in Corolla, on the shoulder of N.C. 12, watching the herd from across the highway. It was a blistering summer day; the afternoon sun burned into my back as I faced east. In the distance the Atlantic was deep blue; closer in, the sea oats were gold against white dunes; just behind Star the yellow shape of a bulldozer threw his black coat into sharp relief.

He looked at me, head high, ears pricked. If I'd been still before, I made myself absolutely rigid. The sentiments Cara felt when confronting the fictitious stallion were born at that moment. There was something about Star, something "un-horsely" that reached across the highway and held me breathless while he made his inspection. After a moment, he lowered his head and began to graze. I was accepted— at least, the respectful distance I was keeping was accepted.

I stood there a long time. Cars whizzed by; the mustangs mosied; a frolicking foal took a sudden turn toward the highway. My heart leapt, and I leapt with it, dashing to the edge of the road, waving my arms at an approaching car. The foal danced safely back to the herd. The driver looked at me as though I were crazy and drove slowly, sullenly, past.

When I returned home, I began the story of Cara and Lee, and the mustangs of Walking Dune. There were many times I pictured Star, remembered how striking he was with his head held high against the backdrop of a bulldozer. *Now there's contrast for you,* I thought. *Flesh and metal, life and lifelessness, past and future.*

Melodrama? I wish it were. If something isn't done, it seems inevitable that the wild Spanish mustangs of North Carolina will become a thing of the past.

You see, as I wrote the conclusion of this novel, I was unaware that the real-life Star had been killed scarce weeks earlier. It seems his four-year-old son tried to cut a mare out of the herd, he and Star began to fight, and the son bolted onto the highway. An approaching driver slammed on brakes, missed the young stallion, and collided with Star. I was told he died instantly.

Now the mustangs have a new leader—a four-year-old black who looks a lot like his father, though not as majestic, some say. At the end of this novel, the mustangs are galloping toward a bright future. In real life, their future is entirely questionable. The Corolla Wild Horse Fund continues to work for their welfare. If you'd like to help, or want further information, write: Corolla Wild Horse Fund, P.O. Box 361, Corolla, NC 27927.

As for me, I invested about a year in writing a story inspired by a black horse I once saw standing by a highway. So if you find this hokey, I'm afraid that's just too bad.

Thanks, Star. Goodbye.

—Marcia Martin
September, 1991